HERB WILLIAMS-DALGART

JINGLE BOYS

A Novel

Fancy Raven Books

ISBN: 978-1-7356184-1-8
eBook ISBN: 978-1-7356184-2-5

Fancy Raven Books
Rancho Santa Margarita, California

For Dad.
You believed in me, and that meant everything.

A ship in harbor is safe, but that is not what ships are built for.

—John A. Shedd, *Salt from My Attic*, 1928

Contents

1

US War Bonds

Brooklyn, New York, December 1943

Wally Lipkin sat in a rusted deck chair on the rooftop of his Kensington brownstone, knowing it would soon be his time to die. Now that Roosevelt's War Department had lowered the draft age to eighteen, Wally's number would be up in a week. Before long, he'd find himself aboard a battleship like Mel Lieberman from apartment 2-D, flying a fighter plane like Ralphie Feldman from down the hall, or trudging knee-deep through European muck like his pal Johnny Milhouser. All three had enlisted, gone through basic training, and shipped off like the millions of other brave men of his age. But Wally wasn't like Mel or Ralphie or Johnny. Deployment would mean the end for a guy like him, plain and simple.

He fastened his helmet's chinstrap, buttoned his coat against the stubborn New York cold, and squinted through the air-raid warden binoculars he'd been provided by the civilian defense captain. He aimed the lenses past the belching smokestacks of Brooklyn's riverside factories toward the sunset sparkle that danced across the East River. His gaze followed the winter chop to the giant troopships that cut the frosty white wakes, charging toward ports unknown. For months now, the Brooklyn Navy Yard had teemed with steel vessels heading into and out of the waterway. The yard was the pride of Wally's borough, and arguably the most important place in New York, feeding soldiers to the insatiable war that devoured men like candy.

Wally let the binoculars fall to his chest on the strap around his neck, closed his eyes, and blew a frosty cloud into the air. He listened to the distant cries of seagulls, squealing their irritability in D-sharp. Their cacophony did nothing to ease the anxiety that percolated in his gut like a pot of his mother's rationed coffee. Even the gulls knew he was doomed.

The white leather belt of his new uniform rode up his waist, a reminder of how poorly his air-raid warden role suited him. He was slender, had a weak constitution, and was prone to attacks of "anxiety neurosis," the name for the way his brain regularly betrayed him, the villain with whom he persistently grappled. It was a condition for which there appeared to be no cure, and his fear of it was why he'd worked so hard to keep it secret from everyone.

Since the war began, Germans had been targeting Jews like him all over Europe, giving Wally a particular sense of purpose, a need to do his part to stop the violence, to end the treachery, to defeat the Nazis no matter the personal price. After all, Jewish stories were filled with tales of sacrifice, and Wally's ancestors would expect nothing less of him. Like those men aboard the ships leaving Brooklyn, he, too, would feed the voracious appetite of war, even if that appetite leaned kosher.

He had taken the air-raid warden job to prepare for his inevitable military duty, to help him grapple with his condition, to steel his nerves in the relative safety of his own neighborhood, before he had to put it all on the line for himself, his fellow soldiers, and his country. Now, after six weeks of civilian service training, it was Wally's role to keep a vigilant lookout three nights a week, fill out an evening log, pass fliers around the neighborhood warning of chemical attacks or aerial bombings, instruct Brooklynites to turn off their lights, and to take part in air-raid drills like the one tonight, his first since taking the job. If he could pull this off, maybe he could heed the call of his country and his people, defeat his betraying brain, and avoid passing out on a battlefield when his time came.

The sound of creaking metal drew his attention to the roof's edge, where Audrey Milhouser, Johnny's seventeen-year-old sister, was climbing off the fire escape.

"There you are," she called, and strolled over.

Audrey's hair was nut-brown and cut short, though tonight it appeared to hold more curl than she usually gave it. Her blue eyes were filled with curiosity. Her lavender wool coat was bright and clean, which Wally thought was impractical for climbing fire escapes. He had known her since before she'd started to curve, and even though Audrey was a month older than him and smarter than he was by a fair measure, he still saw her as Johnny's little sister. In the months since his friend and neighbor Johnny had deployed, Audrey would find Wally whenever she was bored or lonely, even when her timing was terrible. And tonight, it was terrible.

"You shouldn't be here," said Wally.

"When's it supposed to happen?" said Audrey, chewing her Beech-Nut gum.

Wally leaned back in his chair and withdrew his uncle's silver pocket watch from his warden's vest.

"It's five twenty. Air-raid drill is at five thirty-two, right after sunset."

"Perfect." Audrey dragged forward her own deck chair and took a seat. She exhaled into the icy air, enveloping Wally in a peppermint cloud, and then sang the Beech-Nut Chewing Gum jingle.

> *"The minty taste of Beech-Nut gum*
> *I've got to go and get me some.*
> *The minty taste—it lasts so long*
> *And makes me sing this Beech-Nut song."*

Audrey's vocal skills were impressive, honed from years in the vocal ensemble and church choir, but today she was just getting in the way.

"I mean it," said Wally. Feathery steam from his own breath rose between them. "I want to be alone."

Audrey rolled her eyes. "No one wants to be alone, Walter."

Wally wished Johnny were still around to keep Audrey out of his hair and explain to her that there were some things guys needed to do without distraction. But Johnny was exactly where he wanted to be, in the thick of danger. He was one of the fearless ones.

"Audrey—"

"I'll stay out of your way." She ran her forefinger in an X across her heart. "Promise."

Wally shook his head, suddenly feeling the beads of sweat that had begun to freeze along his hairline, heeding the winter chill. He closed his eyes and counted Mississippis, a trick that sometimes kept him focused and steady. The last thing he wanted was a girl to see him faint, even if that girl was Audrey.

Wally's anxiety neurosis had first manifested when he was thirteen, in the basement of the Etz Chaim temple. He had hyperventilated and passed out when Eleanor Getzman tried to kiss him at his cousin Herschel's bar mitzvah reception. After the attempted osculation, Wally came to on the sticky floor, surrounded by concerned family members. He blamed the incident on the lack of air circulation and the rising room temperature from everyone's vigorous hora dancing. No one argued the point. His aunt Betsy could really put out some heat.

Eleanor Getzman was too embarrassed by the unwanted attention to contradict his story, but even then, Wally knew something was wrong with him.

Similar fainting episodes continued throughout his adolescence, brought on by sudden fear, overexertion, or surprise. They happened in parks, on subways, and once in the Liberty High School theater. Blacking out sometimes made Wally late to events, occasionally left him bruised from falling, breathless, confused, or disoriented. Nevertheless, because he was most often alone when such episodes happened, and because he was largely able to avoid such situations, no one understood the severity of his condition, including his own family—and that's how he hoped to keep it.

To ensure these embarrassing incidents remained secret, or to explain them away on the rare occasions when others were present, Wally had grown adept at concocting plausible excuses, reasons for his sudden loss of breath or lapses of consciousness. In short, his condition had helped him hone a singular ability: he had become an accomplished liar.

He took no pride in this skill. But how could he tell anyone the truth, especially now, when bravery was required of every young man?

Audrey eyed his air-raid warden uniform. "You look like a real soldier."

"I suppose," he said, yet Wally knew no real soldier would faint or hyperventilate when things got hot. Revealing his secret to the military would earn him a 4-F and spare him conscription, but men who shunted military service for such reasons were sent to the sanatorium. Wally didn't want to be locked up for the rest of his life at Brooklyn State Hospital like his uncle Sherman, who had come home from the Great War with a medal, a pocket watch, and his own anxiety neurosis. Wally's choice was simple: the war or the funny farm. And if he had to die, he'd rather die serving a cause, defending the Jews, not rotting away in a loony bin like his poor uncle.

Through a second-floor window in the brownstone across East Third Street, Wally glimpsed a family eating their dinner. He heard their plates clinking and the melodic sounds of a piano concerto from their radio. He clenched his hands into fists and blew hot breath across his cold fingers, the tools for playing his own piano. His family Wurlitzer was the one thing that ever gave him peace, and playing it had become his evening ritual, which he used to distract himself from the increasingly persistent thoughts of his own demise. Hearing the neighbor's music only stirred a longing for his family's upright piano, but, of course, he couldn't drag a piano up to the rooftop, let alone onto a warship or across a foreign battlefield, when its calming effect would be needed most. Wally would have to learn to cope without his precious Wurlitzer.

He eyed Audrey chewing her gum and wondered if she might have a stick to offer, but decided it was better not to engage her in further conversation. Instead, he replayed her Beech-Nut jingle in his head, fingering an imaginary piano on his knees, trying to find solace while sitting in his deck chair.

"You okay?" said Audrey.

"Fine," said Wally. "Just stay clear, okay? The precinct captain is counting on me."

"Where'd they put the lever?"

"There." Wally pointed to the flagpole that stood like a sentry at the corner of the rooftop, aimed toward the darkening sky. "Below the siren."

Each Brooklyn neighborhood had installed sirens and levers in strategic locations, a means of warning Brooklyn citizens of enemy attack. News of these installations, and Wally's overly detailed and fear-provoking fliers, had forced people to consider what they'd face if the war found its way onto American soil again, so soon after Pearl Harbor. Wally's precinct captain had explained that, like the devastated Hawaiian base, New York was on a coast; had planes, ships, and soldiers; and would be a target the Japanese or Germans would be keen on destroying. It was a thought Wally had a tough time shaking.

"Looks fun to pull," said Audrey.

"Wardens are our first line of civilian defense," said Wally, quoting his training manual. "Sounding the siren isn't supposed to be fun."

"Can I pull the lever when it's time?" Audrey asked.

"No one's gonna touch that lever but me." Wally thumbed his chest. "I already told you—you shouldn't be here."

"It's a free country." Audrey crossed her arms and settled into her chair.

"I intend to keep it that way," said Wally, suddenly concerned that he had oversold his role in all this.

He looked to the winter sky, which held remnant streaks of purple like spilled Manischewitz across a Hanukkah tablecloth. He inhaled another long draft of air and savored the way it chilled his lungs. He often imagined his chest filled with bagpipes, imbuing his body with a calming song each time he took a breath. It was another ritual he'd employed to manage his anxiety, to keep him standing on his own two feet.

Audrey followed Wally's gaze across the expansive heavens and exhaled deeply as if she, too, had a chest full of bagpipes.

"You're brave," she said. A mint cloud whirled around them.

"Quiet," said Wally. "I need to concentrate." But failing concentration wasn't what was wrong with him.

He reached again into his vest to retrieve his uncle Sherman's pocket watch. Unlike his uncle, the watch still functioned when it returned from the Great War. With each movement of the second hand, Wally felt his anxiety rise.

"Two minutes," he said, and then tucked the watch back into his pocket. "Get ready."

Dusk had fallen and lights around Kensington had started to switch off one by one, as if counting down to Wally's big moment. The family across the street had finished their meal, turned off their radio, and switched off their lamps. Citizens had read their fliers and were abiding by the drill guidelines. They were doing their part.

Wally rose from his deck chair, set the binoculars in his empty seat, and tugged again at his belt. It was time.

He strode toward the flagpole and Audrey followed, but halfway to the siren, the blood left his head, and his legs grew weak. A sudden rush of nausea caused his stomach to lurch, and he stopped dead in his tracks.

Audrey stopped too. "What's wrong?"

His heart raced and his throat began to close. "Oh, no."

His mouth went dry, and it felt as though he'd swallowed a lump of sawdust. He tried to count Mississippis, stop the first domino from falling.

He searched the space around him for the scents of Audrey's gum or the sounds of radio jingles, anything to keep him anchored.

His cold palms grew slick, and his fingers quivered as though trying to play a piano that wasn't there.

The air grew thin, and he began to wheeze.

Just then, Audrey's seven-year-old brother, Carl, sprung to the rooftop from the fire escape. "Found you!"

Carl's sudden appearance startled Wally like a first-round sucker punch to his heaving gut. He took a knee, fell to his side, and gasped for air.

"Carl!" Audrey swatted her brother's head, knocking loose his Lone Ranger cowboy hat.

"What'd I do?"

Wally rolled onto his back and faced the kaleidoscope of stars overhead, the faces of his Jewish ancestors gazing down with disappointment.

"Walter!" Audrey's blue eyes radiated through the darkness. She raced over and grabbed his hand. "Walter? What's wrong?"

Some distance away, a siren rang out in what sounded like a C note, followed by another and another, carried by the winter breeze, as Wally's fellow borough air-raid wardens did the job they'd been called upon to do.

Carl spun to face the neighborhood. "It's happening!"

Wally locked eyes with Audrey. "Pull it—!" he gasped, his breath a thin white wisp.

She laid his hand on his chest, her eyes betraying a look of conflict between concern and joy. "It'll be okay, Walter," she said, and ran to the flagpole.

"Now!" he barked, and the shadows began to take him.

Audrey pulled the lever and the siren cried out, filling Wally's head with a shrill, howling sound. Or maybe that was just the triumphant song of his enemy, the sound of his worst fears coming true.

From his seat at the family's upright Wurlitzer, Wally could hardly contain his excitement. He folded the *Brooklyn Daily Eagle* in half, and then in half again, exposing the upper right corner of the newspaper's seventh page—the article that spelled his salvation, the Hannukah miracle he had been wishing for. A fast reader might have missed it, as Wally almost had. But there, in black and white, was the answer to his prayers.

"Read that!" Wally exclaimed. He handed the paper to his brother, Max.

Max perused the page, knitting his thick brow as he read in silence.

"Out loud," called their red-haired friend Frankie from across the Lipkins' small family room. "I wanna hear it too."

Max chuckled and his big belly jiggled. "Okay, okay." He then read aloud with authority: "'WKOB, the Voice of Brooklyn, Hosts War Bond Jingle Contest.'"

"Jingle contest?" said Frankie.

"Shh," Wally hissed. "Let him finish."

Max cleared his throat. "'Uncle Sam and WKOB want you! If you're a patriotic jingle writer, the US Army is looking for a jazzy war bond jingle to stir the hearts of your fellow Americans and fund the war effort. Winning jingle gets played on the radio. Writers earn fifty dollars and a job at the US Army Office of War Information in Washington. Performances required at WKOB.'" Max lowered the paper.

"Well?" said Wally. "What d'ya think? Doesn't that have us written all over it?"

Max shrugged. "Says auditions are in Manhattan tomorrow." He tossed the paper over to the sofa. "You think we can write a jingle before morning?"

"Of course, we can," said Wally. "We've been writing and playing music our whole lives."

"That's a pretty snappy turnaround, even for the three of us," said Frankie.

"Oh, come on!" Wally didn't want his desperation to show, so he took a bagpipe breath and fingered a twinkling tune on the Wurlitzer. "This is right up our alley."

Wally's mother, Sadie, was rinsing dishes in the kitchenette and turned off the running water after hearing their banter. "You boys have talent," she said. She wiped her hands on a dish towel. "You ask me, you've got a real chance."

"See?" said Wally. "A real chance. Mom agrees."

"Mom agrees with everything," said Max.

"Only when it comes to my boys," said their mother, "and, of course, you, Francis." She smiled at Frankie.

"Thanks, Mrs. Lipkin."

Max stroked his round chin. "I guess it would be something to hear our own jingle on the radio..."

"Sure, it would," Wally agreed.

"Don't forget the fifty clams," Frankie reminded them. "I could really use that dough."

"Perfect," said Wally. "Then we're all on the same page."

He twinkled out "The Star-Spangled Banner" on the piano, unabashed in his enthusiasm, the tune bouncing off the walls of their two-bedroom second-floor apartment. Frankie could keep the money, and Max could relish the radio attention. What Wally wanted was that stateside government job that would keep him off the front line. After last night's air-raid fiasco with Audrey, winning this contest was now his last and only hope of surviving the war.

His brother, Max, was a year older and had been spared the draft on account of his undiagnosed asthma, though Wally suspected Max had concocted that story to cover the truth that he was rejected for being too fat for service. He wasn't nearly as good a liar as Wally. Frankie had gotten the 4-F exemption owing to his flat feet just three months ago on his own birthday. But for Wally, there'd be no 4-F unless he came clean about his anxiety neurosis, and that was something he was simply unwilling to do. He'd already sworn Audrey to secrecy after she'd witnessed him faint, even got her to promise to insure her brother Carl's silence. In exchange, Wally had agreed to listen to the radio with her after dinner tomorrow. It was an awkward deal, but Wally couldn't risk anyone else learning his secret.

"Okay," Max proclaimed. "But if we're going to write a jingle, we need to get cracking. It's already seven o'clock."

"Don't need to tell me." Wally set his fingers back on the black-and-whites and began to run scales.

Frankie pulled off his moth-eaten cardigan and set it over the arm of the family room sofa, appearing ready for business.

Max retrieved a pad of paper, handed it to Frankie, and then turned to the piano with a bit of ceremony. "Wally, you work out some simple combinations. Keep 'em short and tight. This is a jingle, not the national anthem."

"Got it."

"Frankie," Max continued, "you write 'em out like you usually do, throw out ideas and keep 'em coming. I'll work on lyrics, key the words off Walter's rhythms." Max then pointed his finger gun at them. "If we're gonna do this, we're gonna do it right."

Wally nodded and followed his brother's direction. He plunked out a few notes on a string.

Frankie drew out the music lines, scribbled musical notes onto the page, and showed Wally. "Try it on the lower octave like this," Frankie said. "We can walk it up from there. Jingles usually work on a four-four."

"Most songs work that way," said Wally. "Don't act like you know more than we do."

Frankie rolled his eyes. "Just play."

Wally lifted his spread fingers, moved them along the keys in a fluid motion like some kind of warlock casting spells over a cauldron. He let the melody of the burgeoning composition bounce around the apartment between the lingering smells of his mother's kosher chicken. "How 'bout that?" Wally chirped.

Wally's father, Saul, walked in from the back bathroom and plopped his stocky frame into his corner easy chair. He turned on the lamp and then searched around with agitation.

"Where's my paper?" he barked.

"Oh, sorry." Max stopped his writing to retrieve the newspaper from the sofa and handed it to his father. "Wally just found that advertisement."

Their father gazed at the folded page. "Jingle contest?" he said. "Hrmph." He then wriggled his thin mustache, opened the *Daily Eagle* to shake out the creases, and disappeared behind the day's news.

Max snapped his fingers at Wally. "Back to it," Max commanded. "Play that combination again with the low C."

Wally nodded and played the notes at the lower octave. "How's that?"

"That, I can work with." Max scribbled again on his lyric page.

Wally played his new combination over and over, adding small embellishments, bringing his mission into focus. He had to agree. Lower was better, and this jingle had to be perfect.

His father peered over his paper again, resuming the conversation as though it had never stopped. "It's a lot of fuss over a jingle."

Wally drew his fingers from the keys and sighed. "A jingle's like a girl," he said. "You gotta treat it gentle."

Max guffawed and Frankie laughed outright at how ridiculous Wally sounded, talking as if he knew the first thing about girls.

Even Wally's father shot him a sideways look. "You wanna take your jingle to dinner, too, maybe?" Saul quipped like a Yiddish comedian.

"Leave 'em alone, Saul," said Wally's mother, stifling a laugh. She danced in from the kitchen wearing a floral apron over her striped blouse and pleated skirt, carrying a cup of hot coffee. She set the cup on the end table under the glow of the small lamp. "This ain't vaudeville, you know."

"You can say that again." Wally's father slurped his coffee and chewed away the heat.

Wally was used to hearing his parents lament their old vaudeville days. The pair had toured the Catskills before their boys were born, blending comedy and song into a popular Borscht Belt stage routine until his mother had gotten pregnant with Max. It was that blessed event that had prompted them to reinvent themselves as dry cleaners in Brooklyn, carrying on the Lipkin family tradition of working with garments and clothing, as their Polish grandparents had done before them. Wally's father ran the till and press downstairs, while his mother ran the washers and dryers and performed the alterations. Soon after establishing A-Rite Cleaners, Max came along followed by Wally. Once the boys were tall enough to reach the shop counter, their parents had them running the register and operating the machines. It wasn't a lucrative business, but it was enough to pay the rent, put food on the table and shoes on their feet. Through it all, despite their domestication, the elder Lipkins could not shake their impulse to perform, singing to the shop radio or spontaneously waltzing through the family apartment.

"What's this jingle for, again?" said Wally's mother.

"US war bonds," said Wally. He glided his digits over the keys and added a patriotic punctuation in the form of a C and D twinkle.

"War bonds?" she piped in. "Saul, when's the last time we bought a war bond?"

"We bought three in April when the Milhouser boy shipped off." Wally's father buried his head behind his paper again like a badger backing into his den.

"Such a brave young man, that Johnny." Sadie shook her head and then dashed back into the kitchen.

Wally blanched at her mention of Johnny, somehow irritated that his absent friend's bravery had been invoked amid everything else. His parents would expect no less bravery from him, though he knew they loved him no matter what. Such was the tyrannical equation of Jewish parental love. High expectations somehow had to square with unconditional love.

"You boys want a little pie?" Sadie called. "It's blackberry."

"Blackberry?" said Frankie. "I love blackberry."

"Not now," snapped Wally. "We gotta concentrate."

"I made it with fresh berries from my victory garden." His mother held up the pie with a pair of oven mitts. "Sweet enough, I hardly needed sugar." Wally's mother seemed to think she'd win the war with her windowsill garden full of anemic fruits and dwarfed vegetables.

"But it's blackberry," Frankie repeated.

"Tell you what," said Wally. "We get this jingle done, and my mom can give you all the pie you want."

Frankie hung his head, a strand of his red hair falling over his face. "Okay."

Wally's mother set the pie on a trivet next to the stove and pulled off her mitts, letting the aroma of toasted crust and sweet berries chase away the waning scents of roast chicken. "It'll be here when you boys are ready."

Max licked his lips, apparently just as eager for pie as Frankie.

Wally worked his long fingers and played an elaborate passage from Ravel's *Gaspard de la Nuit*, trying to drown out the phantom song of last night's air-raid siren, which haunted him like a bad dream.

"Okay. Okay." Max snapped his fingers once more. "Give us the low C again, Walter. We still gotta work out the lyrics."

Wally plunked out the note as Max grabbed his steno pad and squinted at the page. "So far, I've got an opening line," said Max. "'Dig in deep and don't complain, war bonds buy our boys a plane.'"

"I like that!" blurted Frankie.

"It's patriotic," Wally agreed. "Right to the point."

Max nodded. "How about this for a second line? 'You may be strapped, but they're strapped too. So, don't make such a hullabaloo.'"

Frankie squinted his doubt. "I guess it rhymes..."

Wally stopped playing the tune. "Telling people not to make a 'hullabaloo' isn't very nice. People don't have a lot of money these days. We already said 'don't complain.'"

"'Hullabaloo' is a weird word for a jingle," Frankie added. "'Stir the hearts,' remember?"

Max slumped. "You're right."

"What if you just continue the idea?" Wally suggested, yielding to his own enthusiasm. "How about, 'You may be strapped, but they're strapped too. A bond's one thing that you can do.' Make 'em wanna help."

"Guilt works," added Frankie. "Trust me. I'm Irish Catholic."

"Don't start with me," Max countered, pointing his finger gun. "Jews invented guilt."

Frankie scoffed and turned to Wally. "Try walking it up from the C on major keys like this..." He showed Wally his composition page.

Wally played the way Frankie had written it, humming along to their new tune.

"Sounds good," said Max. "Bank that." He scratched down the new lyrics. "We got ourselves our first two couplets."

Wally's father glanced up once again from the *Daily Eagle* with renewed interest. "Now you gotta jazz it up."

Max perked. "What d'ya mean, Pop?"

"In my day, we followed a double couplet with a new rhythm. Something snappy to keep the attention. A switch-up."

Max's eyes brightened as if a light had gone on. "A switch-up," he repeated, and scribbled on the page. He then turned his pad around to show the guys.

"Like this?" Wally worked in extra notes on the higher octave to give the tune some dimension and then turned to Max for approval.

Max smiled. "That's it!"

Wally played the switch-up again and Max sang:

"You buy 'em,
They'll fly 'em.
Even a little goes a long way.
Uncle Sam is callin',
Time for you to fall in
And buy a US war bond today!"

Wally's father raised his hand to the air. "Now, that's a jingle! *Mazel tov!*"

"Thanks, Pop!" said Wally.

"First piece of advice is free," said Saul. "I charge for the second." Once again, he buried his mustachioed smirk behind the wartime news.

Frankie neatly printed the tune and lyrics onto a fresh sheet, and they were ready to put the whole jingle to the test.

"Ma!" Max called to the back bedroom, where she had retreated. "Can you come in here?"

Their mother returned, heading to the kitchen. "You boys finally ready for some pie?"

"I need you to sing something first," said Max. "Gotta hear it all together for myself."

Wally's father closed his paper and rose from his chair.

"Hold it! Hold it! You want a performance, you gotta hire the whole act."

Sadie untied her apron and set it on the kitchen table before joining the boys. "A close harmony or call-and-response?" she asked, smiling like a summer morning.

"You kidding?" Saul plucked the sheet from Max's hands and scanned it like an accountant scrutinizing an overdue bill. "Ten lines of music? It's a harmony."

"All right," said Wally's mother. "Ready when you are, honey." She pressed her flushed cheek against Saul's and held the music sheet up high for them both to read.

Wally twinkled out an improvised prelude to give his folks time to catch the tune until they swayed back and forth to the rhythm and sang. He admired his father's resonant baritone, the way it lifted his mother's soft trill between stanzas. It was clear how they had transformed their couple's act into a marriage so effortlessly. They complemented one another.

Each held their notes through Wally's key changes, connecting with his improvisation, until they harmonized at the end of the jingle, singing, "And buy a US war bond today!"

The musical words dissolved into the sweet berry-scented air and settled like a sprinkling of confectioner's sugar.

"Boys," Wally's mother announced, "I love it! And, Saul, I swear, we're buying another war bond."

Saul scowled at Wally. "See what you did? I knew this would cost me."

"Good work, Frankie," said Max. He shook his pal's hand. "You earned your pie."

"And, hopefully, fifty bucks," said Frankie.

Wally smiled at their jubilation but fought the weight of his own expectations. He didn't care about pie, or money, or fame. This jingle had one job to do.

It had to save his life.

The first-floor offices of WKOB sat just off the marbled lobby of the twenty-two-story Bellwether high-rise on Broadway. Two walls of the reception area were adorned with framed posters of their most popular radio programs, a few head shots of their famous stars, and shelves with awards for broadcasting excellence. The two remaining walls were made of glass, facing the lobby, creating an odd feeling that everyone was watching but that no one cared.

Wally felt small and inconsequential in this ceremonious place, like a dislodged shoe pebble in the large, cold room that reeked of cigarettes. The sofa on which Wally, Max, and Frankie sat was lumpy and had a cigarette burn in the cushion. Whatever enthusiasm the trio had garnered the previous night had now disappeared, replaced by an apprehension that grew with every tick of the clock that stared back at them from the wall over the station manager's office door.

Wally looked to the marbled floor, streaked in a pale pattern he thought was designed to induce nausea. Of course, he had felt sick even before they'd entered the ominous, glass-laden building, concerned he might repeat his rooftop air-raid incident here at WKOB and spoil whatever chance they had of winning the contest, and whatever chance he had of surviving the war.

He glanced toward Frankie and Max, each wearing their best and only suits, pressed this morning courtesy of A-Rite Cleaners. Max clutched his hat and composition book in his lap, cleared his throat every two minutes, and appeared ready to speak on the team's behalf. Frankie just kept crossing and recrossing his legs as if trying to keep from pissing his pants and further defiling the furniture.

Wally moved his gaze to the front desk and the pretty brunette receptionist positioned in front of the office where the station manager, Roger Brubaker—the man they were there to meet—could be heard in a heated discussion with someone on the phone. Brubaker's silhouette passed behind the frosted glass panel of his door, his arms gesticulating wildly.

"It's been forty-five minutes since they called us inside," Wally whispered to his brother. "This is torture."

"At least we're not waiting out on the street in the cold anymore," said Max.

Wally recalled the growing queue of contestants huddled out on Broadway and the frightened-looking couple that had exited just as Wally's trio had been called to come in. The husband-and-wife team had hurried out of the building, carrying their coats, appearing frazzled by whatever had happened inside.

Finally, just as the clock struck ten o'clock, Brubaker slammed down his phone and threw open his door.

"Alice!" he shouted.

The receptionist jumped like a mouse on a hot griddle, and a tornado of papers flew off her desk. Even Wally and the others startled.

"Yes, Mr. Brubaker?" Alice quavered.

The station manager appeared beside her. He was a tall, handsome, slender man, with salt-and-pepper hair neatly parted on the side. His shirtsleeves were rolled to his elbows, and his blood-red bow tie was perfect and pronounced at his throat.

"The next time Dawson calls"—he pointed a finger at her face—"I'm not here."

"Yes, Mr. Brubaker."

He aimed his piercing look toward the sofa and eyed the trio. "Jesus, what's with you guys?"

Max, wide-eyed, hopped to attention, barely catching his composition book and hat from sliding off his lap. "Good morning, sir," Max stammered. "We're here for the jingle contest."

"I know why you're here, son," Brubaker chortled. "You look like you're getting ready to take on Hitler himself." He pantomimed the one-two punch, but when none of the guys laughed, he said, "Relax, fellas. I'm a pussycat."

"Yes, sir," Max squeaked.

"Follow me." Brubaker turned to his receptionist. "Alice, hold my calls."

"Yes, Mr. Brubaker."

Wally looked to Alice for reassurance, but her trembling lip only served to agitate him further.

Brubaker led them past his office and down a hall into the depths of the office building to a chilly auditorium, larger than Wally's entire family apartment, with a ceiling twice as high, where bright overhead lights illuminated the room. White speakers were mounted in the four corners of the ceiling and aimed down toward tiers of seating where an audience would presumably sit, like a miniature version of the seats at Ebbets Field. A side wall had been configured with a window revealing an adjacent control room with a bank of equipment sporting dials and levers, the purpose of which Wally could only guess. The opposite wall was peppered with signed photographs of celebrities—Bob Hope; the Marx Brothers; Edgar Bergen; and even Lon Clark from Wally's favorite radio program, *Nick Carter, Master Detective*.

They followed Brubaker to the front of the auditorium, to a small riser stage carrying two black metal stands for scripts or music scores. Between the stands stood a microphone, where Wally imagined Abbott and Costello or Jack Benny cracking wise.

"Welcome to WKOB," said Brubaker. "The Voice of Brooklyn."

It was thrilling for Wally to be this close to the magic of radio broadcast, even if the "Voice of Brooklyn" was actually in lower Manhattan. He tried to take it all in, but the feature that excited Wally most sat at the foot of the stage. An ebony grand piano gleamed like onyx and stood on smooth, muscular legs. It was both imposing and inviting, like a panther at the Bronx Zoo waiting to be stroked while hungry to be set loose.

"We bounce our broadcasts off the big transmitter." Brubaker pointed at the ceiling as if they could see the top of the skyscraper from where they stood. "That baby can reach the whole eastern seaboard and halfway 'round the world." Brubaker closed the studio door and turned back to the trio. "Know the contest rules?" He looked at Max, keying in that he was the team's spokesman.

"One jingle. Piano accompaniment. US war bonds," said Max. "Played on the radio."

"Fifty-dollar first prize," added Frankie.

"And a Washington job," squeaked Wally. His words rose an octave as if he were asking a question.

"Think you fellas got a shot?"

"Yes, sir!" said Frankie.

Max brandished their composition book. "This is the winning jingle right here." He spoke slowly as if defying contradiction.

Wally bit his lip, concerned Max was being too cocky. Even Frankie winced.

"You've got moxie"—Brubaker laughed—"I'll give you that." He looked them over. "You boys patriotic?"

"Course," said Max. "Frankie and I got the 4-F for health reasons, but not for lack of trying. My brother, Walter, is up next week."

The station manager turned to Wally. "That so?"

Wally swallowed. "Yes, sir," he said. "I'm a civilian air-raid warden in Kensington." Though true, his words tasted like one of his lies given his utter failure at the role.

"Attaboy," said Brubaker. He leaned against the wall and crossed his arms, his posture like a dare. "Let's hear what you've got, air-raid warden."

Frankie grimaced and Max nodded to Wally. It was showtime.

They took off their coats and laid them across some of the bleacher seats. Wally sat at the bench facing the polished Steinway and tried to quiet the doubting voices in his head. This piano was much finer than his Wurlitzer back home, and despite his nerves, Wally felt an eagerness to play such a superior instrument. He set his fingers on the cold keys, drew in the smells of the piano's polish, and played scales. He found the keys to be bouncy and pliable. The hammers hit the strings earlier than his piano at home, causing him to play the notes more decisively.

He softened his pounding, worked the pedals, and played out a few more scales on other octaves to loosen his fingers, connect with this new instrument, and tame the panther. After a few moments, his instinct started to replace his discomfort, a feeling of control taking over as though the panther had accepted him, its chime a soft, soothing purr.

"You've got chops," said Brubaker. "Classically trained?"

Before Wally could snap out of his trance and explain that he'd been taught by a pair of vaudevillian Jews, Max answered for him.

"Yessir! My brother can play anything."

"Let's see." Brubaker waved a finger between Max and Wally, instructing Max to give Wally his sheet music.

Frankie crossed himself like a Roman Catholic priest, shooting a glance toward God, or maybe that rooftop transmitter.

Max set the score on the piano, withdrew a small atomizer from his pocket, and squirted spray into his mouth. He cleared his throat and gave Wally the nod to begin.

After Wally's sparkling prelude, Max sang:

> *"Dig in deep and don't complain.*
> *War bonds buy our boys a plane.*
> *You may be strapped, but they're strapped too.*
> *A bond's one thing that you can do.*
>
> *You buy 'em,*
> *They'll fly 'em.*
> *Even a little goes a long way.*
> *Uncle Sam is callin',*
> *Time for you to fall in*
> *And buy a US war bond today!"*

Wally concluded with a sunny up tone, and the three young men turned to the station manager for his verdict.

Brubaker said nothing. Instead, he stood frozen with his eyes closed, appearing to absorb their jingle into his flesh. "It's good—" he finally said. He opened his eyes and raised a finger. "But it's missing something." He then left the auditorium without explanation.

After a silent moment, Max whispered, "Where did he go?"

"Maybe he's getting someone up the chain," said Frankie.

"A producer?" said Wally. He hung on to a vision of himself behind his Washington desk.

"What's it missing?" said Max, uncharacteristic doubt working its way into his voice.

As if in answer to Max's question, Brubaker returned, a bounce in his step. "Fellas, I'd like you to meet Miss Bobbi LaFleur."

Behind the station manager followed a slender, fair-skinned young woman, about Wally's age. She was all legs, in a cap-sleeved yellow dress and white heels. She sported beautiful blonde locks like Lana Turner's, her eyes a striking green.

Wally's cheeks warmed at the sight of her.

"Hello, boys," she sang. Her smile sent a bolt of energy through the studio like a fresh white bulb. Both Max and Frankie ogled her as she sashayed toward the piano.

Wally reminded himself to breathe.

"Bobbi's the station's top vocalist," said Brubaker. "Even performs three nights a week at the Diamond Club on Fifty-Second." He thumbed in her direction. "The Lin-X floor wax jingle? That's her."

Wally recalled hearing that jingle on the radio during *Nick Carter, Master Detective* and admiring her voice.

"A pleasure." Bobbi reached out and shook Max's hand.

Frankie stared at her without a word, slack-jawed, and Bobbi graciously nodded at him.

Then, she eyed Wally. "You must be the fella Roger mentioned. Can't resist a musician."

Wally stood and willed himself to stay calm, gazing into those green eyes. No one had ever called him a musician before. He tried to steady his hand as he offered it to her.

"Walter Lipkin," said Wally.

"Pleased to meet you." Bobbi didn't appear to notice Wally's trepidation, or at least was kind enough to pretend she didn't. She leaned next to him, moving in closer to the piano to read the score.

Wally took shallow breaths, smelled her lilac perfume, and noticed the glow of her skin.

"Looks pretty straightforward," she said. "How about we make some magic, Curly? Ready to give it a whirl?"

Wally shot a glance to Brubaker for permission.

"You heard her, Curly." The station manager laughed. "Make some magic."

With feigned graciousness, Max stepped away from the piano. "Please do."

Wally lowered himself onto the bench and let his fingers move across the keys, which were now warm to his touch. Again, he extended the jingle's intro as he had done for his parents the night before, both to ease his nerves and to give Bobbi a few notes of lead-in.

She tapped her foot, humming along to catch Wally's cadence, and then placed her hand on his shoulder, almost causing his to miss a note. But Wally kept the tempo, surprised to find her touch reassuring.

The air between them buzzed, and as she sang the words the guys had written, Wally added more flourish, working to match the complexity of Bobbi's voice. This time, he instinctively played it slow.

"...and buy a US war bond today...!" Bobbi held the last note until she and Wally punctuated the ditty in perfect alignment as if they'd performed it together a hundred times.

Once the jingle had dissolved into the soundproofed walls, Brubaker applauded.

"See?" he said. "That's what was missing. A dame to dress it up." He nodded at Max.

"No offense, Moxie."

"No offense taken," said Max. "That was perfect."

"Does that mean we won?" asked Frankie.

"The day is young, fellas. Let's just say you're in the running." Brubaker turned to Bobbi. "Thanks, sweetheart. Terrific as always."

Bobbi reached over and tousled Wally's hair. "Helps to have such a talented partner." She then aimed her green eyes at him. "You oughta pop over to the Diamond sometime."

Wally couldn't make words come out of his mouth and, instead, offered a crooked grin.

Bobbi returned the smile and then seemed to float out of the studio, Wally's eyes floating with her.

"All right, boys." Brubaker held their composition in the air. "Got your number. We'll ring you tomorrow morning, first thing." He reached for the studio door and opened it. "Thanks for coming in."

"That's it?" said Max.

Brubaker winked. "We'll be in touch."

Wally buttoned his coat and followed Max and Frankie out onto Broadway, past the other contest hopefuls who awaited entry into the tower, eyeing the trio as if their own fate could somehow be revealed on the faces of the boys.

Wally ignored them, half in a trance. The air was crisp and seemed to freeze his lungs, but Wally didn't care about any of it. The riddle of how he might survive the war had been replaced by a new quandary: How could an awkward, Jewish dry cleaner with a fainting problem win over a beautiful club singer?

They made their way down the boulevard, which was decorated with tinsel and lights for the holidays. Visions of Bobbi LaFleur breathed new hope into Wally's vison of the future, but before he could sort through these new thoughts, he heard his name called from the crowd of holiday shoppers and suited businessmen crossing the street ahead. He searched the herd of approaching pedestrians and spotted Clyde "Rat" Rubinstein, aiming his pointy nose and beady eyes right at him.

"Lipkin!" Rat repeated. He approached the curb, waving. "Wally Lipkin!"

"Ugh," Wally groaned, the phantom smell of lilacs dissipating into the prickly air. "Not him."

Rat bolted forward and planted himself right in the trio's path. He held a small pad of paper, had a crooked tilt to his fedora, and a wool scarf around his throat. He was panting white puffs into the cold, petrol-fumed city air while trying to look relaxed.

"Hey there, fellas!"

The guys stopped short. Max and Frankie groaned aloud, and Wally felt his stomach sink. Rat Rubinstein was the only person in the world Wally really hated, and the sight of him sucked the holiday spirit right out of the December air.

"What do you want?" grumbled Wally.

Rat eyed them all. "The Lipkin brothers and ol' Frankie O'Brien," he huffed. "The gruesome threesome."

"Rat," Frankie snarled. "What're you doing out of Brooklyn?"

"I write for the *Daily Eagle* these days," said Rat. "Heard about the radio contest at WKOB, so I figured I'd pop on over to see which sad sacks from the borough had eyes full of stars." He smirked. "Guess you boys are hoping they don't get a lot of entries, huh?"

The smart-mouthed rodent had been a reporter back in high school for the *Lincoln High Gazette*. "Rat" was the nickname the boys had given him when he had written stories about his fellow students as unflattering as the English language and the journalism teacher would allow.

"Take a walk, Rubinstein," Wally replied. "Go on. Scram."

Wally hadn't forgotten the terrible review Rat had given them during his junior year, despite their honorable mention at the high school talent show, when the boys had performed their first original composition. "The best part of the act came at the end," Rat had written, "because after that, the song was over." Rat's review was insulting and went on to target Wally most relentlessly. "Walter Lipkin must have hated his own performance," he'd penned. "He fell unconscious, just to be spared the experience."

It had been Wally's most public fainting incident. The school theater had been full of parents and students, so it was easy for Wally to blame the episode on the lack of fresh air in the packed venue, just as he'd done at his cousin's bar mitzvah years before. The drama teacher and school nurse who had rushed to Wally's aid had concurred with his quick explanation that the blame rested with the stuffy theater, and their quick and incorrect diagnosis turned Wally's lie into fact. Nevertheless, Rat Rubinstein had been cruel, and his words had forever cemented Wally's animosity toward him.

"Let's go, fellas," Wally said, and pushed him aside.

Max and Frankie followed, bumping Rat as they passed. "Later, Rat," Frankie snapped.

"C'mon, guys!" Rat angled his hat forward and followed them down the sidewalk. "Don't be like that."

Max nudged Frankie. "Didn't realize Manhattan had such a rodent problem."

"Makes me wish I had some rat poison," answered Frankie.

"Oh, please!" cried Rat. "I'm writing an article for the *Eagle* about the contest. A day-in-the-life profile of the contestants. Just trying to give these wide-eyed hopefuls a bit of public attention, you know? A local interest story?"

The boys picked up their pace and didn't respond.

"Don't you want some free press for your little ensemble?"

"What you write isn't press," grumbled Wally. "It's trash."

The boys hurried down the bustling avenue, past a Santa Claus ringing a bell for the Salvation Army, but Rat kept up with them, hopping over St. Nick's near-empty bucket.

"Come on, guys. Can't you see it?" Rat walked backward in front of them, raising his thumbs and forefingers to form a picture in the air. "'Brooklyn's Jingle Boys Dream Big.' Your folks'll be so proud."

When none of them answered, Rat sidled up next to Frankie.

"'Cept your father, right, Francis? He'd rather you be a cop like him."

Frankie stopped and grabbed Rat by his lapels. He lifted him and shoved him against the window of a department store featuring a tinseled tree with gifts gathered around it.

"What the hell d'you know 'bout my business, you little runt?"

"Ain't it true?" panted the cub reporter. People from inside and outside the store began to stare. "I got it on good authority you failed another police exam. Bet that was an awkward dinner conversation at the O'Brien's."

"Why, you little—"

Wally grabbed Frankie's arm before his friend could swing his fist at Rubinstein. With a crowd forming, the last thing the son of a policeman needed was a public scrabble or an imminent arrest.

"Leave us alone," said Wally, sneering at Rat from behind Frankie's elbow. "Beat it."

"I'm a reporter," Rat spat. "First Amendment? Freedom of the press?"

Frankie noticed the people gathering around them and released Rat, letting him slide down the store window to his feet.

"You heard him, rodent." Max aimed his index finger at Rubinstein's face. "Beat it."

The crowd dispersed and relief washed over Wally.

"Look, fellas—" Rat straightened his coat lapels, seeming more self-possessed under the watchful eyes of the store patrons still glancing at him through the window. "There are two ways I can write my story: using the facts as you give them to me or deploying my own prodigious imagination and masterful vocabulary. Either way, I run the article. You decide which way it goes."

Max stepped forward, moving Wally and Frankie aside, and pointed again at Rat. "Report this, Rubinstein: 'Brooklyn's Jingle Boys Ready for Big Win.' Think you can spell all that with your masterful vocabulary?"

"Big win?" Rat's beady eyes widened. "You sound pretty confident."

"Did I stutter?" said Max.

A jolt of fear ran through Wally. If Rat ran his article with Max boasting their victory before the contest was even decided, it could make the guys look overconfident, unworthy. And what if Brubaker, the station manager, was to see that in the paper? Or worse, what if they lost?

"Look," said Wally, "I'm sure this is all small potatoes to a big-time journalist like you. Why not find something else to write about? There's a war on, you know."

Rat ignored Wally, his eyes fixed on Max. "Big win," he repeated. "Got it." He tipped his hat. "See ya 'round, fellas."

As suddenly as he'd arrived, Rat scurried back into the crowd crossing Broadway.

"I hate that guy," Frankie growled.

"Don't worry," said Max. "We've got this in the bag."

Wally swallowed, unable to shake the feeling that, for once, it may have been the rat that had set the trap.

2

Why Can't My Heart Just Do Its Part?

It was early afternoon and the day had moved like molasses. Standing behind the A-Rite Cleaners cash register, Wally twirled his finger in his hair and stared at the shop door. Business had stalled at the dry cleaners since the war had begun, and Wally spent much of his time at the shop counter, staring at that same shop door. Usually, he spent his time worrying about gunship fights on the open sea or bomb explosions in a muddy ditch, wondering how and when his anxiety neurosis might strike once and for all. However, today it was a bombshell of the blonde sort that occupied his thoughts.

Max strode in from behind him and poked Wally's arm. "Gawking at the door won't bring in new customers," said Max.

Wally shook his head but didn't respond.

"Fine," said Max. "Ignore me." He returned to draping customer garments on wire hangers and placing them on the wait rack while whistling to some happy tune along with the shop radio. Even with Christmas just a few days away, fewer and fewer people were dry-cleaning their clothes, and the customers that did show up only seemed interested in pressing holiday tablecloths and napkins or hemming and repairing their old clothes to make them last. Such work was barely enough to keep the doors open, and the Lipkins were grateful for those loyal customers that still relied on them.

Wally's mother exhaled loudly from her stool at the end of the shop's long counter. "Mr. Fleming takes good care of his slacks," she said, pulling a threaded needle through a button on some worsted wool pants. "He's seventy-two and I keep expanding his waistline. I should tell him to lay off those rich desserts Mrs. Fleming makes."

"Don't you say a word, Sadie," Wally's father shouted from his desk at the back of the shop. "Those desserts pay our rent. If you want to help, bake him a pie."

"Oh, Saul." Wally's mother laughed and then peered at Wally over her half-moon glasses. "Walter?"

"Yeah?"

"You've hardly said a word since you boys came back from the radio station. Something wrong?"

"Just thinking about the contest, I guess."

Max emerged from the press through a puff of steam to hang a jacket. "I put our chances of winning at ninety-eight percent," he declared. "That Brubaker fella liked us. I could tell."

"You put our chances at a hundred percent when you blabbed to Rat Rubinstein," said Wally. "I don't think that was such a good idea."

"You worry too much," said Max. "We'll win hands down, and that pest will run home with his tail between his legs."

The contest had gone well. On that, Wally agreed. But the stakes had become even higher, and not just because of Rat Rubinstein. Wally now wanted more than the life-saving job in Washington. He wanted a chance with the knockout jingle singer too.

His mother wagged a thimble-capped finger at her boys. "If those studio men have any sense, you boys will win." She leaned forward and whispered, "I bought another war bond this morning."

"I heard that!" Saul called.

"We do our part," Sadie called back. "Soon enough, our Walter will be off fighting for the Jews and defending democracy. I want him to have all the *mazel* a bond can buy. Call it a Hanukkah present if it makes you feel better."

"I will!"

Wally appreciated his mother's eagerness to contribute to the war effort, and even shared her desire to protect the Jews and everyone else. But what would she say if she found out her only able-bodied son wasn't so able to fight after all? He was no Johnny Milhouser.

He returned his gaze to the door, imagining Bobbi gliding through, singing away his melancholy and filling him with the same sense of purpose she'd filled him with back at the studio.

Max closed the press with another hiss of steam, lifted the lid, and placed a second jacket on a hanger. His work completed, he switched off the press and stepped forward next to Wally's ear. "Still thinking about that girl?" he whispered.

"What?" Wally came out of his daydream. "What do you mean?"

Max snickered. "You can't fool me. When she walked into that studio, you got all starry-eyed. Same look you've got now."

Wally glanced down the length of the counter to be sure their mother wasn't listening, knowing if she heard about his interest in a girl, she'd grill him like he was some Nazi sympathizer.

"I've gotta see her," Wally whispered. "How 'bout we check out that club tonight, the one on Fifty-Second that Brubaker mentioned?"

"The Diamond Club?" Max shook his head. "Too expensive."

"I've saved a few bucks," said Wally. "I'll spring." His meager stash wasn't much, but to see Bobbi again, he was willing to put a dent in his savings. "We can grab Frankie from Mulligan's after work, take a cab straight over."

"A cab?" Max raised an eyebrow. "One dame flashes her lashes, and you're John D. Rockefeller?"

"She's not just one dame," said Wally.

When Sadie glanced their way, Wally hopped off his stool and nonchalantly switched on the industrial dryer, engaging its boisterous rumble, hoping to provide some ambient noise to cover his private conversation. He turned back to Max and kept his voice low.

"The way Brubaker trusts her, it wouldn't hurt our chances to show Bobbi a little support, would it? I doubt any of the other contestants are going to the Diamond Club."

Max's eyes narrowed as he puzzled over Wally's suggestion. "Stacking the deck? Very clever, little brother."

"So, you're in?" Wally tried not to sound desperate.

"I'll do you one better," said Max. "I'll prep the suits we just got from the Edelman bar mitzvah. I noticed three in our sizes—you, me, and Frankie. We can borrow 'em tonight and dry clean 'em again once we're back. We'll look like a million bucks."

As much as Wally wanted to look his best, he'd never borrowed a customer's clothes before. "I don't know, Max..."

"You don't want to show up in the same rumpled old suit from the morning, do you?"

"Rumpled?"

"Don't you want to look good?"

"Sure, I do."

"Great." Max then disappeared behind the clothes racks.

Wally knew better than to argue with Max once he'd set his mind to something, and if going along with his questionable plan meant he'd have his brother's support, he had to relent. He decided to focus, instead, on the night ahead. With their parents distracted, Wally collected the candy tin he had squirreled beneath the shop counter, folded a handful of bills he'd saved into his wallet, and returned the tin to its cubby.

When the workday finally ended, the brothers powered down the presses and fans for the night.

"Don't be too late," said their father upon hearing they'd be out for the evening.

"We'll lock up," said Wally.

After watching their parents leave, the boys grabbed the Edelman bar mitzvah suits, including the one for Frankie, and walked the four blocks to Mulligan's Grocery, where they found Frankie on his knees in the canned foods aisle, placing tins of beans on a shelf.

"How much is this club, anyway?" Frankie asked.

"Don't worry," said Max. "Wally's picking up the tab. Even said he'd spring for a taxi. He's warm for that jingle gal."

Frankie cocked his head. "This is all about a girl?"

"She has pull with Brubaker," said Wally. "Figured we could show her some support."

"Wally thinks she might put in a good word," added Max. "He wants to look good, which is why we nabbed these." He used three thick fingers to lift the trio of suits on wire hangers.

"Max is the one who nabbed them. I had nothing to do with it," said Wally. "I just wanted to make an impression."

Frankie stood once the last can of green beans was on display, brushed the dust from his knees, and looked Wally in the eye. "Call it what you like," he said, "as long as you're paying."

"Just leave your hat and coat here," said Wally. "I'm not springing for any coat checks."

"What about the drinking age?" said Frankie. "You're not eighteen until next week."

It was just last year that Wally had been to his first club. He and Max had slipped through the back door of the Rose Club to avoid questions about his age. It was a small supper and entertainment club in a questionable part of town, which they chose specifically for its reputation for looking the other way when underage men, mostly sailors and soldiers, came looking for a good time. Despite the precaution and premeditation over his intended crime, he'd been too nervous to drink anyhow. Now, he'd spent so much time thinking about the deadly consequences of his age, he hadn't connected it to the privilege of drinking.

Max seemed to key off Wally's concern. "Don't worry," he said. "Even fancy clubs like the Diamond don't care these days as long as you're paying. Course, if you think it'll be a problem—"

"It won't be a problem," said Wally. "Let's just get there."

"No argument from me," said Frankie. "I could use a drink, especially a free one."

With Frankie's work complete, the boys spruced up in the grocery restroom and donned the Edelman suits, which Wally had to admit were quite nice. His blue suit fit perfectly, and so did Frankie's gray one. Max's pigeon-breasted striped suit strained at the buttons but was passible. And Max was right. Wally felt like a million bucks.

Frankie locked up the grocery store as Wally hailed a taxi, and the trio soon made their way over the bridge toward Midtown and the Diamond Club. Wally stared out the taxi window as they approached Manhattan's towers, silhouetted against the cloudy winter sky. He loved the flashy billboards peddling cigarettes, toothpaste, and department store sales, especially during the holidays. He rolled the window down a crack and delighted in the sounds of trains, car horns, and the bleat of the ferries passing beneath the bridge. Once on the Manhattan side of the river, he heard newspaper hawkers calling out daily headlines, watched the smoke and steam that rose from the shoreline factories working around the clock, reveled in the scents of roasted nuts and women's perfume that permeated the streets this time of year. These all gave Wally the sense that anything was possible, even for a guy with a fainting problem in a borrowed suit and just a few bucks in his pocket.

When the taxi finally arrived at Fifty-Second Street, Wally settled with the driver and joined Max and Frankie under the club's twenty-foot-tall sign that formed the words "Diamond Club" in crackling lights over the entrance. Unlike the warmth of the taxi, the air outside was freezing, and since Wally had forbidden them from bringing their coats, he was eager to get into the club. A black-suited bouncer stood at the club's door with his arms crossed over his broad chest. When the guy eyeballed him, Wally immediately felt like a fraud, both for being underage and for showing up in someone else's suit.

"Evening, my good man," said Max, gazing at the brute.

The man ignored Max but continued to scrutinize Wally. "First time here?" said the man.

Wally frowned a little, thinking a broody look might make him appear older. "Second or third," he lied in a voice lower than normal.

The man paused as if having a silent conversation with himself about Wally, and then nodded. "Welcome back, then, sir. Have a nice evening." He opened the door.

Wally breathed out his relief and was the first to step through the threshold into the club. But that quiet relief was quickly replaced by an unexpected breathlessness that gripped him. The space around him seemed to bloom with wild, colorful splendor like the *Wizard of Oz* film, when everything bursts into Technicolor. The club was far larger inside than it had appeared from the street. Ornate fixtures lined the walls, floor to ceiling. Gleaming bulbs shaped like candle flames pulsed with electricity and filled the room with a warm golden glow. An enormous chandelier, strewn with glass baubles, hung from the center of the domed ceiling with its curling arms outstretched like some munificent octopus casting favor on the people fortunate enough to enter. The air smelled sweet like peaches, woven with wisps of cigarette smoke. Men in smart suits and women in bright dresses were seated in booths that lined the club's perimeter or chatted over cocktail tables that encircled the polished black-and-white-tiled dance floor. The place was further adorned with garland, wreaths, oversized colorful tree ornaments, and holiday décor—gilding the lily, so Wally thought.

Like Dorothy, Wally felt transported to an entirely different world.

A dark-haired hostess wearing a revealing, black-frilled uniform approached holding a stack of menus. "Table or booth?" she said with a grin.

"Table," managed Wally. He retrieved a dollar from his breast pocket and handed it to the gal, reminding himself of his mission. "With a view of the stage, if you don't mind."

The hostess looked at the bill but didn't take it. "A good view of the stage?"

Wally pulled out another dollar. "Yes, please."

"Pleasure," she said. She snatched both bills, folded them in half, and inserted them into the depths of her cleavage. "Here to see anyone in particular?"

"Bobbi LaFleur," said Wally. "You know her?" Heat climbed his cheeks.

Max elbowed Frankie, both of them grinning like Wally was some dope. But he didn't care.

The hostess winked. "Sure, I know her. This way."

Wally and the guys followed the hostess through the throng of patrons, none of whom were like the folks in Wally's neighborhood. People here were laughing, drinking, and acting as though they'd never heard of Adolph Hitler, appearing to have money they weren't afraid to spend. Wally doubted any of them had victory gardens, turned in their tins, or kept jars of their kitchen fat for weeks, as his family did. And he was willing to bet none of them had stolen their suits to be there.

The hostess led the trio around tables, maneuvering between busy waitresses carrying trays with tall glasses toward the front of the club. The shining and imposing stage rose above the floor. A crimson curtain hung in the back, fronted by long strands of glass beads like strings of diamonds suspended from the rafters. The hostess stopped next to a table situated front and center.

"How's this?" She gestured toward the table's French-style chairs facing the stage.

Wally gulped. He had hoped to see Bobbi from a safe distance, where a fast, clean getaway would have been an available option he might exercise. These seats offered no such means of escape.

"Perfect," said Max, but Wally felt far from it.

"Swell," said the hostess. "Darlene will be right over to take your orders." She left them with their menus.

The guys all took their seats. Frankie and Max ogled their menus, but Wally left his where it sat and, instead, looked around the club, trying to calculate the fastest route back to the entrance. He was half tempted to click his heels together to see if anything would happen.

"Some place," said Frankie, lifting his gaze from the menu to the club around them. "Heard it started as a speakeasy."

"Paper said a guy was shot here a year ago," said Max. "A gangster or something."

Wally inhaled and set his thoughts like a compass, due north, on Bobbi LaFleur. She was the reason he was here and the only thing that mattered tonight.

Frankie set his menu down and searched the club with a sudden urgency. "I need a drink," he said, scanning for the waitress. "My dad's busting my chops again to join the force. Keeps telling me it's an honorable way to help people, that it's an O'Brien family tradition. 'Policing is a selfless profession,' he keeps saying. I'm just not sure I'm the selfless type."

"You need to tell your dad to give it up," said Max, speaking over the murmur of the crowd.

"I've already thrown the exam twice," said Frankie. He rested his elbows on the table and held his head. "Flat feet may be a problem for the army. Ain't true for the Kensington police department."

"Then just tell him straight," Max urged.

"You're the one with moxie." Frankie's voice was strained. "Besides, it would just make him angry. Stupid Rat Rubinstein was right."

Wally felt for Frankie. He knew their friend didn't want the life that seemed to be chosen for him. Who would? Still, they could sort those things out later. Right now, Wally's issues were more pressing. He moved his attention to the stage, staring up at the glistening beads. What would happen when Bobbi stepped out and saw him? His plans to get here had been simple enough, but he had no plan for what would come next. He had jumped from the plane and forgotten the chute.

"You okay, brother?" asked Max. "You look a little flushed."

"I'm fine," said Wally.

"Don't worry," said Max. "I told you they don't care about your age. You're already in. Order whatever you like."

Wally pondered whether alcohol would help his anxiety or make it worse.

The hostess returned to their table, but before they could ask for their waitress, she leaned down next to them, an urgent look on her face. "Is one of you Walter?"

Wally tensed. "I'm him. I mean, I'm Walter."

"I told Bobbi she had company, and she spotted you from backstage. Said she needed to talk to you right away."

"Me?" Wally scanned the stage, but if Bobbi had been peeking through the curtains, she was gone now.

"I can take you to her. It sounded serious."

Wally looked to Max and Frankie, unsure how to react.

"Leave your wallet," said Frankie. "I mean, you said you were paying, right?"

Wally stood and tossed his wallet onto the table, ignoring Frankie's impertinence. He wanted to see Bobbi, maybe even talk to her at some point in the evening, but figured he'd have more time to wrangle up his courage, maybe bolster it with gin or whiskey. He drew a breath, buttoned his borrowed blue Edelman jacket, and ran his hand along the side of his head to assure the pomade still held his curls.

One Mississippi, two Mississippi...

"Follow me," the hostess said.

Wally trailed her through the din of patrons, the hum and noise of the nightclub waning as they climbed the side stairs to a crew door. They moved deeper backstage into the shadows behind the curtain, where Wally heard the whispers of stagehands dashing about, and smelled talcum powder and the aroma of sweaty costume fabric he thought desperately needed to be dry-cleaned. When they finally reached a dressing room, the hostess knocked on the door and twisted the knob before getting an answer.

"Found him!" she proclaimed. "Break a leg, honey!"

She pushed Wally forward and then pulled the door closed behind her.

The dressing room seemed more like a closet, crowded with racks of gowns, feathered boas, and hats. Wally spotted Bobbi sitting at a corner makeup table. She was carefully applying lipstick while squinting at an oval mirror that hung from a bent nail in the bare brick wall. She saw his reflection and turned on her stool.

"Thank goodness!" she said. She tossed her lipstick onto the table and then dashed over in a fog of perfume to take Wally's hand. Her makeup was pronounced and her green eyes glowed. She was draped in a floral silk robe tied with a sash and wore a pair of glistening silver heels that made her look like a movie star. "I've never been so happy to see someone," she said.

"Why?" said Wally. "I mean, thanks, but why me?" He withdrew his hand, fearful Bobbi might feel the sweat forming in his palm.

"It's fate," she said. "Doyle, my piano man, is a no-show. Split with my five bucks and left me without an accompanist. When I heard I had a visitor and saw you sitting there, I couldn't believe my luck. A piano player right there."

Wally's knees went weak, and he locked them to keep from falling.

"You up to it?" said Bobbi. "I'm good for another five."

"I've never played in a nightclub," he said, haunted by the memory of his Lincoln High School performance.

Two raps on the dressing room door, and it opened again, this time to reveal an angular man in a dark suit with black hair combed straight back from a perfectly horizontal hairline.

"Hey, sweetheart," the guy said, aiming his eyes at Bobbi. "You almost ready?" The man pushed aside a rack of dresses to get closer, appearing surprised to find Wally standing there.

"Hey, Eddie," said Bobbi. "This is Walter." She gestured toward him.

Wally recognized the guy from a picture he'd once seen in the papers. His pointy chin, thin mustache, and deep-set eyes were unmistakable.

"Eddie Diamond," the guy said, extending a hand with a shiny jewel-encrusted watch. "I run this outfit."

"Walter Lipkin," Wally stammered, shaking Eddie's hand.

"Walter's gonna sit in for Doyle," said Bobbi.

"Sounds great, sweetheart." He turned to Wally. "What're you gonna play?"

Again, Bobbi jumped in. "I was thinking, 'Why Can't My Heart Just Do Its Part.'" She grinned at Wally. "Know that one?"

Wally nodded. It was one of his favorites to play, and he suddenly wondered if Bobbi was right. Maybe this was fate.

"It's usually played with a small ensemble," said Bobbi, "but I've always liked it simple. Dressed down. Just me and the piano."

"Sounds terrific," said Eddie, "but you two better get hopping." He looked at his watch. "You're on in three minutes. It's a holiday crowd tonight, and I'm hoping they're feeling generous." With a flash of his toothy grin, Eddie left.

Bobbi turned her back to Wally and dropped her silk gown to the floor to reveal a shimmering silver dress that matched her heels, hugging her voluptuous body like a second skin. She turned and pointed to the undone zipper that traced each side of her spine. "Do me a favor, Curly?"

Wally inhaled Bobbi's floral perfume, steadied his hand, and zipped up her dress.

Three Mississippi, four Mississippi...

"Thanks!" She turned to the mirror, widened her eyes, and then squinted to check her makeup as Wally continued to stare. "Sheet music is already on the piano," said Bobbi. "Play it sweet and slow, okay? Like honey."

Wally nodded, trying not to glance at her cleavage so obviously. He closed his eyes, and silently continued to seven Mississippis.

"You okay?" Bobbi asked, catching his reflection in her mirror. "You look a little pale."

He opened his eyes and drew in the reminiscent smells of lilacs that danced around her.

"Aces," he lied, trying to muster some of his brother's moxie. He forced a smile, raised his chin, and silently pleaded with his demon to give him one chance, one night to be a regular guy. "I'm your man."

Bobbi grinned and slid her hands over her hips, smoothing the creases out of her dress. "Okay, tiger. Let's knock 'em dead."

Butterflies that seemed more like caged squirrels banged around in Wally's gut. He gritted his teeth and followed Bobbi through the dark backstage halls to a place just behind the curtain. Applause rose from the club, welcoming Eddie Diamond, who'd taken center stage.

"Ladies and gents," Eddie announced, "the Diamond Club's holiday revue continues strong with a pretty, little gal who I'm sure you'll see on the silver screen in no time. She's a real beauty with a pair of pipes to match." Someone in the audience whistled a catcall, but Eddie didn't miss a beat. "Tell your friends you saw her here first, folks. Join me in welcoming the talented, the lovely, Miss Bobbi LaFleur!"

The dark velvet and glass-bead curtains rose, the applause rang out, and a spotlight illuminated the stage. Bobbi swayed as she glided to her place in the light like a Brooklyn June bug drawn to a streetlamp, gliding forward as she had back at the WKOB studio. Hooting and hollering ensued at the gleaming angel that had floated onto stage. She seemed born for this sort of attention.

Wally forced his reluctant, knobby legs to follow and moved upstage to the bench of the ostentatious piano, a sparkling-white, diamond-trimmed grand. With all eyes fixed upon them, he entertained the thought that the gangster who Max said was shot here had gotten the better deal.

With a quick glance, he spied Max and Frankie at the front-row table he'd left minutes before, their own eyes wide like dinner plates. He feared he might repeat the air-raid drill incident on the rooftop with Audrey, even before he got the chance to play. He closed his eyes, searched for the calming scent of Bobbi's lilac perfume, his new anchor. He found it, felt his pulse slow, and opened his eyes, focusing on the piano keys. He set his fingers in home position and let the chemical reaction begin.

Without needing the sheet music, Wally began to play "Why Can't My Heart Just Do Its Part." It was a song he routinely played at home, and he found it oddly appropriate for the circumstances—*bashert*, as his mother would say in Yiddish—providence that Bobbi would even suggest it.

His hands on the ivories, he embellished the song's opening the same way he did the last time he had accompanied Bobbi. This piano, though unfamiliar, cooperated with him, quickly taking a shine to his movements, allowing him to shift his attention to Bobbi.

True and steady, her voice filled with melted butter, and she sang.

> *"That chance encounter when we met*
> *Is the one thing I regret,*
> *And now all I see is you.*
>
> *Our first night alone together,*
> *We both knew it was forever,*
> *And now all I hear is you."*

Wally's fingers tingled with excitement. Nervousness channeled away from his knocking knees, her voice and words drawing him in.

> *"But when you gin me up,*
> *And spin me up,*
> *And leave me at the start,*
>
> *My poor heart it breaks,*
> *My poor heart it aches.*
> *Why can't my heart just do its part?"*

Wally opened his eyes as Bobbi crossed the stage, the spotlight following. Her hypnotic voice, her perfect pitch, reached the farthest tables of the club, where her beauty and talent had transfixed everyone.

> *"You come and you go, and you do as you please.*
> *My heart is a door and you've got the keys.*
> *Oh, dear...*
>
> *That night when we both knew*
> *It was just me and, darling, you,*
> *And now you're so, so far from me.*
>
> *The last time we were together,*
> *I had hoped it was forever,*
> *And now you're lost as you can be."*

Just when Wally had settled into his calm space, Bobbi turned from the crowd and faced him. When their eyes met, he almost lost tempo but remembered her advice to play the tune slowly. He savored the notes, borrowing her thoughts of honey, finding opportunities to add his own stylings, careful not to take the attention off Bobbi, where it belonged. Her eyes thanked him, and instead of turning back to her adoring crowd, her gaze remained locked on his.

"But when you gin me up,
And spin me up,
And leave me at the start,

My poor heart it breaks,
My poor heart it aches.
Why can't my heart just do its part?"

Bobbi's words lifted the song's final note on a sweet, delicate breeze. It hung like a veil over the club, which Wally had forgotten was filled with other people. And the moment it ended, a roar of applause hit him like a wake wave off a troopship.

Bobbi smiled at the crowd, took a humble bow, and then angled her open palm toward Wally. She gave him a quick nod and mouthed the words, "Stand up."

Wally rose from the piano bench, fighting the urge to move his eyes off her, to lose the tether that kept him on Earth. He bowed and risked a glance to the crowd, but only for a second. Max and Frankie leapt to their feet with the others, clapping as fast as their hands seemed to allow, joining in the whistling and cheering.

Eddie Diamond appeared from stage right. He scanned the exuberant audience and beamed, trotting to center stage to take back the microphone and the crowd's attention.

"Didn't I tell you, friends? Just fantastic." He looked to Bobbi and Wally. "Quite a pair, right?"

As if on cue, Bobbi rushed over, took Wally's hand, and led him quickly offstage, his legs struggling to comply. The heat of the spotlight left his face once they raced behind the curtain, but he still felt warm all over. She pulled him down the hall like he was a petulant child, passing the next singer, who was waiting in the wings.

"Thanks a lot," the singer blustered as they raced by. "I gotta follow that?"

Once at the dressing room, Bobbi pushed open the door, spun around, and kissed Wally square on the lips.

The moment froze.

He tasted the flavor of her lipstick, smelled her alluring perfume, and tried to stay calm.

Bobbi withdrew and proclaimed, "That was the greatest moment of my life!"

Feather fluff and talcum swirled around him in a tornado. Visions of diamonds and ruby slippers crowded his thoughts. He tried to speak, but no words came. That's when the weight of it all hit him.

His stomach dropped, the room whirled, and his eyes lost focus. "Oh, no."

"Walter?"

Bobbi's voice grew distant, and the room fell dim. Wally's fingers started to quiver, playing their own piano, the song of his shame.

"Walter, what's happening?"

His body's betrayal struck like a house falling on him from the sky. Wally hit the floor, and somewhere in the Technicolor darkness, he heard air-raid sirens sounding out like the laughter of flying monkeys mocking him.

Wally sat up with a start, blinked his eyes, and tried to clear his vision of the diamonds that swirled there. The smell of old fabric made him think he was back at the dry cleaners, but the sight of a pink feather boa made him realize he was lying on the floor of Bobbi's dressing room, and the deep shame of what had happened came flooding into his thoughts.

Not again. Not now.

Bobbi, Max, Frankie, and the hostess came into focus. They stood in a circle leaning over him as if they were playing spin the bottle and Wally was the bottle.

"Walter!" Max chided. "Are you okay?"

Wally sat up, leaned on his elbow. "Yes."

"Guess fame didn't agree with you," joked Frankie.

"I didn't know what to do," said Bobbi. "One minute, you were standing, the next—"

Wally could still taste her lipstick on his lips and didn't need to be reminded of what had happened next. His goddamned anxiety neurosis had once again felled him. The enemy had prevailed.

"Sorry," he said, rising from the floor. "Shouldn't have skipped lunch. Never perform on an empty stomach. Rule number one." He forced an awkward smile but felt himself collapsing inside.

Wally's feigned indifference was ill-conceived, his lie certainly not his best, and he knew it. He dusted powder and feathers off his stolen suit, all eyes still fixed on him. He long believed that passing out in the midst of a battle was the worst thing that could ever happen to him, but now he knew he was wrong.

"Drink this," said the hostess. She handed him a glass.

Wally grabbed it and took a swallow, quickly realizing he'd gulped straight gin.

"Easy, brother," said Max. He patted Wally on the back as he coughed.

"You guys sounded great out there," said the hostess. "Eddie's already asking how to get you both on the schedule every night."

Bobbi leaned forward. "It was Walter who was great," she said. "How can I thank you?"

"Well," said Frankie, "there's the contest."

"Contest?" said Bobbi. "What do you mean?"

"Nothing," Wally coughed, fighting for composure. He shot Frankie a withering look and worked to clear his throat. "Frankie's confused."

"I'm not confused," said Frankie.

"Yes, you are!" Wally slammed his empty glass on Bobbi's makeup table, swallowed against the gin's lingering burn, and pointed to the door. "Outside, Frankie!" He took his friend by the arm. "Now!"

Wally dragged Frankie out of the dressing room, too embarrassed to look back.

"Thanks again!" Bobbi called after them.

With his pulse pounding in his head, Wally maneuvered Frankie through the cluttered backstage area to the club's rear door, which he kicked open to the dimly lit alley.

A pair of roaches skittered behind a reeking dumpster as Wally and Frankie strode out into the chilly winter air, with Max trailing behind.

"What the hell are you doing?" said Frankie, yanking his arm out of Wally's grasp.

"Me? What about you?" Wally's words echoed around them. "Why would you mention the contest to her?"

Max let the door slam closed. "Take it easy, you two."

Frankie's eyes were ablaze. "You said you were gonna make nice to the girl so we can get in good with Brubaker. That's what you said."

"We weren't going to ask her directly!" Wally blared. "That wasn't the plan."

"Blowing our best chance at winning that contest wasn't the plan either," yelled Frankie, smelling of whiskey. He poked Wally's chest. "If you weren't so starry-eyed, you'd have your priorities straight."

Max stepped between them. "We're not missing any chances," he said calmly. "Didn't you see the look on her face? She already knows she owes us. Wally's right."

"That's not what I'm saying," said Wally. "Bobbi doesn't owe us anything."

"Brubaker calls in the morning, and we'll see," said Frankie. "We'll just see."

Frankie handed Wally his wallet, which he quickly realized was empty.

"Perfect," Wally barked. "You cleaned me out. Guess there's no cab ride home now."

Frankie glowered but didn't reply. Instead, the trio walked in angry silence to the nearest subway station. Wally hugged his arms to his chest and lowered his head against the frosty breeze. It was cold and dark, and Wally wished they'd brought their coats after all.

They paid their fare using Max's pocketful of emergency nickels and took their seats for the long subway ride home.

Wally sat two rows in front of Max and Frankie with his back to them as the train hurtled toward Brooklyn. It was a suitable metaphor for the way Wally lived his haphazard life, always alone, barreling into the unknown without a plan, without a clue, praying for miracles that never seemed to materialize. He watched the lights of the subway tunnel flash by his window, as if every hopeful wish he had was disappearing behind him, one after the other.

It wasn't long, however, before the flames of his anger, fueled by gin, soon subsided, and his erratic heart slowed to keep pace with the clackety-clack of the subway tracks. The rhythm put some city music in his head, allowing the melody of New York to draw his fractured thoughts back to his duplicitous and defective brain.

He wasn't angry with the guys. Frankie and Max had dreams of their own, and tonight was as much about theirs as it was about his. He was angry, instead, with himself. A dope with his issues shouldn't dare to have such big dreams, and he'd paid the humiliating price for his audacity. He wanted so badly to be the sharply dressed piano player that Bobbi needed, to be as driven and determined as Frankie, or as self-assured and confident as Max. Instead, he was just a panicked clod in a stolen suit, destined to spend more time on the floor than in the arms of a girl. Since he had first seen Bobbi at WKOB, smelled her enticing perfume, heard her melodic voice, felt her fingers in his hair, nothing else seemed to matter. For the first time in months, Wally was thinking of something other than war, other than the certainty of his death.

"You played great tonight," said Max. He moved up a row, leaned forward, and crossed his arms on the back of Wally's seat, speaking over the railway sounds as the subway traversed the river. "Your performance was the best I've ever heard."

"Thanks," said Wally. He had to admit he had never felt more at home playing the piano than he had onstage with Bobbi tonight. As horrible as everything was that had followed, that part of the night was undeniably great.

Frankie joined Max and leaned forward too. "It was like you were in some sorta trance," Frankie said. "You really connected."

"Bobbi was the real star," said Wally. He kept his eyes on the window, uncomfortable with the praise that was being heaped upon him. He understood that compliments were how guys apologized without actually saying, "Sorry."

"That Bobbi likes you," said Max. "You oughta ask her out."

"Doubt she'll ever want to see me again," Wally said. "Not sure I could face her now, anyway."

"Course, you will," said Max, "when we win the contest."

"We need that money," said Frankie. "You'll see. We'll get the dough, you'll get the girl, and everything will work out fine."

Wally nodded and smiled, but he knew a lie when he heard one.

Under the glow of their Kensington brownstone's interior hallway light, Wally, Max, and Frankie keyed their way back into the Lipkins' apartment, careful not to wake Mr. and Mrs. Lipkin. The guys were exhausted, not just from their trip to Manhattan but from the extra hour it had taken to retrieve their clothes from Mulligan's and to return the Edelmans' suits to A-Rite. They had to dry-clean and rehang the garments to cover their tracks, and that level of detailed deception, it turned out, was a time-consuming, tiring business.

Frankie crashed on the sofa with a Lipkin family afghan blanket, and Max face-planted onto his bed in the guys' bedroom, snoring before his head hit the pillow. Wally, on the other hand, found it harder to wind down from the events of the evening.

He paused at the dresser he shared with Max, suddenly drawn to the hidden heirloom he had long ago secreted away under the clothes in his large top drawer. He quietly pulled it open and pushed his hand into the depth of his folded underwear and socks, feeling around for a ring box he had tucked away at the age of thirteen, the day after his bar mitzvah.

The long-languishing box was a small, smooth wooden cube etched with fine, Hebrew letters, arranged to spell his Hebrew name. Like all Jewish boys, upon his birth, Wally had been gifted a Jewish name along with his given name—a name designed to be used in communal ceremonies like circumcisions, bar mitzvahs, or weddings.

His name was *Shelomo*—Hebrew for Solomon.

He had only heard himself referred to as Shelomo twice in his life, once during Max's bar mitzvah and once again during his own coming-of-age ceremony. It felt odd to have a name designed to fit, but to be used only rarely, like a rented wedding tuxedo or a new funeral suit. He supposed it made sense to give a man a secret identity, like Clark Kent and Superman, for those times when a guy just wanted to pretend his miserable life actually belonged to someone else. But since the Lipkins were not temple-going Jews, this name, Shelomo, now seemed like an artifact, an artifice, a public thing to wear on the right occasion, but meant to languish like his ring box, tucked away for some special occasion that never seemed to come.

Tonight, oddly, for the first time in years, that box called to him.

He pulled it out, slowly pushed the drawer closed with his shoulder, and retreated to his bed, where he sat by the buzzing radiator. He lifted the box open against tiny golden hinges under a wash of moonlight that beamed through his bedroom window, clouded with frost. Inside was a silver ring, a thing of beauty, adorned with Hebrew letters along the band, like those etched on the box. A Jewish star seal on the ring's face shone like an emblem wealthy noblemen might use to endow hot wax with a family crest. This, however, was not the tool of a nobleman. It was a bar mitzvah gift from his grandmother, an heirloom left behind by his grandfather, who had passed when Wally was just seven.

His bubbe Esther had pulled Wally aside after his last bar mitzvah guest had left the temple, while his parents were putting away the leftover challah and brisket. It was a time before anxiety neurosis had become Wally's curse, when remembering his Torah portion and Hebrew pronunciations were the largest of his concerns.

He recalled Bubbe Esther cornering him by the bathrooms, taking his hand, and placing the box square in his palm. "This, Walter," she said, "is for you."

Wally had opened the box and gaped at the shining ring. "Why?" he said, believing himself unworthy and undeserving of such a family treasure. "Isn't this Papa Herschel's ring?"

"It is."

"Shouldn't it go to Max?" said Wally. "He's the oldest."

His bubbe scoffed as though she'd eaten something sour. "Don't be foolish," she said. "Why should being born first make a person more worthy of a gift?"

Wally had shrugged.

"Max has many gifts of his own," his bubbe had said, "and he'll have many more, just because he's first. Your papa Herschel was third in his family, and I was second in mine. This is not a gift for the first born, *tatala*. This ring has always been for you. You were named for Solomon after all. Shelomo was granted the kingdom, even though he was not the first born to David."

"I'm no King Solomon," Wally had said.

"Solomon was many things," Bubbe Esther had replied cryptically. "Even had a ring of his own. Perhaps someday you will understand."

Wally had cherished Bubbe Esther's words more than the ring, particularly the permission her words seemed to grant that he, like his namesake, could be many things. And, after several hours of eyeing the heirloom, imagining all the many things he might one day become, he had returned the ring to its box and shoved it in his underwear drawer, where it had sat for years.

He now angled the open box in the moonlight. He remembered the tale from Hebrew school, a Jewish story about wise King Solomon and his own ring of power, bequeathed by God himself. The ring gave Solomon the ability to talk to animals—and even plants—but, most importantly, it held power over demons like Asmodeus.

The mighty Asmodeus, king of the demons, according to the tale, had threatened the Jewish people, tricked and tormented them, and created mayhem and discord. However, through the power of the ring, Solomon—Shelomo—had overcome Asmodeus, tamed and controlled him, and forced the mighty demon to use his strength and guile to help build the Great Temple of Israel, restoring hope and life back to the Jews.

It was a story Wally now remembered, not just because he shared the wise king's name but because, ever since that stunted kiss with Eleanor Getzman, he had longed for a way to control his own demon. He was tempted to don the ring now and implore it to vanquish the demon inside him, the one that seemed determined to sabotage his life. He wished now to activate the ring and smote the anxiety neurosis that plagued him, dogged him, and unraveled the fabric of his life, to use the ring to end his misery and allow him to dream of a life without his curse.

But Wally knew his answers didn't lie in a ring bequeathed by his grandparents, hidden beneath his underpants. God had not looked upon Wally as he had upon Solomon, and deemed him worthy of divine intervention. Wally's demon was not named Asmodeus. Wally was his own demon, and how did one smite oneself and reap any benefit?

He quietly closed the wooden box as if closing the chapter on his book of childish dreams, stepped over to his bureau, and once again buried such hopeful nonsense back in the depths of his top drawer. When his weary head finally hit the pillow and his delusions faded, his last thought was to wonder why anyone would want the power to talk to plants anyway.

3

Visitors

Wally and Max stood bleary-eyed by the family phone, awaiting Brubaker's call and the results of the jingle contest. There had never been a more important call, and Wally wished he was more lucid as he faced his fate.

"This is like waiting for water to boil," said Max, staring at the phone receiver.

"Huh?" Frankie rose from the Lipkins' couch, the family afghan in a heap beside him. His red hair was uncombed, and he couldn't stop yawning.

"When's this Brubaker character supposed to call anyway?" Saul asked. He stood by the open front door, wearing his coat and hat, clearly eager to get to work.

"He said he'd call this morning," said Max. "He didn't give us a time."

"What kind of *meshuggener* doesn't give a time?"

Sadie, already in the hallway, peeked around the open door. "You boys can use the phone at the shop."

"Brubaker doesn't have the shop number, Ma," said Max. "He's gonna call us here."

"Pop, can't we just meet you at the cleaners?" asked Wally, finally rising to the moment. "It's right downstairs. I don't understand why you even wear your coat and hat."

"It's work, and it's December," his father snapped. "I take work seriously and so should you." He pushed his hat forward as if punctuating his thought. He pressed his fingers to his lips and touched them to the doorframe *mezuzah*, giving his home the traditional Jewish blessing before stomping out the door and down the stairwell.

"Good luck, boys," said their mother. "I'll handle your father. And don't forget, it's the first night of Hanukkah. I'm making a brisket." She blew them a kiss and dashed after her husband.

With his parents gone, Wally closed the door and leaned against it, the pressure of the moment building in his head. "I've never wanted anything so much in my life," he said.

Of course, neither Max nor Frankie knew that Wally's life depended on what Brubaker said on the phone. He needed a Hanukkah miracle.

"Relax," said Max. "Brubaker will call to congratulate us, and we'll be celebrating in no time."

"I need that dough," said Frankie, his voice raspy from lack of sleep and a night full of whiskey. He stretched his arms to the morning and then ran his fingers through his red mop. "Don't jinx it."

Before Wally could ask why Frankie was so obsessed with money, the doorbell buzzed, vibrating the door at Wally's back. When he opened it, Roger Brubaker was standing there in the flesh, wearing a long coat, a bright-blue bow tie under his chin, his hat in his hand. The cool air from the street downstairs still swirled around him in the hallway and gave his cheeks a flushed glow.

"Mr. Brubaker?" said Wally. "We were waiting for your call about the contest."

"Figured I'd pay you a visit instead." The station manager looked in from the doorway like a tourist on some foreign vacation, ogling the scenery. "Place ain't easy to find."

"Don't just stand there, Walter," chided Max. "Invite him in."

"Right. Sorry, Mr. Brubaker. Please, come in."

The station manager walked past Wally into the family room, continuing to size up the place. When he spotted the piano, he pointed at it with his hat. "An upright. Nice. That a Wurlitzer?"

"Yessir," said Wally. "Course, it's nothing like the Steinway at the studio."

"We use what we've got," said Brubaker. "And that there is a lesson."

Wally puzzled over his words but couldn't quite understand his point.

"Please have a seat," said Max. "Can we take your coat?"

"No need. Can't stay long." The station manager sat in their father's chair, rested his hat on his knee, and leaned forward. "I came to give it to you straight and in person, boys." He shook his head. "You fellas didn't win."

The oxygen seemed to leave the room, and Wally's apartment walls felt like they were closing in. Brubaker's single pointed declaration confirmed every fear he'd had. He'd never see Bobbi LaFleur again, and he would die for sure in some European ditch. He staggered over and sat on the piano bench.

"Didn't win?" Max repeated.

"You're talented. All three of you," Brubaker added. "Each of you, standouts. The lyrics, the composition, the playing. All top-notch."

"Thanks, I guess," said Frankie, "but we were hoping for the cash."

"And the radio play." Max hung his head.

Wally just wanted the job, but now, the lesson of his life was clear: broken men were destined for broken hearts. His fate was sealed, and for good measure, Rat Rubinstein would skewer them alive in the *Brooklyn Daily Eagle*. Everything was falling apart.

"Don't sound so glum, fellas. You won second place."

"There's a second place?" Wally perked up.

"You bet there's a second place," said Brubaker. "Second out of fifty-three contestants. That's pretty good in my book."

"What's second place get?" said Frankie, now more awake.

"Second place gets a shot at another jingle. A paid one. That is, if you're interested."

"Sure we are," said Max.

"Another jingle?" said Wally. The air quickly returned to the room, and it smelled like lilacs. "Is there still a job in it? The one in Washington?"

"I suppose jobs could still be on the table," said Brubaker.

Wally's greatest wish burned like the undying Hanukkah *shammos*, lasting beyond the oil that could reasonably be expected to fuel its flame.

"What's the jingle for?" said Max. "More war bonds?"

"Podolor Diaper Service," said Brubaker with more fanfare than Wally thought diapers deserved. "The Podolor ad men are in a pinch and need a jingle, pronto. Think you're up to it?"

"What's it pay?" interrupted Frankie.

"Gig pays thirty bucks," said Brubaker, "ten of which goes to me as your manager in this little arrangement. Anyone will tell you that's a square deal."

"When do they need it?" asked Max.

Brubaker leaned back in their father's chair. "Tomorrow."

"We'll do it!" Wally replied before Max could answer. He didn't know anything about diapers, but the new jingle meant he'd have another chance at seeing Bobbi, another chance to hit up Brubaker for that Washington job, another shot at surviving this god-forsaken war.

Max caught the fever too. "All right," he said. "We're in."

"But it's five bucks to you, and the rest to us," said Frankie. His sleepy eyes suddenly focused like a fox spotting his prey.

"Five's a little thin for a manager, Red."

Frankie pushed back an errant strand of hair and stepped forward. "You came all the way to Brooklyn when you could've just called us on the phone," Frankie said. "I'm betting you've got no one else to pull off this diaper deal by tomorrow."

The station manager fell silent, locking a stony-faced stare on Frankie.

"Without a jingle," Frankie continued, "there's no money to split. And there's gotta be a premium for pronto, right?" Frankie raised his eyebrow triumphantly.

Wally held his breath, afraid Frankie might have ruined their chances, both at the money and at the job in Washington.

"Francis," Brubaker began, using Frankie's real name for the first time. "I like you"—he gestured toward Wally's brother—"but maybe leave the moxie to Max."

Wally was surprised to hear that Brubaker had remembered their names.

Max smirked some quiet victory and Frankie just frowned.

"Let's keep it at ten clams to me," Brubaker pronounced. He lifted his hat off his knee and pointed it at the boys. "Tomorrow, we can talk about your future."

"Sounds fair!" blurted Wally, and Frankie quietly conceded, obviously seeing that money may lie in that future to which the station manager alluded.

Brubaker stood, put his hat on his head, and reached for the door.

"Almost forgot—" He pulled out a folded sheet of paper from the pocket of his wool overcoat. "Those Podolor fellas are quirky. They have some specific requests for their jingle."

"What kinda requests?" said Max.

Brubaker handed him the sheet. "Four-by-four count. Five lines of lyrics. First line's gotta end with the word 'hoist.' Fourth line ends with the name 'Podolor.' They wanna hit some notes on certain measures too. It's all there on that paper."

"Strange requests," said Max, eyeballing the sheet.

"Told you," Brubaker said. "Think you can manage it?"

Frankie snatched the paper and waved it at Brubaker. "You guarantee the pay; we can manage anything."

"Terrific," said Brubaker. "See you boys at the station tomorrow morning, nine o'clock sharp."

With only one day to pull together the new jingle, the trio realized they would have no time for their day jobs. Frankie placed a call to the grocery and got Mr. Mulligan on the line. With his voice still froggy from lack of sleep, Frankie managed to convince Mulligan he was too sick to come in to work.

Wally's father would be a different story.

"What are we gonna tell Pop?" said Wally. "He wasn't exactly supportive this morning."

"We got second place. We tell him there's money in it for us," said Max.

"He's gonna want his part of it."

"So, we bargain," said Max. "You know what he's like."

Wally opened the door, ready to accompany Max downstairs for the conversation with their father, but standing in front of them was Audrey.

"Your mother said I could find you here," Audrey said. Her arms were crossed, and she frowned at Wally like Superman using laser vision to burn a hole through a bank vault.

Panic shot down Wally's spine as he realized that last night's trip to the Diamond Club meant he'd missed his radio date with Audrey, her price for keeping his secret.

"Audrey!"

She returned a dark, angry stare and Wally quickly turned to Max.

"Can you handle things with Pop?"

Max eyed Audrey and then Wally. "Fine, but you owe me."

"Thanks," said Wally. He leaned into the apartment. "Hey, Frankie, help yourself to some coffee," he shouted. "Stashed a jar behind the cornflakes. I'll be right back."

"Already on it," said Frankie, opening the cupboard.

Max strode off to A-Rite as Wally closed the door behind him, stepping into the hallway with Audrey.

"Look," he said, bolstering himself. "I can explain—"

"Save it, Walter." She looked away.

"I'm sorry," he said. "I got distracted by this whole jingle contest." He wasn't about to explain to Audrey that he'd gone to a club to see another girl, but he wanted to express his genuine regret. "I know I owe you."

Audrey looked at Wally, dropped her arms, and softened her stare. "You don't owe me," she said. "We're friends. I'll keep your secret. It's just—I waited for you all night."

"I'm so sorry," said Wally. "I feel like a heel. I want to listen to the radio with you," he said. "I really do."

"Tonight, then?" said Audrey. There was a lilt in her voice, her laser vision now warm and inviting.

"We have to write another jingle tonight. We got second place and—"

"I could help. I mean, with the jingle. You know I can sing…"

Audrey did have a wonderful voice. Wally recalled her solos at the holiday concerts back at school and her constant singing of radio ads. But adding her to the mix would only complicate what was already seeming like a complicated undertaking. He had too much at stake to take any unnecessary risks.

"We're kind of on a deadline," he replied, "and you know how Max gets."

"I understand." Audrey hung her head, and Wally felt more like a heel than before.

"Let's plan another night, okay?"

Audrey's eyes brightened. "How about Monday night, then? It's *Nick Carter, Master Detective*." She knew it was Wally's favorite program, and it was clear she was leaving nothing to chance.

"Sure," said Wally. "Monday's great."

"I'll even make dinner," said Audrey. She flashed a smile and rushed up the stairs.

Wally took a deep bagpipe breath, relieved that she was just as willing to move past his failures as she was to keep his secrets.

He walked back into his apartment to join Frankie for a cup of coffee in the kitchen. After a few minutes, Max returned and sniffed the air.

"Coffee?"

"The last of it," said Wally. He pushed forward an empty cup and filled it for Max.

"I think you may have missed the point of rationing," he joked.

"Then I guess you won't be having any sugar," quipped Wally.

Max raised an eyebrow, reached for the sugar, and heaped in a spoonful. "Very funny."

"How'd it go with Pop?"

"Good and bad," said Max, sipping his cup of joe.

"Give us the good," said Frankie. "We need a win."

"All right." Max set down his cup. "I convinced him to give us the day off to write the diaper jingle."

"That's great!" said Frankie.

"What about the bad?" Wally braced himself.

"I told him we'd write a jingle for him too. For A-Rite Cleaners."

"What?" said Frankie. "When?"

"Tonight. I told him we'd ask Brubaker tomorrow what it would cost to run it on the air."

"Two jingles in one day?" Frankie rubbed his temples, which, no doubt, pounded with the memory of too much whiskey. "I barely have it in me to write the one." He chugged his coffee.

Wally made his way over to the piano, where his mother had already set the menorah and a box of wax candles for the evening's celebration. Thanks to Saul, the Hanukkah miracle Wally had hoped for already had strings attached. Nevertheless, he remained undeterred.

"Let's do A-Rite first," said Wally. "We know more about dry cleaning than diapers, so it'll be a good warm-up."

He lifted the keyboard lid of their family Wurlitzer, which now felt small and dilapidated after playing the polished, shiny grand pianos of both the station and the club. He tapped out some combinations, his fingers buzzing with possibility, or perhaps that was just the coffee starting to kick in.

"You think that Bobbi girl will wanna sing the A-Rite jingle?" said Max.

"Worry about that later," said Wally. But the thought of Bobbi was exactly what he needed to spur his creativity.

Back and forth, the boys worked for hours, taking only one break to snatch leftovers of cold chicken and glazed carrots from the icebox. Together they tooled over their handiwork, music prompting lyrics, and lyrics forcing music, until the coffee ran out and momentum took over.

Max sang aloud, noodling over the words. Frankie wrote them out in time to the tune Wally was crafting, and so it went until they finally had an A-Rite jingle they thought their father would like.

"Okay, Wally. Play like you did last night," said Max.

"Just don't faint this time," said Frankie.

The two burst out laughing at Wally's expense, giddy from exhaustion and Maxwell House's finest.

The heat of embarrassment rose along the backs of Wally's ears. The guys had refrained from bringing up the Diamond Club incident all day, but he realized he couldn't escape their mockery any longer.

"I was tired," explained Wally. "And I didn't feel well."

Max sat next to Wally on the piano bench and collected his composure. "It does make me a little nervous, Walter. It was Liberty High all over again. Maybe you should see a doctor."

"Doctor?" Wally thought again about his poor uncle Sherman, locked away for years at Brooklyn State Hospital, presumably poked and prodded by doctors, wasting away like some sort of criminal or zoo animal with only Wally's mother to visit him. "I'm fine," he lied. "Just sensitive to stuffy rooms, that's all."

Wally placed his fingers on the piano and started playing. He didn't want to spend another second thinking about fainting, and he hated lying to Max.

"Okay," said Max after a wistful pause. "Let's pick it up with the intro." He stood from the bench, lifted his lyric page, and sang the jingle as Wally played.

> *"A pleat that's pressed, a hem that's straight,*
> *Your evening dress that can't be late...*
> *You need a tailor you can trust.*
> *Try A-Rite Cleaners—that's a must.*
>
> *A button sewn,*
> *a tear repaired,*
> *The A-Rite team will show they care.*
> *Just say 'A-Rite,' that's the word.*
> *Kensington corner—Church and Third.*
> *A-Rite Cleaners! "*

Wally lifted his fingers. "Well?"

"I like the two-octave staccato," Max said. "It hops."

Frankie nodded. "You father will like it."

"Even gives the address," said Wally. "Good touch."

"Well, it's good enough to run by Pop when he gets home," said Max. He flipped the page on his steno pad. "A-Rite was the easy jingle. We still have to write the diaper one."

"Where's that list of requests?" said Wally. "The one from Brubaker?"

Frankie handed Max the sheet with the instructions.

"These requests are more than 'quirky,'" said Max, skimming the page. "Guess it makes sense that diaper people are full of crap."

"Very funny," said Frankie, "but what do we know about diapers?"

Max walked the list over to Wally, who started to toy with a few combinations. After some trials and improvisation, lyrics began to swirl in Wally's brain.

"How's this?" said Wally. He played as he sang, "You give your kid a hug, a hoist, and find your tot's a little moist."

"Hey, that's good!" said Frankie, leaning over Wally. "You worked their word 'hoist' into that first line."

Max smiled. "You even talked about piss without actually saying the word. Well done!"

Wally tilted his head. "Still needs a second verse, though."

Max's face betrayed a flurry of thoughts, and he added: "Just send those nappies out the door, and trust that tush to Podolor." He raised an eyebrow. "Can we say 'tush' on the radio?"

"If you say 'ass,' it sounds like a limerick." Frankie laughed.

Suddenly, in the middle of their laughter, the doorbell buzzed again.

Grinning, Wally opened the door to a tall man in a Western Union uniform, a telegram in his hand.

"You the Milhousers?" the man asked.

Wally's smile evaporated and his heart leapt to his throat as if the Western Union man were the grim reaper. Sad telegrams were being delivered all over the city these days with news of fallen soldiers. A telegram to the Milhousers could only mean one thing.

"Upstairs," said Max when Wally was struck silent. "3-B."

The man pulled the brim of his blue cap. "Thanks."

Wally closed the door and turned to Max, whose face was saying what Wally was thinking.

"Johnny deployed in April," said Wally. His stomach knotted at the thought of Audrey and Carl answering their door.

"Telegram could be about anything," said Max.

"Yeah, anything," agreed Frankie.

The guys lacked Wally's skill at deceit, and their attempt to lift his mood failed miserably. He returned to the bench, placed his hands over the piano keys, but held them. His thoughts lingered on the Milhousers and his friend Johnny. He tried to think of the last time he saw Johnny, and remembered it was the day he had shipped off. He'd come home after basic training in New Jersey. He was wearing his uniform and looked years older than when he had first left for the army. Wally's mother told Johnny he looked handsome, but Mrs. Milhouser just cried. Johnny kept things light, smiled at them all, told Audrey and Carl to stay out of his room until he got back, and told Wally and Max to keep an eye on things while he was gone. He then took his mother by the hand and told her everything would be all right.

"Hey, piano player!" Max snapped his fingers at Wally.

"Give him a minute," said Frankie in a rare moment of discord with Max.

"You wanna go up and see Audrey?" asked Max.

It was exactly the thing Wally knew he should do, but the last thing he wanted. Now, more than ever, he had to find a way to get that Washington job, otherwise the Western Union Man would be back.

"No," said Wally. "I'm sure you're right. Could be anything. I'll check on her later." He played a C-major scale to chase away the "rum-pa-pum-pum" of war drums in his head. "Let's get this jingle written."

The boys worked through the last of the Podolor jingle challenge. Wally jazzed up the intro, each note distracting him from his thoughts of war and death. Max checked that all of the Podolor requirements had been satisfied, and Frankie put it all to paper, capturing the best of the improvisations. In the end, they agreed the second jingle also hit the mark.

Before the melancholy from the Western Union man's visit could find its way back into Wally's full conscience, the front door opened and their father entered, their mother just behind.

"You boys got my jingle?" Saul asked, one foot into the apartment.

"Your father closed five minutes early," said their mother. "That's a first."

"Yeah, we've got it," said Max. He motioned to Wally. "Play it."

Wally shook away his haunting thoughts of Johnny Milhouser and played the piano as Max sang with gusto, ending with Wally's favorite part:

> *Just say "A-Rite," that's the word.*
> *Kensington corner, Church and Third.*
> *A-Rite Cleaners!"*

As the last verse left Max's lips, Sadie was quick to pronounce judgment. "It's perfect!"

She grabbed her husband's arm, a tear in her eye. "Saul, isn't it perfect?"

Their father's wide-eyed look jumped between the boys until a smile transformed his face. "Even worked in the address!" He threw his hands into the air. "The address, Sadie! These boys of ours, they make me wanna get back to the Catskills." He tossed his coat and hat onto his chair and then pointed at Wally. "Play it again, Walter!"

Wally breathed his relief and Max sang as they played the A-Rite tune once more.

Their father grabbed their mother by the waist and waltzed her around the coffee table. True performers, Wally's parents sang along to the jingle as if it had been their theme song since the day they first opened.

When the music ended, his father was winded. "Okay," he wheezed. "What'll it cost to run this on the radio...right after that new show Walter likes?"

"*Nick Carter, Master Detective*," said Wally.

"Yeah," his father said. "It's perfect. People who like detective programs like their clothes dry-cleaned."

Wally puzzled over his father's strange logic but decided to leave it alone.

"I'll ask Mr. Brubaker at the studio tomorrow," offered Max.

The doorbell buzzed again, and Wally feared their playing and dancing had disturbed the neighbors. His mother danced to the door and opened it, her face bright with an A-Rite smile.

It was Helen Milhouser. She wore an apron, curlers in her hair as though they'd been there all day, her eyes swollen and red.

"Helen?" Sadie's voice grew small. "Helen, dear, what's happened?"

"Oh, Sadie!" Mrs. Milhouser collapsed into his mother's arms, sobbing. "Johnny's gone," she cried. "He's gone!"

Wally's gut grew tight, a prickly pain crossed his skin, and a chill creeped into his bones. The boisterous fun was over.

Mrs. Lipkin took Mrs. Milhouser by the arm and steered her to the sofa. "Here, dear. Come and sit."

The sobs began anew, and the music faded to memory, replaced by a thick and heavy sadness that fell over the room like a leaden blanket. The three jingle writers hung their heads and quietly gathered their papers, agreeing to complete their work in the hall. And as Wally closed the door behind them, he saw his mother take Mrs. Milhouser's hand in hers and say, "You have the gift of knowing Johnny was brave, Helen. And that is a gift, indeed."

4

Podolor Diaper Service

It was nearly midnight when Wally finally found Audrey on the rooftop of their apartment building, staring at the stars that hung overhead. She wore her lavender winter coat with a blue scarf and was sitting on the same deck chair she'd sat on the night she learned Wally's dark secret. He needed her friendship then, and tonight he suspected she needed his.

"How can you tell if it's an enemy plane and not one of ours?" Audrey asked, her eyes fixed on the sky. She seemed to know Wally was there without even looking.

"Precinct captain gives us a list of planes and flight times," said Wally. He stepped onto the roof and flipped up his coat collar against his ears to ward off the cold. "Course, I just figured the enemy planes would be the ones dropping bombs on us."

Audrey grew quiet, and then said, "I don't see any planes. I was just wondering."

Wally pulled the other deck chair next to hers and sat. "I'm sorry about your brother."

"Why?" Her cheeks were red, her blue eyes glossy under the icy moonlight.

Wally bit his lip. "Sorry" was just what you said when bad things happened. He hadn't considered why.

"Johnny was my friend," he finally said. "He was a hero. We're always sorry when we lose a hero."

"We didn't lose him," she grumbled. "He was killed. And dying doesn't make someone a hero."

Wally recalled his mother's words that Johnny's bravery should serve as a comfort to Mrs. Milhouser. Little did she know that cowardice and fear were the only things Wally had to offer.

"Well"—he drew in a nose full of frigid air—"I'm still sorry."

Audrey tucked her brown hair behind her ear; redirected her attention back to the starry sky as if, somehow, Johnny could be found there; and fell silent.

Wally let her silence stand and directed his attention to the stars as well. It was as if they were preserved, the two of them, trapped in a New York City snow globe like the kind they sold in Times Square. Through the stillness, he heard the late-night sounds of the neighborhood and used the music of Kensington to drown out his own feelings of loss and quell his nagging wish for half the courage shown by his pal Johnny. Dogs barked somewhere in the distance; trucks growled through the borough, and one even bleated its horn. Even this late, people were busy, coming home from Christmas shopping or finishing their Hanukkah celebrations. His family's own Hanukkah celebration had been understandably postponed, the focus turning instead to the loss of Johnny and the comfort they all tried to offer the Milhousers. Wally's mother had thrown together a quick but substantial broth from the leftover kosher chicken and served it with toasted rye bread to Mrs. Milhouser and Carl, the only food they could convince Audrey's mother to eat. Carl devoured the meal eagerly, seemingly out of desperation to fill a new hole that had formed from the news of his brother. Mrs. Milhouser, on the other hand, barely touched her dinner.

After a quarter hour of stillness, Audrey finally blew frost into the air and turned to Wally, an urgent look in her eyes.

"Are you gonna die too?" she asked.

Wally winced, not because Audrey's question was direct or insensitive, but because it was familiar. It was the question he'd been asking himself for months.

"When you enlist," he said with a practiced tone, "you have to acknowledge that death is one of the possible outcomes. You just have to accept that."

"Are you trying to convince me or yourself?"

Wally fell silent.

"What I'm asking is, aren't you worried?"

"Worrying hasn't been working out too well for me," said Wally. He figured Audrey's recollection of their last visit to the roof would support his point, and she didn't even know about the Diamond Club incident. Worry was a constant companion. He wanted to offer her assurances that he was working on a plan, wanted to mention the contest and the possibility of the government job, but even he was uncertain of its likelihood to save his life.

Again, she studied the sky as if reading some sort of story written there. "You're afraid you'll pass out in the middle of combat, like you did up here the other night, aren't you?"

A knot caught in Wally's throat. To hear another person articulate the details of his greatest fear made it more real, perhaps more likely.

"That's exactly what I'm afraid of," he said with more defeat in his voice than he intended. He swallowed against a dryness that had worked its way into his throat.

Audrey faced him again, her pink cheeks newly wet with tears. "Then that's what I'm afraid of too."

A rush of warmth flowed through Wally's limbs at the realization that Audrey was the only person who saw him for exactly who he was: a neurotic coward desperate for an ally.

"Why do you like me?" he asked.

Audrey grew rigid, as though he'd issued the greatest insult she'd ever heard.

"Can't you see anything?" she said, her wet eyes ablaze. "The real question is, why don't you like yourself?"

Before Wally could ponder a response, Audrey's brother, Carl, emerged from the fire escape, this time with more caution and care than when he had inadvertently scared Wally. He was wearing his cowboy hat, boots, and a coat awkwardly buttoned over his pajamas. His eyes were bleary from sadness.

"Audrey, Mom wants you to come home." He sounded congested.

Without a word, she stood from the creaking chair and followed Carl back down the fire escape, relieving Wally from answering her question.

In Audrey's absence, a strange, sudden silence blanketed Brooklyn as if the world were hushed, awaiting Wally's response. He fought an inexplicable urge to race to the flagpole and sound the air-raid siren, to raise a panic in others that mirrored the panic he always seemed to carry within him, a silent alarm perpetually ringing in his head.

Instead, he searched the stars Audrey was deciphering earlier, looking for his own answers. He pulled his knees close and tried to quiet his mind. In that moment, he longed for Solomon's ring of power, understanding clearly for the first time that if you couldn't vanquish your demon, and you didn't care for the things people said, you might at least find advantage in talking to plants.

Wally stood with Max and Frankie in the spartan reception room of WKOB, each of them still in their coats, staring across the desk at Roger Brubaker. They had made arrangements to get to work late, taken an early train out of Brooklyn, and arrived at WKOB, just as instructed, at nine o'clock sharp, ready for business. However, the normally composed station manager now sat at the receptionist desk alone, opening drawers between frenetic gestures that disrupted the thin wisps of smoke rising from the cigarette smoldering between his fingers. The man's neatly parted hair was springing free of its pomade, and his signature crimson bow tie hung unfurled around his neck, his herringbone blazer draped over his chair.

He was a man transformed.

"Damned if I can find anything in this desk," Brubaker said, bits of ash flying around him as he searched. "Why's it so hard to keep a goddamned receptionist these days?"

Wally smelled liquor on Brubaker's breath despite the early hour.

The station manager stopped his search, raised his eyes toward the trio, and pointed his half-ash cigarette at the single sheet of paper Wally had placed on the desk, the one that carried their Podolor Diaper jingle. "If you fellas had all the money in the world, would you still write jingles?"

"I suppose," said Wally.

"Why?" Brubaker scrutinized their faces with his unfocused eyes, leaving Wally to wonder if this was some sort of test.

"For the love of music?" said Wally.

"Is that your answer or a question?" said Brubaker.

Wally just shrugged.

Brubaker shook his head. "If you love music, you write a song"—he shoved a drawer closed—"not a jingle." He stood suddenly, and his precarious ash fell to the pale marble floor.

"Jingles *are* songs," Max countered.

"Yeah, they *are* songs," echoed Frankie.

"Hell, they are!" An assault of whiskey vapor floated across the desk at them. "Songs reveal the truth," snapped Brubaker. "Jingles don't require the truth; good jingles are just good lies." He then pointed at Wally. "And good jingle writers are just good liars."

Wally felt immediately exposed. He'd become adept weaving falsehoods, but never thought of that as a qualification for jingle writing. And when had Brubaker gotten so philosophical about jingles, anyway?

The station manager crammed his cigarette into an amber glass ashtray and then put both hands on the desk. "I'll be damned if I can find your money, boys," he said. "I think that brunette I fired made off with the dough."

"You've gotta be kidding!" said Frankie.

"Don't sweat it, Red. WKOB is good for your twenty clams." Brubaker's focus waned again.

"We're not saps!" Frankie snatched the Podolor composition from the desk and shook the paper at Brubaker. "And we don't work for free."

Wally's heart began to race. The whole jingle deal was unraveling just like Brubaker. He started to count Mississippis, feeling like the long arm of death had found him just as it had found Johnny Milhouser.

"I know you're not saps." Brubaker aimed his dark eyes at them, a quiet seriousness filling his questionable focus. "You just need to know what you're getting into, make your own decisions. That's what I told Dawson."

"Who is Dawson?" said Max.

Brubaker swiped the Podolor page back from Frankie. "Follow me."

Wally and the guys trailed Brubaker through the first-floor reception area, uncertain where he was taking them or how a man seemingly used to control had devolved so spectacularly. Wally glanced around for Bobbi but didn't see anyone else there. In fact, it was strange at a daily radio station that no one was anywhere to be seen on a Wednesday morning.

Brubaker led them past the studio with the Steinway to a service elevator. Without a word, he pressed a button and pushed aside the collapsing metal screen of the elevator cage. Within seconds, the bell rang, and the doors opened. Once they'd all stepped into the wood-paneled elevator car, Brubaker pressed the top-floor button, number twenty-two.

"What's on twenty-two?" asked Max, breaking the silence.

"Fate," said Brubaker.

It was the first thing the station manager had said since they had arrived that Wally understood. This contest was his last hope, and if that government job wasn't waiting for him on the twenty-second floor, his fate was sealed. His demon would have prevailed.

The three young jingle writers stood behind Brubaker as the squeaking elevator rose, the invisible hurricane of Brubaker's liquored breath swirling around them. The station manager used the time to silently read their Podolor jingle page, nodding as the cage ascended, floor after floor.

Out of Brubaker's eyeshot, Frankie gave a look toward Wally and Max, running his finger in a circle next to his head.

When the elevator car stopped, the bell rang, the door opened, and Wally's jaw fell. Through the grated screen, he saw a tall, silver-haired man in an army officer's uniform, standing at attention. He was broad and muscled, his jaw a perfect square, his chest peppered with a puzzle of colorful medals. At the man's side stood Bobbi LaFleur, wearing a cobalt-blue dress with brass buttons and a wide collar. It was as if fate had arranged for Wally's greatest fear and greatest hope to present themselves all at once, and he began to worry he was trapped in a dream.

Brubaker slid open the screen and held the elevator door to allow the boys to step onto the twenty-second floor. The entire space was one big office, filled with row upon row of wooden secretarial desks, each equipped with a chair, a typewriter, a telephone, and a steno pad, all contributing to the notion that this was a place where a considerable effort would normally be underway. Today, however, every desk was empty.

The elevator closed behind them, and Brubaker handed their jingle page to the officer.

"Signed, sealed, and delivered, Colonel," said Brubaker.

The colonel slowly perused the score, his shining gaze moving like the carriage of a typewriter across each line. He then raised his head and smiled at Brubaker. "Perfect," he said, "just as you promised," and handed the page over to Bobbi.

Brubaker sat with a decisive "thud" atop a nearby desk and saluted awkwardly. "Thank you, sir."

The officer seemed momentarily put off by Brubaker's demeanor, but quickly looked back at the team of jingle writers.

"Maxwell Julius Lipkin, Walter Herbert Lipkin, and Francis Seamus O'Brien," he said.

They froze for an awkward moment until Max cut through the quiet.

"Who's asking?" His tone was defensive. He was clearly as unsettled as Wally was, hearing their formal names spoken aloud by a man they'd never even met.

Wally shot an inquiring look to Bobbi. Even in this bizarre moment, she was beautiful, but she didn't meet Wally's stare, didn't give any indication of what was happening. Instead, she kept her gaze aimed at the jingle page.

The military man raised his head. "Let's just say I'm your Uncle Sam, and I need you." He pointed at them like a recruitment poster and laughed in a way that sounded rehearsed.

Wally gritted his teeth and took one step forward. "I'm the one you want," he said, trying to keep his voice steady. "I'm the only one cleared for service. At least, I will be in a few days."

"Very bold of you, Mr. Lipkin." Uncle Sam chuckled. "But we want you all. Wouldn't be right to break up the trio."

"What's that mean?" said Max. "Did we do something wrong?"

"Quite the opposite." The man gestured toward a hallway at the far end of the office. "Follow me and I'll explain everything."

Wally and the group shadowed the enigmatic officer, trailed by Bobbi and Brubaker. They arrived at a brightly lit conference room featuring a long wooden table surrounded by chairs and a capacious glass window overlooking the Manhattan skyline and the sparkling, busy Hudson River. If the circumstances weren't so strange, it would have seemed spectacular.

"Have a seat," the officer commanded.

Wally followed Max and Frankie around the table to a group of chairs, where they each took a seat, ill at ease in their heavy coats. It felt as though they were back at Lincoln High and had been called to the principal's office.

Brubaker pulled out a chair for Bobbi to sit.

"Thank you," she said politely, as if this was all normal.

"You gentlemen have three things we need," the officer said. He clutched his hands behind his back and walked around the table, stopping when he reached the guys. "You're clever, you're fast at writing jingles, and you're patriots."

This close, the officer appeared a foot taller than Wally, filling his uniform like a fist in a glove, and imposing in stature. He reminded Wally of Charles Atlas in the ads on the inside covers of his comic books, showing what a scrawny kid could become with the right motivation and mail-order vitamins.

"Why do you need those things from us?" asked Wally.

"Simple," said the officer. "We need your help to end the goddamned war."

The officer's words hit Wally like a slap to the head and left him just as confused.

"What the hell is going on here?" said Frankie, finally speaking up. "We wrote a couple jingles and won second place in a contest. We just came for our twenty clams."

"You actually won first place," said the officer, resuming his stroll around the table.

"Come again?" said Max.

Uncle Sam stopped when he got to the front of the room and faced them again. "If we had announced you'd won first place, the news might've made the papers, and we can't have your names in papers. We need to keep you secret. Second place doesn't make papers."

Wally remembered their encounter with smarmy Rat Rubinstein and how Max had bragged about their likely win.

Max scowled. "Is this some sorta prank?" He turned to the station manager. "Mr. Brubaker, what gives?"

Brubaker reassembled his bow tie, working to find his usual composure after his whiskey breakfast. "Technically, you fellas should call me 'Major Brubaker.' I'm a recruiter for the US Army."

"Army?" said Frankie.

Wally thumbed toward his brother and their friend. "You can't recruit Max and Frankie," he said. "They got the 4-F. I already told you, I'm the only one who can serve."

The officer leaned toward Wally with New York's skyscrapers tall and impressive behind him. "We know your status, son. But your country needs you all, and the need is urgent."

"You've got to listen," said Bobbi, finally speaking up. "My father knows what he's talking about."

"Father?" Wally almost swallowed his tongue.

"Colonel Howard Dawson, US Army," the officer said, returning to Bobbi's side. "Barbara Ann is part of the team too."

Wally stared at Dawson and then at Bobbi. He instantly saw the same green sparkle in the colonel's eyes that he saw in hers. It was the sparkle of deception.

A slow heat flushed Wally's face. "I thought your name was 'Bobbi LaFleur.'"

Bobbi turned away from Wally's angry glare, appearing half coy, half apologetic. "A girl needs a stage name."

"Or an alias," Max growled.

Wally replayed in his mind each episode with Bobbi that had led to this one: Bobbi's flirtation during their audition, the way she touched his curly hair, her casual invitation to the Diamond Club, her unexpected need of him the night of their performance, and that kiss...

"So, this has all been some sort of act?" said Wally. "You're just a phony?"

"I like you," said Bobbi. "That wasn't an act."

"What about all this?" Wally waved his hand around the room, hearing the anger in his own voice rebound off the walls.

"All this," said the Colonel, "is a chance to do more to stop the war than anyone with a rifle, a plane, or a battleship has been able to do since it started." Dawson's eyes gleamed.

"Major Brubaker and I have been working to develop a secret code that no Japanese, Italian, or German has been able to break. This code is meant to get information to our troops outside our usual cryptographic channels, and in a way the enemy can't decipher and won't understand." He paused, seemingly for dramatic effect. "We'll do it through music. American music. Jingles."

Wally's brain hummed as if trying to track a single bee in a swarm. "What are you talking about?" he said.

"Podolor Diaper Service is the US government, Mr. Lipkin," Brubaker said, his earlier inebriation staring to wear off. He pointed to their jingle page sitting on the table. "And you already proved what you can do."

"How?" said Max.

A knowing smile appeared on the colonel's chiseled face. "In just a few hours, you boys took Major Brubaker's instructions and inserted select words and measures, in a specific order, into a musical arrangement, carrying a meaning we didn't even explain. Don't you see? You've executed the perfect cryptographic messaging system with nearly no time given. If you're capable of that, we can use your talents to hide secret codes in even more jingles, broadcast them all over the world."

Wally, Max, and Frankie exchanged looks, and Dawson appeared to sense their skepticism.

"Even if the enemy listens to American radio programs that carry these jingles," he said, "—and you can bet your britches they will—what they'll hear will be indiscernible from the usual content that goes into our daily Allied broadcasts from the home front."

The bee swarm in Wally's head grew.

Brubaker eyed the guys and cleared his throat. "It's the perfect place to hide our military messages, right there in plain sight, buried in the notes, words, and tempo of your jingles. The beauty of it is, we defeat them by being card-carrying, diaper-buying Americans."

Dawson crossed his arms across his broad, medal-laden chest, looking even more like Charles Atlas than before.

"Hang on," said Wally, squinting. "You think the jingle we wrote can help you beat the Nazis?"

Dawson aimed his green eyes at Wally. "Yes, son. We do." The colonel scanned the occupants in the room. "From the start, Germans have been dead set on deciphering our coded messages between our troops and between America and our allies—key information in advance of our battles... We can usually stay ahead of them, but as the weeks and months of this conflict trod on, that work has been getting harder and harder. And if the Germans are anything, it's persistent. If we hope to get ahead, we need to make bold moves. We need a less conventional way of communicating with our front line."

Max stood abruptly, his chair squeaking on the floor behind him. "Why not get the heavy hitters, the Broadway song men or some Hollywood people? We're just three schlumps from Brooklyn."

Brubaker hopped off the desk. "If we pulled in Rodgers and Hammerstein, don't you think the world would notice? This is supposed to be a secret mission."

"Now I've heard everything," said Max. He stepped away from the table. "Not interested."

Following Max's lead, Frankie stood. "Not interested," he repeated. "You're all crazy."

The two of them headed toward the double door, but Wally remained at the conference table.

"C'mon, Walter," called Max.

Wally didn't move and didn't answer, his eyes staring out through that big window to the world and the bleak winter sky.

"Walter?" said Frankie.

Wally drew a breath. "Wait."

His gut had a bad habit of lurching and dropping, but at the moment, Wally's gut was telling him that the colonel's crazy plan, as unbelievable as it sounded, might be exactly the chance he had been hoping for. This wasn't the means to a Washington job. This *was* the Washington job; it was the chance to serve, to make a difference, without the certainty of a battlefield fiasco. If jingles were lies and he was a talented liar, why not use that talent to help others, to serve his country, to exact justice for the Jews who were being killed by the Germans, the ones his mother prayed for every night?

Wally turned to his friends, aiming his eyes at Max and Frankie. "Why aren't we interested?"

"Cause we just came for the money," said Frankie. "Money they don't seem to have."

"Cause I already got the 4-F," said Max. "And you haven't even enlisted yet."

"But if we can help end the war, shouldn't we try?"

Brubaker, Dawson, and Bobbi stayed silent, watching the conversation between the guys as though observing a tennis match.

"They're nuts, Walter," said Max, flicking his own head. "Their plan will never work. You don't win wars with jingles. You shoot people. You kill people. The last ones standing win. It's all terrible, but that's how war works."

"What if they're not nuts?" said Wally. "What if we can stop people from dying, people like Johnny Milhouser?" He drew another breath. "People like me?"

Max pursed his lips and walked back to the table.

"Walter," he whispered, "even if this is legit, it could be dangerous. These guys have been lying to us all along, and they're probably lying now."

"You have to believe in this mission," said Bobbi, "even if you don't believe in me."

Wally looked at Max, trying to put Bobbi out of his mind. This was no longer about a girl, no matter how beautiful she was.

"I need this, Max," he whispered. "Even if you don't."

Max shot a desperate look to Frankie, but Frankie ignored him and, instead, addressed the station manager directly. "Will you pay us, Mr. Brubaker?"

"Major Brubaker," he corrected, smiling at Frankie. "And standard soldier's wages seem in order."

"Plus the seventy bucks you already owe us?"

Brubaker frowned. "I thought we agreed on twenty."

Frankie put his hands on his hips. "The colonel said we actually won the contest. First prize for that was fifty dollars, plus the twenty for writing the diaper jingle. That's seventy."

"A numbers man, huh?" chortled Brubaker. "Sounds fair."

Frankie gave a nod. "Then I'm in too.

Brubaker eyed Max, still appearing to struggle against the effects of his whiskey. "What d'ya say, Moxie? You're the odd man out."

"Say yes, Max," commanded Wally. "I need you."

"*We* need you," corrected Frankie. "Can't break up the trio, right?"

"I'm a man of...stature." Max sighed. "Not the athletic type. Will this involve running?"

"Doubtful," said Brubaker.

Max looked at Wally. "If there's running, you're gonna be the one to do it."

Dawson started to speak, but Wally cut him off. "What about my service?" said Wally. "My birthday is in a few days. I need to register, and they'll probably ship me off somewhere."

"Let me worry about the paperwork, son," said Dawson. "This is an army operation after all. In the meantime, we gotta keep all this top secret. You can't tell a soul about your mission. Loose lips can sink ships. Got that?"

"What about our families?" said Max.

"Or my work?" added Frankie. "I can't quit and not tell Mr. Mulligan why."

"You don't have to quit anything," said the colonel. "You'll each go about your daily business, and we'll do our work here at the studio on designated evenings. As far as anyone will know, you'll have busy social lives. In the meantime, you'll wait for us to contact you with your orders."

Wally reached into his pocket and withdrew a sheet of paper. "Sir, I don't know how to ask this, but when our father heard about the diaper jingle, he asked us to write a jingle for our family's dry-cleaning business. He wants to know what you charge to get it on the radio. How do I tell him to take it up with the US government?"

Major Brubaker walked over and took the paper, his eyes as wide as his smile. "You wrote two jingles last night?"

Wally nodded.

Brubaker beamed. "Tell him this one's on the house, courtesy of his jingle boys."

On the noontime subway ride home from Manhattan, Wally tried to piece together the events of the morning. Brubaker, a cranky station manager, was really an army major and a military recruiter. WKOB was a front for a secret military operation, and Podolor Diaper Service was the US Army. On top of that, the girl of Wally's dreams was, in actuality, a duplicitous army agent, working for her colonel father, more skilled at lying than he was. It all sounded like an episode of *Nick Carter, Master Detective*.

Even crazier, Wally, Max, and Frankie were told their jingle-writing skills could help end the war. Now, they just had to wait for word of their first mission, instructions that would direct them to return to the studio to begin their work. It was almost too much for Wally's weary brain to ponder, but for some reason, in the depths of all this chaos, he was left with a feeling of hope, as if he had been granted his very own Hannukah miracle.

For his part, Frankie seemed excited at the prospect of all the money he thought they could make, mumbling to himself about soldier's wages and Mulligan's Grocery pay as he worked out the math with his forefinger in the grit on the subway train window.

Max, on the other hand, appeared anxious next to Wally, tapping his foot to the rumble of the train, his look growing darker and more troubled as the train approached Brooklyn.

"What's wrong, Max?" whispered Wally. "Aren't you on board with everything?"

"Yes," Max said quietly. "But it just occurred to me, we gotta find Rat Rubinstein. He can't print that article."

With all that had happened at the station, Wally had forgotten Dawson's pronouncement that their second-place win wouldn't make the papers. If Rat's article ran, the boys' connection to WKOB would be right there in the *Daily Eagle*. They would have undermined Dawson's first rule, and their mission would be over before it had begun, his trust in them lost before they'd had a chance to earn it.

"Jesus," said Wally. "We gotta find him, now."

The subway pulled into the Kensington stop, and Max rushed out of the station with Wally and Frankie trailing.

"What's the big hurry?" asked Frankie.

Once a safe distance from the subway stop, and away from earshot of other people, Max filled Frankie in on the problem.

"I knew Rat was gonna be trouble," said Frankie, punching a fist into his hand.

"For once, it isn't him," said Max. "I was the one who insisted he run the story, remember? This is my fault."

"It's nobody's fault," said Wally. "We had no idea what was going on when we saw him. We just gotta stop him from putting this in the paper."

"Wait," said Frankie. "I don't get it. Won't Dawson have to say someone else won first place? Won't some other jingle team be in the paper?"

"Rat said he was gonna run a local interest story about the contestants, not just the winner, remember? As soon as he ties us to WKOB, he puts us and the whole mission at risk."

Frankie nodded, even though he still looked perplexed. "And just so I'm clear—"

"If some foreign agents figure out what WKOB is up to and tie us to that work," said Max, "our lives and the secret mission could be in jeopardy."

"Foreign agents?" said Frankie.

"Our lives?" said Wally, now growing more concerned than before.

"You've heard the news," said Max. "They keep finding Nazi sympathizers and sleeper agents right here in New York, reporting what they see and hear back to the motherland. You can be sure they read the papers. It's why Dawson wants us to keep quiet, even with our families."

Wally recalled his father reading an article aloud from the *Brooklyn Daily Eagle*, Rat's own paper, profiling a couple of air-raid wardens from Staten Island who were caught counting soldiers boarding ships and then sending letters to the Germans with their findings. Max wasn't being paranoid. The risk was real.

"For as long as we're in this," said Max, "we're as top secret as the mission itself."

Wally imagined Rat knocking away on his typewriter, each word a nail in their coffins. The trio moved quickly down Church Avenue in a race to stop him.

"Does Rat still live in the neighborhood?" asked Wally.

"Think so," said Max, breathless. "Lived with his mother on East Fifth off Beverley."

The guys got to the brownstone Max remembered and found one of the mailboxes labeled "Rubinstein."

"Here," said Wally. "Upstairs. 202-A."

They took the steps two at a time. Max gasped for air, his wide chest heaving, until he caught his breath and gave a handful of frantic raps on the door.

After a moment, a slight, gray-haired woman pulled it open and peeked her head out.

"Mrs. Rubinstein?" asked Max, still slightly wheezy.

The woman looked like an older, female version of Rat, with the same unfortunate point to her nose, squint to her eyes, and unsightly overbite.

"Yes," she answered.

"We're friends of Ra—I mean, Clyde," Max said, quickly stopping himself from calling her son by his unflattering nickname.

"Friends?" The woman sounded surprised. "Please, please, come right in."

The boys entered the warm apartment, which was decorated with flocked wallpaper. Across the far wall were family photos, men and women unmistakably linked through genetic misfortune to the wiry reporter the boys had come to hate, each relative looking like they represented a step in rodent evolution going back to the turn of the last century.

Wally bit his tongue and scanned the rest of the apartment, startled to find that Mrs. Rubinstein had the same taste in décor as his own mother, with floral doilies on burnished wood furniture and the same Sentinel radio on an end table.

"Clyde," she called to the back bedrooms. "You have some friends here." Mrs. Rubinstein leaned toward Wally and whispered, "My Clyde never brings anyone home. I worry people don't like him." She seemed to be asking a question.

Wally looked at Frankie, who bit his lip, and then to Max, who turned away.

Wally smiled back at Rat's mother. "We've known Clyde since middle school," he said.

It was a neutral enough statement that Mrs. Rubinstein could take to mean anything she wanted, and it had the benefit of being true. Misapplied truths were the best sort of lie.

Rat entered the room, his messy hair half covering his face, a shirttail hanging out of his trousers. He stopped in his tracks when he saw Wally and the others.

"The gruesome threesome. What are you doing here?"

"Clyde!" his mother snapped. "That's no way to greet your friends." She put on a smile. "Have you boys had lunch? I have some nice leftover corned beef."

"They don't need lunch," Rat said. He pointed to the door. "Let's take this outside."

The boys followed Rat out the door, down the stairs, and around the rear of the building. Once they got to the dirty alleyway behind the brownstone, Rat tucked his errant shirttail into his trousers and faced them.

"Okay, fellas. What gives?"

"We need you to pull the story," said Max.

"The story?"

Max held his thumbs and forefingers in the air, framing an imaginary headline, just as Rat himself had done when they saw him in Manhattan. "'Brooklyn Jingle Boys Ready for Big Win?'"

Rat squinted. "Right. And why would I pull the story you were so enthusiastic about?"

Wally exchanged glances with Frankie, unsure how Max was going to explain their request, wishing they'd spent more time crafting their plan.

A mischievous smile grew on Rat's face. "Wait," he said. "I get it. You lost." He laughed in a manner that sounded like a cough. "You lost the contest. Oh, that's rich."

Max curled his fist, and Wally worried his brother was getting ready to punch the guy right in his overbite.

"Yes," said Wally, stepping between Max and Rat. "We lost. If you print the story, you'll just have to retract it. Then, we'll all look like idiots."

Rat scrutinized Wally's face. "But, that's an even better story." He raised his thumbs and forefingers to a new headline. "'Brooklyn Hopefuls Lick Their Wounds After Devastating Defeat,'" he said. "Great tragic appeal, don't you think?"

This time, Frankie reacted. Just as he did on Broadway, he grabbed Rat by the collar. "You little—"

"Wait!" Wally pulled Frankie off Rat. "Let him go."

Frankie blustered, "C'mon, Wally! We can't let this twerp get away with it."

"No," said Max, more calmly than Wally expected. "Walter's right." Max unfurled his thick fingers and slowly maneuvered his girth toward Rat with a new, odd confidence. "Clyde," Max said softly, "do you believe what goes around comes around?"

Rat's beady eyes grew beadier. "Maybe."

"Then listen carefully." Max moved in close, his voice reduced to a whisper. "We know where you live, and we know where you work. You're a bright guy. You must realize, there's no place you can hide that we can't find you."

Rat rolled his head as if trying to release a sudden tension in his neck. "What's that supposed to mean?"

Max reached toward Rat's throat, and Rat flinched. But instead of choking the guy, Max straightened his collar where Frankie had ruffled it, wiping away the creases on Rat's wrinkled shirt like he did when fitting a customer for a new suit. "It means just what you think it means," said Max. "It means we know you'll make sure things will work out just as they're supposed to." He winked.

For the first time, Wally realized just how terrifying his brother could be if he put his moxie to nefarious use.

"Let's go, fellas," Max said, pointing his finger gun toward the street.

Wally and Frankie said nothing as they followed Max, leaving Rat alone in the alley.

However, just as Wally looked back, Rat called out, "I completely forgot about the story until you morons showed up here." He then darted upstairs to his apartment.

The boys resumed walking in silence until Frankie said, "You think he'll run the piece?"

"He's a rat," said Max. "He knows when to jump ship. Trust me, he won't run it."

But Wally didn't share Max's confidence. Instead, he was more concerned than ever. Thanks to their own carelessness, the success of their secret mission—and the preservation of Wally's life—appeared to rest in the hands of the person Wally trusted least in the world, and no Hanukkah wish could save him from that.

Back in the deck chair on the rooftop of his apartment building, Wally sat next to Audrey under the snowless winter sky and tried to calm his fretful thoughts. It was the second night of Hanukkah, but Wally was not in a festive mood. The initial hope of his secret mission had faded, and once again, thanks to Rat Rubinstein, he had death and doom on his mind. With the setting sun would come his next air-raid drill, another shot at keeping his cool or surrendering to his demon.

He tightened his helmet chin strap.

"How long?" said Audrey.

Wally lifted his uncle Sherman's silver pocket watch. It read 5:25.

"Eight minutes," he said. He snapped the watch closed, rubbed his frozen nose, and drew in the flavor of the luckless evening breeze that had weaved its way through the Brooklyn streets. His day had started simply enough with a trip to WKOB to get paid for a jingle, but now the world was different, more complex and nuanced, even though, from his vantage above the neighborhood, everything looked the same.

For tonight's air-raid drill, he intended to pull the lever with his own hands and prove to himself, or maybe to Audrey, that no matter what life served up, he'd be okay. Then again, it felt better to have Audrey at his side in case he was wrong.

She pulled her scarf more snugly around her chin and raised her wool collar to her ears. "Things will be fine," she said, sounding like her brother Johnny before he deployed. "I know you can do this."

Audrey's confidence in him was welcome and encouraging, but he couldn't stop thinking about the pain she and her family were suffering. Despite the horrible news about Johnny, Audrey said she wanted things to be normal, wanted to join Wally on the roof, to go about life as simply as she could. Or maybe she'd just run out of tears. Either way, she was now the one offering support when it should have been the other way around.

"How's your mom?" he asked, changing the subject.

"Same as yesterday, I suppose. Sad." Audrey chewed her gum, the peppermint aroma mingling with the steam that rose from her mouth, her blue eyes growing distant.

"And how about you? Any better than your mom?"

Audrey drew and released a long breath. "They told us we won't get Johnny's body back," she said. "Government letter said it was too difficult to ship the dead. I think they meant there's too many dead to ship."

Wally felt the air around him grow colder. "What will they do with his remains?"

"Bury him somewhere out there, I guess." She stared into the sky. "Letter didn't say."

"I'm sorry," said Wally. This whole thing seemed like a burden placed on people that had already been forced to bear the worst burden of all. "That's awful."

"That's war, Walter. It's all awful. If I could do something to end it, I would."

Wally wanted to comfort Audrey, to tell her everything about his jingle mission, about Colonel Dawson, even about Bobbi, if for no other reason than to reassure her that things were being done—absurd and daring things—to end the war, just as she wished. Of course, Wally couldn't tell her any of that. Besides, he was trying to avoid thinking about Bobbi, let alone talk about her. And Rat Rubinstein could end it all, anyhow. For now, he'd have to continue to do what he did best. Lie.

"I'm sure things will get better," he said.

She gnawed her peppermint gum. "My mother told me our grief was our duty, our way to honor Johnny's sacrifice." Audrey's tone revealed she didn't quite agree.

"Guess that's one way to see it," said Wally. He raised the binoculars to his eyes and looked out across Brooklyn. "Duty is...complicated."

"Are we still talking about my mother?" asked Audrey.

Wally lowered his lenses. "What do you mean?"

"Walter, it's me. We both know about your fainting. Doesn't your condition make your own duty...complicated?"

Wally looked at his uncle's pocket watch. "Do you remember my uncle Sherman?" he asked.

"The one in the hospital?"

"Sanitorium," said Wally. "Locked up at Brooklyn State in Flatbush like some kook."

"Yes, I remember. You and Max used to visit him with your mother when we were kids."

"My mother once told me that Sherman faints from anxiety neurosis."

Audrey let out a gasp. "Faints? Like you?"

"Yes," said Wally, hearing a strange, sad defeat in his voice. "Like me."

Audrey's eyes narrowed. "You're not just worried about combat, are you?"

"Even if I can avoid dying in the war, I still run the risk of being sent away like Sherman."

"Does your mom still visit him?"

"Once a month. But she made Max and I stop going about ten years ago. Said a sanatorium was no place for us when we started asking too many questions." Wally looked away. "Now, I can't help but wonder if that's the place I'll end up anyway."

Audrey turned her deck chair to face him. "You aren't like your uncle, Walter."

"How do you know?"

Audrey shrugged. "I suppose I don't, but neither do you. You may be worrying about something that isn't even true."

That idea had never occurred to Wally. He had simply accepted his uncle's curse as his own, carried it around just like he carried the man's pocket watch, ticking and ticking until his own time was up.

"Guess there's no way to know," said Wally. He noticed the time, stuffed the watch into his pocket, and rose from the deck chair.

"Of course there's a way, dummy." Audrey stood and followed Wally to the flagpole. "Go ask him."

"Ask Sherman? At the sanatorium?"

Audrey cocked her head. "Like you said, he's right over in Flatbush. Find out why he faints. Find out if he's like you or if it's something entirely different."

Since Wally's mother had barred him from visiting Sherman so long ago, he had never contemplated defying that instruction, but Audrey's idea was audacious and stirred something in him, placed a question in his head that he realized needed answering.

Wally shrugged. "It's not the craziest idea I've heard all day."

"I can go with you. We can come up with an excuse." Audrey's solemnity had been replaced with enthusiasm, a slowly developing plan.

Wally drew a breath. "My mother can't know," he said. "No one can." The secrets he was sharing with Audrey were beginning to multiply.

"Tomorrow, then?"

"Sure," said Wally. "Tomorrow."

"Perfect," said Audrey. "We'll tell everyone we need to go to the USO office in Flatbush to help with caroling. They're singing every day, straight through until Christmas, you know?"

Wally nodded. "Surprisingly plausible." He knew plausibility was the key to every successful lie.

Both looked to the dimming sky and the stars that were blinking awake. The pair remained quiet until Wally heard an air-raid siren ring somewhere north of Church Avenue. He grew tense, knowing his time had arrived.

"You can do this, Walter," said Audrey, repeating her earlier reassurance.

To his surprise, this time, he believed her. Tonight, he wasn't anxious or nervous like his last air-raid drill. Too much had happened since then, and tonight's drill seemed like the least of his worries.

"Thank you," he said.

Audrey smiled, and somewhere in that smile, Wally found comfort.

He gripped the lever on the flagpole as if ready to activate some Jules Verne contraption designed to set a more hopeful future in motion. He pulled down hard, the lever clicking into place.

A siren cry, like the call of fate, spread across the neighborhood, and a profound, ironic peace flowed through him where once he'd felt only fear. He closed his eyes and let the siren song wash over him. He inhaled his relief and realized that hope smelled like a lot like peppermint.

5

The Gun in the Drawer

When Wally arrived at the curbside in front of A-Rite Cleaners, Audrey was already there waiting. She buttoned her wool coat over her blue pleated dress and carried a matching blue purse. Today she wore pink lipstick and her eyelashes seemed longer.

"All set?" said Audrey.

Wally felt underdressed in his usual cotton slacks and white shirt with worn leather shoes, feeling like he'd misunderstood their plan. Their trip to Flatbush was a secret task to be undertaken without much pomp or circumstance, and the eagerness he'd felt last night had now been replaced with a prickly caution.

"You dressed up," said Wally, buttoning his own coat.

"We're caroling, remember?"

"Should I change?"

"You look fine, silly. Any trouble getting away?"

"Nope. Your story seemed to work. Besides, my dad's been in a good mood since we told him his radio jingle was running free of charge."

"My mom was half asleep," said Audrey. "Seemed glad to hear I was getting out of the apartment and singing. She says I don't do that as much as I used to."

"She's right," said Wally. "You do have a great voice."

Audrey looked away, embarrassed by the compliment. "Let's go," she said. "I told Carl I'd be back to fix his lunch."

With their alibis in place, the two began their walk to the trolley stop.

Audrey drew a breath and sang, "God rest ye, merry gentlemen, let nothing you dismay, for Jesus Christ our savior was born upon this day."

"We're not actually singing carols, you know," said Wally, suddenly afraid his compliment about her voice had unleashed something in Audrey.

"I know. It's just fun to sing them. You oughta try."

"I'm Jewish. Jews don't sing carols. Too ecumenical."

"What do Jews sing? Jingles?"

"That's right." Wally laughed. "Jingles are Jewish carols. The Old Testament is filled with jingles."

Audrey laughed at their banter. "I heard you practicing on the piano the other night. You sounded good, but you really ought to let me join your jingle team."

Wally didn't reply. Audrey had an excellent voice and could certainly lend something to the trio, but now that their jingle enterprise was an army-sanctioned mission, he had to keep his work secret. "I'll see what the guys think," he said.

The trolley squealed to a halt just as he and Audrey arrived at the stop. They hopped aboard, dropped their coins into the slot, and took seats in the middle of the trolley. There were a few other people seated, but Wally spotted two women on the back bench carrying lunch boxes and wearing greasy worker's uniforms. It was a sight more common lately with so many men off to war. The thought of it tempted Wally toward the feelings of guilt he was working to keep at bay.

"Figured I'd grab some sort of pamphlet at the Flatbush USO office," said Audrey. "This way, we'll have some real evidence to back up our story."

"You're a clever liar," Wally said with a curious sort of professional admiration. He suddenly flashed to Bobbi and wondered why he had judged her deception so differently.

"I'm not a liar," Audrey protested. "I'm a creative thinker." She raised an eyebrow. "Don't you want to see your uncle?"

"Sure, I do," said Wally, but today he wasn't as convinced as he had been last night.

"When was the last time you saw him?"

"Been a long time." Wally searched for a tangible memory. "The last visit I remember, I was eight. Max and I were with our mother and visited him during his lunch in the dining hall. I remember thinking it was strange that a nurse and two orderlies had to watch us eat."

"What happened?" Audrey chewed her peppermint gum, appearing eager for a story.

Wally smiled. "Max and I ate our meat loaf and gravy while Sherman and my mother had a conversation, the kind adults have when they think kids don't understand what they're talking about. My uncle told a dirty joke about a traveling salesman and a farmer's daughter, and my mother pretended it wasn't funny. Max and I stuffed our mouths with mashed potatoes, trying not to laugh. Wish I could remember that joke."

"Sounds like he's a nice person."

"As a kid, I thought of my uncle as a friendly man who happened to live in a sanitorium, and that the sanitorium was just a hospital with meat loaf." Wally looked out the window while the trolley rolled toward Flatbush. "Now, he's just a sad family story."

"Why'd they put in him there in the first place?"

"He's been there my whole life," said Wally. "I suppose he went in sometime after the Great War. One night, when I was about ten, after my mother stopped taking us to see him, she came home from one of her visits. She set her purse on the piano and fell to her knees with her face in her hands. It was the first time I ever saw her cry like that. She said that Sherman had blacked out while she was there. Guess it hadn't happened for a while."

Audrey nodded but didn't say a word.

"It was the first time I heard her use the term 'anxiety neurosis.'" Wally's voice wavered, his own emotion surprising him as he spoke about his mother's grief. "She hasn't mentioned it since."

Audrey sat quietly chewing her gum as the trolley rattled on.

"My mother crying. That's all I can think of when I think about Sherman now," said Wally. "When I started fainting myself, I began to think about how much Sherman and I must be alike, how what happened to him was happening to me. How my mother would cry if she knew."

Audrey turned away.

"What's wrong?" he asked.

She reached into her purse for a handkerchief, which she dabbed under her lashes. When she turned back, she looked angry.

"We're going to figure this out, Walter. I promise."

Audrey's determination was startling. Wally had never seen this side of her, so formidable or strong. Yet, here she was, taking charge on his behalf.

"Got any more gum?" asked Wally.

Audrey reached into her purse and handed him a stick. He quickly unwrapped it, stuffed the gum into his mouth, and crammed the wrapper into his pocket. He was happy for the taste of peppermint on his tongue, happy for the sense of hope he now associated with it.

The trolley paused at a corner stop, and the two women with lunch boxes hopped off, heading toward a factory.

"Know what you're gonna say to Sherman?" asked Audrey once the trolley resumed its roll toward Flatbush.

"Not really."

Last night, Wally thought Audrey's suggestion for this visit was optimistic, a way for him to see how different he was from Sherman. Now, after telling his uncle's story, he worried this trip would only serve to confirm his original assumption, that he was destined to the same fate as his uncle.

Searching for a calm center, he stared out the trolley, letting his thoughts carry him to Bobbi. He wondered what she was doing, whether she even cared what he was up to now that her own mission to recruit him had been successful. At WKOB, Bobbi had said she liked him; she had even proclaimed that those feelings were real. But since she'd lied about everything else, why should he believe that? It was why he'd called her a phony. Then again, maybe he was wrong to judge her for lying. Were Bobbi's lies any different than his own?

Audrey elbowed Wally, bringing him out of his trance.

"We're here."

The steel wheels screeched as the trolley slowed. The duo hopped off and dodged cars along East Forty-Second, then walked three blocks to the USO office in direct view of Brooklyn State Hospital. Wally chewed his peppermint gum harder and stared at the sanitorium. A few stories tall and surrounded by trees, the place felt foreboding, like a sleeping giant, presenting a calm exterior, blocking out the low morning sun. He marveled at the size of such a building, large enough to keep a thousand people in its depths.

"There it is." Audrey pointed instead to the USO office, marked by a recruitment poster and a large American flag hanging next to the door. "Be right back."

"Okay," said Wally, his eyes still fixed on the hospital.

When he was there as a boy, he had never pondered the need for such a place to hold so many people like his uncle, people considered unfit for society. Part of him now feared he would walk in only to find the doctors and nurses sense that he was another such person. Would they sound the alarm? Buckle him into a straitjacket and lock him away for good? The thought of being trapped there chilled him, or maybe it was just the absence of sunshine in the shadow of the building.

"Turns out, the caroling starts tomorrow." Audrey appeared and tucked a pamphlet into her purse. When Wally didn't reply, she strode in front of him, stealing his attention away from the sanitorium. "Walter?"

"Yeah?"

"We don't have to do this if you don't want to."

Wally lifted his chin and said, "I want to," but he could hear his own hesitation. He forced his legs to carry him across the street and down the hedge-lined path, with Audrey following close behind.

When they entered the building, they saw a dour-faced reception nurse wearing a starchy white uniform standing behind a counter, a telephone receiver held between her cheek and shoulder, a curling cord trailing down beside her to the phone. She greeted them with her forefinger raised, indicating she needed a moment to finish her telephone conversation before acknowledging them directly. A silver holiday garland traced the edge of her reception counter, reminding them, and perhaps others, that the season was supposed to be festive even if the place wasn't.

"That's right," the nurse said into the receiver. "Only immediate family on the list can visit, and you've gotta have a doctor's signed order. Sorry, ma'am. I don't make the rules."

Wally shot a look to Audrey, understanding from the reception nurse's words that they may have a problem seeing Uncle Sherman together if only family was allowed. Wally was a nephew and might be able to pull off a family visit, but not Audrey. And they certainly didn't have a doctor's order.

The nurse returned the phone to its cradle and turned to them. "May I help you?"

Audrey approached the counter. "My brother and I, Walter and Audrey Lipkin, are here to see our uncle Sherman," she said.

The woman looked them over. "Been here recently?"

"Nope." Audrey kept her eyes on the reception nurse.

The nurse then tilted her head. "Are you expected?"

"It's a Christmas surprise."

"Hanukkah," said Walter.

"Hanukkah and Christmas," echoed Audrey. "Big surprise."

Wally found Audrey's feigned ambivalence inspiring.

The nurse squinted at them. "I see." She lifted a clipboard from her desk, then flipped one page and then the next. "Lipkin? I don't see a Sherman Lipkin."

"No," Wally blurted, "Sherman Abramowitz. He's my—our mother's brother. Different last name."

The nurse flipped the pages back. "Abramowitz. Right. The list shows he has a sister, Sadie."

"That's her," said Audrey. "Good ol' Mom."

The woman shook her head. "Gotta have your name on the list, like your mother's. Doctor's approval required."

Wally felt defeated, turning to Audrey for some ideas. Without hesitation, Audrey reached into her purse and pulled out a one-dollar bill. She slid it across the reception desk. "Dr. Washington approves," Audrey said.

The reception nurse locked eyes with Audrey and pushed the dollar back across the desk. Wally thought that would be the end of their excursion.

"I'm afraid I can only accept Dr. Lincoln's approval," the nurse said. "It is Christmas—or Hanukkah—after all."

Audrey snatched the dollar and exchanged it for a five she pulled from her purse. "I suppose Dr. Lincoln knows best." She offered the nurse a wry smile.

The receptionist took Audrey's five and put it into her breast pocket. "Third floor," she said. "Room 320. Doors only open from the outside and lock automatically, so I'll come get you in twenty minutes."

"Thank you," said Audrey.

"If you see the charge nurse, you tell her Gladys from reception sent you." She tapped her name badge with her burgundy-enameled fingernail.

Audrey gave a single nod to Gladys and followed Wally to the stairwell door.

"Thank you," Wally whispered.

Audrey grinned. "You owe me five bucks."

They ascended the stairs in the dark, musty stairwell to the third floor, where the air began to smell like ether and disinfectant. The scent stirred distant memories of Wally's childhood visits, filling his lungs with an expectant apprehension.

Audrey wrinkled her nose. "I hate the smell of hospitals."

"Doesn't really smell like meat loaf," said Wally.

They opened the third-floor stairwell door to a dim hallway, where the smell of ether and disinfectant was more pronounced. The hall was lined with numbered doors on either side, and each was equipped with a small double-paned window. Through a handful of such windows emitted a ghostly glow. At the end of the hall, they saw a nurse's station with no nurse present.

Four doors down, Wally spotted the room they wanted. Room 320.

"Here it is," he said, pausing at the door. Wally pressed his molars into his gum to keep from grinding them. "Sure you wanna go in?"

"I'm sure," said Audrey.

Wally drew a breath, gave the door two raps, and turned the knob.

The room was small, cold, and dark and smelled more strongly of ether than the stairwell or hallway that had led them there. A window on the opposite wall of the room was curtained with thin muslin fabric that permitted into the room a sickly, filtered daylight the color of aged lace. Beneath the window sat a desk with a lamp bolted to its surface, and in the corner of the room was a metal toilet and a roll of paper beside it on the floor. Kitty-corner stood a tall wardrobe, and against the fourth corner of the room was a single bed and bedside table. All the furniture appeared affixed to the floor.

Both jumped when the door closed behind them with an audible click of the latch, locking them in as Gladys had warned.

Wally's eyes adjusted to the dim room. "Looks like a prison cell," he whispered, scanning the small space.

A man, presumably Uncle Sherman, lay in the center of the metal-framed bed with his back toward them. He wore a thin cotton pajama top, his legs covered by a gray wool blanket, the rise and fall of his body in sync with his heavy, gravelly breathing.

"Should we wake him?" Audrey whispered back.

"I am awake." Sherman's rasp startled them, but its familiar tenor gave Wally assurance that they had entered the right room. Sherman turned his head but did not face them. "Who is that?"

"It's your nephew Walter," said Wally. "I'm here with my friend Audrey."

Sherman turned further and squinted at them over his shoulder, through the thin beams of sunlight that shone through the gaps in the threadbare cotton curtains.

"Walter?"

"Hello, Uncle Sherman."

Sherman rose from the bed, let the blanket fall, and stepped forward into a ray of light. He was naked from the waist down.

Audrey turned away. "Oh, jeez."

Wally tried not to laugh at his uncle's naked body. "I think you lost your pants, Uncle Sherman."

Sherman looked at his bare legs. "Christ." He moved to the wardrobe, withdrew a pair of cotton pants that matched his pajama top, and quickly slipped them on. "Wasn't expecting company." He pushed his feet into cloth slippers and quickly made his bed.

"Can we draw the curtains?" asked Wally.

"Do what you like," said Sherman. "They'll just close them again."

Wally took that as permission and reached over the desk to open the drapes but found there were no cords attached. He drew them by hand to allow some sunlight into the room and noticed iron bars preventing access to the glass. Through the window, down below, he saw a well-manicured courtyard and a fountain with a statue where heckling crows were roosting on the wings of a stone angel. He turned back to get a better look at his uncle.

Sherman flinched against the morning sun, working to adjust his eyes to the light. He looked like an overgrown child in his ill-fitting pajamas. He was tall and had curly hair like Wally's, only Sherman's mop was gray and wild. He had a slight hunch to his shoulders and looked older than Wally remembered, but everyone had grown older since Wally was last there.

Sherman stared at him as if trying to get him into focus. "Where's your mother?"

"It's not her day to come," said Wally.

"Does she know you're here?"

"No."

Sherman nodded as if he understood.

"How are you, Uncle Sherman?" said Wally.

"Just how you think I am." Sherman opened his arms to the room. "Another day at the zoo." He shuffled closer in his slippers and looked Wally over. "You got tall. How old are you now, anyway?"

"I'll be eighteen on Saturday."

"That's right." Sherman rubbed his stubbled chin. "Lost track of what month it was." Sherman patted Wally on the back. "You and Jesus. Two Jews born on Christmas."

"So I've been told," said Wally. It was a Lipkin family joke Wally heard every year as though it were the first time ever uttered. He never found it funny, which was probably why his family kept mentioning it.

"Wish I had a present to give you..." Sherman looked around his barren room until his eyes locked on Audrey. "Who'd you say this was?"

"This is my neighbor Audrey." Wally walked over and stood by her side.

Sherman looked down his nose. "I don't know her."

Wally shot Audrey an apologetic look, and she just offered a crooked grin in response, as if to reassure him she was fine.

He turned back to his uncle. "She's my friend, Uncle Sherman. Just figured she might wanna come along and meet you."

"And why did you come?" Sherman cocked his head at Wally.

"Well, this week is Hanukkah…"

Sherman squinted. "Why did you really come?"

Wally braced himself. "Eighteen is the draft age now. Guess I wanted to talk about your own service before I enlist."

Sherman's eyes widened. "Enlist? Why the hell would you enlist?" His sudden anger made Wally question the wisdom of his visit.

"I want to serve my country," said Wally. "You know what they're doing to Jews? I want to help end the war."

"There is no end to war," Sherman blurted. "And I don't know the last time you read your Old Testament, but Jews don't end wars. They just escape to the desert and pray for miracles. It's certainly what I should have done."

Wally had already been praying for miracles and knew what his uncle meant. Life and its preservation were central to the Jewish faith, but that was exactly where the problem lay. To protect life during a time of war, men were being asked to risk life. It was the conundrum for all humanity, not just the Jews.

"I just know I can help, that's all," said Wally.

Sherman shook his head as if trying to rid his mind of horrible thoughts. "The only one you can help, Walter, is yourself. Run away. Run while you still have the chance."

"But I don't want to run." Wally glanced to Audrey, who was biting her lip like she did during the distressing parts of *Nick Carter, Master Detective*.

Sherman stepped closer, stared into Wally's eyes. This close, Wally saw several days' stubble on his uncle's face, the vessels in his temple pulsing.

"You may not think so now, Walter, but you'll want to run. They'll make sure of it." Sherman's eyes narrowed again. "Every brave thought you have, every courageous impulse, will be taken from you until all you have left is fear and despair." The flatness with which Sherman spoke made his words sound like a pronouncement, a speech he had practice reciting.

"It doesn't have to be like that," said Wally. He hoped his reassuring tone would calm Sherman. "I found a way to help," Wally said softly. "I have…skills." He knew he couldn't share any information about his secret jingle mission and had probably said too much already, especially in front of Audrey.

"Bah," barked Sherman. "I used to think like you back when I was a soldier." He moved next to the desk, raised his eyes to the barred window, and slowed his speech. "Now I know the truth." Sherman's gaze remained fixed on the courtyard. "I'm just a gun."

"A gun?" said Wally.

Audrey leaned forward.

Sherman spun his desk chair around and sat to face them. "When people put a gun in a drawer, they do it to feel protected, to know it's there for a time when they need it. Makes 'em feel safe. But it makes no sense. Guns don't work in drawers, don't you see?"

"No."

Sherman blew a frustrated breath and looked at Audrey. "What's her name again?"

"I'm Audrey." She offered a smile like a wince.

"Audrey," Sherman repeated.

Wally worried that all the talk of guns had upset Audrey, but before he could suggest that she wait outside, she said quietly, "What makes you a gun?"

Sherman's voice grew small. "In the Great War, the first one, they called me 'the gun' because of my skill with a trench rifle. Captain said I shot more enemy soldiers than any other man in our troop, most of 'em right between the eyes. 'Best shot in the army,' he said. Meant it as a compliment. Said I was the secret weapon of the regiment. The gun."

Wally's jaw clenched. Even in the cloying light of his uncle's room, he saw the haunted look on Sherman's face. Wally had never known his uncle outside these walls; Sherman had been here Wally's whole life, and his mother had never shared the details of her brother's military service.

"You helped end the war," said Wally, trying to find a bright spot in his uncle's dark tale.

"Did I?" Sherman looked to the ceiling as though something there had suddenly commanded his attention. He then lowered his eyes to the floor. "You're about to serve in another war. With Germany. Again. I didn't help end anything."

"You were there for your fellow soldiers when they needed you."

"Needed me?" Sherman growled. "They were just guns too, Walter. A gun doesn't *need* anything. A gun is an instrument used by the ones in charge. When you're the gun, you don't make the decisions, and you sure don't have any needs." Sherman shook his head. "I'm sorry, Walter. You don't know a thing about war."

Wally looked away. Sherman's words cut deep, not because they were harsh but because they were true.

Audrey cleared her throat. "Mr. Abramowitz?"

Wally's uncle softened. "Call me Sherman."

"Sherman," Audrey repeated. "Do you—" She paused. "Do you still faint?"

Wally's skin prickled at the word "faint." He hadn't planned on asking Sherman pointed questions about his condition, but now that Audrey had brought it up, he wanted to hear his uncle's answer.

Sherman raised his head. "Is that why you're here?" He looked back and forth between them. "Is my nephew fainting?"

Audrey froze, looked at Wally.

"Yes," said Wally, ready to speak for himself. He swallowed saliva that tasted like ether. "I am."

Sherman stood from his chair and circled Wally, examining him more closely, a darkness now shadowing his features.

"Does anyone else know?"

"Just Audrey."

"Keep it that way." Wally's uncle now had an urgency in his tone. He lifted his curling gray bangs to reveal a thick scar that ran the length of his hairline and leaned toward Wally. "See this?"

Wally nodded.

Sherman let his bangs fall. "They used electricity, they gave me pills, even cut part of me out of my head." Wally's heart skipped a beat. "Had to leave me conscious for the whole procedure. And the damned thing is, I asked them to do it."

Audrey gasped.

"Why?" said Wally.

"Hope makes us do stupid things, Walter. Like you, I didn't want to keep fainting."

Wally bit hard into his wad of gum and tried to steady himself. "Did it work?"

His uncle took him gently by his arm, led him over to the bed, and gestured for him to sit. Audrey followed, sat next to Wally, and took his sweaty hand in hers.

Sherman then knelt in front of them at his bedside. "Nothing stops the fainting, Walter. At least nothing they do." He grew quiet. "Course, that doesn't stop them from trying new things, and it doesn't stop me from hoping, God help me."

A cold realization rushed through Wally's veins. Sherman had been praying for his own Hanukkah miracle. And he'd been doing it a whole lot longer than Wally.

His uncle rose from the floor, his knees cracking with the effort. He returned to the window and looked through the bars. "Why do you suppose they build fountains outside a sanatorium?" Sherman asked, staring at the angel and the ravens.

"For the beauty?" said Audrey.

"For the peace?" Wally offered.

"For the birds," said Sherman. "Some fancy architect must've thought loony people would like to see birds from behind the bars. Maybe he thought it would help us imagine that the birds were the ones in the cage, and we were the ones looking in."

"When did it start," said Wally, "your fainting?" His words had come out as a whisper.

Sherman said nothing, and Wally wondered whether his uncle had even heard the question.

"I know why you're asking," Sherman finally replied. "You're afraid you'll end up here, staring through the bars at the birds. You don't want to be like me."

Wally hung his head, ashamed to be so transparent, and withdrew his hand from Audrey's.

Sherman drew another slow, deep breath, causing his broad shoulders to rise and fall as if he, too, were imagining bagpipes in his chest.

"Here's the thing, Walter. They locked me up because I asked them to."

"What?" Wally was stunned that anyone would want this. "Why?"

"It always made your mother cry when they'd find me in a park or on the street, unconscious, even when we were younger. Got worse when our parents died and all we had was each other."

"You had this...condition before the war?"

"Yes," said Sherman, "and somehow I managed to survive out there anyway. Probably why I got so good at using a gun. Self-preservation. Feels like cowardice but looks like courage." He swallowed. "But there's no denying it. The war made it worse." "Once I got back to Brooklyn, in the months after the fighting stopped, the cops would find me unconscious in the park or in the gutter, week after week, passed out on a bench or on some stranger's doorstep. Assumed I had been on some bender, drinking myself into such a state. After serving, a lot of men were found that way. Haunted like ghouls, roaming the city in a fog of gin or whiskey. But I never touched the drink. They had no idea I was different from the other shell-shocked soldiers. They'd drag me home, your mother would put me to bed, and we'd repeat the whole thing a week later." He shook his head. "Poor Sadie thought I'd be dead in a year if I didn't do something. Coming here was the only sensible choice at the time."

"You don't think that now?"

"First night here, I remember like it was yesterday. I settled into this very room, laid here for an hour. And before I could drift off, I heard the screaming," said Sherman. "Three nights in, I realized the scratching noises that kept me awake weren't the rats. The scratching was from full-grown men clawing at their doors, at their walls. I knew I'd made a terrible mistake."

Audrey covered her mouth.

"I'd already signed the papers, admitted I was a danger to myself and society. It was too late to change my mind." Sherman fell silent for a moment and then turned to Wally. "Your mother seemed so much happier knowing where I was every night. Three square meals a day, heat in the winter, visitors allowed once a week. Coming here was the only thing I ever did that she approved of. Every time she visited, I'd see how she'd changed, how she'd gotten the smile back in her eyes." Sherman exhaled. "Can't take that away from someone you love, no matter what it does to you." His eyes were wet with memory.

Wally began to see his bleak future roll out before him like a red carpet to a movie premiere, welcoming him to a special screening of his horrible fate. It didn't matter whether or not he went to war. Even if he survived, his condition would be right there with him, an unwelcome companion—a demon brought along on the journey.

That's when Wally realized it. His uncle's tale wasn't harrowing because it was shocking. It was harrowing because it sounded like prophecy.

"What should I do?" said Wally, trying to steady his voice. "How do I fight something I don't understand?"

Wally heard Audrey swallow.

Sherman turned back to the window as if the answers were in the fountain. "That's what life is, son: a series of struggles against things we don't understand. We just do the best we can with what we've got for as long as it lasts."

Sherman's words hung in the air among the ether and the anguish.

Wally closed his eyes, closed off the world, searched the emptiness for answers that refused to come. While his uncle's advice was sound, it provided no comfort. More importantly, it didn't solve Wally's dilemma. Perhaps that was the point; there were no answers.

He opened his eyes. "How do I stay conscious?" Wally asked.

Sherman let out a pained sigh, his eyes still on the fountain. "I used to wonder if birds ask themselves such things. *How do I keep from falling from the sky?* But birds don't ask pointless questions, Walter. Birds aren't meant to worry. Birds are meant to fly."

Wally chewed his gum harder and harder, trying to eke out every drop of calming peppermint. He tried to meet his uncle's knowing eyes, to keep his tears from falling. Wally had come here eager for answers but had given little consideration to Sherman's own desperation. His uncle was struggling, not just with his own condition but with the tragic consequences of a choice he had come to regret—a choice Wally still had time to make differently.

The tumblers in the door's lock sang of their undoing, and Sherman's door suddenly opened. Gladys, the receptionist, walked in. "Time's up."

Sherman stood, hugged Wally, and quietly returned to his place at the window, looking at the fountain.

Audrey wiped her eyes and shadowed Gladys out of the room without a word.

Wally followed, but stopped when Sherman called, "Walter?"

"Yeah, Uncle Sherman?"

Sherman faced Wally, his eyes glossy. "I'll understand if you never come back. There's nothing for you here."

"There's nothing here for you either," said Wally, and he forced a smile. "This place is for the birds."

Sherman let out a bellowing laugh that seemed to escape from a place deep within him, and Wally moved to leave. But before he let the door snap shut behind him, he removed the wad of Beech-Nut gum from his mouth and shoved it into the hole where the door latched.

He then raced to catch up with Gladys and Audrey as the door closed behind him with a notable hush instead of the click he had heard earlier. He hadn't gotten any answers for himself, but instead left with a truth he would never forget.

Birds are meant to fly.

Wally and Audrey rode the pitching homebound trolley away from the sanitorium without saying much to one another. The smell of ether and disinfectant quickly dissolved off their winter coats as the trolley worked its way back toward Kensington, and Wally wished his angst could be so easily shed.

He had seen a premonition of the dark fate that awaited him. Far from proving he was different from Sherman, this trip had instead only fueled the feelings of desperation and self-doubt that had brought him there in the first place. His uncle had proven that few choices were left to men like them, and even those choices that were left in their control were likely to have lasting consequences that no man should be forced to endure.

The trolley squealed to a halt at their stop, which Wally would have missed had Audrey not tugged on his sleeve. They hopped onto the sidewalk, where he kept his eyes facing forward along the street, busy with pedestrians.

"How will you help?" asked Audrey, finally breaking Wally's silence now that they were walking.

"What do you mean?" he said.

"You told your uncle you'd found a way to help with the war. You said you had skills."

"Oh, right," Wally stammered, recalling the conversation. "I just meant that I was a civilian air-raid warden. Wardens help win the war, right?" He hated lying to Audrey, but this lie was ordered by the US Army.

Audrey nodded and dropped the subject; however, her silence felt more like sadness the longer it lasted.

"I'm sorry my uncle talked so much about guns and war," said Wally. "You're probably tired of all that, with what happened to Johnny..."

Audrey stopped and faced him. "Walter, don't you know why I suggested we visit your uncle in the first place?"

"You were looking out for me. You wanted me to have answers."

"I'm the one that wanted answers, you dope. I don't want you to end up like Johnny."

Before Wally could reply, Audrey ran the remaining distance to their apartment building. She dashed upstairs and left Wally alone in front of the cleaners, surprised and confounded. He had no idea how much Audrey feared for his life, how the notion of losing him would make her so afraid. He wanted to reassure her, to tell her he would be safe. But was that even true? Dawson's secret jingle mission was an opportunity to avoid death on a battlefield. It didn't promise a cure for his anxiety neurosis. No matter how the war turned out, Wally could end up right where his uncle was.

He pushed the door open and entered A-Rite Cleaners, eager to think about something other than war and loony bins. The bell that hung over the door heralded his entrance.

"Walter!" his mother called from the counter. "How was Flatbush?"

Wally immediately saw that his mother's perky tone was not for his benefit alone. At the counter stood Mr. Edelman. He was a man in his early seventies, roughly Wally's height and build, and appeared perpetually unhappy with his sunken eyes, downturned mouth, sallow cheeks, and skin the tone of mottled ash. He wore a long, black wool coat with a fur collar, and he raised a thick, bushy gray eyebrow at the sight of Wally.

"Hello, Mr. Edelman," said Wally, trying to mirror his mother's cheery tone. "Happy Hanukkah."

Mr. Edelman stared silently at him, and Wally suddenly feared the man had found something wrong with the bar mitzvah suits he, Max, and Frankie had "borrowed" for their evening at the Diamond Club. Despite their exhaustion that night, Wally and Max had been careful to press and clean the suits thoroughly after using them. There was no way Mr. Edelman could have known what they had done.

"Mr. Edelman said he wanted to thank you in person for doing such a fine job, pressing his family's suits," said Wally's mother.

"It was my pleasure." Wally's limbs filled with welcome relief. He approached and shook Mr. Edelman's hand.

"Yes, thank you." Mr. Edelman's voice was steady but held a note of equivocation. He wore a curious, uncharacteristic smirk but didn't take his eyes off Walter.

Wally's mother disappeared to the back of the shop and quickly returned carrying several bagged garments on hangers. "Here are the dresses for your wife and daughters," she said. "We took extra care with these." She hung the frocks on the receiving rack. "Just lovely. They have good taste."

"Thank you, Sadie. I'm sure they turned out just as well as our suits did." Mr. Edelman settled the bill and turned back to Wally. "Perhaps Walter can help me to my car. I'm parked just up the way."

"Sure," said Wally. "Happy to."

Wally grabbed the dresses, draped them over his arm, and followed Mr. Edelman out the door. Three steps onto the sidewalk, the man stopped.

"Is she pretty?"

"What?" said Wally. "Who?"

"Bobbi. Who else?"

At the sound of the name, Wally froze.

Mr. Edelman reached into his jacket and withdrew a crinkled slip of paper the color of blush. "I found this in my suit pants pocket, the pants you cleaned earlier this week. It says, 'Call me, Walter,' and it has a phone number. It's signed, 'Bobbi.'" Mr. Edelman grinned and looked up from the paper. "Beautiful penmanship. Usually, a sign the girl is beautiful too."

"I—I can explain," Wally faltered.

Mr. Edelman resumed walking to his car. "I suppose I should be angry," he said, waving the paper, "but those pants probably got more action on you than they've had on me in thirty years. Please keep that to yourself."

"What?"

"I'm presuming you kept the pants on, but I suppose I don't really know."

Wally's heart knocked, and he feared he might collapse right there in the street at Mr. Edelman's feet. But the man didn't seem to notice Wally's discomfort. Instead, he keyed open the trunk for Wally to unload the dresses.

"So, is she pretty?" Edelman repeated.

Wally swallowed hard. "Very," he answered, placing the dresses gently in the trunk. The thought of her seemed to calm him. "And she smells like flowers."

Mr. Edelman raised his nose to the air and closed his eyes as if trying to smell Bobbi's perfume for himself. "If she's right for you, Walter, make the most of it." Mr. Edelman shut the trunk and handed Wally the paper with Bobbi's number. "Girls like that don't come along every day, especially ones that give you their number."

"Thanks, Mr. Edelman." Wally slid the paper into his own pocket. "I'm sorry about—"

Mr. Edelman gestured with his hand. "Never you mind. Pants are pants." He then got into his car, gave Wally an uncharacteristic wink, and drove away, leaving Wally in a cloud of smog and embarrassment.

He waved away the exhaust and then stared at the street where Mr. Edelman's car had been. Now that Wally had signed up to help Bobbi's father on his crazy mission, it was likely he'd have to face her again, decide how he felt about her deception, and figure out whether he believed her when she said she liked him. It was a quandary for sure, but a better one to puzzle over than the one he'd carried home from Flatbush.

As he stood there on the sidewalk, playing his last confrontation with Bobbi over in his head, a man with a wide-brimmed hat bumped him.

"Oh, sorry," said Wally, self-conscious that he was standing on a busy sidewalk. But the man just strode by without responding and disappeared with a crowd rounding the corner.

Wally dug into his pocket for Bobbi's phone number to ogle her handwriting, see if the paper still smelled of lilacs after having been dry-cleaned. Instead, he withdrew two pieces of paper. The first was Bobbi's pink note that Mr. Edelman had given him. The second was a slip of white paper folded multiple times.

Wally unfurled it and saw typed instructions for crafting another jingle, written like the quirky requests they'd gotten for the Podolor jingle, with directions on measures, key changes, lyrics, and stanza cuts. Across the bottom it read: "Tonight 7:30 pm."

Wally spun to find the guy in the hat who had bumped him, but the man was long gone. He looked again at the paper, ran down the instructions, and felt a smile slowly grow on his face.

If Wally was a gun, someone had just opened the drawer.

6

Del Monte Peaches

Wally, Max, and Frankie stepped off the subway once they'd reached their stop in lower Manhattan. They had spent the entire train ride from Brooklyn sitting in silence, both out of a need to keep their thoughts about their mission secret from the others aboard the subway and from a desire to bolster themselves for what promised to be the most consequential work of their lives. This was no longer about fifty dollars or radio play. This was about war.

They weaved their way out of the station and started their walk through the frigid evening air toward WKOB. The electric streetlamps along the boulevard in front of a department store had been adorned with silver garland and fragrant pine wreaths, and several windows had been decorated with twinkling holiday lights in an attempt to raise spirits and aim people's attention toward commerce, even with so many unlucky men off to the front lines. Wally's own family was struggling with bills as always, and the holidays this year, like most years, promised to be modest. Tonight's third-night Hanukkah celebration had consisted of a hastily mumbled *bracha* over the candles, some warmed, leftover brisket and boiled potatoes, and an exchange of handwritten cards and woolen socks.

Of course, tonight, socks and cards were the last things on Wally's mind. He prayed for his Hanukkah miracle, which had now grown beyond his wish to save his own life. Added to the list was the desire to stay out of the sanatorium and to earn the love of a beautiful girl. The way his wishes were piling up, he thought, it was a good thing there were eight nights of Hanukkah.

Max opened the heavy glass door to the station's headquarters, led the team through the empty, darkened lobby, and when they entered the WKOB reception area, they found Major Brubaker alone at the reception desk once again, this time with his feet up on the desk's leather blotter.

"Right on time, fellas. I like your style."

Wally scanned for Bobbi, but the reception area was empty.

"Got your note," said Max. "We're ready to start."

The major slid his feet off his desk.

"Appreciate your enthusiasm, fellas, but first we need to clear up a few things." His tone was surprisingly terse.

"What things?" said Frankie.

Brubaker stood. "Follow me."

Wally and the others exchanged confused looks as the major led them toward the studio, where, to Wally's surprise, someone was already sitting at the piano bench—and it wasn't Bobbi.

Rat Rubinstein stared bug-eyed at them all. He was bound and gagged, tethered by a rope to the shiny ebony Steinway, his eyes betraying a panicked desperation.

Wally's heart sputtered and seemed to stop entirely like their unreliable industrial dryer.

Max made a noise like "gawp," and Frankie simply froze in place.

"Funny thing," said Brubaker. "This punk reporter showed up this afternoon with more than a few questions. Says he knows you fellas. That true?"

Max looked at Rat Rubinstein with eyes like daggers. "Yes," Max seethed. "We know him."

Frankie drew back his sleeves. "Rubinstein."

"We can explain," said Wally.

Brubaker gritted his teeth. "Said you came to his home and threatened him, told him to keep quiet about the contest. Said that's how he knew there was some sort of story here."

Rat's eyes darted and he tried to speak through the handkerchief that had been wadded in his mouth. "Mrph. Vrmm. Mmmrm!"

"So, tell me, fellas," said Brubaker, ignoring Rat. "Is there a story here?"

Wally turned his back to Rat and faced the major, speaking under his breath so that Rat couldn't hear him. "There wasn't a story until you kidnapped the guy," hissed Wally. "Why didn't you just brush him off?"

Brubaker pointed an accusing finger at Wally. "You're on thin ice, Curly," he snarled softly. "Don't put this on me."

Max leaned in and joined the whispered argument. "Walter is right. We handled him already. All you did was add fuel to the fire. You could've come up with some excuse and sent him on his way."

"Yeah," said Frankie. "This isn't our fault."

Brubaker's face grew red. "It took all of two minutes to see this little twerp isn't the sent-on-his-way type, and, besides, it's not my job to make excuses for anyone. You boys blew this, not me."

Wally looked to the squirming reporter tied to the piano and pondered his next move.

"I can fix this," said Wally.

Brubaker raised an eyebrow. "How?"

"I need you to trust me," said Wally.

"I did trust you," said Brubaker. "Look how that worked out."

"Just let me talk to him. Alone."

The major sized up Wally, seemed to weigh his options.

"Five minutes," pleaded Wally. "At least give me that."

"All right," Brubaker said. He brandished his palm at Wally. "Five." Brubaker waved Max and Frankie back toward the reception area. "You two are with me."

Max shot Wally a look of doubt but followed Frankie and Brubaker out of the studio. Once alone with Rat, Wally moved to the piano bench, where Rat was still squirming. He untied the gag around Rat's face and removed the handkerchief from his mouth, leaving Rat's hands and feet bound to the piano.

"Jesus, Lipkin!" Rat coughed. "What the hell—?"

"Quiet," said Wally. "Just listen."

Rat ran his tongue over his teeth as if clearing his mouth of the taste of handkerchief. "Untie my hands. I swear—"

Wally sat on the bench next to Rat and held up a finger.

"Do you remember Mrs. Holman's civics class back at Lincoln High? You read your paper on Eleanor Roosevelt."

"What are you talking about? Untie me."

"It was the one time in all of high school that I actually respected you. I had expected your paper to be about Hitler or Mussolini or someone horrible. I figured you liked those sorts of people. But you picked Eleanor Roosevelt."

"Who cares?"

"When you read that paper to the class, you talked about your dad, how he had died in the Great War. How you respected his service. How Eleanor Roosevelt understood you and families like yours, poor families who had experienced sacrifice and knew the value of hard work." Wally looked more intently at Rat. "Your family sounded like mine," he said. "It was very moving."

Rat stopped squirming. "I'm a good writer. Better than you. So what?"

"That was more than good writing, Clyde. It was the truth. I saw it in your face. Heard it in your voice. First time I ever thought you actually cared about people. Bet you still do, somewhere in there, even though you act like you don't."

Rat shook his head but didn't reply.

"You're patriotic," said Wally. "We have that in common."

"What the hell are you blathering about? Why did that guy tie me to a piano?"

"Because you walked into something patriotic. Something you might screw up if you keep at this like a reporter."

"I am a reporter, you idiot. Now, untie me." Rat continued to struggle against his restraints.

"Can't do that," said Wally. "You know too much."

Rat drew a deep breath and settled down.

"All I know, Lipkin, is that you and that crazy station manager have something hinky going on, and the cops oughta know about it."

"No, that's the reporter talking. If you're the patriot I think you are, the patriot who believes in what his father sacrificed, then you realize there are things the government is doing to save lives. Things that need to be kept secret from the average person. You know that, don't you?"

Rat fixed his gaze on Wally. "I guess so."

Wally shook his head. "You can't guess so. You need to know so. Are you able to keep a secret? A secret that could help end the war?" He stared into Rat's beady eyes, looking for his humanity, the part of him that was the son of a fallen soldier, the part that had spilled his guts in civics class. "If you could choose between cracking a story or stopping the war, which would you choose?" said Wally. "In your heart, if you had to pick one, who are you, a reporter or a patriot?"

Rat widened his rodent eyes. "Christ, Lipkin. What the hell have you gotten yourself into?"

"I'm being honest, here, Clyde. You're usually mean and petty. Folks call you Rat, and you deserve it. I think you know that too. But what's going on here is more important than any of the name-calling stuff we play at, me or you."

Rat kept his eyes locked on Wally, and Wally kept his on Rat.

"Answer the question," said Wally. "Reporter or patriot? Brubaker's coming back and your answer will matter."

"I'm no traitor, Lipkin. I know how horrible war is. More than most." Rat's voice shook, his tone serious. "And I'm not a rat, no matter what you and your friends call me."

Just then, Brubaker burst into the studio, Max and Frankie close at his heels.

"All right, Curly. Five minutes are up. What've we got?"

"Let me go," Rat blurted. "I know my rights."

Wally shot Rat a cautionary look. "Clyde..."

Rat frowned but shut his mouth, obeying Wally's command.

Wally stood from the bench and faced the major, who looked puzzled by the way Wally had just quieted the reporter.

"Tell him, sir," said Wally. He put his hand on Rat's shoulder, which seemed to surprise everyone, including Rat. "Tell Clyde everything."

Brubaker's eyes widened. "Have you lost your mind?"

"I trust him," said Wally. "His father gave his life in the Great War. He knows what's at stake." Wally raised his head and stood firmly at Rat's side. "Clyde may be a news hawk, but he knows the value of the truth and the importance of keeping secrets. Despite everything else, he's a patriot. If you trust me, you can trust him."

Wally looked at the pathetic reporter tied to the piano, and Rat just stared at back at him, incredulous, speechless for the first time since Wally had met the guy.

"I was wrong about him," Wally added. "He's smart and he's clever. I think the team could use someone like him."

"The team?" barked Max. "Are you kidding?"

"No chance!" said Frankie. "You know this guy. He's no friend of ours."

Rat sneered but kept quiet.

"We can't win wars if we keep looking for enemies," said Wally. "We need allies, and I'd rather have Clyde as an ally."

"C'mon, guys," Rat begged, finally speaking out. "These ropes hurt."

Major Brubaker stared at Rat, and then stepped over to get up close. "How old are you, son?"

"Eighteen," said Rat.

"Why aren't you serving? Did you register?"

Rat looked away. "3-A."

"Dependent deferral?" said Brubaker, cocking his head. "How'd you swing that?"

"My mother wrote a hardship letter without me knowing," said Rat. "Guess she's a good writer like me."

Max let out an audible huff, but Brubaker ignored him.

"You wanna serve your country?"

"I do serve my country," said Rat. "I'm a journalist."

"Bah!" spat Frankie.

"That's important work," the major agreed, ignoring the sounds coming from the peanut gallery. "But what if you could do more?"

Rat raised his head. "Like what?" Rat's tone had grown curious, and Wally saw why the army found Brubaker to be a skilled recruiter.

The major squatted next to the piano bench and untied Rat's hands and feet. As he did, the reporter rubbed at the red indentations on his wrists, but he didn't try to run.

"What if I told you that I'm a major in the US Army and not a radio station manager?" said Brubaker. He rose and tossed the ropes aside.

"I'd say you seem the military type," said Rat.

"And what if I told you the army needed smart people, right here in New York, for a secret mission that could save lives on the other side of the world? A secret mission your friends have already agreed to take on?"

Rat aimed his unblinking eyes at him. "I'd say I've heard stranger stories than that."

Brubaker smiled. "Then maybe Lipkin is right. Maybe you are ready for this. But to be in on the secret, it has to be official. Are you willing to be sworn in to serve your country? Now? Here? Tonight?"

Frankie looked away but stayed quiet. Max just folded his arms.

Major Brubaker thumbed over to Frankie and Max. "These two gave up their 4-Fs to join the team. How about you? Do want that 3-A to stick?"

Rat shot an inquiring look to Wally, appearing to find some new connection with him.

Wally nodded back. "Come on, Clyde. You're good and the army needs good."

Rat rose from the piano bench, puffed out his chest with the awkward pride of someone unused to receiving compliments.

"All right," said Rat. "I'm in." He rubbed his wrists. "I'll tell my editor there was no story here after all."

"Good," said Brubaker. "Phone's in the reception area."

"Can I ask a favor first?" said Rat.

Brubaker narrowed his eyes. "I suppose."

"Can we quit with the rope?" Rat scoffed. "If you wanted my help, all you had to do was ask."

Wally sat at the WKOB's ebony Steinway, twinkling away with his fingers on the keys, conjuring the team's war bond jingle from memory, eager to replace the tension in the room with something melodic.

Rat stood beside him, tapping his foot, appearing to enjoy the music. It was a scene Wally would never have imagined, but the last few days had been filled with strange and unusual situations, and Wally was growing used to it.

Max and Frankie stood at the far end of the studio, shooting distrusting looks toward Rat, whispering conspiratorially.

Rat seemed to notice, stopped his toe tapping, and quickly turned away.

"Ignore them," said Wally. "They'll come around." Wally fueled his voice with reassurance, though he was still unsure whether he'd come around to accepting Rat on the team himself.

"I'll believe it when I see it," said Rat.

Major Brubaker unfolded a card table near the piano and asked Wally and Rat to help set up some folding chairs to create a makeshift writing area for the team.

Wally looked around, longing for Bobbi to join them, to give him the opportunity to clear the air with her. Instead, he had to settle for the uneasy alliance he had formed with Rubinstein. He agreed to answer Rat's questions about the particulars of the mission, now that the major had officially taken Rat into the army's confidence.

When Brubaker left again to retrieve more chairs, Rat leaned toward Wally.

"WKOB?" asked Rat. "What's the story?"

"A government front," answered Wally.

"The whole building?"

"Guess so." Wally had only been on two floors of the skyscraper and wondered what other secrets the skyscraper held.

"What about the jingle contest?"

"A cover to recruit us." Wally smirked. "We actually won the contest after all." He played a twinkling anthem on the grand piano to highlight their victory. "It's why we couldn't let you run the story."

Rat's eyes flashed like he was solving a riddle. "Your jingles have secret messages."

Wally stopped playing, impressed at Rat's swift power of deduction. His silence was all the answer Rat needed.

"Holy shit." Rat laughed. "That's crazy." He sounded genuinely impressed, taking in the news and accepting the truth of it all much faster than Wally had.

Brubaker returned with a stack of writing pads, which he handed to Max. "Crazy may be what works," the major said, hearing the last part of their conversation. "Enemies won't expect it and certainly won't understand it, even though it'll all be there, right under their noses."

Rat nodded, betraying a fiendish respect. "Genius."

Major Brubaker pointed at them. "Now you know why all this needs to be kept a secret, Mr. Rubinstein."

Max and Frankie made their way over to the table and took their seats. Max stared at Rat as if willing him to disappear in a puff of smoke.

"What's with the evil eye?" said Rat.

"You shouldn't be here."

"How are you supposed to help us anyway?" added Frankie.

Rat raised his head. "I have a way with words. Maybe I can help with lyrics."

"Says who?" Max growled.

"I know how to be sneaky," said Rat. "Even you would have to admit that. Maybe I can put together secret messages. That's gotta count for something."

"It does," said the major, stepping forward. "Plus, we could use your eyes and ears over at the *Daily Eagle*. You hear anything that might be a problem for us, we'll count on you to let us know, and to steer things another way."

For some reason, Rat saluted. "Yes, sir, Major."

Brubaker nodded to Wally and the others. "Find a way to work Mr. Rubinstein into the mix, boys."

"Is this really happening?" Frankie looked gobsmacked.

"Yes," said Brubaker. "And I like his style. You three should start saluting too. I am an army major and your senior officer after all."

"What's that make us?" said Max.

"Suckers," whispered Frankie.

"You're all privates," said Brubaker. "And it's about time we get some discipline around here."

"Major, I have questions about the assignment," said Wally in a blatant effort to change the subject. He pulled the folded paper from his pocket, the one he'd gotten from the man with the hat. "These instructions describe measures, notes, and a few of the lyrics. They don't mention the product we're writing a jingle for." He handed the paper to Max, who gave it the once-over.

"He's right," said Max. "No product. What are we supposed to write about?"

"Creative license," said Brubaker. "You decide. Just be sure the jingle works."

Max set the paper on the table.

"It calls for a four-four in the key of C," said Frankie, reading the sheet.

"It says 'sunshine' has to be the first word in the lyric," said Max. "We also have to work in the words 'delicious,' 'treat,' and 'man,' in that order."

"What product does that sound like?" said Wally.

"Could be anything," said Frankie.

"Peaches," said Rat, taking a seat at the table. "Delicious, sunshine, treat. Sounds like peaches to me."

Wally saw the skeptical looks on both Max's and Frankie's faces.

"It works," said Wally. "Don't deny it. If I had said 'peaches,' you would've said it was perfect."

Max shook his head but couldn't argue.

"What kind of peaches?" said Frankie.

"Del Monte?" said Rat.

"Del Monte peaches it is," declared Wally.

A wide grin bloomed across Rat's face.

"Now, you're talking," said Brubaker. "Get to it, fellas. I'll give you two hours." With that, he left the room.

Wally didn't want to be Rat's defender, and yet if things were going to work with the others, Rat would clearly need his support.

"See? That wasn't so hard," said Rat.

Frankie leaned across the table to snatch the paper. "Don't get cocky. That part was the easy part. Now, shut up and let the experts do their jobs."

Wally feared an argument would ensue, but, instead, Rat sat back in his folding chair.

"Okay," said Rat. "Show me."

Max pulled up a chair, pressed his pencil to his lined pad, and started mapping out lyrics. Wally sat at the Steinway to toy with some combinations, softly singing the word "peaches" in different ways. Frankie joined Wally at the piano and flicked the metronome in motion on the piano lid to set the tempo.

Rat watched from his chair but, to Wally's surprise, didn't make any snide or sarcastic remarks. Instead, he was respectful, silent. For once, Rat was behaving.

After an hour of back-and-forth negotiations over lyrics, Wally, Max, and Frankie finally had a working draft. And, while Max seemed happy to sing their new tune, Wally was still hoping Bobbi would float in like an angel and lift their efforts, and his spirits. He longed to hear her melodic voice and wanted to put the past behind them as he had managed to do, at least for now, with Rat.

They sang and refined the jingle over the following hour, but Bobbi never came. Instead, it was Brubaker who finally strode in. Once again, Rat saluted the major.

"Ten hut," Rat called, and jumped to his feet.

Max shook his head at Rat's formality, but he and the others stood and saluted too.

"Much better," said Brubaker, nodding in response to the respect he was now being shown. "At ease, soldiers. It's getting late. You boys need some coffee?"

"Depends," said Max. "Listen to this and tell us what you think." He pointed to Wally, who played their Del Monte peaches jingle as Max sang.

> *"Sunshine peaches from the tree,*
> *Delicious fruit will make you see.*
> *Del Monte peaches, sunshine sweet—*
> *Just try some of this healthy treat.*
> *Summer goodness from the can—*
> *Get some peaches from your grocer man!"*

As Wally sang, the major held the folded paper, reading the jingle instructions, appearing to check their work. Once Wally finished, the boys looked to Brubaker who sighed aloud and lowered the paper.

"Boring."

"What?" said Max.

"Big yawn." Brubaker shook his head. "Says nothing." He tossed the paper back onto the table.

"But all the coded messages are in there," said Max.

"That's not what makes it a jingle, son."

"Oh, come on!" said Frankie. "That wasn't half bad."

"Which is another way of saying it was only half good," the major quipped back. He circled the piano. "Since when is that good enough for the US Army?"

The air thickened with their discomfort.

"Fellas, for this to work, your jingle's gotta sound like the real deal. The Germans have to believe that some highly paid, muckety-muck agency men came up with that. When you wrote the Podolor jingle, you said the name three times. You only said 'Del Monte' once. No ad man from Del Monte would let you get away with that. It can't be half good. It's gotta sell peaches. Del Monte peaches. Period." He folded his arms across his chest.

Wally had to admit, the jingle didn't showcase their usual pizazz. Now that they knew the secret purpose of their jingles, they'd spent too much time focusing on the coded messages and not enough on the product. The guys were distracted by Rat and the requirements of the codes. The jingle fell short. Brubaker was right.

From his seat at the folding table, Rat cleared his throat, the first noise he had made since the boys had begun their jingle work.

"Make the coffee," said Rat. "Take a break. Let me give it a shot." He reached for Max's lyric pad, but as he did, Max slammed his fist on the pad and pinned it in place.

"Get your own coffee," said Max. "I've got the lyrics."

"Yeah," said Frankie, leaning in from his seat. "Max has the lyrics."

"Boys," the major said. "Give Clyde his chance. You had yours, and you've got the basics down. Let's see what he's got to punch it up." He handed Clyde a new, fresh writing pad.

Max threw an icy look at Rat.

"He's just trying to help," said Wally. He wanted things to work for Clyde, if for no other reason than to keep him quiet and out of their hair.

Brubaker stepped over. "Why don't you come with me, Moxie? I can show you where Groucho hides his stash of cigars."

"Oh, come on!" said Max. Major Brubaker raised an eyebrow, daring further opposition.

"Fine," said Max. "As long as I can take one." He pushed himself away from the table, his chair creaking from his weight. He stood and pointed at Rat. "Don't write on my pad."

"You got it, Moxie," said Rat.

"I'll work on the coffee," said Frankie, sounding eager for an excuse to remove himself from Rat's presence. He turned and followed Brubaker and Max out of the studio, leaving Wally alone with Rat.

"Sorry 'bout them," said Wally. "We've been a trio for a long time. Old habits, you know?"

"Don't worry," said Rat. "No one likes me. I'm used to it."

Wally felt a pang of sympathy to hear the guy so resigned to the hatred people had of him. Then again, Rat was complicit in building his own awful reputation.

"You need to try a little harder," said Wally.

"Me?"

"You're the new guy. And for starters, you could be more pleasant."

"How?"

Wally eyed Rat, wondering if the guy had ever tried to make friends. "Take Max," he said. "You should be nicer to him."

"He's arrogant," said Rat. "And mean."

"He's my brother."

"So, you know I'm right. Arrogant. Mean. And fat too."

Wally frowned. "Now who's being mean?"

"He is fat. That's not mean. I'm just reporting the facts."

"Well, you don't have to report anything here, remember? Besides, Max only acts arrogant. He's actually insecure."

"Insecure? That wise-ass?"

"You're not trying very hard."

"Okay. I'll bite. How is Max insecure?"

"He wants people to know he's good at this." Wally gestured to the studio. "All this. Writing. Performing. The business stuff. He wants to be respected. Same as you. Same as anyone."

"So, what's your point?"

"Find his good traits. Focus on those. Make him feel less insecure. Help him get what he wants. That's how you win Max over. Frankie too. It's how you'll earn your place on the team, at least as far as they're concerned."

"You've gotta be kidding."

"A compliment doesn't cost you a cent, and it gives Max and Frankie something to work with. A reason to like you."

"They'll never like me."

"Well, at least give them a reason not to hate you."

"Your brother threatened to ring my neck. O'Brien already tried. You saw for yourself." Wally tilted his head.

"Okay. Fine. I'll compliment him and O'Brien." Rat rubbed his chin. "Just gotta remember how to compliment people." A smirk tugged at his thin lips.

"All right," said Wally. "Show me what you're thinking for lyrics."

"Let's start with what your brother wrote," said Rat, sliding Max's pad over next to his own. He ran his finger down Max's lyric page and then skimmed over the jingle instructions. "Technically, you guys worked all the required words into the right places..."

"But?"

Rat looked up from his pad. "I've always had to write for someone else's approval," said Rat. "Can't say I've ever liked that part of the job, but it taught me how to write one thing in a million different ways, still working in the critical elements. You guys'll just have to learn that too. There's more than one way to do something. More ways than your way."

Wally had to concede, it was good advice.

"Now, give me a few minutes." Rat's pointy tongue moved back and forth as he worked on his own draft, shifting between Max's page, the instructions, and his own writing pad.

Wally leaned in. "Don't forget what Brubaker said about Del Monte. We gotta mention the brand more than once."

"Obviously," said Rat. "Should've figured that one out for yourselves."

Wally sighed. Getting Rat to act in a pleasant way was going to be as much work as getting his brother and Frankie to accept him, and Wally wasn't sure he was up to either task.

Frankie soon walked in with two cups of coffee and put them on the table next to Rat.

"Hot coffee," he said. "Try not to choke on it."

Rat looked into his cup. "I take cream and sugar," he said.

"Tonight, you take it black," Frankie snapped, and left the room.

Rat gave an exasperated look to Wally.

"Give him time," said Wally. "He did bring you coffee."

"I guess," said Rat. "I like his hair."

"What?"

"I'm working on my compliments." Rat smiled. "Did I sound convincing?"

"Keep working on it," said Wally.

He returned to the Steinway to give Rat some time to noodle the lyrics. "Can we at least keep the tune?" he asked.

"Sure," said Rat. "The music part isn't my forte, anyway. But do me a favor and kick it up a bit. Make it more...peachy."

Wally chuckled, yet he knew what Rat meant. He added some higher-octave enhancements to make the jingle brighter, trying to elevate the tone they had failed to achieve with their first try, playing as if Bobbi were there with her hand back on his shoulder.

After a few minutes, Rat joined him at the bench, his new lyrics in hand.

"Sing this." Rat set the pages on the piano's music shelf against the rack. "Tell me what you think."

As Wally reached for the keys, Brubaker, Max, and Frankie returned.

"Any progress?" asked the major.

Rat saluted again.

"We were just giving Clyde's new lyrics a run-through."

Max rounded the piano. "Let's hear 'em," he said. It sounded more like a challenge than encouragement.

"Yeah," said Frankie. "Let's hear 'em."

Rat nodded at Wally. "Keep those high notes you added," he said. "Those sounded great."

Wally squinted his disbelief at Rat's flattery, and Rat whispered, "That was a real compliment. I meant it."

Wally drew a breath, and sang Rat's new lyrics:

> *"Sunshine peaches from the tree,*
> *Delicious fruit from Del Monte.*
> *Sliced in syrup, such a treat.*
> *Del Monte peaches can't be beat.*
> *Flown from the orchard to the grocer man,*
> *Del Monte peaches in the little green can!"*

Wally added a final high- and low-octave C combo to signal the jingle's conclusion. But instead of turning to Major Brubaker for approval, Wally gave a hopeful look to Max.

To his surprise, Max nodded his head.

"I wanted that to stink," said Max, "but it was better."

"I agree," said the major. "Well done."

Frankie scoffed aloud, seeming unable to find anything to criticize.

"Well, the bones were already there," said Rat. "You guys are good, no doubt. I just know more words."

Wally elbowed Rat, who stammered and added, "Of course, I still have a lot to learn. From you. Because...you're better. You are."

"Shut up," whispered Wally. "They liked it."

"A good night's work," said the major. He eyed Frankie. "Think you can put it together on the composition page?"

"I guess," said Frankie, not hiding his reluctance.

Frankie picked up the pages from the table and scratched the music and lyrics onto paper.

"What are the next steps?" said Max.

"We get it recorded," said Brubaker. "Then, it gets broadcast to the front line."

The thought of the front line gave Wally pause. While he and his pals were helping the war effort, drinking coffee in the safety of a New York studio, other guys his age were out on some foreign field, putting their necks on the line. He was glad not to be there, but somehow it seemed unfair.

"You're not gonna let us record it?" asked Max.

"Not this go-round," said Brubaker.

"What's the secret message?" asked Rat. "Combat instructions? Weapon drops?"

It was a question Wally wanted answered too, and the new quartet looked to the major for his reply.

"Top secret," Brubaker said flatly. "You don't have the clearance."

"We wrote the thing!" said Max.

"That you did," said the major. "And soon you'll write another and another." He glanced around at all four of them. "We each have a role to play, gentlemen, and writing jingles is yours."

"Who gets to interpret them?" said Rat. "How does it work on the other end?"

"Yeah," said Frankie, seeming surprised to share the same thoughts as Rat. "Who else is in on it?"

"That, gentlemen, is a conversation for another day."

Brubaker led the guys out of the studio, back through the reception area, to the glass front doors. He pulled out his keys, unlocked them, and let the guys through.

"Stay alert," he said. "You'll receive new instructions in the next forty-eight hours. And remember, loose lips sink ships. That's for you, Rubinstein." He pointed at Rat.

"Yessir," said Rat, saluting one last time.

The four of them exited onto Broadway, leaving the warmth of the studio for the December chill of the street, readying for the long haul home to Brooklyn. Wally made fists of his cold fingers and jammed them into his pockets. That's when he got a whiff of flowers.

"Walter?"

Bobbi LaFleur stepped out of the shadows in a fur-collared coat, a purse over her shoulder and a small, feathered hat in her hair.

"Bobbi?"

"I know it's late," she said, "but can we talk?"

Wally looked to the others, and Max returned a knowing smile.

"See you at home," said Max. He winked at Wally and then turned to Rat and Frankie. "Make tracks, fellas."

As his pals walked away, Wally heard Rat ask, "Who's the dame?" and then heard Max reply, "Mind your own business."

Wally worried that without his presence on the subway ride home, Max and Frankie might turn on Rat and destroy the awkward cease-fire they'd forged. But with Bobbi there beside him, the issues of the newly forged quartet would have to wait.

"Come with me," said Bobbi, her green eyes twinkling like the boulevard Christmas lights. He'd been hoping all night to see her, and her insistence was both exciting and alarming.

"W-where?"

In answer, Bobbi whirled on her heel and headed up Broadway, deeper into midtown.

Wally followed for three blocks, past the stores now closed for the night, off the main thoroughfare, and down a series of side streets, the kind Wally had always avoided. As the noise of automobiles and the buzz of streetlights faded behind him, Wally struggled to keep up, his concern growing.

"Is there a diner or something down here?" he called, but Bobbi kept racing ahead.

Wally longed to be in her presence, to explore whether she might really have feelings for him, feelings like those he had for her. If only she'd stop long enough to talk...

Following her into the darkest parts of Manhattan wasn't exactly what he considered a romantic evening, but her urgent concern hardly implied she had romantic things planned. Despite his misgivings, he followed her closely, guided by the scent of flowers carried in the cold air. Soon, they approached a tall apartment building with a sign out front that read "Elving House, Residence for Women," where Bobbi finally stopped.

"Where are we?" said Wally, working to catch his breath.

"I live here," said Bobbi, a frosty cloud rising from her lips. "And I have a curfew."

"Residence for women?" he read aloud.

"I refuse to live on the army base with my father when I spend most of my time in Midtown at the Diamond Club or at the studio."

"And your father's okay with that?"

Bobbi grinned. "The Elving House is full of girls like me. I think he's happy to keep me away from all those soldiers, anyway."

Wally saw the wisdom of that, but as he attempted to say so, Bobbi spun to face the building as if she'd heard something.

"Quick!" she said. "Go 'round back to the fire escape, up to the roof."

"The roof?" Wally had a million questions, but Bobbi seemed to have plans of her own.

"Mrs. Davidson is a real watchdog, so don't dawdle."

Bobbi hurried to the door, leaving Wally alone and confused on the street. She then keyed herself into the building and disappeared.

Finding no alternative, Wally dashed down the side alley of the Elving House until he reached the fire escape, which rose the full height of the building's three stories. He told himself it was like climbing to his own roof for an air-raid drill, but he couldn't quiet the galloping of his heart.

One Mississippi, two Mississippi, three Mississippi...

He filled his bagpipe lungs and reached for the ladder. He lowered it as quietly as the screeching metal would permit and climbed. The escape was dry and dusty and smelled of rust. Still, Wally kept climbing until he reached the top of the building.

He hoisted himself onto the flat roof and dusted off his trousers. A moment later, Bobbi appeared from the roof access door and rushed over.

"Boys aren't allowed in the residence," she said. "I suppose that includes the roof, but no one comes up here besides me. This is where I hide out when I have serious things on my mind."

It gave Wally a secret pleasure to learn that, like him, Bobbi sought solace on the roof of her home. But what serious things were on her mind?

"Come over here," she said. Bobbi led him to a steel storage box near the roof's edge. She motioned for Wally to sit, and then took a seat beside him, facing the East River and the moon shining overhead. "I didn't like where we left things," she said.

Wally nodded. "Me neither."

She pulled the small, feathered hat from her hair and toyed with the hair clip and hat in her lap. "I know you don't trust me," Bobbi added, "and I'm sorry for that. I kept secrets from you, and I lied." Her words sounded rehearsed but earnest.

"Well, the mission is supposed to be a secret," said Wally. "So, I guess it makes sense."

Wally wanted to tell her he'd already decided to move past his distrust, just as he'd done with Rat, yet he was eager to learn why she had brought him to her roof.

"It's important that you trust me," said Bobbi. "Important that you know why I'm involved in this at all."

"Okay," said Wally, his curiosity piqued.

She aimed her eyes at the sky. "My whole childhood, my father was never around," she said, "always working on this plan or the next, kept getting medals and promotions. The only time I'd see him was at army events where families were expected." Bobbi sighed. "What he didn't understand was what his absence was doing to my mother. She felt abandoned. She drank. A lot. One day, when I was fifteen, I found her on the floor, at the foot of the stairs."

Wally gasped, his breath a hovering cloud between them.

"Guess she must've fallen when no one was home," said Bobbi, "and that was it." Her gaze remained fixed on the sky. "She was gone."

Wally recalled Colonel Dawson, his Charles Atlas shoulders, the colorful decorations on his uniform, the way he spoke. The man had seemed confident and self-assured, all of which had intimidated Wally. There was no sign of the colonel's loss, no evidence of the pain he had wrought. Perhaps, like his daughter, his truth was hidden behind a façade.

Bobbi looked back at Wally. "Since that day, my father has been different," she said. "He's not distant anymore. It's the opposite. He's become overly protective. At first, he'd bring me to his meetings, take me wherever he went, even got top-secret clearance for me, just so I could be in the room with him. When he first brought me into the jingle mission, I thought it was just another way for him to keep his eye on me. But I'm trying to show him that I have skills that are useful, that I can really help." She looked into her hands, still fiddling with her hat and clip. "Still," she said, "it's like every day, he's asking my forgiveness without words, apologizing for what happened to my mother."

"I'm sorry you lost her," said Wally, reminded how grateful he was to have both of his parents, as crazy as they were.

"I miss her," said Bobbi. She aimed her eyes back at the stars. "I don't blame my father for what happened. He thinks I do, but I don't." She lowered her head. "I blame myself."

"Why?" said Wally.

"Because maybe if I had been less dreamy, less self-involved, I would have been enough for her, enough to keep her happy whenever my father was away. Enough to keep her with me."

"You can't blame yourself," said Wally. "You were just a kid." He shifted uncomfortably on the cold metal storage box.

Bobbi didn't respond. She just looked out over Manhattan.

An iciness in the air bit at his nose and ears. They sat silent under the crescent moon, which smiled like the Cheshire Cat over the city, shining above the skyscrapers, boats tugging down the river.

"My father's jingle plan," Bobbi said, finally ending the quiet, "I thought it was crazy at first. The army did too. You should've heard the way they ridiculed him. I expected them to shut the whole thing down. Even my father was starting to get discouraged. Then, you and your friends showed up."

"His plan is crazy," said Wally. "You weren't there tonight. We still don't know what we're doing."

Bobbi laughed, and the sound of her laughter made Wally smile.

"That's just because the thing you're doing hasn't ever been tried," said Bobbi. "At least that's what my father told the army. It may be unconventional, but that's exactly why he thinks this plan will work."

"I hope it does," said Wally.

"Walter," she said in a somber tone, "the war isn't going well. The Germans seem to be one step ahead of the Allies, and men like my father are trying to find a way to get the upper hand. He thinks this plan has a chance, even if the top brass can't see it yet."

"I'm not sure I see it, either," said Wally. "I've never been asked to do anything this important. Neither have my brother or the others. The truth is, I don't know if we've got the chops."

"You're the right team. I know it. You boys have my father excited, and I haven't seen him that way in a long time. He's talking to me again, listening to my ideas. It's like we're getting back to being a family."

"He's a good man," said Wally, though he wasn't sure whether that was true.

"If this team doesn't work," said Bobbi, "they'll cancel the mission, send him away someplace dangerous. This new relationship he and I are building will just...end."

Wally nodded. He saw where her concern was leading, saw what she was afraid of.

Bobbi reached out and grabbed Wally's cold hand in hers. "In a war, men like my father who take risks don't come home, Walter. And I can't bear losing him after losing my mother."

Her eyes welled up and she tried to blink away her tears. Wally thought about Audrey and the Milhousers, and how this war affected more and more people every day; how its victims weren't confined to some theater of conflict.

Bobbi squeezed his hand. "All I've been thinking of since you got angry with me is how much all of this depends on you. I saw how you convinced your brother and Frankie to join. I just need you to stick with this, no matter how crazy it seems. No matter what you think of me."

"I'm sorry I said you were a phony," Wally replied.

"I'm the one who should be sorry," said Bobbi. "You were right." She slid closer to him. "I thought if I could get you to like me, I could convince you to stay. I see, you're more than a good piano player, Walter. You're a good person. And I know now that you want this as much as I do."

Her eyes reflected the winter's smiling moon overhead. Her beauty, her kindness, her vulnerability all drew him in. Wally's heart started to flutter, and he leaned closer.

To his surprise, Bobbi leaned toward him too, her eyes closing.

Finding uncertain courage, Wally moved in to kiss her until the angry screech of a woman cut through the frosty air.

"Barbara Ann Dawson!" A matronly woman wearing a floral housecoat charged toward them from the open rooftop door, carrying a broom. "What is a man doing up here?"

Wally froze.

"Mrs. Davidson!" cried Bobbi. She bolted up, standing with such force she almost knocked Wally off the storage box. "Mrs. Davidson, please! This is just a friend from work."

"I don't care if he's a friend from church!" she shouted. "You know the rules!"

Bobbi spun toward Wally. "I'm so sorry!"

Wally sprung to his feet as Mrs. Davidson raised her broom and lunged, her wild look sending a shock of panic through him.

"What kind of man are you?" she cried.

Words failed him, but Mrs. Davidson wasn't looking for conversation. She swung her broom.

Wally ducked, scrambled around the storage box, and fled toward the fire escape.

"Git! Git!" Mrs. Davidson called. "This is no place for a dirty-minded man."

Wally scrambled down the fire escape ladder, two rungs at a time, his pulse beating in his ears, his erratic breath creating swirls of steam in the cold air. He dropped the final four feet and hit the sidewalk hard, the bagpipes in his chest playing a discordant song.

"Go on!" Mrs. Davidson screamed from above. "Go!"

Wally ran, putting distance between him and the Elving House, growing dizzier with each passing block. He didn't know where he was, and his disorientation only raised his anxiety. It became difficult to breathe and his vision blurred with vertigo.

Oh, no.

Wally slowed to a jog, and then to a hobbling walk like a puppet whose strings had been cut. The world became blurry, and he feared he'd run into a wall or a fireplug.

His legs unsteady, he stumbled into an alley, and started to hyperventilate. He spotted a metal dumpster, where he hoped to find his balance, catch his breath, stop the cascade of lost control.

But it was too late. The stars circled quickly overhead, or maybe those were the lights of the Manhattan skyline set free of their moorings. The shadows darted like crows. He heard a loud clang, the sound of his head hitting the dumpster.

He fell to his back. Pounding rose in his ears.

Moments passed but he didn't recover. In the chaos of his thoughts, he became aware of two figures circling him.

Unable to speak, he waited for the pair to help him, his consciousness waning. But as the darkness closed in, he heard a voice say, "What's he doing?"

Then another voice replied, "He's about to pass out. Just give him a minute. He's gonna make this real easy."

7

Trash Day

The acrid smell of car exhaust filled Wally's nostrils, and he coughed himself awake. Despite being cocooned by his thick coat, his ears were prickling with cold, his toes tingling with icy pain, and his nose felt frozen. He opened his eyes to see a stocky garbage man standing over him, pointing to a spot just over Wally's head.

"Gotta move, pal. Have to empty that dumpster."

Wally sat up from the dirty pavement and looked around. It was still dark. "Where am I?"

"Looks like you may have tied one on a little too hard." The garbage man laughed.

Wally tried to get the man into focus. He was a barrel-chested fellow probably a few years older than him with a boyish smile.

"It's freezing out here," he said. "At least they left you with your coat and socks." The man pointed his gloved hand at Wally's feet. "Hoboes out here take what they can. Times are tough."

Wally looked down to see his icy toes wiggling in his dirty wool socks, his shoes nowhere to be found. He rose to stand in the filthy alley, remembering the events of the night, his legs sore, his head aching, his nose and ears stinging as his blood began to circulate. He dug into his pocket for his uncle's watch, relieved to find it there. He raised it to his face and popped open the lid.

"Is it really five o'clock?"

"Trash day," said the man, pointing again at the dumpster. "And I need to get at that dumpster." A garbage truck idled in the street behind him.

"Crap," said Wally. He'd been unconscious for hours. His family would be waking up soon to open A-Rite Cleaners. He reached into his other pocket for his wallet but wasn't so lucky.

"Took your wallet, huh?" The garbage man shook his head. "Where you going?"

"Brooklyn," Wally huffed.

The man pulled off a glove and extracted a handful of coins from his shirt pocket.

"I'm from Brooklyn too," he said. He handed the coins to Wally. "Should be enough to get you home."

The man offered his hand to help Wally to his feet.

"Thanks. I'm Wally."

"Leo," said the garbage man. "If you're in a hurry, you can catch the F Train right off East Broadway." He thumbed toward his left. "Few blocks that way."

Wally gestured toward the dumpster. "Sorry 'bout that."

"Not the first time," said Leo. "Prolly not the last."

"Come by A-Rite Cleaners at Church and Third," said Wally. "I'll pay you back."

"Don't worry about it." Leo put on his glove. "Just do me a favor and stay outta trouble."

Wally raced to the street in his socks. He was grateful for Leo's kindness but realized that staying out of trouble was going to be harder than ever. The fainting spells he thought would only be a problem on a battlefield had left him vulnerable and alone in an alley in the middle of winter. He was lucky he had only lost his shoes and wallet.

He boarded the F-Train with twenty-five cents to spare and plopped into an empty seat, trying to hide his shoeless feet from the handful of other early birds on board. He looked out the window, wriggled his cold toes back to life, and willed the train to get him home fast. What would he say to his parents? How would he explain where he'd been all night or what had happened to his shoes?

A single transfer got Wally to the Church Avenue stop, where he jumped out and ran in his socks to his apartment. Just as he reached for the door to his building, he heard the hiss of a whisper overhead.

"Psst! Wally!"

He looked up and saw Max hanging out their bedroom window above the fire escape. "Climb up. Hurry."

Wally hesitated. He'd had enough of fire escapes for now.

"Come on!" barked Max. "There's still time!"

Wally didn't know what Max meant, but his tone was urgent. Feeling déjà vu, Wally climbed the icy metal escape. Once he got to his bedroom window, Max helped him through.

"You smell like garbage," said Max. "Where are your shoes?"

"I'll explain later."

"I covered for you at breakfast," said Max. "Told Mom and Dad you overate last night and weren't hungry. I was about to tell them you were sick and couldn't work today."

"Thanks," said Wally. "Sorry you had to lie for me."

Max shot him the finger gun. "I'll put it on your tab. Now, get dressed fast!"

Wally rushed into their shared bathroom and threw off his dirty clothes. He brushed his teeth, ran a shard of old soap under the faucet, and then rubbed it under his arms, rinsed off, dried himself with a towel, and changed into a fresh-pressed shirt and pair of pants. He found some old loafers that had never quite fit right, but they were all he had now.

Once dressed, he pulled a comb through his curls and followed Max out to the family room where his parents were waiting.

"You boys were out late," said their mother. "Did you have a nice time?"

"Just looking at the holiday lights," said Wally. The drumbeat in his head was a persistent reminder of what he'd really been up to.

"Let's go," said their father. "I want to straighten up the shop before that jingle of ours hits the air. When did they say they'd run the thing?"

"Not sure, Pop," said Max. "I'll ring over and ask."

Wally had nearly forgotten about the A-Rite jingle, but it was now the least of his worries.

"Oh, Saul," said Sadie, "you're getting it for free."

"I know," said their father. He turned to Max. "But don't forget to call, okay?"

"Top priority," said Max.

After their parents had started down the stairs, Max held Wally back.

"Did you kiss her?" whispered Max, grinning.

"No," said Wally. He recalled the swinging broom that had put an end to that.

"Why did she come for you? What did she want?" said Max.

Wally took a breath, trying to replace the smell of the alley with his memory of Bobbi's perfume. "Guess she just wanted to be understood," said Wally. "She wants what we want."

Max smiled. "So, you did kiss her!"

Wally shook his head and followed his family downstairs.

Once at the shop, the Lipkins trudged through another slow day. Even with Christmas just a day away, fewer and fewer people were dry-cleaning, and the customers that did come only seemed interested in pressing holiday tablecloths and napkins or hemming and repairing their old clothes to make them last. Such work was barely enough to keep the doors open.

Max rang the station to learn from Brubaker that it would still be a day or two before the A-Rite jingle would run. Saul grumbled his dissatisfaction and disappeared into the back office to pour over the books. Sadie darned some wool socks and then worked on repairing a dress hem, guiding the fabric through an old sewing machine. Max noodled with the radio, searching for jingles, apparently trying to brush up on his songwriting skills. Wally figured he was still sore at being shown up by Rat Rubinstein.

All the while, Wally sat perched on his stool at the register, trying to imagine the kiss that Mrs. Davidson had stolen from him. Yet even in his daydreams, today he couldn't focus on romance; his thoughts kept turning to his fainting problem. How could he ever hope to have a normal life if that life was always threatened by the betrayal of his own body? He half-contemplated going back upstairs to retrieve his old bar mitzvah ring, to call upon God and the power of King Solomon to help him control his demon. How fitting would it be that the answer to his prayers was sitting under a pile of his own underwear all along? Of course, he knew his problems wouldn't be solved with Jewish magic or Hanukkah wishes.

The shop door opened with the sound of the overhead bell, and Audrey walked in.

"Hello, Lipkins." She wore a striped blue dress, her brown hair pulled into a smart ponytail with a tie. Wally noticed she was wearing makeup too.

"Well, hello, dear," called Wally's mother from the sewing machine, looking at Audrey through her half-moon glasses. "How are you? How's your mother?"

"The same, I guess." Audrey shrugged. "She's fine for a bit and then cries over nothing."

"Oh, my dear. I'm so sorry. Please remind her that we're here if she needs anything. I plan to bring over a pot roast tomorrow."

"Thanks, Mrs. Lipkin. I know she'd love that. She's still trying to decide whether we should have a funeral for Johnny without his body. It's just...well, she'd love the pot roast and the company."

"Of course, dear."

Wally looked Audrey over. "Why are you so dolled up?" He tried to keep things light and casual after she had run off from their Flatbush adventure.

"I'll take that as a compliment," said Audrey. She sounded as eager to put the prior day's awkwardness behind them as he was. "I'm going over to the shipyard to get some work. Figured my mother could use the help. In truth, I could use to get out of the apartment myself."

"Well, that's sweet," said Wally's mother. "I heard they were hiring girls now. Such times... Who'd have ever guessed?"

"Mind if I step outside for a minute with Audrey, Ma?" asked Wally.

"Go ahead, honey. Your brother and I can handle things."

Max stood from his chair and pointed at Wally. "I'm keeping tabs."

Wally followed Audrey out the door and down the block to a clear part of the sidewalk. She swept the length of her striped skirt beneath her and sat on the curb. Wally joined her, pedestrians moving behind them as if they weren't even there.

"I waited up for you," said Audrey. "Watched out the window, and finally gave up after midnight. Where were you?"

"Working on our jingles," he said, revealing only part of the truth. "It's a lot of work, you know."

She reached into her purse for a pack of gum and offered Wally a stick. "Beech-Nut?"

"No, thank you."

"My offer still stands, you know."

"What offer?"

"To help with your jingles, dummy." Audrey sang, "'The minty taste—it lasts so long, and makes me sing this Beech-Nut song.'" She stuffed the pack back into her purse.

"I'll ask the guys, see what they say." Of course, he had no intention of doing so.

"That's what you said last time. Every jingle needs a girl's voice, you know," she said. "You listen to the radio."

Wally fought the urge to tell her they already had a girl's voice and the thought of Bobbi brought back the memory of Mrs. Davidson's swinging broom. He didn't want to discuss that with Audrey but was eager for advice about what had happened after.

"I wasn't just late because of the jingles," said Wally.

"What do you mean?"

He looked down the sidewalk to the shop and then back at Audrey. "I passed out on my way home," he said. "Woke up a couple hours later in an alley and realized some hoboes had stolen my shoes and wallet."

"Walter, that's horrible!" She grabbed his arm. "You could've been killed."

"I know."

"It's the middle of December. You could have frozen to death. You really need to see a doctor."

"You know I can't do that."

"I know you *won't* do that," Audrey muttered. She released his arm. "And you're being ridiculous. Doctors don't lock you away for fainting."

"Tell that to my uncle."

Audrey scoffed and stood from the curb. "You can be a real dunce, you know?"

"Audrey, listen—"

"I've gotta go," she huffed, and marched off.

Wally wanted to stop her, convince her he had everything under control, but he knew that would just be another lie.

He had hoped to avail himself of her problem-solving skills, come up with a plan, one that could help him get his anxiety neurosis under control. But now he realized, if he was going to solve the riddle of his condition, he'd have to figure out how do to it all on his own, without Audrey and without magic Jewish rings.

Alone at the curb, he stared at the murky, morning water that flowed in the gutter behind his heels, watching the filthy current carry cigarette butts, sticks, and leaf fragments toward the New York sewer system while pedestrians continued to walk behind him. He could make out the faint aroma of trash, wondering if the smell came from the gutter water or the alley filth that still lingered in his hair. It was in that moment he felt a pathetic kinship with the flotsam in the drainage stream, unable to control where fate was taking him, powerless to avoid the flow of destiny. This was the persistent offering of his condition, the promise of his demon: inevitability, the promise of death, or worse.

He rose from the curb and walked back to the cleaners, self-conscious about the smell of garbage that clung to him like his curse.

When he pulled open the shop door, something fell from the doorframe to the space between his ill-fitting shoes. It was a lined piece of steno paper, like the one that had been slipped into his pocket by the mysterious man in the hat. This one had been folded into an origami boat, the kind he had made as a boy out of chewing gum paper or old receipts.

His mother looked up from her sewing machine as Wally entered, stuffing the boat into his pocket. "That Audrey is a lovely girl," Sadie said. "Such a modern thing to do, to look for work at the shipyard."

Wally ignored her and returned to his stool by the register. He hastily withdrew the boat and unraveled the paper in his lap with his back to her only to find new instructions, not just for one jingle but four. Each set of directions appeared more complex than the last.

"Holy shit," Wally said aloud.

"Walter!" his mother chided. "Watch your language."

"Sorry," he said, cramming the paper back into his pocket. "Just realized...I lost my wallet. I need Max to help me find it."

Max perked to attention at the ironing board and looked to Wally. "Your wallet?"

"Will you tend the register, Ma?" Wally asked.

"Sure, honey."

Wally grabbed Max by the arm. Three strides out of the shop, he pressed the dismantled paper boat into Max's hand. "Read that," said Wally.

Max ogled the sheet. "Four jingles?"

"And hardly a day after the first one. They're crazy."

A smile grew on Max's face. "They're not crazy. They finally understand how good we are."

Wally shook his head. "Last night was rough, and that was just one jingle. How do you think it will go with four?"

"Better," said Max with a burgeoning confidence Wally didn't share. "We're good at this, Walter, and we're getting better. Soon, we'll be the best there is. You'll see."

Wally opened his mouth to protest, but Max held up his hand. "Don't say anything to spoil my mood. Let's just call Frankie."

"And Clyde too," said Wally. "Don't forget he's on the team now."

"I told you not to spoil my mood," said Max. He suddenly wrinkled his nose and sniffed the air. "Something stinks."

Wally hung his head. "No kidding."

At seven o'clock, back at the WKOB studio, Wally, Max, Frankie, and Rat sat in folding chairs around the same card table Brubaker had set up the night before, right next to the Steinway. After work, Wally had finally showered, washed his hair, and tried to don a new attitude as they dove deeper into their mission. He wanted to move forward, focus on the opportunities ahead and not the demon that doggedly nipped at his heels. He eyed the piano, eager to create something new, something hopeful to replace the gloom that had taken root like mold in his bones.

Major Brubaker paced around them, his hands behind his back. "Last night's Del Monte peach jingle hit the mark, gentlemen, but getting there wasn't smooth or easy." He looked them over. "Nevertheless, it proved that this team is capable of great things if we work together."

Frankie trilled his lips in mockery, and Wally kicked him under the table.

Brubaker stopped, leaned toward them. "I'm going to tell you something that hasn't made the papers," he said. "The battle for Europe is going badly. Our boys need some fast intel if we hope to turn the tide against Uncle Adolph. That means our work is more important than ever."

Wally remembered what Bobbi had told him, that the army remained unconvinced of their potential for success. It seemed on top of everything else, Dawson's hastily assembled team still had something to prove.

The guys straightened in their chairs, their sense of duty growing more palpable, more consequential.

"Your Podolor Diaper jingle was a good opener," Brubaker said. "Already made a difference to our Allies in the north."

Wally felt a warm rush of accomplishment. They wrote the Podolor jingle without even knowing it was for a mission.

"We hope your Del Monte peaches jingle will push things further," said Brubaker. "But now we have to pick up the pace."

"Four jingles," said Max. "We got the paper, Major. We're ready."

Brubaker nodded. "I like the can-do, Moxie, but tonight we're gonna do things a little differently. Each of you is gonna take a shot at one jingle apiece, and then rotate to a partner to punch up your work."

"What's that supposed to accomplish?" asked Frankie.

"Assembly-line approach," said Brubaker. "Reduces conflict, raises productivity. Besides, the punch-up approach worked yesterday, and we oughta learn from our own success." He pointed at the folded paper in the center of the table. "I'll be back in an hour to check your progress. Don't forget, gentlemen: jingles save lives."

Rat rose and saluted, but Wally and his pals stayed silent until Brubaker had left the studio. When the door closed behind him, Frankie pushed back from the table and folded his arms. "This is nuts."

"I like the idea of pairing up," said Rat with a fresh enthusiasm Wally had never seen before. "I know how to write words; I just can't write music. I could use the help."

"You can say that again," Frankie mumbled.

Wally moved to the piano. "Like it or not," he said, "we have our orders, direct from the US Army." He pounded out the opening to "America the Beautiful," trying as much to convince himself to move forward as he was the rest of the team.

"Wally's right," said Max. He grabbed the paper, tore away the instructions for each of the four jingles and handed the pieces around, seizing the leadership role. "Here's how we'll do it," said Max. "First person picks a product that matches their instructions. Don't get fancy. Keep it simple. In the next hour, knock out the best lyrics and music you can manage on our own. Do what you can. Leave what you can't. When you're done, trade with your partner; he'll work to complete the jingle. Don't get precious. It's just a first draft."

Frankie and the others nodded.

"Wally," Max added, "we're the first pair. Frankie and Rat, you have complementary skills. You're the second pair."

"Got it," said Rat. "Makes sense."

"Hell, it does!" shouted Frankie. "Rat can't even write music. You heard him."

"That's why Rat is paired with you," said Max.

"His name is 'Clyde,'" said Wally.

Rat turned to the team, his eyes focused on Frankie. "I need you, O'Brien," said Rat. "You're the expert." His compliment even sounded authentic.

Frankie rumbled like a thundercloud but didn't object further.

Wally looked over his instructions. They were fairly straightforward, calling for a four-four time signature and five lines of music with a few notes and half-notes on two octaves that looked easy enough to implement. The challenge was finding a product to match the words: "brighter," "wonder," "clean," "away," and "twice." He flicked the metronome on the piano to get his brain and heart aligned with a rhythm. With the click of the pendulum, he closed his eyes and let his assigned words float around his imagination until a product came into focus.

Toothpaste.

He wasn't quite sure how all the words would work together, but "clean" and "twice" reminded him of the feeling and frequency of brushing his teeth. The words had to be in the order required by the instructions, and he pondered how such words would amount to any reasonable order for the soldiers who would receive them. He figured the tempo, the notes, and half-notes meant something, as did the lyrics, but what? Would Major Brubaker ever share more of the code's details with them? And who were these messages going to?

After jotting down some lines, erasing them, and rewriting them, Wally played a few notes on the piano's lower octaves to get an angle on the tune.

As soon as the Steinway rang out, he was quickly "shushed" by Frankie. "Don't play anything yet," Frankie barked. "I'm still working out my phrasing. You're screwing me up."

"Sorry," said Wally. "I think better through the piano."

"Fifteen minutes," said Max. "You can play after we swap."

The time passed quickly, and the guys handed their pages to their partners, hammered out the rest of their jingles. Before long, just as Brubaker predicted, they had four roughly hewn jingles, each created with none of the conflict that had characterized their previous effort. And, as an added bonus, after Rat's compliments of Frankie's work, the two of them seemed to be getting along, or at least refraining from killing each other.

Before they could test their jingles with Wally at the piano, the studio door opened. Wally expected the major to re-enter and ask for a run-through, but it was Colonel Dawson who strode in. He was accompanied by Bobbi, who was wearing a dark-crimson dress. Tonight, however, she wasn't beaming or smiling as she usually was. This time, she was sullen and seemed distracted.

Wally's smile faded too, and he wondered if something had happened with Bobbi since he'd last seen her on her rooftop, since that near-kiss he had been thinking about all day.

Rat leaned over to Frankie. "Who's that man with the dame?"

"The dame is Bobbi, our jingle singer, and the man is Bobbi's father," said Frankie, "Colonel Dawson. He's the head of this whole operation."

Rat stood and threw his hand to his brow in a fast salute. "Colonel Dawson, sir!" he bellowed.

Wally and the others stood and saluted too.

Dawson raised an eyebrow. "You must be the new recruit." The colonel walked over to Rat. "Clyde Rubinstein, is that right?"

Rat looked uncharacteristically speechless, but then pulled himself together. "Reporting for duty. Yes, sir!"

"At ease, Rubinstein." Dawson shook Rat's hand. "We expect great things from you, son."

"I'll do my best, sir."

Dawson nodded and looked to the others. "I can't express enough the importance of your work, gentlemen." His features grew somber. "But, as with all important work these days, there's risk."

"Risk?" said Wally.

Major Brubaker suddenly entered the studio and seemed surprised to see the colonel. "Colonel Dawson, sir." Brubaker saluted.

Dawson stopped his discussion of risk and, instead, returned Brubaker's salute. "At ease, Major." He gestured toward the crew. "I see you've got things moving along here."

"Four jingles," replied Brubaker. "Dividing and conquering."

"Well, don't let me interrupt," said the colonel. "I just need a moment with Walter."

Wally's cheeks grew warm at being singled out. Was he the risk the colonel mentioned? But how could he have learned about Wally's condition?

"Be my guest," said Brubaker. "The rest of you, over to the piano. Let's hear what you've got."

Wally wanted to ask who would play the piano in his absence, but his concern over the colonel's words compelled him to quickly follow Dawson and Bobbi to Brubaker's back office.

Wally tried to get a bead on the situation from Bobbi's expression but couldn't read her.

Dawson closed the door, sat in Brubaker's chair, and gestured for Wally and Bobbi to take the two seats that faced him across the desk. Brubaker's desk was more organized than the reception desk he'd ravaged back on the day Wally had been recruited and gave no sign it was even being used, save the amber glass ashtray and the handful of crushed cigarettes crumpled in a heap.

"I received a troubling telephone call late last night from a very agitated woman named Mrs. Davidson," the colonel said almost affably.

Bobbi fidgeted in her seat. "Father, I told you—"

"Barbara Ann, please let me finish." His tone had suddenly grown stern.

Bobbi crossed her arms and fell silent.

"As I believe you know, Mr. Lipkin, my daughter has chosen to live on her own at the Elving House here in Manhattan. It's an arrangement to which I have agreed, provided she follows Mrs. Davidson's very reasonable rules."

It hadn't occurred to Wally that Bobbi's father would learn about his visit to the Elving House. "Sir, I can explain—"

"And the fact is," Dawson continued, "last night, my daughter elected to break the simplest of those rules." He paused, allowing his pronouncement to sink in. "You must know, Mr. Lipkin, I do not hold you accountable for this in any way. You made no agreement to follow any such rules. You've barely joined the team and have had no training whatsoever on the chain of command or standards of protocol. This...infraction...is entirely Barbara Ann's responsibility, and she already knows how I feel about it. I just wanted to set the record straight with you."

Wally shifted uneasily in his chair, unsure if he was being asked to respond. When no one else said anything, he ventured to speak.

"Sir, may I say something?"

"You may."

"Bobbi—Barbara Ann—knew I was concerned about our mission, sir. She just wanted to be sure I was on board. We only went to her place so she could make curfew and still have that important discussion. And she had the good sense to meet outside on the rooftop, assuring the rules were being followed. Nothing happened between us."

Dawson smirked. "I know."

"You do?"

The colonel leaned forward. "If anything had happened, Mr. Lipkin, we'd be having a very different conversation."

Wally glanced to Bobbi, who was looking at the ceiling as if searching for an escape hatch.

Dawson stood. "Now, I'll leave you to finish your assignments," he said. "I'm sure the major explained how important your work is. We'll save our chain-of-command discussion for another time."

"Risk," said Wally.

Dawson tilted his head. "Yes?"

"You mentioned there's some risk. What risk were you talking about, sir?"

Bobbi moved her gaze from the ceiling to face her father as if she were as eager for his answer as Wally.

For the first time since he met the colonel, Wally saw discomfort on the man's face. Dawson lowered himself back into Brubaker's chair.

"I suppose it makes sense to tell you directly," he said. "Did you hear about those men in Staten Island they caught, Ernie Lehmitz and Erwin De Spretter?"

"The traitors?" Wally recalled his father had read aloud a series of recent articles from the *Brooklyn Daily Eagle*, reporting that the two men the colonel named had volunteered as air-raid wardens, just as Wally had. But these guys were caught sending secrets to Germany. They had counted soldiers, ships, and armaments in the harbor after chatting with some careless sailors. It was why the local civilian defense precinct had amped up recruitment of younger air-raid wardens like Wally, young men who didn't have ties to foreign countries and whose patriotism they believed could be assured.

"Those two were part of a Nazi ring," said Dawson, "right here in New York." His tone softened and a seriousness filled the room. "Turns out, among other things, those men were watching *me*."

Bobbi's eyes flew wide, and Dawson reached across the desk to take her hand. "It doesn't appear they knew any details about this operation," he said slowly. "Their correspondence made no mention of WKOB, though we remain uncertain whether any previous communications about me, or our work here, ever made it to their intended recipients. But it does mean we have to be careful, more careful than we've ever been." He turned to Wally. "And I mean all of us. I intend to tell Major Brubaker, but perhaps you can share this caution with the others."

The weight of the news sent a chill down Wally's spine. "Of course, sir." If the Nazis were watching Dawson, they might be watching Bobbi. And if they were watching her last night, they could have been watching him as well.

"Travel separately and vary your routes to get here and home," the colonel continued. "Make plans to spend more time here at the studio, where you can't be watched. The major and I will have more instructions for you tomorrow." The colonel kissed Bobbi's hand and stood.

Wally swallowed. He had a million more questions, but it seemed they would have to wait.

"Gotta get back to the base," said Dawson. He then left Bobbi and Wally alone in the station manager's office.

"I'm so sorry," said Bobbi. She rose from her chair, her face flushed. "First, Mrs. Davidson nearly kills you, then this whole scene with my father about last night, and now this talk of Nazis. You must wish you had never met me."

Wally shook his head. "I meant what I said last night. I know you've only been trying to keep the mission on track. This Nazi business just proves how important that is." Wally realized the words he was speaking, intended to comfort Bobbi, were actually comforting to him.

Bobbi's eyes grew glossy. "You still think this mission is the right thing to do?"

"I know it is," said Wally. A slow, warm resolve started to fill his limbs. "If your father is a threat to a Nazi victory, that means we all are. And isn't that the whole point? Isn't that why we're here?"

Bobbi nodded. "Well, when you put it that way..."

"Let's get back to work," said Wally.

Bobbi and Wally returned to the studio, where they found Major Brubaker seated at the Steinway, playing a jingle. He was sporting reading glasses that Wally had never seen him wear before, leaning toward the piano's music rack to read a composition page while playing with surprising skill.

"We took it up an octave there," said Frankie, pointing to the page. "That's what the instructions called for."

"Good," said Major Brubaker. "Very good." He glanced over to Rat, who was standing quietly at Frankie's side. "Figured the best work would come from the Lipkin brothers," the major said, "but you two sure held your own."

A grin overtook Frankie's face, and Rat put his arm around him. But, instead of scoffing, Frankie just rolled his eyes and tolerated Rat's affection, taking everyone by surprise.

"Anything for me to sing?" Bobbi asked once at the piano.

"You can sing Walter's jingle," said Max. "We were saving it 'til he got back."

"Perfect," she said.

Brubaker stood from the Steinway and waved Wally over. "Take a seat, slim. I can fill in, but I'm no maestro like you."

"Thank you, sir," said Wally. He sat at the piano and turned to Bobbi. "My jingle is for Pepsodent toothpaste."

Bobbi sat next to him on the bench. "Is this okay?" she whispered.

"Sure," said Wally, but he scooted slightly to the left to leave room between them, recalling her father threatening "a very different conversation" if anything was to happen between them.

Max placed Wally's jingle page on the piano, and Wally played a few bars of his intro for Bobbi to sing:

"The brighter white of Pepsodent
You'll wonder where the yellow went.
The clean, fresh feeling makes you say
Pepsodent chased those stains away.
Pepsodent, Pepsodent, twice a day!"

Bobbi nodded at the last note. "Very catchy!" she said.

Frankie knotted his brow and ran his tongue over his teeth. "Anyone have any water?"

"Terrific job," said Brubaker. "All of you."

"I missed the others," said Bobbi. "What'd we get?"

Brubaker pointed around at each team member. "Cigarettes, coffee, and shoe polish," he recited. "With Walter's toothpaste, we've got all the essentials."

"Fantastic!"

"All right, fellas," said Brubaker. "Let's send you on your way. Bobbi's gotta record these jingles before her curfew."

Frankie stepped forward, straightening his shirt with an odd formality. "Major," he said, "traveling here and back on the subway every night is costing us some real money. Any idea when we'll start getting those soldier's wages the colonel promised?"

Brubaker furrowed his brow. "No checks mailed to you yet, eh?"

"No, sir," said Frankie.

"Guess the paperwork we filed hasn't come through." Brubaker reached into his pocket and handed over a few dollars. "Let's start with subway fare. How's that, Red?"

Frankie looked at him deadpan, and Brubaker laughed. "Tough customer." He opened his wallet and pulled out some bills. "Let's get you boys square for the week. But watch that mailbox."

Frankie grabbed the dough and distributed it among the other guys. "Works for me."

Rat saluted, and the boys made their way to the door.

Wally looked over to Bobbi. "See you tomorrow?" he said.

"Better believe it." She added a wink.

Wally grinned and led the others out the door. They made their way past light posts and fireplugs sparkling with frost, past a row of buildings festooned with tinsel and angels, along a string of windows traced in flashing holiday lights. Once the guys were a few blocks away from the station building, Frankie stepped up to Wally and nudged him.

"What's the deal with the girl?" said Frankie. "What did her father want?"

"That's easy," said Rat, jumping in. "Wally's warm for her, she's warm for him, and her father figured it out. Colonel was just laying down the law."

Max squinted at Wally. "That true?"

The heat of embarrassment rose along the edges of Wally's ears. He wasn't ready to talk about his feelings for Bobbi, but leave it to Rat, the reporter, to figure it all out.

"Not exactly," said Wally. "Our conversation was more complicated."

"See?" said Rat. "I'm never wrong."

Wally stopped walking, looked around to be sure they hadn't been followed, and pulled Max and the others into a side alley between a department store and a hat shop.

"What gives?" said Max. "Is that girl causing trouble?"

"Nazis are the trouble," whispered Wally, half shadowed in the alleyway.

"Nazis?" said Frankie. "What Nazis?"

"You heard about those traitors from Staten Island?" said Wally.

"Covered 'em in the paper," said Rat. "Degenerates. What about 'em?"

"They were following Dawson."

"Jesus, Mary, and Joseph," said Frankie.

"He thinks the mission is still okay," said Wally, "but he wants us to be more careful. Take alternate routes. Travel separately. He wants us to spend more time at the station."

"Screw those traitors," said Rat, his jaw fixed with determination. "We have a job to do."

"We can't keep walking around like we've been doing." said Wally. "If the Nazis already know about Dawson, they could know about us."

"Wally's right," said Max. "Fun and games are over."

"Listen," said Frankie, a peculiar urgency in his voice. "My father taught me every train and subway station between here and New Jersey. I know the schedules better than anyone in all the boroughs." He drew a long breath. "I'll give you each a plan to follow to stay safe, but you have to do exactly as I say."

Max and Wally exchanged looks. "Okay," said Max.

Rat laughed. "I had you all wrong, O'Brien."

"What do you mean?"

"You already act like a cop, whether you know it or not." He gave Frankie a playful punch in the arm.

Frankie made a growling noise. "I'm not getting paid nearly enough."

8

All Who Follow

Morning had come, but Wally found the hazy December sunshine outside his bathroom window irritating. It was winter and there had been no snow at all. There had been no neighborhood snowball fights among the children, no snow slope in the vacant lot where he and Max used to sled, and no laughter in the streets. Holiday cheer had been replaced for many by loss or by the persistent fear of a war that might find its way onto the Eastern Seaboard. It seemed the conflicts that raged in Wally's own life were being reflected by the very world around him.

He stood in his new pajamas, last night's Hanukkah gift—a light-blue cotton number with dark-blue piping his mother had sewn herself—and stared into his bathroom mirror, hardly recognizing the sunken eyes of the man he saw looking back. All things considered, he should have felt a deep delight. He and the others had learned that their first jingle had advanced the army's secret mission. Their second jingle had proven their skills as a team to their army commanders, and now they'd written four more jingles in a single day. All of that meant Wally's plan to stay clear of the battlefield while helping the war effort was working better than he could have ever imagined.

But Wally's glass seemed perpetually half empty. Thanks to the Staten Island traitors, he and his friends now had to look over their shoulders and vary their movements. On top of that, the colonel seemed wise to Wally's feelings for his daughter and had implied that if Wally acted on those feelings, there might be undesired consequences. And, of course, underlying all of this was Wally's demon companion, who seemed determined to complicate everything.

"Good news," said Max, peeking into the bathroom in his own new green pajamas.

"I could use some good news," grumbled Wally.

"Thanks to some fast thinking on the part of yours truly, we can now spend more time at the station."

"Dad agreed to your plan?"

"I told him we had more jingle work coming and that we had to reduce our hours at the shop, at least until the new year. Before he could argue, I pointed out that would mean we'd have to forego our usual meager salary, which he appreciated given the shortage of customers. Let him think it was all his idea."

"What about Frankie and his job?"

"Frankie says Mulligan has been threatening to cut back his hours anyway. He took the news better than I thought."

"Figured Frankie would put up a fight," said Wally.

"Oh, he did," said Max. "But I pointed out that the jingle gig meant he'd be home less often, making it easier to avoid his father."

"Wow," said Wally. "You really do have moxie." He turned back to the mirror. "What've I got?"

Max squinted. "Come on. Buck up, brother. No one should be so glum on their birthday."

With all his distractions, Wally had totally lost track of the days.

"And don't forget Merry Christmas," Max added. "Happy birthday to you and Jesus." He chuckled at his own joke, the same one their uncle had told.

"Every year." Wally sighed, looking back at the circles under his eyes.

"Never gets old," said Max.

"Says you."

Max patted him on the shoulder. "When we're done at the station tonight, we can grab a drink, take in a show to celebrate. My treat."

"If you say so."

"Oh, and Mom told me to have you stop by the shop before we head over to WKOB," said Max. "Didn't sound like 'no' would be an acceptable answer."

"When is 'no' ever an acceptable answer with her?" Wally quipped.

Once Wally was dressed and ready in his old shoes, the brothers donned their coats and walked downstairs, out to the street in the cold air of Christmas in Brooklyn.

"You know the plan?" said Wally. He blew heat into his bare hands, hoping for new Hanukkah gloves this year.

"Frankie has me on the F Train straight into town," said Max. "He and Rat take trains from other stations and make transfers. You follow on the next F Train twenty minutes later."

"Got it," said Wally. "See you there."

Max lifted his collar against the cold, stuffed his hands into his coat pockets, and left Wally alone.

Wally pulled open the A-Rite door, setting off the ringing bell. By the counter, he saw a young, barrel-chested man talking to his mother over the register.

"Oh, Walter!" said Sadie. "This nice man found your wallet."

The man turned, and Wally recognized Leo the garbage man, the kind fellow who had found him at the dumpster downtown and who had given him fare for the subway. He now wore dungarees and a leather coat instead of his garbage-man uniform.

"Merry Christmas," said Leo, an odd look on his face. "I had the day off and decided to come by. Turns out I live pretty close."

The hairs on the back of Wally's neck rose as a rush of emotions ran through him, each progressively more alarming. The first emotion was fear that Leo may have revealed to his mother how he had found Wally unconscious in the middle of the night in Manhattan. It was a secret Wally had kept from her and everyone except Audrey.

The second feeling was surprise at Leo's possession of his wallet. That morning in the alley, Leo had said hoboes had taken it, but if that were true, how'd Leo get ahold of it?

That led Wally to the most alarming feeling of all: terror. If Leo were lying and had been the one to take his wallet in the first place, that could mean he wasn't a garbage man at all, but one of those Nazi agents who Dawson warned about. Wally had given the guy his address, and now he was here, talking to his mother.

Panic shot through Wally's limbs.

"Oh, hey, Leo," said Wally, trying to keep his voice steady. "What a surprise. Guess I owe you."

"Don't worry about it," said Leo. He sounded calm and jovial. "Just glad to see you made it home okay."

"Home okay?" said Wally's mother. "What happened?"

Wally was relieved that his secret remained intact and quickly tried to recover. "When I lost my wallet, I had no money. Leo came to my rescue."

"Where was this?" Sadie asked.

"Manhattan," answered Leo.

Wally's mother tilted her head, puzzling together her own version of what had occurred. "You must have been on your way home from the station."

"You work at the subway station?" said Leo.

"No," Sadie replied. "Our Walter wrote a couple jingles for the radio station. WKOB. We're so proud."

A new wave of distress replaced Wally's relief and made Wally's knees go weak. If Leo was a Nazi agent and hadn't yet figured out Wally's association with the radio station, Wally's mother had just connected the dots.

"Interesting," said Leo. "Radio station jingle writer. You must be very talented."

"Oh, he is," said Sadie. "His brother, Max, too."

"Your brother too?"

"Be quiet, Mom," said Wally, a little too firmly.

"What?"

"I mean, you're embarrassing me. I'm sure Leo doesn't want to hear about all that."

"Not every day I meet an honest-to-God jingle writer," said Leo. "And your brother's in on it too? Your mom has a right to be proud."

She gave Wally a victorious look, which only made his anxiety grow.

"Probably none of my business," said Leo at Wally's silence. He reached to the counter, where he had set the wallet, and grabbed it. "Here you go." He handed it to Wally. "Guess I'll see you 'round. I don't do much dry cleaning, but now I know where to find you."

In light of Leo's dubious intentions, Wally took his kind remark as a threat.

As Leo turned to leave, Wally felt an impulse to act. Should he follow the guy? Interrogate him for answers to his suspicions? Whack him on the head with his mother's iron?

Leo reached for the door.

"Where are you headed?" said Wally.

"Soho," said Leo. "Meeting a couple guys from work for a Christmas lunch."

"Taking the subway?"

"Yep."

"I'm going that direction too," said Wally. "We can ride together." The words came out before he could muster a plan, but he didn't want to take his eyes off Leo until he figured out whether the garbage man was a problem.

Leo shifted uncomfortably. "Oh, sure."

"Before you go," said Wally's mother, "your dad and I wanted you to have this…" She reached under the counter and pulled out a small wrapped package, the size of a cigar, sporting a blue ribbon. "Happy birthday, dear."

"Thanks, Mom," said Wally, distracted by the possible Nazi at their door. "Mind if I open it later?"

"Take it with you. Open it when you like."

"Happy birthday," his father called from the back. "You and Jesus!"

Wally just shook his head.

He put the small gift in his back pocket, leaned over, and kissed his mom on the cheek. "Gotta run, Mom."

"Love you, dear."

Wally smiled. "Love you too."

"What am I, chopped liver?" said his father.

"Love you too, Pop."

Wally followed Leo through the ringing door, seeing him eye the shop as they left.

"You have a nice family," said Leo.

"Thanks," said Wally, now worried for their safety too.

The cold air needled his skin, or maybe that was just fear poking him into caution. He jammed his fists into his pockets and tried to focus on his companion, feeling his heart race as though he had joined a tiger on a walk into the jungle.

The two strode down Church toward the subway station.

"Why don't you like to talk about your jingles?" said Leo. "Sounds like you're pretty good."

The two descended the stairs to the subway platform.

"It's no big deal," said Wally, sporadic white breath clouds betraying his trepidation.

"Seems like a big deal," said Leo. "Lots of people listen to those. Sometimes they're better than the actual program."

"I guess." Wally pulled his coins from his pocket for the subway fare. "So, what do you do besides collect the garbage and save unconscious guys in alleys?"

Before Leo could answer, they paid their fare and jumped onto the train toward Manhattan. The train was busy and full, even though it was Christmas. Some folks were dressed for church or holiday parties, some carried gifts, and others just looked miserable as though traveling to their own execution. Wally wondered if that was what he was doing.

Leo and Wally maneuvered their way through the crowd to a corner of the subway car, where they stood and grabbed an overhead handle. When Leo reached up to steady himself, Wally saw a holster and sidearm under his leather coat.

His eyes flew wide, and Leo appeared to notice.

Leo released the bar, lowered his arm to conceal his weapon, and raised the other arm to the subway bar as the train lurched forward.

"I'm a security guard," fumbled Leo, clearly seeing the need to explain a gun on a subway.

Wally's heart banged like an angry neighbor at the door. "That so?"

"Part time. First National Bank in Manhattan. It's not far from WKOB."

"You know where WKOB is?" said Wally. A hard knot formed in his throat.

"It's a good second job," said Leo, ignoring Wally's question. "Helps make ends meet."

"Garbage doesn't pay well?" said Wally, prodding.

"Times are tough, right?"

Wally nodded calmly, despite his heart racing as fast as the subway. He couldn't afford to pass out—not in such tight quarters, and not with Leo at his side. The loud clamor of the train made small talk impractical, so Wally began to count Mississippis to the rhythmic clack of the tracks, like a metronome, trying to stay calm.

One Mississippi, two Mississippi, three Mississippi...

What if Leo really was just a nice garbage man, and this whole thing was some strange misunderstanding?

Four Mississippi, five Mississippi, six Mississippi...

Then again, who brings a gun on a subway or to a Christmas party?

Seven Mississippi, eight Mississippi, nine Mississippi...

The guy had about thirty pounds on Wally and seemed more athletic. Each option for action he could think of all ended with Wally sporting a hole in his head.

The subway finally slowed to a stop.

"Here we are," said Leo.

The two hopped out, took the stairs, and emerged at street level in lower Manhattan. The air was streaked with wispy clouds, thin like Wally's grasp on the situation. Pedestrians walked by, and Wally contemplated asking one of them for help. But what could he say to a stranger that wouldn't sound crazy? *Hey, Merry Christmas, mister. Can you help me tackle my friend here before he tries to kill me?*

"How do you go about writing jingles?" said Leo.

The guy had a one-track mind, and that track kept leading him back to Wally's jingles, which gave Wally an idea.

"Wanna find out?"

An odd look washed over Leo's face. "What do you mean?"

"Why not?" said Wally, working to replace his fear with a manufactured resolve. He ignored the tightness in his shoulders, which felt tense like a trolley cable. "Come with me. I can show you how things are done at the station...unless you'd rather get to your Christmas party."

Leo paused, but then said, "Guess I can't pass up an offer like that, can I?"

The guy sure didn't sound like a Nazi to Wally, at least not like the ones in Wally's radio programs who praised their führer with exaggerated German accents. Even so, Wally wasn't ready to let down his guard. Bringing the guy to WKOB would give Wally the advantage of numbers, presuming his friends had already arrived following Frankie's detailed travel plan. With any luck, Major Brubaker would have his own pistol for just such an occasion.

They walked a short distance farther, and Wally thought his heart might explode, his cold hands now slick with perspiration.

He drew a breath, grabbed the station door, and opened it. "Here we go."

The instant they entered, Wally spotted Frankie, Rat, and Max standing in the lobby outside the glass doors of the WKOB office, talking to Brubaker. Before Wally could alert the others to the danger, he saw the major lock eyes with Leo.

"What the hell are you doing here, Copulsky?" said Brubaker.

"Sorry, Major," said Leo. "Found his wallet in the garbage and went to return it. When I got to his shop, he was leaving for the studio and invited me along."

Wally's heart skipped a beat, and his eyes darted between Brubaker and the garbage man.

"You know each other?" said Wally.

Leo offered Wally his outstretched hand. "Army Specialist Leo Copulsky," he said.

"I thought you were a Nazi," said Wally. He wiped his hand on his trousers, and then shook Copulsky's hand, adrenaline still coursing through his veins.

"So, you brought him here?" said Frankie. "Are you nuts?"

"A good move," said Brubaker. "Safety in numbers."

The major approached, patted Wally on the shoulder, and turned to the others.

"Colonel Dawson and I assigned each of you a security detachment. Specialist Copulsky was assigned to Walter. Can't be too careful."

"No one followed me," said Rat. "I can tell you that."

"Me neither," said Max. "And I was careful."

"All of you were covered," said Brubaker, "whether you realized it or not."

Wally didn't know whether to be angry or relieved. It had been days since he first met

Leo in the alley, even before Dawson revealed he'd been under Nazi scrutiny. How long had Wally and the guys been covered by army security?

Just then, the lobby doors opened, and Bobbi entered with Colonel Dawson at her side. Today, she was all smiles.

"Happy holidays," said Bobbi. She wore a cotton blouse with wide shoulders and a pleated skirt. She looked like a blonde Rita Hayworth, and her very presence helped to quiet Wally's nerves.

When Dawson stepped forward, Rat stood at attention and saluted, as did Brubaker and Leo, prompting the others to follow suit.

"At ease, gentlemen," said Dawson, his medals gleaming. He turned to acknowledge Leo. "Didn't expect to see you here, Copulsky. What happened to 'undercover'?"

"I was made, sir," said Copulsky. "Just went along with it."

Colonel Dawson grinned at Wally. "Well done, Mr. Lipkin. Specialist Copulsky is as good as they come."

"Thank you, sir." Wally puzzled over Dawson's characterization of Copulsky. It hadn't taken much for him to spot Leo's gun, and the guy flat-out showed up at his shop. Not too stealthy, in Wally's opinion. If Copulsky was their best, maybe his safety wasn't as secure as the colonel believed.

"Sorry to have brought you fellas in on Christmas," said Dawson, "but the war doesn't stop, and neither can we." He nodded at the group. "I need a word with the major. Why don't we head to the studio?"

The major withdrew a ring of keys and opened the door to the WKOB offices off the lobby. Bobbi sashayed next to Wally. "Outsmarted Copulsky, huh? Not bad."

Wally grinned and tried to muster some keen reply, but before he could think of anything clever, the roar of a car engine from the boulevard caught his attention. It was so loud, the whole team spun back to face the building's glass entrance. Wally feared that some drunk driver may unexpectedly plow into the WKOB lobby.

Instead, a cacophony of machine-gun fire rang out, shattering the frosted glass of the entrance doors, debris and bullets whizzing by his head.

Before Wally could react, Copulsky yelled, "Get down!" He leapt forward, arms spread like wings, knocking Wally and Bobbi to the marble floor.

Bobbi screamed over the gunfire, which ended as quickly as it had begun with another roar of the car's engine.

After a moment, Copulsky stood. "Stay down!" he barked and drew his sidearm.

But Bobbi wouldn't listen. She rose from the floor and raced over the broken glass alongside Copulsky to the entrance where her father lay, his eyes blinking at the tall lobby ceiling.

"No!" she cried and dropped to the colonel's side.

Wally sat up and saw Max, Rat, and Frankie peek out from behind a bullet-ridden lobby sofa.

He moved his gaze back to the front entrance to see Major Brubaker leaning against the side wall, blood streaming from his left shoulder. The major moved haltingly into the WKOB reception area and over to the reception desk. He opened the top drawer, withdrew a pistol, and then dashed through the jagged remains of the building entrance, disappearing onto Broadway and into the cold morning.

A winter gust from the street blew through the lobby, swirls of sparkling glass dust still floating through the air.

Wally rose to his feet, shaken.

Rat, Max, and Frankie stood and brushed themselves off, appearing uninjured but equally dismayed. Before Wally could ask if they were okay, the relative quiet was disrupted by the coughs of Colonel Dawson, sputtering from his injuries on the floor where he lay.

"No, no, no!" Bobbi repeated. She threw her arms over her father.

Copulsky knelt next to her. "Let me help him," the specialist said softly. "You phone an ambulance." Bobbi sat motionless as if she didn't hear him until Copulsky touched her arm. "Barbara Ann. Please?"

Bobbi stood and ran to the reception desk in the WKOB office.

"Walter..." Dawson gasped in whisper. He tried to lift his head. "Get Walter."

"Yessir," said Copulsky. He waved Wally over. "Lipkin, get over here."

Wally rushed to the colonel's side, where he saw what seemed like a dozen bullet holes peppering Dawson's broad chest, outnumbering his medals. The man's olive uniform was soaked with blood, which now flowed through the thick fabric into a sick crimson pool on the marble floor around him. Wally bit his lip to keep his horror to himself.

"Walter," Dawson repeated. Blood rose through the his lips, the man's once booming voice now shallow. "Trust her."

Wally knew who he meant. "I do, sir."

"No"—Dawson coughed—"you don't. But she'll need you to." The effort of talking suddenly sent him into spasms.

Copulsky held the colonel. "Easy, sir. Try not to speak. An ambulance is coming."

Bobbi rushed back over with a small canvas bag labeled "US Army—First Aid" and handed it to Copulsky, who began to dig for supplies.

"This is all I could find!" she cried.

Wally stood back to give Bobbi access to her father.

"Stay with me, Dad!" Bobbi pleaded. She grabbed his hand and laced her fingers through his. "We'll fix you right up," she said, but her sobbing undermined her reassurances.

Copulsky tore open a package of sterile white fabric dressing, but it was too late.

Dawson's eyelids fluttered until he fixed on Bobbi. "Sweet girl," he whispered. "I'm so sorry." With that, his head fell to the side, his last breath a horrifying, wet rattle.

Copulsky tried to resuscitate the colonel but couldn't.

Bobbi let out a wail and fell over her father once again, her sobs shaking them both.

Everyone else hung their heads in solemn silence.

A hard stone had formed in Wally's throat, and the whole scene seemed like a horrible dream. Bobbi had hoped for reconciliation with her father through this mission, a chance she never had with her mother. Now, that chance was also lost.

Wally looked over to Max, Rat, and Frankie, seeing sparkling glass dust in their hair and on their clothes. Otherwise, they appeared okay. Copulsky had managed to save their lives. Maybe he was the best the army had to offer after all.

Brubaker returned from the street outside, stepping carefully through the jagged maw of the entrance. He stuffed his gun into the back of his trousers. The December cold now moved freely through the reception area, bringing a haunting chill to the studio.

"Bastards made off," the major announced. "Broad daylight. The public is starting to gather—" His words halted when he spotted Dawson on the floor.

Copulsky rose from Dawson's side. "The colonel is gone, sir."

Brubaker stared at the colonel's body, and Bobbi still huddled at her father's side, crying.

Wally hoped the major would say something profound or reassuring, but instead he just stared in silence at Dawson, his commanding officer, his friend.

Wally wanted to speak up, find some way to fill the horrible silence, but the solemn quiet was cut by the sound of glass crunching under someone else's footsteps. He turned to see a figure enter from the boulevard, stepping through the frame of the broken door.

Copulsky drew his gun and aimed. "Freeze!"

That's when Wally saw the person's lavender coat.

There stood Audrey in the demolished lobby, wide-eyed, carrying a wrapped birthday present in her hands. She looked around at the chaotic scene, spotted the dead colonel in a pool of blood, and dropped the gift to the shard-covered marble floor. She covered her mouth.

"Stop!" Wally leapt in front of Copulsky and raised his palm to face the barrel of the specialist's gun. "She's my friend."

Wally felt his worlds collide, the comfortable, familiar world of his Brooklyn brownstone and the dangerous, shattered, bloody world of secret missions, the very worlds he'd been working so hard to keep separate.

Audrey gaped, motionless. "Walter? What's happening?"

"She can't be here," said Copulsky. He lowered his weapon.

Wally searched Audrey's frightened eyes, worked to keep his voice reassuring, tried to stay calm, not just for his sake but for hers. "I can explain," he said, though he was uncertain how words could bring sense to the madness that surrounded them. He hardly understood himself.

"Your mother said you were here," said Audrey. "I came to surprise you." She retrieved the gift from the dust and glass. Her hands were trembling, and Wally feared she was going into shock. "I sorta hoped I could audition for the jingles too."

"You can't be here," said Wally.

"None of you can be here," said Brubaker, finally gaining his composure. He put his hand on his wounded shoulder, to the blackened, bloody spot on his herringbone coat where a bullet had hit him. He turned to Copulsky. "Get them to safety. I'll meet the ambulance, sort things out with the police, help Barbara Ann."

"You've been shot, sir," said Copulsky.

"I'll be fine. Ambulance will take care of me. Just get them home, and I'll meet you at the Lipkins' as soon as I can."

"You're sending us home?" said Wally.

"Our families," said Max, putting things together faster than Wally. "If Nazis tracked Dawson here, they may know about us. And if they know where we live—"

"Nazis?" said Audrey.

"It's just a precaution," said Brubaker. "But a necessary one."

"Walter?" said Audrey. "What is he talking about? What's going on?"

Wally looked to Brubaker, uncertain of how to respond.

"Go ahead," said the major. "Tell her. Doesn't matter now anyway."

Wally swallowed. "But, sir, what about the mission?"

Brubaker drew a long, solemn breath. "Look around, son. The colonel is gone, the station's been compromised. The mission is over."

Wally chewed his lip, staring through his family's kitchen window down to the street, watching Leo Copulsky pace the curb, smoking a cigarette at the sidewalk outside A-Rite Cleaners. The army specialist who had saved their lives now stood sentry in front of his home in case the Nazis had somehow connected the Lipkins to Colonel Dawson and WKOB. It was ironic to Wally that earlier that day he thought Leo, himself, was a Nazi. Now, he needed the guy's protection from the real threat, though it remained unclear how much the Nazis knew about the jingle mission, or about Wally, his friends, or his family.

He turned back to his small family room, where Max had called everyone to gather. Wally's mother sat alongside Mrs. Milhouser and Carl on the Lipkin family sofa, Wally's father sat in his usual armchair, and Audrey was seated on the piano bench, still looking haunted by what she had seen at the station. Frankie was sitting next to his own father, Officer O'Brien, still in uniform, in chairs taken from the Lipkins' kitchen table. Rat stood in the doorway leading to Wally's parents' bedroom, and Mrs. Rubinstein sat in another displaced kitchen chair beside her son. If one didn't know any better, it would have seemed like an impromptu Christmas party with family and friends. But there was no holiday punch, no exchange of gifts, no singing of carols. Instead, nearly everyone Wally cared about sat riveted with eyes on Max, who stood in the center of the room, commanding their attention like Roosevelt giving a fireside chat.

Max told them everything—about the contest, the boys' recruitment by the army, and the details of Dawson's crazy jingle plan. Throughout Max's detailed explanation, Wally's mother made small, gasping noises, and Carl kept leaning forward. It didn't hurt that Max was a good storyteller.

He talked with pride about the modest success the mission already earned and offered his apology, on behalf of the boys and US Army, for keeping them all in the dark, even though it was a necessity, mandated by Colonel Dawson himself. The mission was, Max explained, a matter of life and death, as evidenced by the horrible incident that had just happened at the studio. Clearly, the Nazis were eager to stop whatever they were doing.

"Thank God you're all right," Sadie proclaimed after Max was through.

"You boys," said Saul with glistening eyes. "Patriotic, every one of you."

Officer O'Brien looked at Frankie intensely. "Francis, don't ye see? This is why ye'd make a fine officer of the law." His Irish brogue was filled with both charm and earnestness. "Ye know what's right and nothin' scares ye. Not a dern thing."

Frankie turned a deep shade of red.

"This is all so confusing," said Mrs. Milhouser. "What does Audrey have to do with any of it?"

"She was there today," said Wally. "She saw what happened." He turned to Audrey with regret. "And because she's our friend, she may be at risk. You may all be at risk."

Just then, there were three quick raps on the door, which gave Mrs. Milhouser a start. Max strode over and opened it to find Major Brubaker framed in the threshold like a photograph. His military uniform had replaced his station manager's coat and bow tie, his arm now in a sling, his wound apparently cared for. It was the first time Wally and the guys had seen Brubaker out of his herringbone suits, and Wally found it disconcerting. His medals were impressive, his hat low on his brow. He was still tall and commanding, only now he looked troubled.

Rat immediately stood and saluted. "Major Brubaker, sir." The other guys saluted, and Wally did as well.

Brubaker nodded, but he lacked his usual bolt of enthusiasm. "At ease, gentlemen."

Wally was reminded that, however horrible the day had been for him and his friends, it was worse for Brubaker. He'd not only lost the mission, he had lost his friend and his commanding officer.

Wally's thoughts turned to Bobbi, to the memory of blood on her blouse, her weeping, and to the last request her father made of him, imploring Wally to trust her. It made no sense, but then again, today had been filled with senselessness.

"Major," said Max. "How's your arm?"

"Not the first time I've been shot, Mr. Lipkin. I'll be fine. Thank you for asking." Brubaker seemed more irritated by his injury than anything.

"Come in, sir," said Wally. "Max was just explaining everything to our families."

"Good," said Brubaker. "Saves me the trouble."

Max closed the door as the major strode to the center of the room, where Max had been. Wally's parents and the rest of the families stared at Brubaker as if he were the embodiment of the war, strolling into this humble Brooklyn apartment, his medals catching the lamplight like a hypnotist's watch stealing their attention away from Max.

He scanned their faces and removed his hat using his good arm. "Thank you all for gathering here," he said. "I'm sorry to spoil your holiday. I can see from the looks on your faces, you probably have questions."

"I do," said Mrs. Rubinstein, aiming her beady eyes at the major. She had been quiet until that moment and stood from her chair. "Why in the world would you think something so ridiculous would work? And why involve our boys?"

Wally immediately saw that the apple hadn't fallen far from the tree. Mrs. Rubinstein was every bit as blunt as her son.

Brubaker paused and seemed to consider his words carefully. "How many folks in the world do you think know how to read music, Mrs. Rubinstein?"

"Well, I'm sure I don't know."

Brubaker tilted his head. "Half the world? Less?"

Mrs. Rubinstein looked around, seeming uncomfortable with questions being directed back at her. "Far less than that, I'm sure."

"That's probably true. And of those in the entire world who can read music, how many do you think are in the service, the military service, in whatever country they live in? Maybe half of those?"

"I'd guess fewer than that."

"Yes, I agree," said Sadie. "Fewer than half."

"Far fewer," chimed in Saul as if he were participating in some sort of radio game show, playing against his wife and their houseguest.

"Okay, then," said Brubaker. "So, of all those folks in the world who can read music, and the percentage of those who are in military service, how many do you think can discern a note or a change in a measure, just from hearing the music out loud?"

"A very small number?" posed Carl, seeming eager to contribute to the conversation.

"Very good, young man," said Brubaker. "You're probably right. It is a rare skill indeed."

Carl nudged his mom, grinning.

"So, of that small number who can read music and who are in the military, and who can suss out a note or a measure change, how many of those work for our enemy and how many of those listen to Allied radio?"

"Just about none," declared Officer O'Brien, seeming irritated. "What's your point?"

"Well, Officer O'Brien, let's assume, for the sake of argument, there exist more than a few who can and do. Oddball turn of fate, maybe. Shall we assume a small number, tuning into an Allied broadcast, can read music, hear the notes, and spot the subtleties over the radio?"

"Fine," said Frankie's father. "A few."

"Great," said Brubaker. "Now, imagine that Uncle Sam's army had dozens of such men, say fifty of them, specifically trained to do all of that, and that each of them was stationed in key places all over Europe where battles were taking place, tuning in to specific radio broadcasts, listening to the music, discerning the music's subtleties, knowing there are secret messages buried in the notes. What if those men had a way to decode what they were trained to hear—like translating morse code, only better—turning those codes into secret orders. Wouldn't that be something special? Something...helpful?"

"Sure would!" said Carl. He was now standing.

Mrs. Milhouser tugged at her son's sleeve. "Sit down, Carl."

Brubaker drew a breath. "Folks, this is not some fancy story I'm telling to entertain you. This is the mission I've been leading, the ones your boys have been serving. It's an experiment in the name of peace. It's the work Colonel Dawson gave his life for. And your children, your talented children, have helped write, perform, and encode jingle music. Their work has already saved lives and may help us save more."

Helen Milhouser exchanged looks with Officer O'Brien and Wally's folks. Their faces all bore the same reluctant understanding that Wally felt the day he and his pals found out about the mission.

Wally faced Brubaker once again. "I thought you said the mission was over, Major. That the Nazis won."

"I did say that, Lipkin. And it very well may be true. But as long as I have a breath to breathe, I'll fight. And if you still want to help, the mission may still have a chance."

Wally's mother cleared her throat. "Excuse me, Major Brubaker."

"Yes, Mrs. Lipkin."

"Is it still dangerous? This thing you want our sons to do?"

"I'm not going to lie to you, ma'am. We found out today it's more dangerous than we thought, certainly more dangerous than doing nothing would be. And even though we've got army investigators and local police hunting down the ones responsible for today's brazen attack, the threat to our success can't be ignored. As I've learned from my years in the army, no work in this fight comes without risk. I want to be honest about that."

"This whole thing scares me," said Mrs. Rubinstein, whose voice now sounded more sympathetic.

"I understand," said Brubaker. "This war has had a way of stealing from our young people the privilege of a carefree youth. It's usually older folks who are forced to contemplate their deaths and, if they're lucky, prepare for what may come. This generation has had no such privilege. We're all facing death and uncertainty, whether we want to or not. Whether we're ready or not. I'm not offering any guarantees, ma'am. I'm just looking for a chance to do good. To help stop this horror and bring back some semblance of...calm and certainty."

"I'm still in, Major," blurted Rat.

Mrs. Rubinstein turned to her son. "Clyde, I know you're angry about my deferral letter. Tell me you aren't doing this to spite me. I just can't bear to see you in danger."

"Ma, please," said Rat with an odd and surprising tenderness. "If the mission is going forward, I gotta be part of it. Don't you see? I can't sit home anymore, not when every other fella is putting it all on the line, not when I know I can do something."

Audrey stood. "I can sing, Major Brubaker."

"Pardon?"

"I saw another girl there today at the studio, the one who lost her father. I'm betting she's a singer. Well, I can sing too."

"I see."

Mrs. Milhouser stood, a frantic look on her face. "Audrey!" Her desperate voice bounced around the Lipkins' apartment. "I already lost your brother. Isn't that enough?"

No one else spoke, and Wally felt the tension between them rise.

"It is enough," said Major Brubaker. "More than enough, ma'am." He turned to Audrey. "Miss, I appreciate what you're offering, but I'm sure we'll do just fine without your help."

"No," said Audrey. "I'm tired of standing around and waiting to see what men will do to save us. Hasn't it occurred to anyone that men got us into this mess? Maybe you need a few more women to make things right."

Wally flinched. He felt responsible for Audrey being there, felt as though her involvement was somehow his fault. If she wasn't his friend, would she even be interested in this crazy mission?

"Audrey," he whispered. "Don't—"

She ignored Wally and strode from the piano to the sofa to take Mrs. Milhouser's hand.

She knelt beside her. "Mother, I loved Johnny as much as you. I'm sick that he's gone. But if this war doesn't end, it'll be Carl next, and more and more until we run out of boys to throw at the problem."

Carl's eyes went wide, and he sank in his seat.

"You taught me to be strong," Audrey urged, "to speak my mind." She lowered her voice. "I should be able to do what I can, just like Johnny, to keep us all safe. Don't make me feel like I'm anything less than him."

Mrs. Milhouser's eyes filled with tears. "God help me," she said softly. "You sound just like your brother."

"What do we do?" said Max, his eyes fixed on Brubaker. "What's next?"

"Yeah," said Frankie. "What is next?"

"Well," said the major. "This is where things start to get complicated."

"*This* is where they get complicated?" scoffed Officer O'Brien. "I'm still doin' the math on who can read music and who can't."

"First and foremost, we need to attend to your safety," said Brubaker. "All of you. That is, until we can be sure there are no threats against you."

"How do you do that?" said Carl.

"I know a place to take you," said Brubaker. "A safe place, right here in Brooklyn." The major leaned over to the window to look down to Copulsky. "Just gotta get there."

Wally's father stood from his recliner. "Then we'll hail a taxi!" he proclaimed. He scanned the crowd in the family room. "Three or four taxis if we have to." His willingness to spend money on cab fare told Wally that his father needed no further convincing to support the mission.

"That's very generous," said Major Brubaker. "And safer than taking the subway. But we gotta go now. We've been sitting here too long already, even with Specialist Copulsky out at the curb."

"What about our things?" said Wally's mother. "If we're going to be gone long, surely I've got to pack some clothes."

"I'm sorry, ma'am," said Brubaker. "Just grab your coats and hats. We'll sort out the rest later."

With no more time to waste, the families grabbed what little they could and made their way down the stairs.

"Out the back," said Frankie, directing the others to the alley behind the brownstone. "It's safer."

Officer O'Brien grinned at his son as he and the other family members headed to the street and down the block, through the biting chill of the Christmas afternoon toward the corner of Third and Beverley where they hailed four taxis.

To Wally's astonishment, his father handed money out to each of the families as if doling out chocolate Hanukkah gelt. Meanwhile, Brubaker sent Copulsky off on his own task. When the major returned, he gave instructions to have the taxis take them all to Fort Hamilton via different routes. The fort was the old coastal artillery battery near Bay Ridge, where Wally and the others had taken a school field trip back in elementary school. Wally had heard they were using it again as a staging area for the war, but he didn't know what sort of help Fort Hamilton could provide his family and the others.

Rat and his mother paired up with the O'Briens in one taxi, Max joined Wally's folks in the second, and Brubaker hopped in with Mrs. Milhouser and Carl in the third taxi, giving Wally time alone with Audrey in the last cab.

"Fort Hamilton," said Wally once he and Audrey were seated.

"Sure thing," said the driver.

Once on their way, Wally leaned toward Audrey and lowered his voice. "I'm sorry I lied to you," he whispered. "Out of anyone, you were the one I wanted to tell the most."

"Don't apologize," said Audrey. "It all makes sense now."

"It does?"

"You've been acting so strange, staying out late, keeping secrets. Now I understand everything. You're trying to help end the war. You're brave."

Wally recalled his uncle's pronouncement that "self-preservation feels like cowardice but looks like courage."

He looked over to assure the driver wasn't listening and, once he had, whispered back, "You don't think it's all crazy?"

"Of course, I think it's crazy," said Audrey. "But you're still willing to try. That's what I want too, Walter. Since Johnny left, no one gives me the time of day, but this is my chance to finally do something important. Something brave. Like you. Like him."

Wally was suddenly filled with a strange mixture of appreciation and shame.

"That reminds me," said Audrey. She reached to her feet and lifted a box. It was the gift she had brought to the studio, and it still had glints of glass dust clinging to the wrapping. "I've been trying to give you this all day. Happy birthday."

It felt odd to Wally that he should be accepting presents or even acknowledging his birthday on such a horrific, tragic day.

"Thank you," he said. It was then Wally remembered the gift from his folks. He reached into his back pocket and pulled out the small gift the size of a cigar. "Almost forgot, my folks gave me this too."

"Well, don't just sit there. Open them."

"Here? In the taxi?"

"It's still your birthday in a taxi," Audrey asserted.

Wally pulled off the wrapping made from the funny pages that Audrey had taken from the *Brooklyn Daily Eagle* and opened the box. Inside was a pair of new leather shoes.

"After you told me you lost yours in that alley," she said, "I knew what I wanted to give you."

Wally blanched at the reminder of his further lies to Audrey.

"I was going to send those loafers to Johnny," she said, "but he died before I could send them." She drew a breath. "You're both a size ten. It seemed a waste not to use them."

Wally hung his head.

"What's wrong?" she said.

"It's just...this is too much," said Wally. "Are you sure you don't you want to save these to remember him?"

"They were never really his," said Audrey. "Besides, they don't remind me of him. They remind me of you."

A knot formed in Wally's throat, and he couldn't speak. He used the moment to kick off his own ill-fitting shoes to slip on the new ones.

"How do they feel?" said Audrey.

"Like guilt," said Wally. "I really do wish Johnny could've had these."

"I know he would have approved," said Audrey. "They're yours now."

It was humbling to have someone like Audrey whom he could trust in his corner, especially after all the lies he'd told. Surely, she deserved a better friend than him.

"Now open the one from your parents."

Wally tore through the wrapping, and the gleaming gift inside immediately made him smile. "It's a harmonica," he said, turning it over in his grip. "They even inscribed it." He held it so that Audrey could see it in the light coming through the windows of the taxi. He read the inscription aloud: "'Wherever you go—music.'"

"Well, isn't that something?" said Audrey. "I didn't know you played."

Wally ran the harp along his lips. "It was my first instrument, even before the piano. In fact, the one I learned on belonged to my Uncle Sherman."

Audrey nodded. "Well, now you have one of your very own."

The thought of Sherman reminded Wally of their visit to the sanatorium. "I didn't tell you something about my uncle," he said.

"What is it?"

"I didn't think it was fair that he was locked up in that place," said Wally. "Not after everything he told us."

"I agree," said Audrey. "It was sad."

"When we left his room that day, before the door closed, I stuck the gum you gave me into his door latch."

"To help him escape?" A grin grew across Audrey's face.

"I know I shouldn't have—"

Audrey let out a howling laugh, which momentarily caught the driver's attention. He gave them a look and a smile, and then looked back at the road.

"Wish I'd thought of that!" said Audrey. "I can just picture him out on the street in his pajamas."

"You're assuming he remembered to put them on!" Wally laughed, recalling Sherman standing half naked in front of them.

Audrey's laughter filled Wally with a joy he hadn't felt in weeks.

"Do you think he's out there?" she asked, turning her gaze out the window to the streets they were passing.

"No idea," said Wally.

"You shouldn't feel bad, Walter. He didn't deserve that place. No one does."

Before Wally could remind her that the sanitorium may be the place he'd wind up in himself, the taxi slowed to the stop.

"Fort Hamilton," said the driver.

Wally stuffed his new harmonica back into his pocket. He then tucked his old shoes into the now empty shoebox Audrey had given him and abandoned it under the passenger seat, choosing to leave them behind. He handed the fare to the driver. "Thank you," he said. "Merry Christmas."

Wally and Audrey stepped out to join their families and friends at the front gate of Fort Hamilton as the taxis drove off, one after the other. The air smelled of the sea, and Wally could hear the crash of waves beyond the walls of the fort at the perimeter breakwater. They all stood for a moment, gaping at the stone gate and the walls that rose before them, the setting sun now relinquishing its influence to the chill in the air.

Wally's first and only trip to Fort Hamilton happened long before the Japanese had belted Pearl Harbor. He and his young classmates had learned that this Brooklyn stronghold had been used back in the Great War, the first one, as a launching area for troop mobilization. Now, the newspapers said the military had resumed using it as a gateway to Europe and the Pacific, training soldiers to fill the troopships Wally had seen launching from the Brooklyn Navy Yard. With traitors shooting up radio stations in front of his very eyes, battleships floating in the harbor, and the fort hard at work preparing soldiers, it was now clear to Wally that the war had been there in New York all along. He had been foolish to think he could ever escape it.

Brubaker led them forward to a manned window, where he spoke with a duty sergeant at the gate's entrance. He then returned. "Follow me," he said.

Wally noticed the major wince as he adjusted his sling. Whatever painkillers he'd been given after the attack must have started wearing off. Still, he was managing to lead, on this horrible day, carrying a certainty that Wally could only admire. He was ashamed he had ever been reluctant to salute this man.

They followed Brubaker through the entrance in the buttressed stone walls, and Wally noticed old cannons resting in turrets, aimed at the harbor. Bunkers and sleeping quarters that he didn't remember from his childhood visit had been constructed everywhere. Soldiers were running drills on the expansive grass fields, even as the rest of Brooklyn was at home with their families enjoying a Christmas meal and opening presents. But these men were readying for battle, preparing to face a danger that Wally had worked hard to avoid.

Brubaker led them to a brick and clapboard administrative building, where they were greeted by two officers and a private. "This is Captain Ellis, Sergeant Rollins, and Private Bailey," said Brubaker. They're aware of our...unusual circumstances and will set you up in family quarters for the night, get you some grub, prepare you for your debrief in the morning.

"Good evening," said the man named Captain Ellis. He had a thin mustache and a cleft chin. He reminded Wally of Errol Flynn and seemed to carry a similar charm. "Bet this isn't where you thought you'd spend Christmas Day."

"We're just grateful for your help," said Wally's mother, warming to the captain's magnetism. "And thank you, Major, for taking care of us and our families."

Brubaker shrugged. "I should be thanking you, Mrs. Lipkin, all of you. It's not every family that's asked to support the war effort in this extraordinary way. I'm grateful."

"We've always supported the effort," Saul chimed in. "Bought plenty of bonds, I can tell you that."

Max rolled his eyes at Wally.

"Follow me," said Captain Ellis, but as the families strode ahead, Brubaker asked Wally to hold back for a moment.

"Lipkin?"

"Yes, Major?"

Brubaker paused to watch the families walk away and then lowered his voice. "Best not to mention to any of the folks here at the fort that you boys are enlisted."

Wally tried to discern the strange look on Brubaker's face. "Why not?"

"Well," said Brubaker, "because you aren't. None of you are."

The sun sank below the horizon, and Wally felt an odd sinking too. "What do you mean?"

"I mean, your work on the mission has been...off the books." He adjusted his arm in its sling, pursing his lips from what Wally assumed was physical pain, and then looked Wally in the eye. "I'm afraid the colonel and I weren't entirely upfront with you fellas about a few things."

Wally felt a strange sensation like an imaginary sandcastle collapsing in the center of his body. "What things?"

9

How Things Break

It was a scene out of Wally's wildest and most nonsensical imagining. In the far corner of Fort Hamilton's largest mess hall, among the throngs of enlisted men serving in all branches of Uncle Sam's armed services, the Lipkins, Rubinsteins, O'Briens, and Milhousers sat at a long table sharing an unlikely Christmas dinner. Despite the rationing practiced by all New Yorkers and within each division of the military, the families had been served a special holiday meal, the same one all the enlisted men at the Fort had been served: roast turkey, string beans, corn bread, and mashed potatoes with actual gravy. They even enjoyed soft dinner rolls with real salted butter. It all seemed at once oddly familiar and yet entirely incomprehensible, another discordant note in the song of Wally's life.

He'd hardly touched his turkey and was using a spoon to stir his mashed potatoes into a runny cream that flowed beneath his beans.

"This is the best Christmas ever," said Carl. He gaped at the soldiers in all manner of uniform that surrounded them, appearing impressed by the scope of the effort underway and the scores of men it took to support it.

"Carl, quit gawking and finish your dinner," said Mrs. Milhouser. She seemed less enamored with their situation than her son.

A crew of nearby sailors were the most jovial, not to be outdone by the airmen who seemed to know one another well. But the real miserable hordes were the army soldiers, the bulk of the men, seeming more somber than the rest. They appeared to know what came after the Christmas festivities.

Max eyed Wally's plate and the mashed potatoes that were now unidentifiable. "What's wrong?" he whispered.

"You'll find out," said Wally.

"What does that mean?"

Wally lowered his voice. "Brubaker asked to meet with us after dinner," he said, "without the parents. Said he'd explain everything."

"Okay," said Max, but it was clear Wally's meek explanation only raised new questions for his brother.

Once the meal was complete and the families had retired to their quarters, Max and Wally gathered Frankie and Rat outside the mess hall under a glowing streetlamp. Of course, Audrey refused to be left behind, pulled on her coat, and joined them.

"What's going on?" she said.

"Yeah," said Rat. "What gives?"

"Ask him," said Wally. He pointed to Brubaker, who approached from the shadowy path connecting two administrative buildings.

"Evening," said Brubaker. He tossed aside a cigarette, smashed it with his boot, and blew smoke over his head into the December sky.

Rat and the others saluted, including Audrey, but this time, Wally simply frowned at the major.

Brubaker nodded as if he knew he deserved Wally's disdain and said, "Follow me."

The crew followed the major across the well-manicured lawn, the smell of New York Harbor and the sound of distant bells from seafaring vessels hovering in the crisp winter air.

"Wish it would snow," said Rat. "That would make it seem more like Christmas."

"Nothing about today seems like Christmas," said Frankie, "or a birthday." He put his hand on Wally, who silently agreed.

They soon entered another brick and white clapboard building, where the major led them to a small briefing room, warmed by a rattling radiator. The room looked like a classroom with desks facing a podium and a chalkboard on wheels off to the side. They took off their coats, hung them over their chairs, and sat at the desks.

"Okay," said Wally once Brubaker had closed the door to the briefing room. "Tell them what you told me."

The others looked at one another uncomfortably, appearing to react to Wally taking charge in a room where the major was clearly the ranking officer.

Brubaker took off his hat, set it on the podium, adjusted his sling, and faced the team.

"Our mission," he said. "There are things you don't know."

"What don't we know?" said Max.

"Your involvement—it wasn't exactly sanctioned."

Max's brow tightened. "What do you mean?"

Wally faced his friends. "He means none of us were actually enlisted." The pronouncement fell over the team like a bucket of cold water tossed onto hot coals. "He lied," Wally said to further punctuate his point. "Lied to all of us."

Frankie's eyes gleamed, piecing it together. "That's why you paid us cash from your own pocket," he said. "I knew something fishy was going on!"

"Why?" said Rat. "Why tell us we were enlisted?"

"The colonel and I hoped to enlist you eventually."

"Eventually?" said Max.

"The colonel was trying to prove himself," said Brubaker, "prove to army command that our mission could work. To make that happen, we needed men like you—talented men who couldn't be redeployed. We needed to show progress as well as gain your commitment. By telling you that you were enlisted, he figured we could spark your loyalty. We needed you all-in."

"We were all-in," said Max.

Brubaker drew a breath. "None of you except Walter was subject to enlistment, and we hoped to resolve this before today. His birthday."

"I still don't get it," said Frankie.

"This mission wasn't given the kind of support Colonel Dawson needed, the kind he deserved. It took months to get as far as we did when we were first given the resources, and the army barely provided enough for a trial."

"Trial?" said Rat.

"To prove the mission could work or let it fail early before any real effort was wasted. They clearly weren't ready to commit. We had no funding and, before you, just a handful of enlisted men stateside and in Italy. Needless to say, the first attempt didn't work."

Wally noticed Audrey leaning forward, hanging on to every one of Brubaker's words.

"We weren't the first attempt?" said Rat.

"Before we recruited you all," said the major, "they sent us a half dozen young soldiers with some musical training, ready to follow orders. But none of them had that extra gift, that chemistry or that talent we needed, not like you fellas. And none of them believed in what we could do. They had doubts and didn't take the work seriously." A new sparkle animated Brubaker's voice. "Dawson knew we needed jingle writers with real experience, real chemistry, a team with a true passion for music, not enlisted men distracted by their duty or the details of the military parts of the mission. We needed civilians." He shook his head. "And, of course, the army refused to allow it. The best Dawson got was permission to bring Barbara Ann on board. But having her around only made it clear that we needed more people like her, different than the handful of rank-and-file soldiers they gave us."

Wally recalled his night on Bobbi's roof when she pleaded with him to stick with the mission, told him that the army brass still needed convincing. He had no idea this was what she meant.

"Dawson had only one chance to make things work or else the whole shebang was lost for good. That's when we concocted the idea for the contest." The major eyed the team. "Until today, as far as the army leadership knew, everything we've achieved with the mission was done with a handful of enlisted men, not civilians. Not you. That's why we couldn't enlist you yet."

A pained look darkened Max's features. "So that nonsense about not getting Broadway or Hollywood writers. It wasn't because it would have drawn attention. It was because you couldn't afford them."

"None of that mattered once we found you fellas." Brubaker left the podium and got closer to the team. "We used the stateside soldiers like Specialist Copulsky to provide security instead, and to run the coded ciphers," he said. "But Colonel Dawson was right. This jingle team is what made the difference. You made the missions work, the music work, and he was ready to tell the army. Ready to tell them what we'd done."

"And then he was killed," said Wally.

"Yes."

The room got quiet, and Wally recalled the colonel's final moments on the floor of WKOB, when Dawson implored Wally to trust his daughter, when his mission and his life ended.

"You said 'until today,'" said Rat, breaking the silence. "Does the army know now? Do your commanding officers know that civilians were the ones who actually made the plan work? That *we* made the plan work?"

"They do," said Brubaker. "I told them everything. That's how I got them to agree to protect you and your families here at Fort Hamilton."

"They must not be very happy with you," said Rat.

"That assumption would be correct, Mr. Rubinstein. They are not." Brubaker sighed and adjusted his sling. "Now," he said, "they're discussing next steps."

"Next steps?" said Frankie.

"He thinks they're gonna sack him," said Rat, watching Brubaker shift uncomfortably.

Wally turned. "That true, Major? Are you getting sacked?"

"That would be a court-martial. And I don't know, son. It's out of my hands now."

"But Dawson was your commanding officer," said Max. "You were following his orders."

"I believed in the mission," said Brubaker. "And I gave orders of my own. Whatever you think of the colonel, I was his willing partner. I did the job he asked of my own volition. This doesn't just fall on him. It's my job on the line."

"Your job doesn't matter," said Wally. "It makes no difference whether they sack you or not."

"Walter!" said Audrey. "Don't be rude."

"You heard him," said Wally. "He lied to us, put us all at risk." Wally felt heat rise up the back of his neck, felt that sinking feeling like he was right back at the start of everything, when the war was upon him, and his death was a certainty. "Now our families are hiding in a fort and who knows whether any of you will be able to go home."

"Any of us?" said Audrey. "What about you?"

"I know what's in store for me," said Wally. "I'm the one person here who still has to serve, remember." He met Brubaker's somber look. "Isn't that right, Major? The colonel said he'd take care of my paperwork, but he didn't file that paperwork, did he?"

Brubaker shifted uncomfortably. "No, Lipkin. I'm afraid he didn't."

"So, let's just get it over with," said Wally. "I'm sure they have someone at Fort Hamilton who can help me enlist. Today, I'm eighteen after all."

"Hang on," said Max. He turned to Brubaker. "What about the mission? You said it succeeded. Doesn't that count for something?"

"Yeah," said Rat. "Back at the Lipkins', you made it sound like the mission still had a chance."

"Or was that just another lie?" said Frankie.

"It wasn't a lie," said Brubaker. "My superior officer, Colonel Renshaw, has taken my report and has heard my recommendations. He was the one who sanctioned the work we've done so far, at least the part he knew about. He'll be here tomorrow to meet with me in person, and we'll know more then." With his good hand, the major grabbed his hat off the podium and put it back on his head. "Until then, I suggest you get some sleep." Brubaker opened the door and, before leaving, turned back to the team. "For what it's worth," he said. "I'm sorry." With that, the major left.

Wally stared at the door. He was back to square one. The mission had been a side game, a distraction that only served to raise his hopes unnecessarily and cause him to put his entire family in harm's way. Now, it looked like that mission had little chance of continuing, and without a stateside assignment, Wally would be shipping off like all the other soldiers there at the fort, being distracted from their horrible fates with turkey, potatoes, and salted butter.

Maybe he was getting exactly what a coward like him deserved. Max and Frankie would go back to enjoying their 4-Fs, Rat Rubinstein would still have his 3-A intact, and Audrey would go back to the sidelines she hated in the long shadows cast by her brother. And, to top it all off, he'd probably never see Bobbi again. Of course, he had no idea how to feel about her anymore, anyway.

"I, for one, think the chances of continuing the mission are good," said Rat. "Nothing is more convincing than results, and we got those."

"Didn't you hear a word Brubaker said?" barked Wally. "He thinks he's a goner. And if he's gone, we're gone."

"He better not be gone," said Frankie. "The guy still owes us money."

"Don't worry," said Max. "He doesn't think he's a goner."

"But you heard what he said…"

"I did," said Max. "I also heard him in our family room, and I heard him back at WKOB. I've heard him all along. Brubaker believes in us, Walter. He's a good recruiter. Hell, he convinced us to join, didn't he?"

"Technically, he tied me up," said Rat.

Max pointed toward quarters. "Brubaker got our families eating Christmas dinner in the middle of a military installation, even had our father doling out cash for taxis! That man is good at his job, and he has one job left to do, one more person to recruit to the cause—this Colonel Renshaw. And tomorrow, he's going to make it clear to Renshaw that this mission has to continue."

Wally looked at Max intently. "And if he doesn't?"

"Then I'll eat my hat," said Max.

Rat opened his mouth to speak, but Wally raised his finger. "Don't you dare say Max will eat anything."

"I wasn't going to say that," said Rat with a mischievous twinkle in his eye.

"I saw it on your face, Clyde. You thought it."

"So now I'm in trouble for thinking?"

"Knock it off, both of you," said Max, seeming to allow the joke at his own expense.

"All I'm asking is that you believe in Brubaker. Trust him to do his part."

"Easier said than done," said Frankie.

"It's Hannukah, Christmas, and Wally's birthday," said Max. "Make a wish and have a little faith."

By the end of the long and painful day, Wally, Audrey, and the others quietly made their way toward the quarters they'd been assigned. Wally and the guys had been provided a small converted storage bungalow nearby, equipped with four cots, a small desk with a table lamp, and a wardrobe bureau they had to share, filled with military pajamas in varying sizes. Audrey's quarters were with her mother and Carl in separate rooms along with the rest of the parents, in a building typically reserved for visiting dignitaries, away from the rank and file.

After stopping outside the guys' quarters, Audrey said she was ready to get some sleep.

"I'll walk you," said Wally, joining Audrey and letting the others wind down for the night.

"Thanks," she said.

The air still smelled like the sea, and Wally could hear the waves crashing against the fort's breakwater like his dark thoughts beating on the shores of his subconscious. On any other evening, this might have been a pleasant holiday adventure, but Wally remained troubled.

"It's been a big day," said Audrey. "Not the Christmas I was expecting, nor the birthday you hoped for, I'm guessing."

"That's putting it mildly," said Wally. He looked down at his shoes. "At least I got some great shoes."

"Are you okay? I know what this mission meant for you. What it could still mean."

"It must seem selfish for me to worry about myself, especially when Bobbi lost her father today."

"I'm sorry he died," said Audrey. "I know he believed in you."

"First dead person I've ever seen up close." Wally tried to rid his mind of the memory.

"Not mine," said Audrey.

Wally remembered that Audrey was at her father's bedside when he passed away from cancer in the hospital two years earlier. She was still mourning him when she lost her brother to war. "How do you get over it?" he said. "How do you make make sense of it all? The death, the loss, the confusion?"

"You don't," said Audrey. "You just try to think of them when they were alive. If your mind lets you."

"This mission was supposed to keep me safe," said Wally. "You were supposed to be safe. Our families were supposed to be safe. Now, everything is different. It'll always be different."

Audrey stopped walking.

"That's how things break, Walter. There are no clean edges." She moved her gaze to the stars. "I knew with my father and again with Johnny, before they died, that their deaths were possible. But when their deaths happened, it was still surprising, still painful. They both left so much behind, so much left to do. I realize now that's how it always is. Nothing in life breaks neatly. Everyone dies with more left to do, leaving questions that have no answers."

Audrey sounded so calm, so centered. Wally tried to see what she saw in the stars, but all he found there was darkness.

"I don't want that," he said. "I want to do something important while I still can. I want to answer my own questions."

"Me too," said Audrey. "That's why I have to be in on this mission."

"You mean if there is a mission. It seems unlikely, with Dawson dead and all his lies out in the open."

"Maybe," said Audrey. "Or maybe that's exactly what needed to happen for things to move forward."

"Guess we'll find out tomorrow."

They arrived at Audrey's quarters and said good night. Wally walked back down the path, breathing the cold, salty air, the growling waves still assaulting the breakwater. Back at his bungalow, he found Max standing next to his cot in his white tank top and boxers holding a slender pair of army-issued pajamas in his plump outstretched arms. Max's eyes were wide with disbelief. "They've gotta be shitting me. Are these meant for a toddler?"

Wally grinned. "Maybe you should make a wish and have a little faith."

Max scowled. "Don't make me hurt you on your birthday."

After a restless night's sleep in his musty army cot, Wally put on the clothes he'd worn the previous day and joined his friends back at the mess hall. Gone were the holiday decorations and the homestyle cooking of their Christmas dinner. Instead, among the bare walls of the mess hall, they shoved their mouths full of chalky oatmeal and cold toast with jam. The restrictive rationing practiced every other day was now back in full force, and it seemed a suitable wake-up call for a day destined to deliver disappointment.

After his concrete-flavored breakfast that sat like a stone in Wally's gut, he joined Audrey and the guys at the light post outside the mess hall while their parents and Carl were taken on a tour of the fort by the dashing Captain Ellis, given proper distractions as though they were on some sort of family vacation. Private Bailey, the young soldier from the prior night, retrieved Wally, Audrey, and the crew and led them down a grassy path across Fort Hamilton's grounds. They strode in silence in a single line between soldiers marching through basic training until they reached a small auditorium.

The inside of the building reminded Wally of the Lincoln High School theater, with a small stage and sloped seating for an audience of around two hundred. But as they arrived at what he expected to be an empty theater, Wally spotted two people already seated in the second row: Leo Copulsky and Bobbi LaFleur. Copulsky now wore his uniform and looked more like a real army specialist than a garbage man. Bobbi was dressed in a subdued skirt and a cream-colored blouse, her cheeks flush as though she'd been crying. The two of them turned and faced the entrance as Wally and the others made their way down the aisles toward the seats.

"What'd we miss last night?" said Copulsky, addressing Max, who now led the procession.

"Turkey dinner and lies," said Rat, which caused Copulsky to cock his head in confusion.

Wally locked eyes with Bobbi. She offered him a strained smile but didn't say a word, leaving him to wonder if she knew that her father's lies had now been exposed.

"Poor thing," Audrey whispered at Wally's side.

Wally remained silent, struggling to reconcile his pity with his resentment for Bobbi's part in the whole charade that had left him and his friends duped.

Private Bailey remained at the entrance while the team found seats in the third row behind their two other teammates.

"You okay?" Max asked Bobbi softly as he sat.

Bobbi nodded but didn't say a word.

The doors to the theater opened again. This time it was Major Brubaker, accompanied by Sergeant Rollins from the night before. They were joined by a tall, stout, uniformed man with a corpuscular nose, an iron jaw, and sharp focused eyes like an eagle. Wally figured the man must be Colonel Renshaw, the commanding officer Brubaker had mentioned. The man looked angry, which Wally took as a bad sign.

Copulsky was the first to stand and salute, prompting Wally and the others to do the same, including Audrey, who seemed to appreciate the protocol.

The procession of military men took the stage, and it felt as though Wally and his friends had been included in some sort of judgment panel. Wally tried to read the look on Brubaker's face, tried to get some sense of whether the major was being reinstated or court-martialed. But Brubaker's features remained inscrutable.

Once on the stage, Colonel Renshaw stood before a wooden podium, cleared his throat, and addressed the small crowd in the deep, resonant voice of an experienced orator.

"At ease, gentlemen," he said. He then eyed Audrey and Bobbi. "And ladies."

They all sat.

"I'm Colonel Abner Renshaw of the United States Army, and I've been made aware of the circumstances that brought you all here." He looked down to Bobbi and softened his tone. "First, let me express my deepest sympathies for your loss, Barbara Ann. As you may know, your father was not just a seasoned, decorated military officer, he was my friend. The army will suffer his loss and so will I."

Bobbi nodded her appreciation at the colonel's words, looking as though she was fighting back new tears.

Renshaw lifted his head again and resumed his booming declarations, despite the scarcity of the crowd. "I know none of you expected to be here today," he said. "It's not often we bring civilians onto a working military facility, especially during wartime, and on Christmas day, nonetheless. But ours are less-than-ideal circumstances and these are unusual times." He cleared his throat. "I've now spent several hours in discussion with Major Brubaker. He's briefed me on the many...irregular tactics taken by him and the late colonel to form this team and to execute their mission. And, while the achievements to date have been laudable, the methods used were unacceptable, both to me and to the US

Army. The ends don't justify the means, even at a time of war. Protocol is what defines us. Order and decency are what make us different from those we seek to defeat. We can't just ignore the rules when we don't agree with them, and let's be clear: several important rules have been broken in the service of this mission."

Wally felt his heart break and looked to the major, who stood solemnly at Renshaw's side. He expected to see some sign that Brubaker's heart, too, was breaking. However, the major's eyes remained fixed on Renshaw, and it looked as though he was willingly taking his licks as some sort of penance, receiving the harsh criticisms he knew he deserved. As mad as Wally wanted to be with his commander, he couldn't help but feel bad for the guy, standing there, wounded in his sling, taking a beating on top of his incomprehensible loss.

"These times," Renshaw continued, "have required many men to make hard decisions, choices, not just between right and wrong, but choices between easy and hard, between one risk and another, between one crazy idea and the next. War has a way of bending good men in directions they didn't think they could bend."

Audrey suddenly grabbed Wally's hand and squeezed it.

"We lost one such good man in Colonel Howard Dawson. Since his death, I've struggled to find a way to reconcile the man he was with the choices he made, the choices he's now left me to make." He looked at Bobbi. "Forgive me for saying so, Barbara Ann."

Bobbi nodded gently.

Wally saw the shame on Bobbi's face, started to see where the speech was going, where his fate was taking him. The large auditorium started to feel very small, and Wally's destiny was seeming more certain. It was clear Renshaw was going to pull the plug and Wally was heading toward the very fate he'd hoped to avoid.

"Sir?" Wally was standing before he realized it.

"Please take your seat, son. I'm not finished."

"I know, sir...and I'm sorry. I just want to say, we're not victims."

"Victims?"

"I think I speak for all of us when I say that we believed in the mission too, sir. We still do, even knowing...what we know. Major Brubaker, Colonel Dawson—they didn't do anything to harm us. We were there because we wanted to be. We volunteered. We wanted the same thing they wanted. To make a difference. To end the war. And it was working, sir. Before you shut us down, won't you give the mission one more chance?"

Renshaw turned to Brubaker, who looked just as surprised and irritated by Wally's outburst. "Who is that?" Renshaw asked him.

"That's Walter Lipkin, sir. Our piano player." Brubaker shot Wally a disapproving look.

Renshaw turned back and squinted at Wally. "Mr. Lipkin, I appreciate your words, but I need you to have a seat—"

"Please, sir, don't shut us down. If you do, you may be stopping the very thing that could make a difference."

Renshaw's jaw tightened. "I understand you have not been trained in protocol, young man, but you really do need to take a seat. Decisions have already been made, and I have more to say."

"Sit down, Lipkin," barked Major Brubaker.

Wally lowered himself onto the wooden seat, embarrassed to have let his feelings take control so completely. But how could he just sit there and let all hope of the mission, of his survival, die in front of him?

Audrey grabbed his hand again and squeezed it. "Easy, Walter."

Renshaw took another breath. "As I was saying, and as Mr. Lipkin has just proven beyond a doubt, Howard Dawson and the team he comprised has been anything but conventional."

Renshaw shot a wilting look at Wally, causing him to slump further in his seat.

"Nevertheless, it's also clear the colonel's team hasn't lost his vision, his determination, or his hope for winning the war. Howard Dawson didn't just believe in the US Armed Forces or in this work. He believed in each of you."

Bobbi raised her head a little higher.

"I know this Nazi business drove you from your homes, probably has you more than a little afraid," Renshaw continued. "I wouldn't be surprised if you had your doubts along the way before any of that transpired. Let me just say this: I've had my doubts too. Still do. Major Brubaker has them, and Howard Dawson had them, God rest his soul. But be assured, nothing good in this war has been accomplished without fear or doubt, right on up the chain."

Colonel Renshaw set his gleaming eyes. "I had a choice to make today," he said, "to end the mission, seek punishment for Major Brubaker, and disband this team, or to find a way to continue the colonel's work, but within the reasonable boundaries of US Army protocol, to honor the work done by a good man with a vision, no matter how desperate that work may seem."

Wally froze and it seemed everyone in the theater was holding their breath.

"Didn't sleep much last night, I can tell you that. But I've decided after some consideration to change Major Brubaker's rank," he said, and the team gasped in unison. Wally figured a demotion was better than a court-martial, but then Renshaw added, "I'm advancing him in rank to lieutenant colonel."

Wally felt his jaw drop and saw he wasn't alone in his surprise.

"While I can't say that I've agreed with all of the decisions he's made, I also cannot deny that he has shown leadership, demonstrated creativity and tenacity, and proved his readiness for increased command duties, even in the way he's taken full responsibility with me for all that has passed. If there's one thing thirty years of service has taught me it's that character counts. And I'm convinced, in this case, it counts more than anything else that may have happened."

The team burst into applause, which was apparently not the right response. Private Bailey, Sergeant Rollins, and Major Brubaker all spun to face the team with surprised looks.

Copulsky turned in his seat and frowned at the others. "Shhh," he chided.

Rat flinched and sat on his hands.

"Quiet," said Renshaw, gaining back his control. "Quiet, please." He cleared his throat again. "I've elevated now colonel Brubaker's rank because I've asked him to take on enhanced duties, a new mission." Renshaw turned to Brubaker. "I'll let him explain further."

Renshaw stepped away from the podium to join Rollins and Bailey on stage left as Brubaker strode forward and saluted the colonel with his functioning arm. He then stood at the podium and scanned the faces of the team with eyes that held a softness Wally had never seen there before. He adjusted his sling and cleared his throat. "Back at the station," said Brubaker, "Colonel Dawson had intended to ask each of you some questions. Now, I'm left to ask them in his place." He paused, letting the echo of his words dissolve into the walls of the theater. "I'm asking each of you to accept the fear Colonel Renshaw described, but to set it aside, to do your best, even when you have doubts. I'm asking you to serve your country in the name of all the brave soldiers who are dying to protect us, even if it means putting yourselves at risk."

Max and Frankie exchange puzzled looks.

"I know what I'm about to ask is no small thing," he said, "especially after yesterday's horrible tragedy. But I'm asking anyway. Can each of you serve your country, officially, and work toward ending this war despite the risk?"

"Yes, sir!" barked Copulsky without hesitating. He then turned with disappointment to the team.

This time, they all shouted their reply: "Yes, sir!"

It was in those urgent proclamations of fealty that Wally realized the mission wasn't just personal for him; the mission had become personal for everyone else too, including Audrey, whose eyes were riveted on Brubaker. It was a chance for her to avenge her brother, to feel useful, a chance for Frankie to prove his worth to his father, a chance for Rat to finally earn trust instead of scorn, a chance for Max to truly become a leader, a chance for Bobbi to see her father's vision through.

"Then we agree," said Brubaker. "We move forward with the mission—officially. That means, this time, you'll all be properly enlisted in the United States Army."

"Me too?" asked Audrey.

"I'm presuming from your prior statements that's what you want, Miss Milhouser. Is that still true?"

"Oh, yessir!" she said and squeezed Wally's hand so hard he thought she'd break his fingers.

Wally's stomach spun like one of A-Rite's industrial dryers. If this pronouncement was the outcome he and the others were hoping for, why was he suddenly nervous?

Colonel Brubaker looked at Bobbi directly. "Barbara Ann, the plan is for us to launch Operation Teacup." He squinted. "You up for that?"

Bobbi's eyes widened as if she understood too clearly whatever Brubaker meant, even if no one else did. "Yes," she said, though her tone sounded as if she were using that moment to convince herself. "Yes, I am."

"Operation Teacup?" said Wally.

Rat pursed his lips. "Sounds fancy. What does it mean?"

"It means," said Brubaker, "that like most every other soldier here, we're leaving New York. And I hope none of you gets seasick."

10

Edmund B. Alexander

Wally lugged his army-issued duffel bag over his shoulder as Max, Frankie, and Rat followed close behind. They shadowed a young army soldier down the stairs of a constricted companionway to the lower decks of the US Army transport *Edmund B. Alexander*, the crown jewel of army troopships, anchored at the port of Boston Harbor.

Their tight new boots sent metallic echoes all around the claustrophobia-inducing passageway as they descended farther into the darkening bowels of the ship. "Watch your skulls," said the soldier in the lead. He directed their attention to a tangle of pipes that ran overhead, through the passageway, and into the depths of the enormous steel troopship. The soldier was a trim young man around Wally's age with a clean haircut. "These pipes are built to take a beating," he said. "Your melons aren't. Stay alert."

As they proceeded, Wally played over his last moments with his parents back at Fort Hamilton. His mother had cried, so had his father, but they had never looked prouder. Then again, as Jewish parents, they would have been proud even if he shit his pants.

"Wear thick socks," his mother had urged. "And don't start smoking. It'll ruin your clothes and make your teeth brown. You saw what happened to Edna Milner's son, Vincent."

"It's the service," his father had snapped back. "If they smoke, they smoke." He had eyed both Wally and Max. "Just come home in one piece, would ya? Someone's gotta run the register when you get back."

They'd all had a laugh, indulged more than a few additional tears, and hugged until their arms ached. Too soon, the driver of the transport bus had sounded its horn. Wally and Max boarded the bus destined for Boston Harbor after Frankie, Rat, and Audrey had similar exchanges with their own families. It was a privilege none of the other men at Fort Hamilton had. They had left their own families weeks earlier in whatever towns they came from.

Of course, Wally's privilege came with a price. Neither he nor his teammates had time for much basic training. In the few days after being formally enlisted, before departing Fort Hamilton, the guys had been taught how to assemble, load, aim, and fire a pistol and a rifle; how to make a bed without creases; how to wash their clothes; pack a satchel; and obey commanding officers, following the chain of command. They were told to act like proper infantrymen, though Wally had no idea what an infantryman did. Of course, serving as an average infantryman wasn't going to be his role, anyway. Brubaker told them they were heading to London, where they would be setting up shop similar to how things were at WKOB. The gals would have their own separate duties consistent with their gender. The rest of the details would be provided upon arrival.

Their families, meantime, would remain safe in Brooklyn, housed at Fort Hamilton for the time being, at least until the army was certain they could be made safe from any stateside threats. And for good measure, Specialist Copulsky had agreed to stay behind to assure their families had everything they needed.

It all should have been a comfort to Wally, but since leaving the fort, a slow, insidious sense of doom had haunted his thoughts, set his anxiety to boil on a slow, constant simmer, raising new concerns about whether any of this would matter. His original goal of staying safe by staying stateside was now officially abandoned. What lay ahead was anyone's guess.

A loud clang and a sharp pain in his head snapped Wally out of his silent musing.

"Told you to watch your melon," the guy with the haircut said with a chuckle.

"You okay?" said Max, trying to keep from laughing.

"Fine," snarled Wally. He rubbed the bump that was forming at his hairline, cursing the pipe and the whole damn ship. He preferred his seafaring vessels at the far end of his binoculars.

"It's no joke," said their guide. "I know three guys who gave themselves concussions down here before even setting sail. It's small inside, no matter what it looks like on the outside."

From the docks of Boston's busy harbor, the *Edmund B. Alexander* had looked like the biggest ship Wally had ever seen, and he'd ogled quite a few in Brooklyn's Navy Yard. He'd long thought the last place he wanted to find himself was aboard an army troopship like this one, but ever since he saw the jingle contest ad in the paper, nothing had worked out as planned.

"You're wearing an army uniform like us," Rat said to the soldier, ducking an overhead conduit. "Isn't this a naval ship?"

"Most of the army ships were turned over to the navy," said the young man. "The *Edmund B.* is still in service to Uncle Sam's army. Only a handful of these left."

"Left?" said Wally, but the guy only shrugged.

As they moved farther down the corridor, deeper belowdecks, the afternoon sun vanished, and their pathway was lit instead by flickering overhead bulbs creating odd patterns of shadow and light that only served to heighten Wally's distress.

He tugged at the starchy collar of his private's uniform, knowing none of the guys particularly liked their army attire. Max had to have his shirt tailored to fit his wide neck and his pants let out to accommodate his broad waist. Apparently, they didn't get many infantrymen of Max's dimensions. Despite the humiliation of it, Max said the army's precision needlework was second only to their mother's.

Frankie complained that his drab olive uniform only drew unwanted attention to his red hair, and Rat had to roll up his sleeves that hung long on his scrawny arms. Even Brubaker had a change of uniform. After giving up his station manager's bow tie and herringbone blazer for a major's uniform, he now wore the insignia of a lieutenant colonel, taking full command of the team now that Dawson was gone. Win or lose, Brubaker was the new man in charge.

While the fellas were being shown quarters, Colonel Brubaker was off somewhere with the captain of the vessel getting Bobbi and Audrey situated. Audrey had bonded with Bobbi back at Fort Hamilton, helping her navigate the loss of her father. Despite their common bereavement, each shared a fondness for singing, as well as a mutual love of New York. It was a natural friendship, yet it made Wally uncomfortable. Audrey knew nothing of his feelings for Bobbi, whatever those feelings now were.

"Watch your step." This time, the soldier pointed to the lip of a door port, which Wally carefully traversed.

"You want us to watch our head or watch our step?" said Frankie. "Not sure we can do both at the same time."

Wally started to laugh, but with a painful "clank" hit his head once again on an overhead pipe. "Son of a—!"

"You'll get the hang of it," laughed the young soldier.

"Doubt it." Wally stopped to rub the growing knot on his forehead, feeling more misery than pain.

Despite the dim flickering light, Wally and the others kept pace with their guide from one corridor to the next, hunching over as they moved past dozens of other young men. As Wally trod slowly, Max pushed past him to follow the soldier. His breathing was heavy, and he struggled to move his wide girth down the narrowing passage. Wally quickly understood why Max had gotten the 4-F declining his service in the first place. He wasn't built for this.

"How much longer?" huffed Max.

"Getting close," said the soldier.

The farther they got from the hatch, the louder the rumble of the ship's oil-fired boilers grew. Wally tried to draw a bagpipe breath to calm himself but found the ship's interior was stifling hot and dank, humid with perspiration, and not at all like the Boston chill they'd left topside. Wally attributed the dense air belowdecks to the hordes of other young men he saw aboard, thousands like him who had no idea what was in store for them, sweating in clothes not their own, in a town not their own, heading to a place they'd never been, to face an enemy they hardly understood.

He called ahead to their guide: "Hey, where'd they take the girls?"

The soldier stopped and looked around as if making sure no one could hear their conversation. He lowered his voice. "Your CO took them up to the first officer's quarters to keep them hidden," he whispered. "Girls probably ain't safe on the *Edmund B.* with this many lonely guys, not that we ever get any girls here. Told me to keep it quiet and you should too. Only a few of us know."

Wally eyed the crowds of men around him and nodded.

"'Sides, girls don't want to smell sweat, barf, and farts, right?" The guy winked and continued forward, but Wally wanted to tell him that no reasonable person, regardless of gender, wanted to smell those things.

The vessel was now only an hour away from departure. Charging into war contradicted every instinct Wally had and, despite the certainty he and his friends had expressed back at Fort Hamilton, that resolve was quickly evaporating.

"Here we are," said the soldier when they finally arrived at their quarters. Wally stared at the shallow bunks, three high, floor to ceiling, on both sides of the space assigned. The bunks barely offered enough room for their duffels, let alone their sleeping bodies.

"We're supposed to sleep here?" said Wally.

"How long is this trip?" said Frankie, his voice cracking.

"Eleven days, give or take," said the soldier. "My advice is to get topside as much as you can. Watch the horizon. Get your sea legs. Fresh air helps."

"I call bottom bunk," said Rat. He tossed his duffel onto the lowest bed to the right.

"Me too," said Frankie, choosing the one on the left.

"Chrissakes," said Max, nearly out of breath. "You guys trying to kill me?"

Frankie looked at Max's protruding belly. "All right," he said. "But don't blame me if I step on your face when I need to get down to use the can."

Max sighed, exasperated. He dropped his duffel at his feet and mopped his brow, bathed in sweat, with a handkerchief. "Eleven days…"

"How many fellas are on this ship, anyway?" asked Rat.

"Five thousand and change," said their guide.

"Jesus, Mary, and Joseph," Frankie murmured. He crossed himself. "I'm an only child. Never even shared a bathroom."

"That's about to change," the guy chortled. "Could be worse, though. You fellas got first shift. You get to sleep at night."

"What do you mean?" said Wally.

"When you wake up in the morning, you'll swap your bunks with another set of guys who'll sleep here during the day. With ship's capacity nearly doubled, that's how they make things work. Half at day, half at night. Be sure to leave room for their duffels too."

Five thousand men sharing bunks hardly sounded to Wally like it was making things work. Then again, if the Americans had any hope of winning the war, they had to be willing to do whatever it took, even if that meant cramming themselves into a sardine can floating out to sea. It was a good reminder that Wally wasn't the only person aboard who was uncomfortable. In fact, he couldn't imagine a single man on board who would be.

"See you topside," the guy said. "Remember, best way there is straight on through." He pointed in the direction he was heading and vanished farther into the guts of the ship.

Wally wondered how Audrey and Bobbi were getting on. He figured if they were in the first officer's quarters, that meant they could avoid triple-stacked bunks. He hoped he'd see them at some point during their journey, but nothing was predictable anymore.

"Gotta get some air," said Max. He was still wiping his forehead, which flowed like Niagara Falls.

"Me too," said Frankie.

There were no portholes on their deck that sat below the waterline, and Wally was beginning to feel claustrophobic. On top of everything else, the last thing he wanted to do was faint in the belly of a troopship. "Let's all go," he said.

The team made their way farther down the passageway, encountering scores of other men like them packed into adjacent spaces, rucksacks littering the walkways.

"Remember where we were," said Rat over the rumble of the engines. "We're section one-eighty-three." He pointed to the numbers painted on the steel reinforcements as they moved through each of the quarters, trying not to step on anyone.

The guys finally found another companionway and climbed the stairs as if they were clawing their way out of their graves. When they emerged topside, they saw that thousands of sailors and soldiers had the same idea as them. Men crowded the deck, perched themselves in open hatches, or lined the ship's railings, catching one last glimpse of Boston before braving the open sea and whatever waited for them abroad. Of course, Wally never even had a first glimpse of Boston before this morning's haul from Fort Hamilton. He'd never even set foot out of New York.

"Hurry," said Max, pointing. "I see a spot by the left rail."

"Port rail," corrected Rat.

Max ignored him and maneuvered his way quickly between a crowd of other men using his girth to shoehorn space for the lot of them. Wally saw dozens of other troopships anchored in the harbor, each brimming with soldiers and sailors. No families were on the docks to see off their enlisted, not that Wally's family would have been allowed there anyway. This was a secured port, designated only for departing servicemen and the Gray Ladies, the women from the Red Cross who offered coffee and doughnuts to the throngs that were shipping off. It was a cruel irony to Wally that, despite the crushing crowd around him, everyone on the ship was, in a profound way, completely alone.

He turned toward the horizon, toward the morning glow of the rising sun, reminded that this was the last day of Hanukkah. His wish had been to avoid this very moment, this very circumstance, heading blindly and hopelessly toward his likely death. And yet his actions, his choices, had put him right here, in the churning Boston Harbor, watching tugboats pull enormous troopships like the USAT *Edmund B. Alexander*, filled with thousands of other men like him, out to sea. It was much different than seeing such ships through binoculars from his Kensington rooftop. Among the hundreds of thousands of others already serving or leaving ports like this one, Wally was just one nervous, fainting army private who hoped to make a difference. It was ridiculous to ponder, yet too late to change his mind. So many people he cared about were on this ship, heading into the same unknown, all because they trusted him. He had convinced Max and Frankie to enter the contest and to accept the jingle mission back at WKOB. He was the first to urge that mission forward after Dawson had been killed. He had recruited Rat and even drawn in Audrey. He figured that meant he was now responsible for all their fates as well as his own.

He inhaled, hoping to marshal a little courage and quiet the bubbling anxiety in his chest. But the air he drew in was filled with oil smoke and the heavy, sweaty musk of five thousand other men.

The ship's horn bleated a series of low F sharp quarter notes ending in a long F sharp, announcing their departure. The gangplank was drawn, and the anchor retracted. Men cheered and raised their fists into the air, but not Wally. He had nothing to cheer about.

A mighty tugboat pulled the ship away from port, led the *Edmund B.* confidently toward the sun like Icarus, the hero from the Greek myth Wally had read about in school. Wally closed his eyes and counted Mississippis, remembering how Icarus's wax wings had melted like the last Hanukkah *shammos*, a punishment for his hubris, believing himself capable of more than he really was. Icarus fell to Earth and drowned, having lived only to serve as a warning to others. Clearly, Wally hadn't gotten the message.

The first two days at sea went by quickly despite the scarcity of tasks Wally and the others had been given. Apparently, there were more men than there were jobs to do aboard the *Edmund B. Alexander*, leaving many like Wally to find things to do to keep themselves busy as a means of forestalling their existential crises. Rat had found comfort reading past issues of the *Brooklyn Daily Eagle*, a stack of which he had taken from Fort Hamilton and packed into his swollen duffel. Wally had found Rat circling stories printed in the last two months, underlining sections, and tearing out specific articles from one paper to the next.

"What are you doing?" Wally had asked.

"I'm bored," Rat had said. "Figured I'd dive into a new project."

Wally didn't pretend to understand Rat and decided it was better not to ask. He was just happy the guy had found something to keep himself busy and out of the team's way. Instead, Wally spent much of his time during the first two days at sea helping Max deal with nausea. Wally had modeled his support for his brother after Audrey's usual answer to everything and suggested Max start with some Beech-Nut gum, a pack of which Wally had purchased at the Fort Hamilton base exchange before they left.

By their second morning, when the waves had gotten higher and the pitch of the troopship had rattled everything and everyone on board, even the gum provided Max with little comfort. "Chuck buckets" had been strategically placed throughout the ship, with many sailors and soldiers like Max huddled over the pails and latrines or leaning over the main deck rails. Turned out, even the most stalwart and purposeful men aboard the *Edmund B.* were inexperienced seafarers.

With so much illness and discomfort aboard, it may have been a good thing that the military only fed them twice a day, with rationing practiced even on the high seas. No longer were Wally and the thousands of others aboard the ship being offered turkey dinners. It was now reconstituted powders and canned foods. It was the same on the troopship as it was everywhere: too many mouths to feed and not enough to go around.

By the third day in open water, the guys had participated in a few games of craps and a handful of card games, joining two fellas from New Jersey who completed the last two of the six bunks in their quarters. None of them had any cash, so they gambled mostly with matchsticks, combs, cigarettes, packs of gum, and pots of pomade. Once his stomach had settled, Max proved to be an excellent gambler and had managed to win enough gum to last him the entire journey. He began to teach the other soldiers how to bluff convincingly, how to hold cards until the right moment, how to track where and when the face cards might show, all for a small cut of their eventual winnings. Wally had to admit, his brother did have moxie and knew how to use it.

Frankie, predictably, kept track of their winnings and used their army-issued journals to keep a pocket tab of all they'd earned.

Still, the anxiety, physical stress, and the idle reflection had begun to take its toll on the men aboard. Of all the members of Wally's team, only Rat appeared entirely unaffected by the churn of the sea and the crippling stress of their circumstances.

"Why is he always so perky?" said Frankie in the mess hall after Rat had left the table to return his dinner tray.

"Rats love ships," said Max. "He's right at home until there's trouble, and then he'll be the first to jump."

"I just wish I had what he has," said Frankie. "I'm sick of being sick."

Wally scanned the mess hall and the faces of the men that huddled over their rations at each standing table. Those men who dared to eat did so in shifts to accommodate the throngs of them, though not all of them chose to eat every day.

Wally searched the mess hall and found no sign of Bobbi or Audrey. "Where do you suppose the girls eat?" Wally asked.

"Probably dining on prime rib and caviar with the captain and Brubaker like they're at some swanky supper club," said Rat, retaking his seat.

"Why do you guys keep talking about food?" Max groaned. He hadn't touched his dinner.

"Guess we won't see the girls until we get to port," said Wally quietly, wondering which port they'd land in to get them close to London. All Wally knew was that, if New York had proved unsafe, no place a ship could take them would be any safer.

"Hey," said Max, finally showing some perk. "What was that birthday present Mom and Pop gave you? They were so excited about it, but things got crazy after that. Never got to see what it was."

Wally reached into his back pocket and pulled it out. "It's a harmonica," he said. Opened it in the taxi on the way to Fort Hamilton. "They even inscribed it." He flipped the shiny mouth harp over and read the inscription aloud: "'*Wherever you go—music.*'"

"Little did they know," said Max. "Sounds like good luck."

Wally put the harmonica to his lips and played their US war bond tune, the jingle that had started everything.

Max peered around at the others in the mess hall. "Better not play that," he said. "Shouldn't even talk about things until we get with Brubaker."

"Guess you're right," said Wally. He put the harmonica back in his pocket. "I'm gonna take a walk."

"Want some company?" said Rat.

"That's okay," said Wally. "Just wanna clear my head."

Wally was in no mood for Rat's enthusiasm and felt pained at each reminder of Max and Frankie's discomfort. They were suffering, both of them, and it was all Wally's fault. There had been no time to consider the implications of their mission, no time for anyone to back out. They had all been so affected by the death of Colonel Dawson and the wish to press forward, none of them questioned the mission when Brubaker announced they'd be heading overseas. Everyone seemed committed to seeing it through, even though the details of how it would change their lives had not been fully explored. If Wally hadn't been so eager to save his own neck, to prove his worth, Max would still be pressing shirts and Frankie would still be stacking cans.

His family, and the families of his friends, had had their lives upended too, each of them now living at Fort Hamilton until their safety could be assured. He wanted to apologize to them all, to beg their forgiveness. But even if he figured out the right words, put them all in a letter, it would be weeks before such a letter would reach them, long after the damage had been done.

He made his way out of the mess hall, past the throng of men in the chow line. He grabbed his coat and made his way up the companionway to the deck of the rolling ship.

With the *Edmund B.* over its proper capacity, Wally could barely find a spot to be alone, even with nearly half the men asleep belowdecks. He finally spotted a small alcove near the lifeboats and took a seat by a thick coil of rope. Other guys walked by, but none noticed him there. It was just the privacy he needed.

He stared out at the churning, dark Atlantic, watching the ship's hull cleave the frothing brine. The sun was setting on their convoy, throwing shards of gold light through the leaden clouds, creating disruption amid the hundred shades of dismal gray. Wally wondered what life was like aboard the other smaller ships that flanked the *Edmund B.*, charging out to sea. He figured fellas aboard those ships were pondering, as he did, the troubling fact that the closer they got to their destination, the more dangerous things would become.

He reached into his coat pocket and pulled out his army-issued journal. Wally had been using his journal to write love songs about Bobbi. He had hardly spoken to her since her father had been killed and, though he was initially upset that she'd kept his enlistment status a secret from him, he'd once again moved on, forgiven her as he had when she manipulated him at the club, and now longed for a moment where they could be alone again as they had been on the roof of the Elving House. Writing love songs to her was the only outlet he had to take his mind off his troubles, and he was keeping his work, and his feelings for her, secret from the others. He flipped the pages to his latest stream of lyrics.

She's all smiles or she's all tears,
She's so much more than she appears.

She has my heart but doesn't know it.
Too afraid, I dare not show it.

Wanna be there to let her see.
The kinda man that I can be.

Oh, I gotta girl but she ain't mine
I think about her all the time.

Oh, I gotta girl but she don't know.
How can I say I love her so?

The thought of Bobbi brought a smile to Wally's face, but when someone approached, he quickly snapped closed his journal and tucked it away.

"Lipkin?"

Wally looked up. "Colonel Brubaker." He stood, his heels and toes together, and saluted, just as he'd been taught to do at Fort Hamilton.

The colonel stood tall beside the alcove, his slender frame and pronounced shoulders silhouetted by the setting sun that sparkled in his peppered hair. Seeing Brubaker in his uniform, two columns of buttons down his jacket front, medals on his chest, cuffs lined with gold stitching, and his wounded arm still in a sling, Wally thought the man looked downright heroic.

"At ease, Private Lipkin. Where are the others?"

"Mess hall," said Wally. "I just needed some air."

"I understand that," he said. The newly minted colonel looked out to the Atlantic, which glowed like a sea of gold, drinking in the waning light of dusk. "How're you holding up?"

"Haven't heaved a meal since yesterday," said Wally. "Can't say the same for Max."

"Big fellas have it the worst," said Brubaker. "Tell him to keep his eyes on the horizon."

"How are the girls?" said Wally.

"Same as you, I suppose," said Brubaker. "Eager to reach dry land."

"Do we get to see them?"

Brubaker pursed his lips. "Most of these men don't even know there are women on board," Brubaker replied. "Probably better to keep it that way."

"I understand," said Wally, but he remained unsatisfied.

"Glad I ran into you, though," said Brubaker. "Just wanted to say I had a ship-to-shore communiqué with your pal, Copulsky. Says your folks are fine. They're proud of you and Moxie and wanted to be sure you both were keeping warm."

Wally laughed. That sounded exactly like something his mother would say, always worrying about the wrong things.

"Colonel, sir?" Wally asked.

"Yeah, Lipkin?"

"Will Bobbi be okay?"

Brubaker gave a broken smile. "She's like her father. She's tough when it counts."

Wally just nodded.

"See you soon, Curly."

Brubaker marched off, and Wally saluted, left to his own thoughts.

Bobbi had been through so much, first losing her mother and then her father. Now, like Wally, she was charging toward danger rather than away from it. He wanted to be there for her, or perhaps he wanted her to be there for him. Either way, it was clear he'd have to wait.

Wally drew in the scents of the Atlantic, focused on the sounds of the seabirds and the crash of the waves against the ship's hull. It seemed daunting to spend six more days at sea, the risk growing each day they drew closer to the action.

Why, then, was he more concerned about telling a girl how he felt?

On their tenth day at sea, their last before scheduled landfall, Wally and his friends again stood at the mess hall tables, huddled over plates of reconstituted powdered eggs. They were exhausted and at the edge of their sanity. Christmas had been marred by death; Hanukkah had ended with their departure from dry land; and New Year's Eve had come and gone at sea with no resolutions, champagne toasts, or sweetheart kisses. He'd spent his time, instead, with a bunch of miserable men who were hardly in a mood to celebrate. But what was there to celebrate anyway?

"These are horrible," said Wally, pushing around the mess on his plate. "I can't do it." He put down his fork beside the beige pile of food. "Can't put another bite in my mouth."

"I don't even bother anymore," said Max. "It just comes right back."

"I like 'em with ketchup," said Rat. He shoveled a load of the mixture into his mouth, grinning as he chewed.

"Something inside you is defective," said Frankie.

Rat downed the remains of his food. "It's not that bad. Besides, everything tastes better the closer we get to the UK. Never been to England...or anywhere, really."

Max gnawed a piece of dry toast, averting his eyes from Rat's breakfast. Wally figured his brother must have lost ten pounds in the days since leaving Boston.

"I hear British fish-and-chips are great," said Rat. "They eat 'em with vinegar."

"Oh, Christ," said Max. He set his half-eaten toast onto his tray.

Wally wasn't particularly eager to reach England. He'd read about the Blitzes in '40 and '41, had seen the newsreels that showed the destruction, and remembered thinking that no one was safe in the United Kingdom. Of course, no one was safe anywhere anymore thanks to the Germans.

Just then, a short soldier with a cap pulled low over his brow stepped up next to Wally and the guys. He pushed aside Wally's tray of abandoned "eggs" and set his elbows on the stand-up table. "You fellas look kinda glum," the guy said in a familiar voice. He smelled like peppermint.

"Audrey?"

Wally glanced beneath the brim of the soldier's cap and saw Audrey's face, her hair tucked under her hat.

She smirked and shot him a knowing look. "Hello, Walter."

Wally searched the mess hall to assure none of the nearby soldiers had noticed her.

"What are you doing here?" he whispered urgently.

Frankie, Max, and Rat quickly realized what was happening. They moved around the table to positions, trying to obscure any view of Audrey by others in the mess hall.

She pulled her hat a little lower, sank into her baggy uniform, and leaned forward. "Couldn't stand being cooped up anymore," she said. "Needed some fresh air."

"Ain't so fresh in here," said Frankie.

"Are you getting better food than we are?" asked Wally.

She glared at the mystery mound on his plate. "Same," she said. "Except we have to eat and sleep in the first officer's quarters. Feels like we've been in prison. Captain did give us a few bars of chocolate, though—and whiskey. Never had whiskey before. Can't say I like it much."

"I'm sure it's better than powdered eggs," said Wally.

"Can we stop talking about food?" pleaded Max.

"Whiskey..." said Frankie. His eyes drifted skyward like those kids in the poem about sugarplums.

"Bet you're happy to be in some nice quarters," said Wally. "We're sleeping in bunks, three high."

"I got a bed," said Audrey. "But I'm sharing it with Bobbi."

Wally perked at the mention of Bobbi's name and the thought of sharing her bed. "Is she okay?" he asked a little too quickly.

Audrey scrutinized him before replying. "Most nights she cries. Most days she keeps quiet." Audrey shook her head. "It's hard. Her dad died right in her arms."

Wally gave a solemn nod. "Her mother too," he said. "She told me she found her dead at the bottom of the stairs when she was younger."

Audrey gasped. "That's horrible. She didn't mention that."

"Poor thing," said Max.

"Don't think she talks much about her mother," said Wally. He recalled Bobbi's distress that night on the roof when she told him her sad story. Now her sad story had gotten even sadder.

"This whole trip has me thinking about Johnny," she said. "He wrote me about his own troopship when he deployed to Italy. Said it was crammed with other soldiers like this." She looked around the mess hall. "He would have never guessed I'd be on my own troopship someday."

The group grew quiet, and Wally felt the pang of his own culpability. Johnny would never have approved of the danger Wally had put Audrey in.

The shipboard horn player, a tall fellow named Alvin Mayfield from Alabama who bunked near Wally, walked to the front of the mess hall. He lifted his bugle to his lips and trumpeted the end of dinner. This meant they had to clear out for the next wave of soldiers.

"Will you tell Bobbi something for me?" said Wally.

"Sure," said Audrey, but Wally couldn't decide what message he wanted her to deliver. The guys collected their trays and turned to leave.

Audrey cocked her head. "Walter?" she prompted. "What's the message? I gotta run."

"Tell her—" He stopped. What did he want to say? "Tell her to meet me topside by the aft lifeboats at seven."

"Is that safe?" said Audrey.

"You're here, aren't you?" said Wally.

Audrey looked around as if searching for a reason to deny Wally's request.

"Please?"

"Fine," said Audrey. "Seven. Aft lifeboats. But I can't guarantee she'll want to risk it."

Something in Audrey's tone sounded angry, but she hurried into the depths of the ship before Wally could ask what was wrong.

"Glad Audrey is getting through this all right," said Max, slipping his tray into a rack with the others.

Wally nodded, but his thoughts were still on Bobbi. "I'm gonna take a walk," he said.

"And I'm going back to my newspapers," said Rat.

"No problem," said Frankie. "We have a poker game to win."

"Got that right!" said Max. He shook Frankie's hand as if they were part of some sort of conspiracy.

Once the others had left, Wally made his way across the mess hall and over to Mayfield the bugler. Mayfield was a lanky fellow, curved like a snap bean. He walked like he had all day to get where he was going, but what he seemed to lack in intelligence, he made up for in eagerness, and Wally genuinely liked him.

"Hey, Mayfield," said Wally.

"Oh, hey, Lipkin. How's it going?"

"Ship smells like an outhouse and I'm going stir crazy. How 'bout you?"

Mayfield just looked at Wally, perplexed.

"Can I ask you a favor?" said Wally. "It's a little...unconventional."

"Favor?" Mayfield stood taller like someone being noticed for the first time. "Name it."

Wally sat against the base of a topside bulkhead looking out over the massive deck of the *Edmund B. Alexander*, marveling at the herculean effort that must've gone into the giant vessel's construction. How could so much steel float? One deck alone could support thousands of men, eager, clueless souls floating on the deep-blue sea. Then again, one German torpedo could put it all to the test.

Wally drew what he hoped would be a calming breath and, instead, filled his lungs with sea air tainted by the stench of motor oil and barf. After so many days at sea, the aroma no longer sickened him. It just reminded him that he was far from home. He longed for the smells of his mother's pot roast, the scents of his father's pipe tobacco, or the fragrance of roasted chestnuts from Manhattan street vendors, but feared he'd never smell those things again.

He stood from his perch, gathered his army-issue service coat around him, and focused instead on his journal, scribbling more lyrics onto its pages as dusk began to fall. He had spent most of the journey filling it with love songs, writing the words he didn't know how to say out loud.

But at that moment, words escaped him. He was too distracted by the plan he'd set in motion. He stuffed his journal inside his coat, pulled out his uncle's pocket watch, and saw that it was ten minutes until seven o'clock. Suddenly, two large sailors climbed to his place above the bulkhead carrying an amplifier box and three microphones on stands.

"You Lipkin?" said one of the guys.

"That's me," said Wally.

"Where d'ya want these?"

"How about right there?" Wally pointed to a clear spot, just beside him, facing the deck below.

As the two sailors set up the equipment, Mayfield arrived. "I got O'Neill to take the second dinner shift," the bugler said, his voice bouncy like a child's. "And I brought my horn like you asked." He held up his bugle.

"Thanks, Mayfield. That's perfect."

Wally knew what he had planned could get him in trouble. It meant breaking the first rule, to lay low. But he'd go crazy if he didn't try something, even if it was something impulsive and rash.

The thought made his heart race and his cheeks flush.

One Mississippi, two Mississippi...

He pulled his harmonica from his hip pocket and played "Oh! Susanna," a song he'd learned on his Uncle Sherman's harmonica which he'd gotten as a gift from his mother when he was seven. It was his "Hanukkah Harmonica," and it had been a gateway to his love of music and of the piano. In fact, once he'd moved his interest to the piano, he'd lost that first harmonica. Now, this new one from his parents drew him back in time, putting music right in his pocket where he needed it tonight.

"Hey, you're pretty good!" Wally heard.

He jerked out of his thoughts and stopped playing, realizing a small group of soldiers had gathered below, next to the lifeboats.

"Oh, thanks," said Wally.

"Don't stop on our account," said a towheaded guy with freckled skin. Three others clambered over and leaned against a railing.

"Yeah," one of them called. "Ain't heard music in days. Keep playing."

Wally took a shallow breath, counted three Mississippis, and tried to stay composed.

"How about 'In the Mood'?" said Wally. Somehow, that song seemed fitting.

"You bet!"

Wally looked slyly to Mayfield. "Those microphones ready?"

"Yessir!"

"And the big guys?"

"Right there." Mayfield thumbed over to the two large sailors who had brought the equipment. They stood on either side of his platform where the stairs descended to the main deck, their arms crossed like bouncers at the Diamond Club. It had cost him ten bucks, but those guys seemed worth it.

Wally nodded, stepped over to a microphone, and played "In the Mood" on his harmonica. At first, he was struck by the echo of his harmonica song, its amplified sound bouncing around the ship's deck, replacing the crash of waves, the loud rumble of the ship's engine, and the murmur of unhappy men. Once he got used to the way the harmonica music sounded, he found himself picking up the pace, tapping his foot, and playing faster and louder with each stanza until he was really cooking.

A couple soldiers clapped along. Soon, a half dozen others had come over to listen.

Purple and pink clouds streaked the foreign skies above him, illuminated by the setting sun. But it was Wally's music, not the colorful skies, that drew the soldiers' attention until his audience had grown to more than a hundred.

When he finished playing, he gave a loud and breathy crescendo and got an inordinate amount of applause. Mayfield nodded, appearing impressed with Wally's playing.

"Encore!" called the towhead. "Let's hear another, fella."

"Uh, sure." Wally enjoyed playing music again after so many days away from his piano, but what if his plan didn't work?

"Need a singer?" someone called from behind.

An electric charge ran through Wally, and he spun toward the source of the voice. It was Bobbi LaFleur, seven o'clock on the nose. She had emerged from a door behind him and appeared like a vision from a dream. However, she wasn't in disguise as Audrey had been in the mess hall. Bobbi wore a daisy-yellow blouse and a pleated green skirt, her golden hair curled and buoyant. She wasn't pretending to be anything other than the beautiful singer she was and didn't seem to care who saw her. Or maybe that was exactly what she desired: to be seen.

Wally's heart leapt and, apparently, his was not the only one. The crowd of men, now numbering around two hundred, started hooting and whistling at the sight of Bobbi, stirring memories of Wally's night with her at the Diamond Club.

"Bobbi!" said Wally. "Glad you could make it."

The two big sailors that Mayfield had recruited came forward to stand guard around them, just as Wally had instructed.

Bobbi beamed at the attention of the crowd below and stepped up to the microphone. "Hey, boys!" she called. She gave a ceremonial wave like the queen of a hometown parade, and the men went wild again, the crowd growing now to several hundred. Pale, sick faces were transformed by smiles. Even Bobbi appeared joyful.

Wally's plan had worked.

"How about 'Boogie Woogie Bugle Boy'?" said Wally. He elbowed Mayfield, interrupting his longing stare at Bobbi.

"Right," Mayfield stammered. "I know that one." He blew into his horn's mouthpiece to clear it.

Bobbi touched Wally's arm. "Thanks, Walter. I needed this."

Wally smiled. "I figured."

"Wait here a second," she said.

Bobbi raced back to the aft-side door and pulled out Audrey who looked stunned to be revealed so unceremoniously to the troops. Audrey was still wearing a soldier's uniform until Bobbi pulled off Audrey's hat to reveal her locks of nut-brown hair.

"Bobbi, what are you doing?" she snapped.

"You only live once, honey."

Wally feared Audrey was out of her element and would only get angry at the reveal of her hair. But when she faced the crowd below and heard them cheer for her too, she smiled.

"All right," Audrey said. "I'm in."

Wally watched the fervent men surging below the bulkhead staring up at Wally, Mayfield, and the girls and feared the wild audience could quickly get out of control, but the men in the crowd just gawked. Of course, the pair of muscular sailors guarding their flanks and the bulkhead behind them didn't allow for much else.

Bobbi smiled at Wally and Mayfield. "Hit it, boys."

Wally and Alvin leaned toward their microphones and began to play the song's intro on the bugle and harmonica. To Wally's surprise, after only a couple measures, Mayfield proved adept at matching Wally's cadence. The amplifier raised the sound of the harmonica to match the power of the bugle, so their tune resonated throughout the crowd and across the ship's deck.

When both gals jumped in to sing the lyrics, a roar rose from the wide-eyed men as though they were hearing music for the first time in their lives.

The biggest surprise, however, was how Audrey's voice created a perfect harmony with Bobbi's. Her singing had started softly, but as the song progressed, she seemed to grow more confident, singing about how the company jumps when the bugle boy plays reveille. Her voice filled with a richness that not only seemed to astonish Bobbi but everyone else on board, whom Wally now thought of as members of Company B about whom the girls sang.

Audrey's vocals and movements became more certain. She appeared to take joy from it all. Wally knew Audrey could sing, but never knew what a good performer she was, and finally understood why she had persisted in her efforts to join their jingle crew.

During Mayfield's impressive solo interlude, the girls improvised a dance together, drawing from a friendship no doubt honed from sharing quarters for the entire journey. They moved in synchronicity, the bugle punctuating each step and hand wave.

The men in the crowd cheered and clapped along. And, in a flash, Wally was transported away from the *Edmund B.*, away from war and longing, to a place of pure and perfect music.

Bobbi was smiling, something he hadn't seen her do since his horrible birthday, and it made it all worth it.

When the song ended and Mayfield's echoing bugle sound dissolved into the sea air, the crowd erupted with applause, calling for more. However, before the performers could comply, one of the big sailors dashed over and whispered into Mayfield's ear.

The bugler's shoulders slumped. He lifted his horn and, instead of playing a song, played the tune that signaled the changing of sleeping shifts.

The power to the microphones was turned off, the crowd groaned, and the show was over faster than it had begun. Apparently, someone in command had decided the fun was over. The once happy hordes of men grumbled as the magic of the performance ended and the reality of their situation returned.

Wally turned to thank Bobbi, to connect with her. But she and Audrey quickly disappeared back through the door from which they had come, heeding the imposing reality of their circumstances.

The disgruntled crowd dispersed, the colorful clouds succumbed to nightfall, and soon the dry-cleaning jingle boy found himself alone with the disconcerted bugle boy under the darkening sky.

"Did that really happen?" said Mayfield, still swooning.

Wally faced the horizon, his heart sinking in the sea. "No," he said. "That was just a stupid dream."

From his top bunk, Wally stared at the overhead pipes. He had hit his head on those damn pipes every morning since they'd arrived, and this morning, his last aboard the *Edmund B. Alexander*, had started no different. The knot on his skull had now formed a knot of its own, and he wondered, if he kept at it, whether he might eventually knock some sense into himself.

He swung his legs over the side of the bunk and leapt forward, landing softly in his socks like a cat burglar on the cold metal deck, careful not to wake Rat, Frankie, Max, or the fellas from New Jersey in the bunks beside him. He rubbed his sore head and decided to skip the salty shower. Instead, he dressed in his uniform, pulled tight the laces of his boots, and pushed his arms into his warm wool coat, all before Mayfield played the morning reveille.

Despite his headache, his nagging nausea, and his persistent fear of fainting, today Wally had something to be happy about. Today was scheduled landfall. His plan to coax Bobbi out of seclusion had worked, even though he hadn't had a chance to have a real conversation with her. Today, however, that would all change.

Wally crept quietly past the sleeping soldiers, held his breath through the compartments thick with the scents of men, and climbed to the main deck, which shined with the rays of the dawn sun.

He gazed east, toward the bow, over the throngs of exhausted night-shift soldiers staggering around the main deck like the woken dead. It was there he spotted a familiar figure at the portside rail, smoking. It was a privilege allowed only above decks and only in daylight hours. A lit cigarette at night, it was said, could be seen by an enemy from the air.

Wally walked over. "Morning, sir." He saluted.

Colonel Brubaker faced him, his lips pinching the last inch of a dying cigarette.

"Morning, Lipkin. Ready for that?" Brubaker pulled the cigarette from his lips and used it to point toward several dark spots on the horizon.

"Is that land, sir?"

"British Isles." Brubaker blew smoke into the pink sky. "Should land in Wales in a few hours." He flicked his smoldering nub into the sea. "After that, straight on to London."

Wally looked around to assure they were alone. "Sir, what happens in London?"

"We pick up where we left off, Private Lipkin. Jingles, secret messages, battles won, lives saved." He rubbed his arm still hanging in its sling.

"How do we do this without Colonel Dawson?"

"Now that is the question, isn't it?" Brubaker turned his inscrutable face back toward the land mass and let his words hang like the salt in the air.

Wally looked away, trying to mask his concerns. He faced the sea spray that blanketed the bow as the ship charged onward.

"Look, Curly," Brubaker said. "I knew when you joined the mission, you never had any plans of getting aboard a troopship. All you kept asking about was the Washington job. But you convinced me you could make a difference here, now. Has that changed?"

"No, sir."

Brubaker gave a half smile. "I'll make you this promise, then: I'll do my damnedest to keep you out of harm's way. That a deal?"

Wally looked at Brubaker's injured arm. "Not sure you can make that deal, sir," he said.

Brubaker laughed. "'Fraid trying is the best I can do, the best any of us can do. But try I will."

"Then I guess I'll take it."

Brubaker nodded. "You gotta promise me something, though. No more stunts like the one last night."

Wally had hoped beyond reason that his performance with Bobbi had escaped Brubaker's attention.

"I saw the show, and I gotta admit, I was entertained. I know you wanted to impress Barbara Ann," he said, "but it puts the whole operation at risk when you ignore my orders. You can't expect me to keep you safe when you work against my efforts to do that very thing."

"Sorry, sir. Just figured she needed a little music."

Their conversation was interrupted by the sudden approach of Frankie, Max, and Rat. They each saluted Brubaker, and then continued an argument that seemed to be underway.

"You can't make me skip breakfast," said Rat. "It's the most important meal of the day."

"Powder ain't a meal," said Max. "'Specially if you can't keep it down. Besides, I can't bear to watch you eat anymore. You're like a stray dog at a dumpster."

Frankie squinted into the distance. "Is that land?" He pointed ahead, over the waves.

"It is," said Brubaker. "Keep your eyes peeled for U-boats or planes, though. They tend to cause trouble 'round here."

"U-boats?" said Frankie. His eyes grew wide, and he searched the surface of the waves for the phantom sea vessels that could be haunting the waters. "You gotta be kidding."

"I'm sure things'll be fine." Brubaker laughed.

"I'm gonna go check for periscopes," said Rat, and he climbed to a higher deck.

"That's it," said Frankie. "I'm throwing him to the sharks." He raced to catch Rat, leaving Max and Wally alone with the colonel.

Brubaker looked to Max. "How're you holding up, Moxie?"

"Looking forward to some real food, sir."

"I think we might be able to manage that," said Brubaker. "Now, if you excuse me, I've got some final arrangements to handle before landfall."

The brothers saluted and Brubaker saluted back. He then turned on his heel and disappeared through a door into the ship's interior.

The sound of Mayfield's reveille put a final punctuation on the moment, announcing the changing of sleeping shifts one last time. However, with the UK only hours away, Wally figured few men would be hitting the bunks today.

"Was Brubaker angry with you?" said Max. "I heard about your little number last night with Bobbi and Audrey."

"He wasn't happy."

"Do me a favor," said Max. "Stop being so reckless."

"Reckless?"

"That stunt with Copulsky when you thought he was a Nazi? That was reckless. Now you're disobeying Brubaker on the high seas. Reckless again. Trust me, Walter, one day your luck will run out."

Wally sighed and then faced the churning sea, his eyes on the horizon and the dark land ahead. "What makes you think it hasn't already?"

11

Skeletons of the Past

I t was nightfall by the time the *Edmund B. Alexander* led a dozen US vessels toward the mouth of the river Mersey. The name sounded a bit like "mercy," which seemed fitting since the river spelled the end to the suffering that had plagued the crew and passengers for days. The waters that fed the river were serene, and the ship was now steady, pulled by a tugboat toward the port. Despite the calm, Wally felt like his body was still swaying to the ocean waves. It was how he had felt for the entire journey, his entire life, searching for some sort of balance he could never seem to find.

To gain his footing and get a better view, Wally clutched a belaying pin along the troopship's guardrail. He stood beside Max, Frankie, Rat, and Mayfield the horn player, who had begun to shadow him ever since their impromptu performance with Bobbi. Wally liked Mayfield and had formed a friendship with him over the days aboard the ship. Nevertheless, they'd part ways soon enough, and Wally tried not to let himself or Mayfield get too attached.

"Liverpool," said Mayfield. "Never would've guessed I'd end up here."

"Don't think anyone on this boat figured they'd end up here," said Wally. He drew in the scents of their new surroundings and thought the Mersey smelled a lot like the East River, a blend of fish and machine fumes; only, here there was an added layer of anticipation.

The sky above was filled with silver barrage balloons tethered to buildings on either side of the river, twinkling under the early moonlight. The balloons were shaped like mini Hindenburgs, hovering over the port as if they were part of some sort of welcoming parade for the ships that traveled by. Wally knew the barrage balloons were intended to disrupt enemy fire from above but questioned how effective they were when he noticed the upside-down hull of a wrecked ship and the mast of another, sunken at the portside mouth of the river, skeletons telling the tale of past danger. The sight of them sent a chill through him. The war in Britain had noticeably progressed beyond the air-raid drills and victory gardens of New York.

Farther downriver, just a few hundred yards from the river's banks, heaps of mortar and bricks, the shattered remains of buildings, sat piled amid toppled smokestacks, the staggering result of enemy bombings.

"Jesus, Mary, and Joseph," said Frankie, crossing himself.

"Holy crap," said Rat.

Max just stared and said nothing.

Wally wondered if the British simply lacked the resources to fix the port, or if it was left in such disrepair to warn new soldiers of the horrors they could only imagine, the danger that awaited them. Whatever the reason, despite the damage, the port continued to receive new troops like those aboard the ships in their convoy. The machine of war churned on.

Bleached stones along the banks were strewn with rotting seaweed and peppered with mussel shells. Gulls dove and dipped through the air, playing as though the surrounding destruction was meaningless to them, and he supposed it was. Wally wished he had their ignorance but remembered the lesson he'd learned at the sanatorium. Birds are meant to fly.

He moved his attention to the top decks, hoping to spot Bobbi among his shipmates, but couldn't find trace of her anywhere. No doubt Brubaker had chided her and Audrey just as he'd chided Wally, urging them to follow orders and keep a low profile until ordered to disembark.

Wally slid his hand into his coat and clutched his journal full of love songs. Aside from his friendship with Mayfield and the memory of his ad hoc performance with Bobbi, that journal was one of the few positive things he had to show for his time aboard the *Edmund B. Alexander*. Owing to her seclusion, it had been the only way he'd been able to express his hopeful feelings for her. Still, he had no idea what he wanted to say to her once he finally got his chance.

"Can't wait for solid land," said Frankie.

"And solid food," said Max.

That's when an announcement was made over the ship's comm.

"All hands, all hands, this is your captain. As you can see, we're approaching the port of Liverpool. Disembarkation will happen in groups and in an orderly fashion."

The captain went on to describe the process, which would start with the night-shift soldiers of certain rank and end with the day-shift soldiers.

"Ugh," said Frankie. "This is going to take forever."

Suddenly, Brubaker pushed forward to meet Wally and the team at the portside rail. "Glad I found you fellas. Hang back a moment."

"Colonel?" Wally perked at Brubaker's eagerness.

"We're first to disembark," he said softly.

"Oh, thank God," said Max.

Mayfield overheard the colonel's words and grabbed Wally by the arm. "Well, Lipkin," said Mayfield, "I'm just a regular grunt, so I guess this means we gotta say goodbye." Mayfield held a sadness in his eyes that pinched at Wally's emotions.

"Guess so." Wally held out his hand to shake Mayfield's. "It's been a real pleasure, Alvin—"

"Don't get sappy on us, Tuscaloosa." Colonel Brubaker stepped forward and pointed at Mayfield. "You're with us too."

"Huh?" Mayfield's jaw dropped.

"Heard you and Private Lipkin last night up there at the bulkhead. You make quite a musical pair," said Brubaker, "and we happen to need a horn player with signal experience. I reviewed a lot of files of men on this ship, and yours caught my attention: high marks in signal corps training, great field ratings during basic, excellent music skills...and you earned the trust of Private Lipkin, whom I consider an excellent judge of character." At Mayfield's incredulous look, the colonel took his hand and shook it. "You're a fit, Private Mayfield. You're on the team. Go get your bag."

Mayfield's mouth opened to reveal a smile full of crooked teeth. He gave an enthusiastic salute and said, "Got no idea what that means, Colonel, but if you're needing me, I'm in!" He turned to Wally and hugged him like he was squeezing a giant tube of toothpaste.

"That's great!" Wally squeaked. It seemed his net of doom had roped Alvin Mayfield into whatever danger awaited them, and a pang of guilt squeezed Wally's heart like the onslaught of the bugler's embrace. Still, he knew the team could use all the help they could get, and he'd rather have someone like Mayfield at their side, whom he knew he could trust.

Given the unknown risks ahead, however, the real question was whether Mayfield could trust him.

Donned in their uniforms and heavy coats, and laden with their rucksacks, Wally and the others climbed the stairs toward the main deck to gather at the gangplank one last time. Wally was eager to say goodbye to the *Edmund B. Alexander*'s powdered food, sour puke smells, and crowded latrines. He confirmed his journal was in his pocket; shifted his duffel to his other shoulder; and followed Max, Frankie, and Rat as they said their own goodbyes to soldiers with whom they'd become friendly. Given the state of the war, Wally figured it was a crapshoot whether they'd ever see those men again, but promises were made to stay in touch and reconnect, nonetheless.

Rat strode beside Wally, looking around nostalgically. "Place wasn't so bad when you think about it," he said.

"I'd rather not think about it," said Wally. "Get moving."

"Wait for me," called Mayfield. He had both his bugle case and a trumpet case tied with twine to the bag he carried over his shoulder.

Managing to stay together amid the surging crowd, the team arrived above decks under the darkening sky and made their way through throngs of enlisted men in the cold air to the gangplank where the captain of the *Edmund B.* stood with Audrey, Brubaker, and Bobbi at his side. Wally's heart leapt at the sight of Bobbi, and he fought the urge to call out her name over the loud chatter of men. She and Audrey both wore women's khaki-colored army uniforms, tapered slacks, and jackets with gold buttons down the front, sleeve cuffs sporting two white stripes. They looked official, confident, and more ready for duty than he was.

Rat was the first to salute the captain and colonel.

"Sirs!" Rat shouted, and the others repeated his call.

The ship's captain, a stocky man with a graying beard and a row of medals along the breast of his black wool coat, saluted them all, and Brubaker followed suit.

"At ease, gentlemen," the captain said. He then turned to Brubaker. "Roger, in the name of Howard Dawson, I wish you and your team the best of luck." He then nodded at Bobbi. "Barbara Ann, your father was one of the finest men with whom I've ever had the pleasure of serving. I'm sure he'd be proud of you, whatever it is you and Colonel Brubaker have brewing."

"Thank you, Captain," said Bobbi. She saluted and then broke protocol to hug him, a gesture he seemed more than happy to allow. Wally tried to imagine himself on the receiving end of one of those hugs.

"Keep her nose dry, Charlie." Brubaker gave the captain a final salute.

"Always have. Always will."

The men shook hands, and with that, the crew followed Brubaker down the gangplank, past the line of other waiting servicemen. Soldiers eyed the ladies, gawking as they passed, and a few even whistled, but the team faced forward and tried to ignore the attention.

Once at the dimly lit dock, Brubaker led them past a row of small buildings to a gray van awaiting their arrival. Beside the van stood a driver, a slender man of medium build in his twenties, wearing a Royal Navy uniform and round glasses. The young man took one last drag of his cigarette, crushed it under his boot and blew out a puff of smoke.

He saluted Brubaker when the crew approached. "Evening, all," he said, "and welcome to the British Isles." His East London accent gave him an air of authority.

Bobbi was the first to reply. "Well, hello," she said flirtatiously. She saluted like a pinup girl. "I'm Bobbi."

"Petty Officer Niles Drummond," he replied with a nod. "At your service."

Wally seethed when he saw Drummond peer over his glasses and wink at Bobbi while retrieving her bags.

Who did this guy think he was?

The rest of the team followed Bobbi, tossed their duffels into the rear of the vehicle, and moved to take their seats in the van.

Brubaker took the passenger seat on the left of the driver.

"Forgot they drive on the wrong side here," said Frankie.

Drummond closed the van's rear doors and stepped over to help the others take their seats. "Yanks got it wrong," he said. "Brits drive on the proper side. The whole thing was decided over tea, right after you lot left for the colonies."

The group all laughed except Wally, who did not find Drummond's humor amusing.

The petty officer helped Bobbi into the van, where she chose the seat furthest in the back. Wally climbed in and sat next to her, hoping to find time to talk during the drive. He figured he'd start by mentioning her excellent performance of "Boogie Woogie Bugle Boy" or compliment her on how nice she looked in her sharp uniform. But the pair was quickly joined by Audrey, who sandwiched him in.

"Glad to be off that ship," said Audrey, but all Wally did was nod. It seemed the world did not want him alone with Bobbi.

The others piled in after them, and once they were all seated, Drummond took the driver's seat and strapped himself in.

Rat gawked out one of the van's side windows toward the troopship. "Gonna miss that old girl," he said, though no one shared the sentiment.

"Good riddance," said Frankie.

"Sorry we couldn't get you on a train," said Drummond, turning the engine and switching on the headlights. "Most of the main rails to London are still quite damaged."

Wally had read in one of Rat's newspapers that the '41 Blitz and the string of subsequent German attacks had delayed road and rail repairs across the UK, with so many men and so much British steel being given over to the war effort.

"Can we get around?" asked Max. "Is it dangerous?"

"Germans have their eyes mostly on Russia and the continent these days," said Drummond. He used a long gearshift to set the van into motion. "I'll get you to London safely, not to worry."

"Our hero," sang Bobbi, which made Wally bristle.

"How far to London?" said Wally, already eager to get out of the van.

"About three hundred fifty kilometers," said Drummond.

"What's that in miles?" asked Frankie.

"About two fifty," said Brubaker. "Should arrive near dawn."

With one hand on the wheel and one bespectacled eye on the road, Drummond reached into a small satchel by his seat and grabbed some packages of British biscuits. He tossed them around the van.

"Not our finest," said the petty officer, "but these might take the edge off, as you Yanks say."

Wally scowled. "We don't say that."

The others munched away while Wally simmered, and Drummond eyed the rearview mirror. "You blokes hear the news about the US Fifth Army?"

"No," said Rat through a mouthful of biscuit mash.

"Your lieutenant general Clark's troops," said Drummond, "they finally took the Bernhardt Line. First big step toward retaking Rome. Real hit to the Nazis."

The crew hooted and cheered, though Brubaker did not appear surprised at all, nor did Rat, who seemed more enthralled with his biscuits.

"Mark my words," said Drummond. "Uncle Adolph's days are numbered."

Wally wanted to share the petty officer's optimism, but he'd already learned that nothing was certain where the Germans were concerned.

Bobbi, too, wore a solemn look, losing her earlier flirtatious perk. Perhaps she was thinking the same thing.

Drummond steered out of the port city and onto a country road lined with English oaks and marching lines of birch trees, white with moonlight. The van's headlights beamed into dense forests along the way, wild shadows casting about them with each turn and bump. Wally found traveling down the left side of the road entirely disconcerting, and the darkness only seemed to make things worse.

"You're all welcome to get some shut-eye," said Brubaker. "We'll stop on the way in case you need to use the facilities."

"I can hold it," said Rat.

"Well, I can't," said Audrey. "Not the whole trip."

"We'll stop in an hour," said Brubaker. "How's that?"

"That works," said Audrey. She pulled off her army jacket and folded it into a pillow roll, where she rested her head against the window and closed her eyes.

Happy to have Audrey distracted, Wally turned to Bobbi, hoping he might start a quiet, private conversation with her.

"Good idea," said Bobbi, eyeing Audrey. She, too, folded her jacket into a roll, and within a few minutes, both girls were sound asleep on either side of Wally.

He let out a quiet sigh, leaned his head back against the seat cushion, and glared at the inside of the van as if he were right back aboard the *Edmund B.* in his top bunk staring at the overhead pipes, cursing his luck. However, after a quarter hour, Bobbi shifted in her sleep and laid her head on Wally's shoulder. No one appeared to notice, and that suited Wally just fine. It wasn't the private conversation he'd hoped for, but he, too, allowed himself to drift, and in the quiet rumble of the van, he entertained the fleeting thought that maybe England wouldn't be so bad after all.

A ray of dawn sunlight struck Wally's face and startled him awake. He heard himself make some noise like a grunt at the end of a snore, but, luckily, no one heard. They were all looking out the van's small side window at a glistening river.

"Where are we?" asked Wally. He licked his dry lips.

"You slept the whole way," said Audrey. "We're in London." She pointed through the window at the river. "That's the Thames."

Wally leaned forward to see the river full of tugboats, barges, fishing boats, and ferries, each churning out smoke or steam and zigzagging in a network of maritime traffic that made New York's East River look like a placid lake.

"No worries, mate," said Drummond. "Almost there."

On the other side of the road they traveled, Wally saw warehouses, char-stained smoke-stacks, and tall apartment buildings. London looked a lot like New York, except the whole city seemed to be made of blackened red brick. Drummond rolled down the driver's window, allowing a rush of freezing air to fill the van, which now smelled of coal smoke and gasoline fumes with hints of sardines.

Wally wrinkled his nose, and Drummond noticed in the van's mirror.

"That is the enticing aroma of East Wapping," Drummond said. "Quite floral, don't you think?"

Max and Frankie laughed, Rat smirked, and Audrey giggled at Drummond's humor, but Wally still found the guy annoying. He turned to Bobbi, but she was quiet, not participating in the team's curious inquiries. Instead, she stared out the van's second side window, clearly burdened by thoughts she was choosing not to share. Wally hadn't had the moment alone with her he'd hoped for and was, himself, burdened with feelings he hadn't shared either.

The van angled north, off a high street lined with shops, and into an industrial area teeming with black cars. Several buildings stood tall like monuments built to celebrate industry, stained with dark streaks, residue from the industrial pollution that filled the air. Other structures held damage of the kind Wally had seen along the river, half-toppled buildings like fallen stacks of toy blocks.

Drummond pointed at the destruction, his voice now tinged with seriousness. "The bloody Blitz took out a few factories along here and over there," he said. "Took some time to recover from the fires, especially down by St. Katharine's. Still get the occasional strafing. Germans won't stop, so neither can we."

The sight of the damaged buildings and the gravity of Drummond's words began to sink in. London wasn't just another city; it was a target that had been hit by the Nazis over and over, and Wally and his team had been delivered right into the center of it.

Brubaker turned from his front passenger seat. "The place we're headed is a lot like

WKOB," he said. "A secret communications facility run by His Majesty's Naval Service."

"How close are we?" said Rat.

"Six blocks," said Bobbi, finally speaking.

Wally perked up. "You've been here before?"

Bobbi didn't reply and just continued to stare out her window.

"Look at that!" Frankie called, his voice trailing off. He pointed away from the street to a crater the size of a baseball field filled with a thirty-foot-tall pile of scorched debris, a mound of broken bricks and bent steel. It looked like the aftermath of a violent bombing, the kind Wally saw in the monochrome newsreels back home, the ones that were hard to believe.

"That pile of rubble," Drummond said softly, "was a hospital."

Audrey gasped and the others fell silent.

Wally's stomach dropped at the callousness of the Nazis. His air-raid warden duties had seemed important during his drills in Brooklyn, but to see the actual devastation wrought by real bombs gave his former role a whole new feeling of necessity. What was it was like for the Londoners here in East Wapping to see their community half demolished? If a bomb ever dropped on New York, if even one building ever fell at the hands of an enemy, there would be hell to pay, and both the city and its people would never be the same. So much for Brubaker's promise to keep them safe.

"Here we are," announced the petty officer.

Drummond navigated the van toward a unremarkable six-story brick structure, one that sat off the main drive, back from pedestrian or motor traffic. There were no directional markers, no clear signage on the building, and its windows were covered by inside shades. If this was a Royal Navy communications center as Colonel Brubaker suggested, there was no way to know it from the outside.

Drummond pulled the van around back, alongside the rear entrance. He parked, switched off the engine, and hopped out.

Brubaker opened the passenger door, adjusted his weakened arm in his sling, and put on his lieutenant colonel's hat. "Will you bring our bags, Drummond?"

"Aye, sir!" Drummond replied with a salute.

"Colonel, may I change first?" said Bobbi. "This jacket is giving me a rash."

"Of course," said Brubaker. "See you inside."

Wally trilled his lips at being separated from Bobbi once again but was beginning to see she was in no mood for conversation anyway.

He followed the others out of the van, weary from the long drive.

Audrey walked to the van's sideview mirror and arranged her hair with her fingers. "I look like an unmade bed," she laughed.

Mayfield pulled his cap off and just gaped at the building.

Rat did a few quick calisthenics behind the van, starting with a quick succession of jumping jacks, counting, "One, two, three…"

"Where the hell do you get that energy?" said Max. He arched his back and pushed out his protruding belly.

"Gotta stay fit," Rat puffed. "We're soldiers now."

Frankie stepped forward and put his arm around Wally. "How you doin', Wall? You seem distracted."

"Just tired, I guess," said Wally.

"All right, gang," said Brubaker. "Fall in and follow me."

With a set of keys provided by Drummond, Brubaker unlocked the facility's window-less back door and led the team to another set of doors that required the use of a second key. Once through the double security, Colonel Brubaker led them down a corridor, around a series of offices, toward the building's front reception area.

Unlike WKOB with its excessive glass and ostentatious marble floors, this building was a simple bureaucratic office with few windows and little décor. It was old, smelled like books, and was quiet like a morgue. Somehow, this comforted Wally. There were no glass doors through which an unexpected shooting might occur.

The only sign this was a government facility was the Union Jack that hung from an eight-foot standing post by the reception desk. There was no directory for visitors, and the space seemed empty except for a single slender young woman in a long-sleeved white blouse who sat at the desk, scrutinizing a file behind a small name placard that read "Miss Davies." She wore her hair in a bun.

Miss Davies looked up as they approached, surprised by the team's abrupt arrival.

"You have keys to the back door," she said, as if speaking both to the crowd forming in the reception area and to herself. She folded the file in front of her and set it aside. "May I help you?"

"Sorry to surprise you," said Brubaker, stepping up to her desk. "I'm Lieutenant Colonel Roger Brubaker of the United States Army." He raised his good hand and thumbed in the direction from which they'd come. "I've just arrived with Petty Officer Niles Drummond. Here to see Chief Officer Finch."

Miss Davies peered down her nose. "You're a bit out of date, Colonel Brubaker. The chief officer is now Superintendent Finch. Advanced two months ago."

Wally loved the receptionist's accent, more refined than Drummond's. Even Frankie appeared taken with her, staring wide-eyed as she interacted with the colonel.

"Of course," said Brubaker. He nodded to himself. "Old habits. I'm here to see the superintendent."

The young woman seemed to intuit the scrutiny she was under and turned to Frankie; she returned his smile and then gave Brubaker discerning look. "Very well," she said. She dialed a number on her phone and exchanged whispered words into the receiver. She then hung up, rose from her seat, and rounded her desk.

"Follow me, Colonel," she said. She withdrew her own key from a hip pocket in her long blue skirt and opened a door. "This way."

Frankie nudged Wally as if he were entertained by their circumstances, or maybe he was just taken by Miss Davies, but Wally just shrugged.

Brubaker and the team followed the young woman to a spacious conference room with a wall that featured a large map of Europe. In the center was an oval wooden table surrounded by a dozen chairs. The room reminded Wally of the one at WKOB where he, Max, and Frankie were first recruited. That seemed like a lifetime ago.

"Please have a seat," Miss Davies said. "I'll inform the superintendent you're here."

Brubaker addressed the team: "At ease."

Everyone took a seat around the table. Frankie's gaze followed the receptionist as she closed the door behind her, leaving them alone. Wally sat next to Brubaker and eyed the door, wondering when Bobbi would join them.

They sat in silence for a few minutes until Wally leaned over to Brubaker to whisper, "Sir, did the superintendent know we were coming?"

"Not exactly," said Brubaker. "I had Drummond keep things on the sly."

Wally felt as though he'd been punched in the gut. Brubaker had dragged the team over the Atlantic, through the woods, and across London to a place they were not expected. If this Operation Teacup had been coordinated with the Royal Navy, why would their arrival be a surprise?

When the door opened again, Brubaker stood and saluted, prompting Wally and the others to do the same.

"Superintendent Finch," said Brubaker.

But the person who entered was not at all who Wally expected. Superintendent Finch was a woman.

She was dressed in a blue Royal Navy uniform, an angular blue hat, a white shirt and blue tie, a freshly pressed double-breasted jacket with pockets full of medals, and a matching blue wool skirt. She was poised with a glow about her, but when her eyes met Brubaker's, her attractive features transformed to something that looked like anger.

"Roger Brubaker," she said slowly. She strode forward and, without warning, slapped the colonel's face.

Wally and the team gasped.

Brubaker flinched, yet he didn't look surprised by the superintendent's actions.

He quickly regained his composure. "Hello, Delphina."

Finch looked around the table. "Where is Howard? I told you both I wanted nothing to do with you or your ridiculous schemes."

Brubaker removed his hat and let the energy of her anger dissolve into the crackling air between them. He then met her searching eyes. "Howard's dead, Delphi."

The colonel's pronouncement hung in the room. He lowered his head. "I'm sorry to come unannounced, but I wanted to tell you myself, and in person. Didn't seem appropriate for a telegram."

Finch's perfect face froze in a place somewhere between anger and confusion. Wally thought she might slap Brubaker again.

Suddenly, her lower lip began to tremble, and she eased herself into an empty chair.

"How?" she said.

"Shot," said Brubaker. "At WKOB in New York. Nazi cell must've tracked him there. Shot up the whole place."

Wally looked to Audrey, fearing Brubaker's recounting of that tragic day might stir in her the memory of the event that almost put her into shock. Yet Audrey kept steady even if it had, riveted as Wally and the others were by the confusing drama that was playing out before them.

Finch stared at the floor, seeming to sort out Brubaker's words. She then looked back at him, at his sling. She reached to touch his arm. "You were hurt too?"

"I'll be fine."

Finch withdrew her hand and turned her addled gaze to Wally and the others.

"This is the team," Brubaker explained. "Howard's team. They're here because he believed in them. They want to make a difference, and I think you'll see they're just the people to do it."

Before Finch could reply, the door behind her opened and Bobbi entered, her army uniform now replaced by a flowing cream blouse and a smart powder-blue skirt. Her hair was combed straight, and her makeup was Max Factor perfect.

The superintendent rose from the chair when she saw Bobbi, her eyes widened. "Barbara Ann," Finch said, her voice soft with surprise.

Bobbi lifted her chin and locked eyes with the superintendent.

"Hello, Mother."

For the first time in days, Wally lay motionless, the pitch of the troopship becoming a slowly fading muscle memory. Tonight, he finally lay in an honest-to-goodness bed, safe in a warm dormitory bedroom, courtesy of His Majesty's Naval Service. There were no smells of vomit and no pipes above his head upon which to concuss himself. Yet, despite the improved accommodations, he'd never felt more uncomfortable.

He shared the room with his newest teammate, Alvin Mayfield, who slept with his mouth open, snoring with the snarl of an Alabama wildcat. Wally, on the other hand, remained wide awake, still reeling from the morning's revelation that Bobbi's dead mother was not only alive but was a member of the Women's Royal Naval Service who matched Lieutenant Colonel Brubaker in rank, despite the fact that she was a woman.

Shortly after the surprising reunion in the Naval Center conference room, Bobbi and the superintendent had retreated to some other part of the building, no doubt to discuss the long and difficult road that had led Bobbi to London. Or perhaps they talked about Colonel Dawson and his shocking death. Maybe they discussed what had driven them apart in the first place, whatever that may have been. Any thoughts Wally had on the matter were pure speculation. The story Wally had been told was different. It had been a lie.

After Finch and Bobbi departed, Brubaker had explained to Wally and the others that Colonel Dawson and Superintendent Finch had met at the end of the Great War here in England, where they'd worked together, each of them serving in the respective militaries in similar assignments. He didn't share anything further, but nothing more was necessary. The woman whose death Bobbi had proclaimed to see firsthand was very much alive, and much of the sympathy Wally had garnered in her favor was based on that falsehood. That sympathy was now gone.

Wally was no longer sure who Bobbi LaFleur—or Barbara Ann Dawson—was. Everything about her now seemed untrue, just like every word in every song he had written for her aboard the *Edmund B. Alexander*. Her deception felt personal.

Wally tried the best he could to put her and her duplicity out of his mind, and his effort was assisted by Drummond, who had arranged for the team to enjoy a proper British breakfast of fried bread, poached eggs, stewed tomatoes, and beans. Like the US military, the British observed strict rationing. However, as a gesture of international kindness, Drummond had arranged for this feast. No one was happier about their breakfast than Max, who ate Audrey's leftover tomato and used her untouched fried bread to clean Wally's plate of the runny egg yolk. Even Rat had to admit it was better than reconstituted egg powder.

Once Brubaker left to coordinate with British officials, Drummond had used the rest of the daylight hours providing Wally and team a tour of the Royal Navy Communications Center, which he revealed was only temporary, as a new facility was being built underground in Scotland. This facility, and the people in it, seemed nice enough. Wally learned that the center was charged with monitoring Allied transmissions, directing key British propaganda campaigns, and handling sensitive and secret troop communications on the European continent. Enlisted personnel lived on the upper floors of the building and worked on the lower floors, where there was also a functioning mess hall, a billiard table, and space for recreation.

Drummond had shown the team the facility's briefing rooms and recording studios, boasting about the United Kingdom's advanced radio technology, letting the team noodle over the maps of the European theater for which they had clearance. Audrey was wide-eyed the entire time, and it occurred to Wally that she now had greater clearance than even her brother Johnny must have had. The entire place seemed to be run with the British precision and planning Wally had seen in newsreels and read about in the papers back home. The Brits had, after all, been at this longer than the Americans.

After a full day's orientation and an early dinner of boiled cod and broccoli, the crew had been assigned accommodations on the upper floors of the building. Wally had been paired with Mayfield, Max had been paired with Frankie, and Rat had a room to himself. Audrey was told that once Bobbi returned from her day's meetings they would continue the roommate arrangement they'd had aboard the troopship.

Yet, despite the comfort of his accommodations and Drummond's reassurances over the superiority of the British equipment and technology, Wally remained unsettled. He wanted to talk to Bobbi, confront her about her lies, discuss how she'd used those lies to put him and his friends in danger. Or perhaps what he really wanted to discuss was how her lies had drawn feelings out of him he didn't know he could have, feelings he thought were the truest he'd ever experienced. Now, he had to rethink everything.

With the team sleeping restfully or, in Mayfield's case, sleeping loudly, Wally was still awake and more troubled than ever. He stood from his bed, slid on his Royal Navy–issued slippers, donned his jacket over his cotton pajamas, and left his dormitory room. He searched for and found the stairs, climbed to the roof, and opened the access door to the frosty evening air. On the roof, Wally spotted a utility box facing the Thames and took a seat. It reminded him of his rooftop at home in Brooklyn, and the feeling gave him some measure of familiarity and comfort despite his current disposition.

The Thames wasn't the East River, though it also sported fishing boats and ferries bobbing in harbors, ship bells ringing in the distance, and mariners' lights twinkling with optimism. He closed his eyes and tried to draw in the scents of London to calm his nerves but only smelled the same odors of coal smoke, motor oil, and sardines that Drummond had called the "enticing aroma of East Wapping." He listened to the quiet hiss of the streetlamps and the rumble of car engines below until the sounds of the city were suddenly interrupted.

"Lipkin?"

Wally turned to see Rat striding forward.

"Went to your room thinking you were there," said Rat. "Figured I'd wake you up."

"Nope," said Wally. "Too much on my mind."

Rat took a seat next to Wally on the utility box without asking and stared at him intensely. "Saw the door to the stairwell open and took a chance you were here. I have something to tell you."

Wally huffed, making no attempt to hide his foul mood. "So, tell me."

Rat drew a breath that seemed to fill his bony chest and he spoke through his exhalation. "I cracked the code."

From his back pocket, Rat withdrew his army-issued journal. Unlike Wally's journal, which held secret songs for Bobbi, Rat's dog-eared journal was crammed with newspaper clippings and handwritten notes falling out of its pages.

"On the troopship," Rat said, "I tracked back the news of American combat, the battles that followed each of the team's jingles. Scoured the newspapers, pulled out the stories that fit our timeline, puzzled it all together."

"Cracked the code?" Wally repeated. "How is that possible?"

"I had to think about how it all worked." Rat gestured in the air like a teacher, pointing to an invisible blackboard. "Measures, words, lines of lyrics all had to mean something, right? I took a stab that maybe they were connected to longitude and latitude or names of cities, troop movements." He thumbed his chin. "Course, I also had to figure that the codes might change along the way, right? Names could mean something different too. It wasn't easy, I'll tell you that."

Wally stared at Rat, a newfound respect challenging his old resentments. "You decoded the jingle messages?"

Rat nodded. "Back at your apartment in Brooklyn, Brubaker said we'd helped the Allies in the north. When Drummond told us that the Fifth Army broke the Bernhardt Line, it all clicked, all the battles that led to that final win. Each of those battles followed our jingles. It had to be us."

"We did that?" Wally warmed with a rush of pride.

"There's more," said Rat. He rifled through his journal. "Tonight, I worked my way backward through it all just to be sure, and I realized I had one thing wrong. Well, at least not a hundred percent right." He squinted his small eyes at Wally. "I need to tell you something," said Rat, "and you're not gonna like it."

"What is it?" said Wally. "Tell me."

"The battles we won, we won because we had the element of surprise. But every last one of them took a heavy toll."

Wally nodded. "Okay."

"No," he said. "You don't understand. Each of the battles were sacrifice plays. The intent was to send men into harm's way with no hope of winning. Over three hundred of our men died—and it was our fault. We killed them, Walter. Every one of them."

12

Truth and Consequences

On the rooftop of the secret Royal Navy facility, Wally spent an hour going through the contents of Rat's journal, each page more troubling than the last. As annoying as the guy had been, Rat was a good investigative reporter. He'd managed to do what Dawson and Brubaker had hoped was impossible for the Nazis; he'd cracked their secret jingle code. Of course, unlike the Nazis, Rat knew where to look and what to look for. Still, his success was unsettling. If Rat, alone, could figure it out, how long would it be until Hitler's crew of specialists could do it, too, once they figured out where to look?

However, it wasn't the risk of codebreaking that bothered Wally most. What made his blood run cold was Rat's realization that the jingles they were told would save people came at a horrible price. There, in the pages of Clyde Rubinstein's grubby journal, was proof that more than three hundred men had died following the orders buried in the team's jingles, the orders Wally and his team had given.

Wally's mind began to buzz. In every battle that Rat had linked to their mission, each had the same horrifying characteristics. There were too few men for the operation and no avenue of escape. The jingles appeared to have worked exactly as intended, but not the way Wally and his team were led to believe they would. The element of surprise had led to a win, but it required the sacrifice of the men they sent.

"Jingles save lives," Brubaker had said.

Wally knew war came with sacrifice, but wasn't that a choice made by individuals? When had Americans become *kamikazes* like the Japanese? When did we send men in as sacrifices like lambs to slaughter?

He tried to contain the wave of emotions that pounded his brain like the angry Atlantic against the hull of the *Edmund B. Alexander*.

"I saw you writing in your own journal back on the ship," said Rat. "I wondered if you were figuring it out too."

"No," said Wally. "I was just writing songs."

"Whole songs? By yourself?"

"Seems ridiculous compared to what you did," said Wally.

"So, now what?" said Rat as if the next steps were entirely up to Wally.

But what could be done? Wally was already whirling from the lies that Bobbi had told. Now he was reeling further from the ones told to him by the colonel and by Brubaker. They were not saving lives, they were spending them like currency.

Wally had trusted the wrong people, brought his friends and family into their wild plans, and now had to answer for his ignorance.

"We're in the middle of a country we've never been to," said Wally. "And we're being led by people who lie, people who have our families in protective custody back in New York. If we don't continue to cooperate, what happens to my folks, your mom?"

Rat's eyes widened. "We need to tell the others," Rat said. "They need to know."

Wally looked at Rat. "What's gotten into you, Clyde? You've changed."

"What do you mean?"

"You seem like...like you care about other people."

Rat fell silent for a moment. "Lipkin, for the first time I can remember, I'm part of something bigger than myself. People are counting on me, and I don't want to let them down." He looked away. "Does that sound sappy?"

"No," said Wally. "It doesn't."

"You're the one who convinced me I could make a difference, Lipkin. You said I could save lives. Lives like my dad's. Remember?"

Wally recalled his speech imploring Rat to join the team. He had counted on Rat to see that the mission eclipsed their trivial concerns, to see that their goal was worthy of the risk. Now, he regretted pulling him into this, regretting sucking everyone into this like a whirlpool. Rat was just another victim of Wally's naiveté.

"I'm sorry, Clyde." Wally stood to leave. "I made you believe in this whole thing, and now I can see I was wrong."

Rat grabbed Wally by the arm to keep him from going. "No, you weren't. You wanna do what's right, Lipkin, and you made me want that too. You're a patriot. We both are. That hasn't changed."

"How can you say that after what you learned? It was wrong of me to drag everyone into this, Clyde. I was an idiot to trust—" Wally stopped short of saying Bobbi's name.

"The girl?" said Rat. He let go of Wally's arm.

"Yes," said Wally. "The girl."

Wally looked out over the Thames. Life seemed so much easier on his own rooftop when his biggest challenge was pulling a lever, following instructions, staying conscious.

"Okay," said Rat. "So, what now?"

It was nearly three in the morning, and Wally was suddenly far from tired. He felt crazy standing outside in his pajamas, crazy like his uncle. But maybe crazy was exactly what the situation needed.

"Wake the others," said Wally. "Everyone but Bobbi. I have an idea."

The frosty dawn air nipped at Wally's ears and nose as he stood like a gargoyle on the Naval Center's rooftop, peering motionless at the lights of the fishing boats as they rose and fell with the sleepy heave of the Thames' current. He moved his gaze to the delivery trucks on the riverside streets, conducting their early-morning enterprise as though nothing was out of place, as if nothing had changed. But Wally knew better. He filled his lungs with briny air that smelled like fish, and then turned away from East Wapping toward the tired faces of his friends, who sat in a semi-circle around him, each still stunned by what he and Rat had just revealed.

"The whole time?" asked Frankie. "Every mission?"

"Seems so," said Rat.

"I should have asked more questions," said Max. "Brubaker has always been cagey."

"More than cagey," said Frankie. "He lied." His face was red with anger. "Again!"

Everyone was still in their pajamas, including Audrey, who paced anxiously while wrapped in her bathrobe. Rat had intercepted her in the women's restroom without raising suspicions from Bobbi, who was still asleep back in her quarters. This conversation was not for her.

"I can't believe it," said Audrey. "It feels like I'm still asleep and having a horrible nightmare."

It had taken a quarter hour for the team to bring poor Mayfield up to speed. He didn't know them any more than he knew about their secret mission. But now that he was a member of the team, he had to be told everything.

"So, are we the good guys," said Mayfield, "or the bad guys?"

"We're the good guys," said Rat. "But we weren't told everything we needed to know."

Mayfield cocked his head. "You expect senior officers to tell you everything?"

"Well, yes," said Rat. "When it's important."

Mayfield chuckled. "You fellas ain't been in the army that long. They tell you what they want to tell you, and that ain't much."

"They told us we'd be saving lives," said Wally. "And now we found out that we sent a lot of men to die."

"So that makes the colonel and that Bobbi girl the bad guys?"

Wally envied Alvin Mayfield's simplistic view of the world, the way he sorted things into columns of "good" and "bad." It was a practical way of making decisions, the way Wally's father had managed their shop finances: things that helped the bottom line versus things that harmed the bottom line. But nothing about their situation was simple, and these people proved difficult to sort into such buckets.

"They're the bad guys in my book," said Frankie. "This is a disaster."

By Rat's account, the battles connected to the team's jingles had helped further the Allied efforts to achieve some notable victories like General Clark's success at the Bernhardt Line. Such efforts were impressive, Wally had to concede, and, arguably, worth some sacrifice to achieve. But if the team had known the price of their labor, it's doubtful they would have participated in the work. And Wally knew who was responsible for their participation.

"It's why I woke you," said Wally. "I needed you all to know how sorry I am for dragging you into this."

Max stepped over and poked Wally in the chest. "That's enough," he said.

"What do you mean?" said Wally. Of all people, he thought Max would rally with him.

"Walter, you insult us all if you think you dragged us into anything." Max gestured to the team. "We all chose to be here. We accepted the risks ourselves. We didn't just trust you; we trusted these people too. They're the ones to blame, not you."

"But I pushed you," said Wally. "Convinced you. I was so sure..." Emotion hardened in Wally's throat like a river stone. "I'm so, so sorry." He tried to stop his lip from trembling. "Three hundred men, Max—"

"That's not on you." Max put his hand on Wally's shoulder. "That's on them."

"Max is right," echoed Frankie. "You didn't know. None of us did."

Audrey shook her head. "Those men who died. They were just like Johnny."

Wally tried not to think about Bobbi, embarrassed that he was so struck by her beauty, so willing to let his feelings get the best of him, that he'd let down his guard and trusted her.

Rat shrugged. "What can we do?"

Wally swallowed against the stone in his throat. "I have a plan," he said, "but we've all got to be on the same page for it to work." He drew a bagpipe breath and extended his hand to the space in front of him. "From now on, I don't decide anything for anyone unless we decide together. We have to agree on that as a team."

Max placed his hand on top of Wally's. "Agreed. I'm in."

Audrey came forward and placed her hand on Max's. "Me too."

Rat and Frankie followed next and chimed together, "We're in."

The last to approach was Mayfield. He walked slowly and put his hand in the center of the friend circle, where he held it before committing. "So, we're the good guys?"

"Yes!" they all said at once.

Mayfield nodded. "Okay, then, I'm in too." His crooked smile quickly faded, and he scanned the faces of his team. "Now, can someone tell me exactly what that means?"

Wally and the crew sat at a breakfast table in the mess hall on the Naval Center's brightly lit first floor, awaiting Drummond to escort them to their morning briefing. Paintings and photographs of British heroes lined the walls, severe, dour-faced men in military attire with thick white mustaches or beards and bushy, wild eyebrows, but Wally couldn't name a single one of them. It was a reminder of how far he was from New York, out of his element, and in over his head. Young British enlistees sat at tables around them, chatting away, obviously familiar with one another and their heroes on the wall, eager for their day's work to begin. Wally's teammates, by contrast, were quiet and sullen, knowing what they were about to do.

Wally shifted in his seat, uncomfortable in his US Army uniform. Judging by the way Rat and Frankie were pulling on their own collars, Wally figured they were just as uneasy as he was. Even Audrey looked restless, dunking her teabag over and over in a cup of hot water, not drinking a drop. Frankie stirred a bowl of runny oatmeal but didn't eat a thing. Mayfield just stared at the walls, looking like he was trying to fathom the stories behind the

British military portraits. Only Max had an appetite, picking stewed prunes from Wally's untouched bowl after he'd eaten his own.

Bobbi had told Audrey she was joining the superintendent for breakfast, and Brubaker was off with the British officers in a separate dining hall, which suited Wally just fine. Those two were the last people he wanted to eat with this morning.

The team had worked through the dawn hours on a plan that Wally had crafted, a plan that required each of them to be in full agreement. And while they wore their exhaustion plainly on their haunted faces, Wally was fidgety with nervous energy, concerned that their plan would quickly fail if his restlessness was to become too overwhelming and he were to pass out in front of everyone.

In that moment, he felt trapped like his uncle, imprisoned in a room of his own making, half crazy with anger and fear while riddled with guilt. Wally drew a breath, closed his eyes, and searched for peace. He imagined himself at home at his Wurlitzer, playing a soothing song, surrounded by the smells of his mother's Hanukkah latkes, and the thought seemed to help.

"Jolly good morning, lot," said Drummond, striding forward full of perk and dragging Wally out of his reverie. "Time for your morning briefing, if you'll follow me." The petty officer gestured down the hall for the team to join him, clearly presuming they held a similar enthusiasm.

Instead, they marched in silence to the briefing room where the prior day's events had unfolded, and each took a seat. Soon, Brubaker entered with Finch at his side and Bobbi following last. Wally worked hard not to look at her lest he upset the tentative calm he'd managed to render.

The team only offered half-hearted salutes to their senior officers and then retook their seats without speaking.

"Good morning, team," said Brubaker, appearing to notice their lackluster reception. "I have news for you that may lift your spirits." He lifted his chin. "The superintendent has agreed to help us." He motioned toward Finch. "Operation Teacup is officially launched," he said. "We can begin new operations right here in London and get back to business."

Wally stood. "No," he blurted. "That's not what's going to happen."

Brubaker frowned. "Beg your pardon?"

"I said no," Wally repeated, worried he might throw up. He closed his eyes and thought of his piano back home.

"We all say no," Audrey added, and shuffled up next to Wally, seeming to recognize his need for support.

At the sound of Audrey's voice, Wally opened his eyes. Hearing her speak, feeling her at his side, bolstered his confidence.

One by one, the others stood around the table. Audrey sent a withering look toward Bobbi, who grimaced, clearly confused.

Superintendent Finch searched their faces and then looked at Brubaker. "Roger, what is this all about?"

"It's about lies," answered Wally, gaining his composure. He faced Bobbi. "Lies we won't listen to anymore."

"Stand down, Private Lipkin," said Brubaker, his face an angry scowl.

"Does the superintendent know?" said Wally.

"Know what?" said Brubaker.

"You may address me directly," said Finch. "Go on. What has you so upset?"

Wally looked to the superintendent. "Ma'am, do you know what we've done? What the colonel and...Barbara Ann made us do?"

"I'm familiar with your mission, if that's what you mean."

"She's been briefed, Private Lipkin," Brubaker growled.

"Does she know about the three hundred men we killed?"

Brubaker's eyes widened.

Silence blanketed the room, and Wally figured everyone could hear the tremendous pounding in his chest, like a jackhammer on a Brooklyn sidewalk.

"Three hundred men?" said the superintendent.

Bobbi stepped forward, her eyes pleading. "This isn't necessary, Walter."

Wally ignored Bobbi and focused on Finch. "Colonel Brubaker told us we were saving lives, ma'am." Wally pointed at Bobbi. "And your daughter told me you were dead. Those both turned out to be lies."

"This is insubordination, Mr. Lipkin," said the colonel.

Finch's eyes grew more focused. "Go on..."

"We had no idea what we were writing into our jingles, ma'am, until Clyde figured it out." Wally thumbed toward Rat. "He cracked the code."

"Impossible," said Brubaker, his voice breathy like a whisper.

Rat pulled out his stuffed journal and tossed it onto the table. "It's all there," he said. "Every mission. Every death."

Finch stared at the journal and then looked at Bobbi, who hung her head.

"Ma'am," said Wally, "we're telling you that our mission was to sacrifice men. To send them into battles they couldn't survive. We sent Americans to die." Wally rallied his courage. "And now that we know, we refuse to do it anymore."

The pounding in Wally's ears grew loud like a drum, and he tried counting Mississippis.

"Colonel Brubaker?" said Finch. "Anything you wish to say?"

Brubaker's eyes were ablaze at Wally. "It's not as simple as you make it sound, Lipkin."

"Colonel Brubaker has our families in protective custody in New York," said Wally, addressing the superintendent. "And we're afraid they may be in danger if we don't continue to cooperate. We're asking for your help, ma'am." Wally puffed out his chest. "We're asking for asylum in the United Kingdom."

Although the room again fell silent, the beating in Wally's ears seemed loud enough for others to hear, and yet, somehow, with Audrey beside him and his friends surrounding him, he managed to keep from passing out.

Brubaker raised his good hand as if he had the power to catch the tension in the palm of his hand. "Hold on. Hold on." He shook his head. "I'm not going to harm your families. Jesus Christ. Let's just settle down, everyone, before you each do something you can't undo."

"Why would we believe you now?" Wally snapped.

"You need to understand the full story," said Brubaker. "The whole truth."

"I agree," said Finch. "I think we should all hear what your colonel has to say."

"There is no explanation," said Max.

Frankie leaned forward and pointed at Brubaker. "That's right. No explanation."

"Those men, those three hundred men"—Brubaker barked—"they gave their lives for this country knowing the sacrifice they were about to make."

Brubaker's proclamation fell on the room like cold rain on a fire.

"They knew?" said Audrey.

Brubaker hung his head. "They did."

"All of them?" said Rat. "Who asks that of three hundred men?"

"It was wrong!" cried Bobbi. Tears streamed down her face in trails of mascara. "I told my father the same thing, but he wouldn't listen."

Bobbi's sobbing did nothing to sway Wally. "So now you want us to believe you didn't agree with your father?" he said.

"She's telling the truth," Brubaker said softly. "You should trust her."

Brubaker's words echoed the dying plea of Bobbi's father. Lying in his own blood, Dawson had implored Wally to trust Bobbi. Could the colonel have foreseen this moment, when trusting his daughter would be brought into question, when her trustworthiness would be the turning point of their mission?

"So what?" said Wally. "Even if those men knew what they were getting into, you lied to us about it." He remembered the night he almost kissed Bobbi on the roof of the Elving House. "You lied about everything."

"You're out of line, Private Lipkin," said Brubaker. "You've defied my orders, committed insubordination, and have now shared state secrets with a member of a foreign government." He gestured toward the superintendent. "That's treason. And there is no asylum for soldiers defying a legitimate and direct order."

"You can't just lie to us," said Wally. "And we can't just send men to die."

Superintendent Finch walked toward Wally and placed a gentle hand on his shoulder.

"Tell me," said Finch, "what did you hope to accomplish when you joined this mission?"

Wally steadied himself. "We wanted to save lives, ma'am, if that's what you mean. We wanted to help, but not this way."

Finch turned to Brubaker and raised an eyebrow. "Roger, it seems like you, Barbara Ann, and I weren't the only ones who found Howard's plans unacceptable. If you had bothered to speak honestly with your team after he passed, it sounds like they would have told you so themselves. A little trust could have spared you all this trouble."

Wally puzzled over Finch's words. "What are you saying, ma'am?"

The team stood perplexed.

The superintendent turned back to face Wally. "Both Barbara Ann and Colonel Brubaker share your misgivings. They have from the start." She gestured to the front of the room. "They even expressed their grave concerns directly to the colonel himself, at risk of their own insubordination, and yet he pressed on. Perhaps he didn't agree that the risk of lives was too high, or perhaps he thought he didn't have a choice. I suppose we'll never know." She peered into Wally's eyes. "I don't wish to speak ill of the dead, Private Lipkin, but ignoring serious concerns is the very reason Colonel Dawson became my ex-husband."

Bobbi looked away.

"War has a way of changing people, Mr. Lipkin, and not always for the better."

Wally recalled Colonel Renshaw saying something similar back at Fort Hamilton: "*War has a way of bending good men in directions they didn't think they could bend.*"

Finch took Wally's hand, seeming to lock in on his concerns. "I admire your resolve, Mr. Lipkin. And I assure you, we're all in agreement, including your colonel and my daughter, even though they could have surely handled things better." Finch turned to Brubaker. "For this mission to continue, we need to trust one another."

Wally's pulse slowed. There was something comforting in Finch's touch, her tone, a precision in her words he found hard to question.

She released his hand and walked toward Brubaker. "We need to accept that there will be death and loss," she said. "That's the price of war. It hasn't dissuaded those brave soldiers on the front lines, and we can't let that difficult truth dissuade us from our own duty. As much as it pains me, battles are fought by men with guns who kill each other in the name of the things they want. That's what Mussolini did, that's what Hitler is doing, and, dare I say it, that's what Churchill and Roosevelt are doing too. We can't be afraid of that duty, but that doesn't mean we have to be resigned to it or invite such sacrifice either. No one says we have to carry on without caution." She turned back to address Wally. "I'm not Howard Dawson, and as I told Colonel Brubaker, if we move forward, we do so under my command, under my rules, not his. Charging into battle when the risk is the greatest is never the first option I consider. Nor is it an option I take off the table." She turned to Brubaker. "Colonel," she said, "are you willing to let this misunderstanding pass?"

Brubaker eyed his team. "That would be my preference."

"Private Lipkin," she said, "are you able to accept that? Are you able to see past your anger, past this incident, to continue the mission under my command?"

The entire crew appeared as flummoxed as Wally was.

"It's not just up to me, ma'am," said Wally. He turned to his friends. "It's up to the team."

"Then why don't you take a moment to discuss it," she said, and with a nod to Brubaker and Bobbi, the three left the conference room.

Once the door had closed behind them, Wally and the team took seats around the table, their exhaustion now at its peak.

"I like that lady," said Mayfield with a sigh. He gave a forlorn look to the door. "Her voice is like an angel's."

"The question is not whether we like her," said Wally. "The question is whether we can trust her, whether we can believe Brubaker and Bobbi anymore."

"What do you think?" said Max.

Wally rubbed his temples. "When Dawson was killed, Brubaker was ready to give up. He told me the colonel was the brains of the whole thing."

"Why didn't he tell us about all the sacrifice?" said Frankie.

"We're grunts," said Mayfield. "I told you, no officer ever tells the gory details, 'specially when he doesn't agree with his commanding officer."

Wally recalled his uncle Sherman's words at the sanitorium. He was just a gun, and the ones in charge decided how guns were used. Maybe Brubaker had just been a gun too.

"Back on the troopship," said Audrey, "Bobbi told me she loved her father, but they didn't always see eye to eye. When I asked her what she was talking about, she clammed up." Audrey looked to the space where Bobbi had been standing. "A girl can tell fake tears from real ones. Hers were real."

Wally gritted his teeth. Bobbi's beauty was undeniable, those green eyes, those curves, that voice... But she had played with his feelings to serve her own ends. She was a liar and a manipulator, no matter what she thought of her father's actions. There was no getting around that. But his feelings were no longer the issue.

Wally stood. "If Finch is calling the shots," he said, "if the plan is to protect and save lives before we put them at risk, I'm willing to see where it goes."

"I agree," said Audrey. "That's how Johnny would've wanted it."

Max nodded. "Our work can't be to sacrifice men. We work for a victory."

"Yeah," said Frankie. "A victory."

"All right," said Wally. "Sounds like we're not seeking asylum anymore. We're seeing this thing through to the end as US soldiers." He looked around. "Who agrees?"

Everyone raised their hand, including Mayfield, who stood with enthusiasm. "Now we sound like the good guys."

"Great," said Wally. "Then it's decided."

The team nodded, a cautious resolve washing over them.

"Now," Wally said, "how does a guy apologize for treason?"

After their second dramatic morning at the Royal Naval Communications Center, and considering the team's very obvious exhaustion, Finch decided to give the group the remainder of the morning to rest while she and Brubaker regrouped to hash out the details of the new mission with their European counterparts. Most of the team used the time to gather in the mess hall writing letters to their families, which Dawson and Finch had promised to send at once. They said it was only fitting given the concerns they'd voiced about their families' safety. Bobbi, however, retreated to her room, alone.

Wally and Audrey decided to forego letter writing for the moment and, instead, donned their coats and climbed the stairs to the building's rooftop, just as they used to do in Brooklyn when they needed to gather their thoughts. They sat on the utility box and faced the Thames under the wistful January sun.

Wally pulled out his uncle's pocket watch and opened it. He flipped it over and remembered that on the inside lid, opposite the watch, was a compass. He rarely used the compass since he never left New York and always seemed to know where he was going. But, at the moment, he had no idea in what direction he was heading, actually or figuratively. He held the compass and read aloud the delicate inscription that rounded the lid: "The right place at the right time."

"What does that mean?" said Audrey.

"Guess it's a play on words since the watch is also a compass," said Wally. "It's meant to help you find your place and time."

Audrey nodded as if that all made sense to her, and why wouldn't it? She was a person in complete control of her life, always seeming to know what she was doing and why she was doing it. By contrast, Wally's life felt like a runaway train. He was not in control, and that lack of control made him feel more like his uncle than ever before.

"I've been imagining my uncle out in the city, starting over," said Wally. "Like this fainting thing isn't a death sentence after all."

"It isn't," said Audrey, "for either of you."

Wally saw the compassion on her face, and her kindness made him feel warm.

"You're brave, you know," she said.

"What are you talking about? I'm a mess."

"This morning. The way you stood up to Brubaker, to Bobbi. I know that was hard. I know you were nervous, but you didn't pass out. You kept your cool." Audrey smiled. "You did that for all of us, Walter. You stood up for what you thought was right. You showed courage."

He looked away, unable to accept her compliments. "Max says there's a fine line between courage and recklessness," Wally said. "Guess I'm still trying to figure out where that line is."

Audrey touched his arm. "If you need help, just ask. I'll keep you on the right side of that line."

Something in Audrey's touch caught Wally's attention. He looked at her, surrounded by the morning glow, and felt something new, something electric. He no longer saw his neighbor. He saw the blue in her eyes, the gentle perfection of her skin, the honesty in her dimpled smile. He didn't see Johnny's little sister. For the first time, he saw a woman. A lever in his brain had been switched on, a siren activated, a truth that had always been there finally revealed to him as if a blindfold had been removed.

He felt his jaw slacken. Audrey was not just a good friend, not just a good person. She was an intelligent, courageous, amazing young woman. A woman who cared for him. And she was beautiful.

How had he missed that? All this time.

Wally's heart galloped with a new thrill, a thousand buzzing bees traveling through his veins. It had taken the absence of Johnny coupled with Wally's own abandonment of Bobbi to create the space for him to notice what had been there all along.

Audrey Milhouser was a beautiful young woman who actually liked him.

What a fool he had been.

The fog of East Wapping dissolved around her, evaporating with the heat of recognition, and the moment seemed like a dream. He gazed into her robin's-egg-blue eyes, which sparkled as if she were privy to his new thoughts about her, as if they were having some unspoken conversation.

The edges of her mouth turned up with recognition, and she leaned toward him like a magnet drawn to its pair. Her lids lowered and her lips drew close to his. But just as his mouth reached hers, something in his chest tightened.

He stopped but was unable to speak.

Audrey opened her eyes. "Walter?"

The sun leapt around the sky like a pinball in one of those machines they used to have at Coney Island. Audrey's shape grew distant, and the bright morning fell dark. The world folded in his vision like he was being pulled down a drain away from her. He fell from the utility box onto the rooftop.

"Walter, say something!"

He looked at her as if from a distance, managing to squeak out one word: "Audrey." But his voice was strange, small.

She cried out his name again, as if calling down a well into which he had fallen. "Walter!"

But he couldn't call back. The darkness wouldn't allow it. He fell to his back and succumbed to a cold, dark emptiness that grew like a living ink stain, a Rorschach blot that clutched him, pulling him deeper into the well with every pulse of his heart.

He knew his demon had reached its judgment.

He did not deserve Audrey.

13

The Wrong Place at the Wrong Time

The caw of crows filled his ears like conspiratorial laughter, and Wally opened his eyes. A cold sky, the color of bad luck, hung over him, the air infused with the smell of sardines. Wally sat up, realizing he was still on the roof of the Naval Communications Center. He blinked away the gauzy haze from his eyes, his mind following thoughts of Audrey like a trail of popcorn leading out of a forest. He searched for her but, instead, found Max standing over him.

"Jesus, Walter. You were out for twenty minutes."

Wally ran a hand through his hair and remembered what had happened there on the roof with Audrey, or, rather, what hadn't happened. He rubbed his eyes and saw Audrey standing behind Max, and the longing in his heart quickly returned.

"I'm sorry," said Audrey once their eyes met. "I had to get help. I was so worried. The last time, you woke up right away."

"Last time?" Max snapped. "When you fainted at the club, you said it was nothing. How many times has this happened?"

"I'm fine," said Wally, avoiding the question. He rose as steadily as he could, both out of defiance toward his brother and to show Audrey he was okay.

But, of course, he wasn't. If trying to kiss her was enough to put him out, how could they start any sort of romantic relationship, even if she were interested in him that way?

"Don't you dare tell me you're fine, Walter." Max pointed at him. "For someone who says he hates liars—"

"I've got it under control," said Wally, painfully aware that those words were another lie.

Max's eyes grew wide, his nostrils flaring. "I told you not to be reckless, remember? I told you not to take risks. What if you had passed out and fallen over the edge of this roof?" Max pointed angrily toward the Thames. "What if you had fallen off the troopship?"

"Neither of those things happened."

Wally understood these were reasonable fears, yet in that moment, he was less concerned about falling off a building than he was about falling for Audrey.

"I trusted you, Walter! This is serious."

"I heard you. Audrey heard you. Half of London heard you!"

As the tension swirled between the brothers, Audrey came forward and put her hand on Max's arm. "Can I talk to Walter alone?"

It seemed like Max was going to say no.

"Please?" said Audrey.

Max closed his eyes and then slowly opened them. Without a word, he headed for the door of the stairwell but turned back before leaving. "Chrissakes, Walter. Get the hell off this roof. The last thing I need to do is tell our parents you fell off a building."

Once Max had gone, Audrey rushed over, embraced Wally, and put her hand on his cheek, a new intimacy seeming to have formed between them.

"Are you okay? Tell me you aren't mad at me. You know I had to tell someone, don't you?"

"I'm not mad at you," said Wally.

"You seem mad."

"I'm mad at myself for putting you through this. I should've told Max about all this a long time ago. That's not on you. It's on me."

Audrey looked him over. "Are you hurt? You fell hard."

"I'm sorry. I didn't mean to scare you."

Audrey moved closer, took his hand. "When I couldn't rouse you, it put me right back to the day we lost Johnny. I couldn't do anything to help him either."

Wally drew a breath. "Audrey, I—"

"Ever since Johnny died," she said, "I keep coming back to a single thought, a wish for a moment when I could have said something that might've made a difference, something that would've made Johnny think twice about taking the chances he took."

Wally swallowed. "War is dangerous," he said. "Johnny understood that."

Audrey let go of Wally's hand and stared into the distance, toward the river.

"We found out Johnny was running reconnaissance when he got shot. He volunteered for that duty, the most dangerous duty there was." Audrey's eyes grew glossy. "No one was there to talk any sense into him."

"I'm sure there was nothing you could've said to stop him," said Wally. "You know how he got when he set his mind to something. Besides, he probably saved a bunch of other guys. Johnny knew the risks he was taking."

"Maybe he did," said Audrey. She turned to face Wally. "But do you?"

"What do you mean?"

"Maybe Max is trying to do for you what I couldn't do for Johnny—say something to keep you safe, get you to think twice before you put yourself at risk. One day, Max may think this was his moment and he'll feel exactly like I do. Like he missed his only chance."

Wally saw the desperation in Audrey's eyes. "You think I shouldn't be here," he said softly.

She reached over and placed in Wally's palm his uncle's compass-watch, which had fallen when Wally fainted. *"The right place at the right time,"* Audrey said, repeating the inscription. "You're exactly where you're supposed to be."

"So, you understand," said Wally. "No matter what happens, I have to see this mission through to the end. For you. For Johnny. For myself."

"I do understand," said Audrey. "But no one says you have to hurt yourself. Just promise me, if you faint again, you'll see a doctor."

Wally looked in her eyes and knew what he had to do. "I promise," he said. And while he didn't think a doctor could solve his problems, a plan was forming in his mind that would make the need for a doctor unnecessary. For now, for Audrey's sake, he'd keep his wits about him, minimize his risk of overstimulation, and steer clear of situations that might trigger his anxiety. That meant he'd have to keep his distance from Audrey until their mission was over, or at least until he had solved the riddle of his anxiety neurosis. Despite what his uncle's watch said, when it came to Audrey, he was just in the wrong place at the wrong time.

It was late afternoon by the time Wally finally shuffled to his empty quarters, exhausted from his sleepless night and the stressful morning that had followed. His brain ached and so did his hip where he had hit the roof.

He had cut things short with Audrey, told her he needed his rest, ignoring the ache in his heart that urged him to hold her in his arms. She seemed to understand, though it was clear she had hoped to spend more time with him alone. His new plan, of course, would not allow that.

He'd written long letters to each of his parents, taken a break for a small meal in the commissary, and now threw himself onto his bed, face down on his pillow, hoping to get a nap and keep his roving mind off Audrey. The call of his new feelings was strong. At each turn, he thought he smelled the sweet scent of her nut-brown hair, the knowing wisdom in her sky-blue eyes, the summer simplicity in her dimpled smile, and he hoped beyond reason that sleep would quiet his longing. However, before he could turn his brain off, the door flew open and Mayfield stomped in.

"Atten-hut!" Mayfield whacked the bottoms of Wally's feet. "Up and at 'em, soldier."

Wally shoved his face farther into the pillow and pretended to be asleep.

"I saw you move," said Mayfield. "C'mon. Get up!"

Wally turned over and faced his roommate. "Why, Alvin?"

Mayfield snatched his bugle and his trumpet from under his bed. "Drummond said it's time for our new mission briefing, and he promised some music-making." Mayfield lifted his bugle and blew. "I finally get to be part of this whole shebang."

Wally gave an exasperated sigh and sat at the edge of his bed. "Be careful what you wish for."

"After all the carrying-on this morning," said Mayfield, "don't you wanna see if we can actually take these people at their word?"

"I suppose."

"First you say you don't trust 'em, then you say you do. What better way to know if you can than to see 'em in action? If anyone should be wanting this, it should be you."

Wally marveled at Mayfield's unexpected logic. He made a good point. The team had agreed to trust Finch. But they still needed to see whether that trust was justified. And maybe heeding the call of the mission, diving into service of a higher calling was the very thing he needed to keep his mind off Audrey.

Wally stood. "You know what, Alvin? You're right."

Mayfield lowered his shoulders and raised his head like a rooster. "Don't say it like it's such a surprise," he said. "You ain't the only smart one."

The two made their way to the reception area, where Petty Officer Drummond was waiting with Frankie, Rat, Audrey, and Max.

Wally offered Max an apologetic smile, which Max returned with a pained smirk, leaving Wally to wonder whether his brother would ever forgive him. He prayed Max would at least keep the incident on the roof to himself and let Wally work things out in his own way without alarming the rest of the team. The last thing he needed was a lecture from Frankie or a million questions from Rat.

Audrey walked over. "You okay?" she whispered.

"Yep." Wally kept his answer terse and brief, working to keep his eyes from scanning the curve of her body, which now seemed to glow with magnetic energy. "Thanks."

Audrey squinted at his brevity but didn't reply.

"Very good," said Drummond. "You're all here."

"Where's Bobbi?" said Rat.

"Miss Dawson will meet us in the studio," said Drummond.

Hearing Bobbi's name sparked a cinching in Wally's gut. Now that something new with Audrey had developed, it seemed wrong that he'd ever had feelings for Bobbi. But had those feelings been real if everything he knew about her had been false? And, assuming he could put the past behind him, how could he work with her after he'd publicly berated her?

"Follow me."

Drummond led them up a flight of stairs to a large broadcast studio, much like the one at WKOB. They hadn't seen this space during their tour, but it was clear it would serve as the center of their efforts to come. It was a cold, open space with high ceilings, equipped with small risers, providing seating for a studio audience, a raised stage, metal music stands, microphones, recording equipment, and worktables with wooden chairs, songbooks, and pads of lined music pages, all ready for the team's use. But Wally's eye had already drifted to a burnished wood-grain grand piano with a polished lid and ornately carved music rack at the foot of the stage. It was the first piano he'd seen since leaving New York, and it was exactly what Wally needed to move his focus off his romantic quandaries, off his thoughts of betrayal, away from his persistent demons, and onto the mission.

"Rosewood Chappell concert piano," said Drummond. "Finest in London, in my opinion. Handcrafted, hand tuned, built right here in England. My grandad taught me on one of these."

Wally hardly heard a word Drummond said as he floated like a leaf, tugged by an invisible breeze, toward the piano, all thoughts of Audrey and Bobbi abandoned for the moment. He took a seat at the bench, rested his fingers in home position, where they instantly buzzed with connection. He was half tempted to belt out a tune but abandoned any thought of asserting himself and, instead, yielded to the call of piano song.

He intuitively ran scales. The keys grew warm under the tips of his fingers as the chords vibrated in the wood, in the air, in his body, in the room. The delicate, almost imperceptible smell of the piano's wood oil tickled his nose, and his ears filled with its music.

The others seemed to ignore him, which was fine with Wally. Instead, they checked out the room and the equipment, but all grew quiet, including Wally, when Colonel Brubaker entered the studio with Bobbi.

When he stopped playing, the team stood silent at attention to offer an awkward salute to Brubaker. It was a gesture charged with tension after their morning insubordination, and the quiet thrill of the Rosewood Chappell quickly left Wally, replaced by cold discomfort.

He summoned the bagpipes in his chest.

"At ease," said Brubaker, though it was unlikely any of them could be.

Bobbi walked over to a table in the corner, averting her eyes from Wally and the others. It was clear she felt even more uncomfortable than they did.

"Get familiar with this space," the colonel said. "Review the songbooks, check out the equipment. We'll begin the briefing when the superintendent arrives."

Wally sat back down at the piano, eager to lose himself once again in its musical embrace, but when he looked up, Brubaker was striding over like a blitzkrieg bomb finding its target.

"She's a beauty, isn't she?" said the colonel. He ran his hand along the piano's lid. "These Brits don't fool around."

Brubaker's friendly tone and demeanor seemed to imply he was ready to move on from their morning confrontation or perhaps pretend it had never happened, but Wally still felt the echo of it lingering like the tang of sardines in the air of East Wapping.

"Colonel, about this morning—"

Brubaker held up his hand, looked around, and then quietly said, "Follow me." He headed toward the rear of the studio.

Wally rose to follow, his stomach tying itself into an unwelcome knot. *So much for avoiding nerve-wracking situations.*

The colonel led him through a door into an adjoining hallway lined with closets and empty administrative offices. Once the door back to the studio had closed behind them and they were alone, Brubaker faced him. "Back on the troopship," he said before Wally could say a word, "I told you never to ignore my orders. Do you remember that?"

"Yessir," Wally said softly. "I remember."

"And yet, this morning, you did that very thing. Again. You defied my order requiring you to keep our mission secret. You questioned me in front of everyone—that's insubordination—and then shared our mission details with a British superintendent without knowing whether I had already done so—that's treason." The colonel narrowed his eyes. "Would you say that's an accurate description of what happened, Private Lipkin?"

Wally lowered his head. "Pretty accurate. Yes, sir."

"As your commanding officer, in light of these infractions, protocol obliges me to place you in front of a court-martial."

"I...I understand." Wally's fragile plan to prevent distress, to defeat his fainting problem, and to find his way back to Audrey was already failing, not an hour after putting it into play.

Brubaker stared at him, his gaze so close in the constricted hallway that Wally could see his own reflection in the man's dilating pupils. "Perhaps the part you don't understand," said the colonel, "is that I didn't agree with my superior either, and yet, I obeyed his orders. I did what I was told to do for the good of the war because that is what was expected of me. This appears to be something you have a hard time doing."

"I'm sorry, sir."

Brubaker took a breath, lowered his gaze, his voice growing softer at Wally's timidity. "It would be a lie to say I didn't think about defying the colonel myself," he said. "What he proposed was...challenging for me to accept. Yet, for the military to work, the chain of command has to prevail. And you need to know I believe in the chain of command. That's why I followed Colonel Dawson's orders and why I told Colonel Renshaw everything. It also happens to be why he trusted me to continue our mission."

Wally swallowed but didn't know what to say.

"I know Colonel Dawson was faced with horrible choices, Mr. Lipkin. And he died never knowing whether he'd made the right ones. He died with uncertainty." Brubaker narrowed his eyes again. "I may have had trouble with the man's methods, but I understand that dilemma now that I have his command."

Wally tried to look away, but Brubaker took Wally's arm, requiring his full attention.

"I've learned that uncertainty is the burden of leadership, Mr. Lipkin. Making the hard choices without knowing the outcome is the duty of command. The price of leadership.

Do you understand?"

"I think so, sir."

"This mission, our mission, is my chance to make sure that the sacrifice of those three hundred souls wasn't for nothing. To do that, I need you. That's why you're on the team and why I have to trust you. It's the one thing keeping you out of the brig. That's my decision, not the superintendent's."

"Yes, sir." Wally suddenly realized his mission had just gotten more complicated. Instead of Wally watching and waiting to see whether he could trust his colonel, Brubaker was now working to see if he could trust Wally. Trust would be a two-way street.

It was then, in the confines of this barren hallway, that his uncle Sherman's words returned to him. *A gun is an instrument used by the ones in charge. When you're the gun, you don't make the decisions.* It sounded unfair when Sherman said it, but from Brubaker's point of view, freedom from making difficult decisions was a gift from those in command to the poor saps like Wally who had to follow their orders. Brubaker bore the ramifications of tough calls so that Wally wouldn't have to; in return, Wally simply had to agree to the whole charade.

"We can only win this war if men like me can rely, unconditionally, on men like you, Private Lipkin. I know I have to earn your trust, but for now, I'll settle for your obedience. Are you prepared to offer that?"

Wally was far from trusting the colonel unconditionally. Nevertheless, he knew the answer that Brubaker expected, the answer that would keep Wally on the team and out of the brig.

"Yes," Wally lied. "I'm ready."

"Very good. Then let's consider the matter closed and get on with it, shall we?" Brubaker did not wait for Wally's reply, turning back to the hallway door and disappearing into the studio.

Wally took a moment to collect himself. He now realized that, as much as he was ready to abandon the habit of lying—the habit that had failed to generate any laudable results—there was still at least one lie he had to maintain. It was a lie mandated by the US government, and, by design, it provided a clear and prescribed path for him to follow that would keep him out of trouble. For that, he was grateful. Suppressing his feelings for Audrey was causing enough trouble as it was.

He shook out the tension in his limbs, reached for the door, and returned to the studio, pleased that he had managed not to pass out there in the cramped hallway.

Frankie and Max were now huddled over a songbook; Rat penciled away on a pad near-by, somehow inspired to write something. Audrey chatted with Mayfield as he assembled the mouthpieces of his trumpet and bugle, and she eyed Wally as he returned to the room.

Bobbi still sat alone at the corner table, miserable like a winter storm.

Wally used the team's distraction to make his way back to the piano bench, eager to reconnect with the magnificent rosewood grand, to ease his mind, calm his nerves, and make sense of the confusing and seemingly contradictory rules that now governed his life: to earn the trust of the colonel, he'd have to set aside his own distrust of him; to win the object of his affection, he'd have to keep his distance. He longed for the simplicity of Brooklyn, when his biggest worry was pulling a lever.

Before Wally could lose himself in piano song, Superintendent Finch arrived at the studio with Petty Officer Drummond at her elbow. Again, the team stood and saluted.

Finch raised her head. "Ladies and gentlemen, welcome to Operation Teacup, a top-secret effort between US and British communications teams and JASCO, the European Joint Assault Signal Company."

A strange relief fluttered in Wally's chest. The superintendent's flowery proclamation reminded him of the way things were at WKOB, when the team was full tilt into their jingle work, when the mission seemed simple, straightforward, and within their grasp, before the Nazis had shut them down and deception had undermined them.

"I know you're all uncertain about the duties that lie ahead," she continued, "and I've assured you that sacrificing our soldiers is not the point of our work. But make no mistake. Lives are on the line. People will die, either because of what we do or despite it." She returned a stare back at Max and Rat. "That's the truth," she said, "whether you're ready to hear it or not, and I'm committed to the truth."

Wally watched how Finch held herself, watched the certainty in her eyes, saw her leadership in action. If Brubaker was bold and Max had moxie, Finch had downright confidence. It was something Wally could only dream of.

"This team has the skills our work requires," she said, one arm raised to the air. "If we can move past the concerns of the morning, if we can rebuild the damaged trust among us and use those God-given skills, I believe we can turn the tide, end the blight upon the world, and do our part to bring this war to an end."

Wally looked to the others, saw in their eyes a reflection of his own fears. Like him, they knew the grim stakes, had seen them firsthand in the dying eyes of Colonel Dawson. Wally didn't need Finch to remind him that Nazis wouldn't stop until they marched down Fifth

Avenue over the bodies of American citizens. He'd seen the warnings of what Nazis could do spelled out in his neighborhood fliers; he'd lost his pal Johnny to their bullets and read in the papers about what Jews were losing every day across Europe, disappearing into the work camps of the enemy. Yet, to hear Finch speak the goals of the mission aloud in front of him and connect his work to the consequences on the ground somehow made the stakes more real.

"The amount of work to be done is considerable," Finch added, "and Colonel Brubaker assures me you can write jingles better and faster than anyone he's ever seen. He tells me you are the best, and I'm afraid that's exactly what we'll need from each of you: your best."

Finch fell silent and lowered her arm, letting her words wash over them all.

"Pardon me, ma'am," said Rat, using Finch's dramatic pause to interrupt her speech. "What if we can communicate more?"

The superintendent aimed her eyes at Rat. "You have something in mind, Mr. Rubinstein?"

Rat stood. "Since cracking the code, I realized we're going to have to get more complex in our work, to stop others from doing what I did."

Frankie rolled his eyes at what sounded like Rat bragging.

"What do you suggest?" said Finch.

"What if we could write songs longer than jingles?" said Rat. "Couldn't longer songs communicate more information, give more room for our code's complexity, maybe carry more secret information to our troops?"

Brubaker cocked his head, but something in Rat's knowing look made Wally nervous.

"Do you write such songs?" Finch asked.

"I don't," said Rat. He reached into his pocket and set a journal on the table. "But Walter does."

A swift horror clutched Wally by the throat. He fumbled in his empty jacket pockets to confirm what he saw was real. Rat had lifted his most secret possession, his journal full of love songs written for Bobbi back on the troopship—and there it sat on the table.

Wally bolted upright from the piano bench. "Clyde!" He suddenly grew light-headed and grabbed the piano to steady himself.

Audrey rose, walked over, and touched Wally's arm reassuringly, as if she could sense his anxiety and control it with her presence. She then looked over to Rat. "Clyde," Audrey repeated softly. "Did you take Walter's journal?"

"Well, yeah," said Rat. "He told me that he wrote a bunch of songs, whole songs all by himself. So, it just got me thinking—"

Audrey held up her index finger like a schoolteacher. "We're supposed to build back trust with one another, remember? How can anyone build trust with you if you take their things?" She stepped over and retrieved the journal from Rat's table.

Rat slumped in his chair. "I was just trying to help."

Audrey ran her thumb along the journal's pages, and it looked as though she was about to open it. Wally bit his lip, fearful she might read the words he'd written for Bobbi, emotions expressed that he no longer felt.

Instead, she walked the journal back over to the piano and handed it to Wally as if handing him his own beating heart.

"Here you go, Walter."

He stuffed his journal back into his pocket as fast as he could and exhaled his relief. "Thank you."

"Taking private belongings from others is inappropriate, Mr. Rubinstein," Finch chided, "but you may be onto something. Our coding team has been looking for ways to make the ciphers more complex, and full songs may give us the very real estate we need."

A small grin grew on Rat's face.

Finch looked around the room. "What do you think, team? Can you write full-length songs?"

Max rose, a glint in his eye. "Ma'am, writing songs is what we do. It's why we're here."

Drummond peered at Max over his round spectacles. "They can't just be any songs, you realize," the petty officer said. "The enemy has to believe they're popular radio tunes if they're to work as well as your jingles did."

"He's right," said Brubaker. "Your jingles worked because they were convincing. Proper songs will have to be even better if we hope to use civilian radio airwaves to send them."

Max thumbed the lapels of his jacket as if taking credit for the team. "We can do it," he said. "You'll see. Piece of cake."

"Right," said Frankie. "Cake."

"Yep," said Wally, but it sounded more like "gulp."

"Very well," said Finch. "I'll contact my colleagues at BBC Radio and make the necessary arrangements." She turned and left the studio with Drummond close at her heels.

"All right, people," said Brubaker, clapping his hands in command of their attention. "You heard the superintendent." He walked over to the piano. "Fall in. Let's put this team to work."

Everyone, including Bobbi, made their way over to the rosewood Chappell. It was the closest Wally had been to Bobbi since he'd accused her of being a liar a second time. He tried to make eye contact with her, tried to imagine what she was thinking, feeling. He wondered if she, like Brubaker, had decided that it was Wally who had been the betrayer of trust, not the other way around. After Brubaker's chiding in the hallway, even Wally wasn't sure anymore.

"We have all the material things we need at our disposal," Brubaker said. "The piano, composition pages, equipment, logistics personnel...the works."

Mayfield held up his bugle and his trumpet. "And my horns!" he said.

"Right," said the colonel. "But what matters most is our ability to work as a team."

The crew all looked at each other like strangers, and Wally wondered if that was even possible anymore.

"Get familiar with the equipment and materials," Brubaker said. "Write what inspires you at the moment. I'll work with the coding team to get them prepared for what's coming."

The group nodded their agreement, and Brubaker turned to leave. Before he exited, he said, "And, team, it's nice to be back in business."

Wally looked again to Bobbi; however, she had already retreated to her table, where she sat by herself, flipping through a songbook. She was not the effervescent, confident gal Wally had first met in New York, the one who floated into rooms or tousled people's hair. She'd lost her father, been forced back with her mother, and had been shunned by the very team she had helped put together. That was at least partially Wally's doing, even if her own lies were the catalyst for his actions.

Max and Frankie moved to another table to try their hand at a tune, Rat scribbled away on a pad, and Mayfield cleaned his trumpet alone. The team was not acting like a team.

Audrey made her way over to the piano bench, where she sat next to Wally. "You never got to tell me how you're doing," she said.

"Better since you got my journal back," he said. "Thank you." He was careful not to meet those inviting eyes.

"I know what that journal must mean to you," she said. "Every day on the troopship, I'd put on that baggy uniform and sneak out to get fresh air. Each time, I'd see you by the life rafts, writing in that thing. I wanted to come over, but you were so focused and distracted. That's why I came to the mess hall that day instead. Guess you were writing songs on the ship, huh?"

"Yeah," said Wally, reluctant to talk about his songs.

Audrey looked over to Bobbi and then back to Wally. "Did you write them for her?"

Wally froze at her question, and a shot of regret filled him. It felt wrong that he'd ever written anything for Bobbi, and it was the last thing he wanted to discuss with Audrey.

His hesitance was all the answer Audrey needed. Her gaze returned to Bobbi, who continued to read through music pages by herself.

"She's pretty," said Audrey with a pained melancholy, "like a pinup girl. I can see why you'd want to write songs for her."

"Audrey—"

She ignored him and stood. "Hey, Bobbi!" Audrey called. "Come over here a second."

"What are you doing?" Wally hissed.

Audrey leaned toward him. "You two need to patch things up or we'll never get this ball rolling."

Bobbi walked over and finally looked at Wally.

"Hello, Walter." Bobbi's voice was uncharacteristically soft.

"Hello," he said in a way that stripped the word of any meaning.

"Okay," said Audrey. "Let's not make this awkward. You two have some things to work out, and I think a song may help." She gestured to the piano. "How about a duet? Something upbeat like 'Don't Sit Under the Apple Tree'?"

Bobbi nodded. "Okay by me." She seemed suddenly animated like a bird being freed from a cage.

Wally tried to think of a reason not to comply, tried to come up with one of his convincing lies. But he was tired of lies—tired of the ones he'd told and tired of the ones he'd heard. He decided it was best to power though, keep his lying tongue settled in his mouth. Without a word, he returned his hands to the keys, eager to focus back on the rosewood angel.

He straightened his back and played the intro to the song by heart.

At the sound of the musical introduction, Mayfield scrambled over with his trumpet. "Hey, I know this one!"

Wally filled his lungs with air and reluctantly sang the man's portion of the song, imploring Bobbi not to sit under that apple tree with anyone else but him, working to keep all emotion out of his words.

The rest of the team gathered at the piano and snapped to the song as Mayfield joined in with his bugle. Bobbi sang the second verse, echoing the first, begging Wally not to go walking down lovers' lane with anyone else but her.

Wally listened to the lyrics and grew increasingly uneasy, as if he and Bobbi were actually having a conversation about waiting for one another under a tree. However, in Wally's mind, Audrey had become the "anyone else" in the song that Wally had hoped to kiss, and playing the tune was creating more tension than it seemed to be resolving, at least for him.

Desperate to end his misery, Wally played the final stanzas with none of his signature flourish, reluctantly pulling his hands away from the piano at the last note and stomping the pedals to quiet the music as soon as he could.

Bobbi, however, seemed delighted. For her, the duet had achieved what Audrey had hoped for, a break in the ice, a reconciliation. She held her head a little higher, tucked her blonde hair behind her ear, and smiled. "Thanks, Curly," Bobbi said to Wally. "That was terrific." She then tousled his hair, just as she had done the day they'd first met.

However, unlike that first encounter when Bobbi's touch had filled him with excitement, now it just felt uncomfortable and wrong. It was Audrey whose touch Wally wished for, and yet he'd forbidden himself from confessing those wishes.

The others appeared energized by the performance as well and began to review songbooks together, talk about song themes, and sing favorite lyrics with one another. Even Mayfield had been accepted into the fold, encouraged by the team's compliments for his expert trumpet playing. The moment orchestrated by Audrey was just what the team needed, just what Brubaker had hoped for, a chance to bring the crew together, to find their connections, not just to the mission or the music, but to one another. Everything appeared to be falling into place.

Why, then, for Wally, did it seem everything was falling apart?

A bright midnight moon shone through the slatted window blinds of Wally's sixth-floor quarters, casting shadows like prison bars across his face as he lay awake staring at a crack that ran along the ceiling. He thought he had closed the blinds tight as he was asked to do, and as was the custom since the Blitz, to shield any light that could be seen from enemy planes seeking a target. He rose, pulled the twine to close the slats more tightly, and sat back down on the bed's edge.

Mayfield's log-sawing snore only fueled Wally's distress, but, in truth, Mayfield could have been silent, the room pitch-black, and still Wally would have remained awake, troubled and confused. The people he'd named as liars seemed to have forgiven him, the team he'd convinced to seek asylum had now embraced their mission, and the scope of their work was now furthered by the involvement of both the British Navy and the European JASCO allies they'd been told were poised and ready to help. The work would be strengthened by new coding algorithms, new ciphers, and a commitment to creating full-length songs. By all reasonable measures, Wally should have been excited, ready to end the Nazi blight, join his friends in their enthusiasm, and get down to business.

They had come so far from Kensington and left so fast, he'd hardly had time to catch his breath. He and the others had scrambled so quickly from his crowded Brooklyn apartment that he hadn't even had a chance to consider grabbing his grandfather's ring from his bureau drawer on the off chance it carried secret powers.

Instead, he was trapped in a longing for Audrey he couldn't admit, feeling like a bloodthirsty mosquito ensnared in amber. These problems, of course, were his own fault, not the workings of a demon nor the result of lies others had told, and the truth of his culpability only added to his anxiety. So loud was the chiding voice in his head that he almost didn't hear the soft rapping on his door.

He hopped out of bed, slipped his feet into his Royal Navy-issued bedroom slippers, and pulled a striped bathrobe around him. He opened his door to find Bobbi, her hair in a bun, a similar bathrobe wrapped around her, a look of concern on her face. Her makeup, however, was impeccable.

"Did I wake you?" she said.

"No," said Wally hesitantly, nervous to find himself facing her alone. "Couldn't sleep."

"I didn't want to make a scene today in the studio, but I think we still need to talk." She looked away and then back to Wally. "I guess *I* still need to talk."

Wally looked over to Mayfield, who was snoring away, and decided he didn't want to risk inviting Bobbi in. He stepped out into the hall and closed the door behind him.

"The roof?" said Bobbi.

Wally recalled one of the things he liked most about Bobbi was her shared affinity for rooftops. Then he remembered his brother's plea and his agreement to stay away from places where there was a danger of falling. "How about the mess hall?" he said.

Bobbi agreed, and they made their way downstairs to the dining area, where a lone naval enlistee was mopping the floor with a broom that smelled of sour water and bleach. When the young man saw them enter, he gave a simple nod and then disappeared into the kitchen.

Bobbi chose a table with two chairs, and Wally sat across from her. "Should I see if I can find some cocoa?" he said.

"No," said Bobbi. "I don't want to be any trouble."

Wally looked for the man with the mop, searching for some way to delay the awkward discussion he figured was coming.

"Honest," said Bobbi. "I'm fine."

Wally shrugged. "Okay."

"Look," said Bobbi. "Here it is, straight." She leaned in and aimed her emerald gaze directly at him. "I manipulated you. I was flirty at the station when we first met, I set you up at the Diamond Club to rope you into the mission, and I told you my mother was dead to make you feel sorry for me, to keep you from leaving." She looked at the table between them. "I kept the details of those men's sacrifice from you for no better reason than to protect my father and my own shame. You called me a liar, and, the fact is, I am."

"Bobbi—"

"Let me finish, Walter," she said. "I had some apricot brandy, and if I don't get through this, it may wear off."

"Okay." Wally wondered where Bobbi had found apricot brandy in this place, despite British rationing, but realized that wasn't the point.

"My father knew I had feelings for you," she said. "Real feelings. That's why he talked with us back at WKOB. I was letting those feelings get in the way of the mission." Bobbi looked to the ceiling and then at Wally. "What he really wanted was for us trust each other."

Wally remembered Dawson's dying wish, a request Wally had failed to honor.

Bobbi blinked away her tears. "When my parents split, I was confused. My mother may have left him, or maybe he left her, but at the time, it felt more like they had both left me." She looked away. "All I knew was that my mother had ambition and my father had his own ideas about the world. I guess they were never really meant for one another."

Wally saw the pain on Bobbi's face and felt for her. Despite how crazy his own parents were, or because of it, there was never any doubt they were meant to be together.

"My father was my hero," she said. "He loved me for who I was. He included me in his plans, shared his ideas with me, confided in me, and trusted me. My mother just wanted me to live with my grandparents in Sheffield. She didn't want me involved with any of this. I was young. I thought that meant she didn't believe in me like my father did." Bobbi wiped a tear with her knuckle. "After they split, my mother moved me to London, but I fought her. Once I was old enough to travel on my own, I made a choice to return to New York to stay with my father. She and I lost trust, and it cost us everything. Now, I realize she just wanted to keep me safe, same as him. They just had different ideas of how to do that."

Wally watched Bobbi carefully, listened to her words, and heard the truth in them. He recalled those instances when she'd manipulated him, told him the very things he wanted to hear. In hindsight, he should have read the signs. But here, now, she seemed different. She was not dressed seductively or in urgent need of his help; she was in a bathrobe, her hair in a bun, sharing her painful story with breath that smelled like apricots.

"I'd understand if you never believe me again, Walter. I haven't done anything to earn your trust. But if you can at least forgive me for doing you wrong, maybe we can go from there. Maybe we can start over."

"Look," he said, "I know you lied because you wanted me to stick with the mission. You thought it was the mission that I was struggling with." He turned his eyes to the ceiling as if seeing straight through to the starry sky and the faces of his ancestors imploring him to strengthen his resolve. "I did have struggles," he said. "Still do. But not with the mission."

"What do you mean?"

He looked into Bobbi's earnest green eyes. "I mean, I have a secret too." Wally's heart knocked against his chest like an animal trying to escape. "I've lied to cover it up, just like you lied to cover your secret. And now that you've come clean with me, I think for things to be right between us, I need to come clean with you."

"Hang on," said Bobbi. She reached into her bathrobe pocket and handed Wally a small bottle. "Sounds like you could use some apricot brandy too."

Wally unscrewed the cap, lifted the bottle, and took a swig. The sweet, velvety alcohol rushed through him to his fingertips and toes, giving him a warmth like home cooking. He immediately understood how alcohol could be mistaken for courage and took another slug.

"Remember the Diamond Club?" he said, putting down the bottle. "After I played for you, after you kissed me?"

"I remember," she said, a playful gleam in her eye.

"I passed out right there on your dressing room floor."

"Right," she laughed, but then seemed to notice from the look on his face that the memory did not bring with it the same fondness she felt for it. Her tone grew more somber. "I remember that too."

"Well, that wasn't the first time I'd lost consciousness," said Wally, "and it wasn't the last." He looked away. "It's been happening since I was thirteen, and it happened again the night your landlady chased me off. I fainted in an alley on my way home." He turned back to face her. "It happened again today on the roof. The fact is, I have a fainting problem."

To hear himself say it out loud in front of someone other than Audrey felt surprisingly liberating. Instead of the panic he had expected, a strange peace filled him, or maybe that was just the apricot brandy working its magic. It was as though he'd been released from captivity, like his uncle set free from the sanatorium.

"Walter!" Bobbi's face lit with concern. "I had no idea."

"Please don't be upset," he said. "And don't make it a big deal either. I'm trying to handle it on my own."

"Why is it happening?"

"I have an uncle this happens to also. It may just run in the family," said Wally. "It's why I tried to win the jingle contest in the first place. I hoped to get that government job and serve the war effort stateside while staying out of situations that might trigger my fainting."

Bobbi put her hand on her chest. "And then I came along and pulled you right into the thick of it," she said. "Oh, Walter. I'm so sorry.

"Don't be. I wanted in on this mission all along, even when things got dicey. Still do." Wally shrugged. "At least it's safer than fainting in a foxhole, or on a ship or fighter plane."

They both fell silent, knowing from the events at WKOB that there were no safe places where Nazis were concerned.

"What can I do?" said Bobbi. "How can I help?"

"Please, don't do anything," said Wally. "It's a secret. My secret. And I want to keep it that way. Only Audrey and Max know, and that's plenty. I don't want anyone treating me differently, and I sure don't want anyone's pity."

"I understand," said Bobbi. "Your secret's safe with me."

"I know," Wally said, marveling at the fact that he meant it. "And telling you is my way of saying I trust you. And forgive you. I guess I'm asking you to forgive me too."

Bobbi reached across the table and took Wally's hand, tears returning to her eyes. "Oh, Walter. I can't tell you how relieved I am. Maybe we can start things over. See where things go?"

Wally recalled her statement about having feelings for him and realized that this conversation was not complete, couldn't be complete until all his secrets had been shared. He reached for the brandy and took another swig, a long one, and then put the bottle down.

"There's something else I need to say," he said. He drew a long breath. "I have feelings for Audrey."

Wally braced himself and watched Bobbi for her reaction.

At first, she remained still, her green eyes staring straight through him. She released his hand, and then she, too, reached for the brandy, finishing it off. "Okay," she said, and set the empty bottle on the table. She wiped her lips with the back of her hand. "I understand. She's really wonderful."

"I didn't realize I felt that way about her until today," Wally explained. "We've known each other our whole lives, but it sort of snuck up on me. I'm a real dunce."

"Fellas can be pretty thick about things," said Bobbi. "She really is great. I can't argue with that."

"I'm sorry, Bobbi. I care for you, but—"

Bobbi stood. "Thanks, Walter. I'm glad we're resolved. I wish you luck with Audrey." Her face was inscrutable, yet Wally thought he'd somehow hurt her feelings.

"Bobbi—"

"I'll keep your secrets," she said. "Both of them." She gestured with pinched fingers beside her lips and gestured as if turning a key. She then offered a reassuring smile.

Wally nodded, unsure what he had left to say or what was left to ask. Trust had not come easily between them, and yet it finally felt right, even if the words to get there had been awkward.

"Good night, Walter." Bobbi tightened the sash on her robe and, with a simple nod, walked out of the mess hall, leaving Wally alone with the empty brandy bottle and the flavor of apricot still on his tongue.

It was a puzzling irony. Bobbi was now the only person who knew his deepest secrets, all of them, even though she had been the one person he'd trusted least in the world only twenty-four hours earlier. She hardly seemed happy to learn of his feelings for Audrey, but at least he had been honest with her, and, in that, there was some small victory, some sort of progress. That honesty, that trust, meant he had finally granted her father's dying wish. Now, he just had to figure out how to keep his feelings for Audrey in check, and the thought made him wonder where in the building he could find more apricot brandy.

14

Kaboom and Kaboom

I t had taken weeks, and Wally would never say so out loud, but he now had to admit that Petty Officer Drummond's fondness for the rosewood Chappell piano was well founded. The gorgeous burnished wood piano was the greatest he'd ever played. Its strings were tight and resonant, its ivory keys soft to the touch, compliant, and familiar, and its pedals responsive and buoyant. The sounds it made were superior to any other, and it had become an extension of Wally's body and mind. Given the volume of songs he had played and the pounding he had given it since they'd first arrived in London, the piano had fared better than he had, and the work was beginning to catch up with him, especially after a day like this one where the work had begun at oh-six-hundred and gone straight on through the day.

Wally gazed around, bleary-eyed, to see his teammates strewn about the Naval Center studio. Max sat with Frankie at a nearby table, both resting their chins in their hands, staring at the blank wall as if willing new songs to appear there. Rat noodled away on the same page he'd been scribbling on for three days, and Mayfield lay asleep on the first bench of the studio risers, though he still provided a valuable service. The rhythm of Mayfield's snoring happened to follow a perfect four-four cadence like a metronome, and Wally had been using his friend's nasal rumbling to help compose new songs until he, too, had run out of steam. Audrey and Bobbi had returned to their quarters for what Bobbi called "some beauty rest."

They'd all been at it this way for weeks on end, relying on their newfound trust and partnership to craft new songs. Just as Finch and Brubaker had promised, Operation Teacup had been running very differently from their work at WKOB. Each member of the team now had increased security clearance and was privy to the goals and results of each mission. And, instead of being handed a list of required counts, words, phrases, and rhythms to incorporate into their music, the team was expected to write the songs and music first. Rat had joined the British code writers, and based on his knack for codebreaking, helped offer methods through which their music could deliver the needed messages in a more complex way. Based on the prior jingle work, Rat and the coders created ciphers and corresponding code sheets, designed to encode and decode messages hidden in their songs. The cipher code sheets were then provided through secret channels to high-ranking Allied officers who had been trained there at the Naval Center, now deployed across the continent where they awaited public radio broadcasts of the songs they were meant to decrypt. By keeping the code sheets and songs separate, the mission itself would be kept safe, at least as safe as they could make it.

The JASCO leadership had sent several dozen men through training there at the East Wapping facility, where they learned how to decode the messages being built into their songs. For several weeks, small batches of men would come through, each of them musicians in their civilian lives, able to read music and decipher notes they heard aloud, just as Brubaker had described back in the Lipkin living room on the day the mission had been laid out for their families to hear. These young men were trained, put to the test, and retrained to assure they could do the work on the receiving end of each song Wally and his team would create. Max would lecture these recruits on the importance of their roles, the stakes of their work, and the beauty of using music as a tool for bringing down the Nazis, as though he were some sort of army commander himself with the duty of inspiring and directing Allied forces in the same way Dawson had done before when Wally, Frankie, and Max were the new recruits. Brubaker and Finch seemed to allow it, amused by Max's disposition and the warm reaction of the soldiers of his age.

Wally would eye these men, lined up day after day in the risers of the studio, trying to memorize their names, their faces. Even after they had deployed, he'd try to keep them in his mind as he crafted or played each song, imagining them listening, decoding, and running the directions to their own commanding officers. He understood that it was their lives on the line, their safety the codes and songs were intended to protect. But as each week passed, and more men came through, their personal details became hard for his mind to carry.

Frankie, on the other hand, had found greater happiness. He had struck up a relationship with Miss Davies, whose first name they learned was Dorothy. He'd arranged his breaks to coincide with hers and often had to be retrieved from the reception desk, where he flirted with her shamelessly every day. She seemed to relish Frankie's attention and had managed to secure clearance to come hear the team play whenever she could. Their mutual affection was sweet and tender, and it made Wally happy for his friend, even as he tried to set aside his own feelings for Audrey.

Wally stood from his chair and shook away these thoughts. He then staggered like a sleepless ghoul to the corner table and turned on the radio to combat his lack of sleep. Thanks to Finch, the team's songs were getting played in heavy rotation through the BBC's *General Forces Programme*, along with other songs and popular entertainment, removing the tunes from suspicion as instruments of war. Each week, after several days of airplay ahead of key battles, the songs were then rebroadcast on Allied radio, when they could be decoded for the messages they carried to the troops. Code sheets were scheduled to be delivered and changed weekly with each new batch of songs that followed.

The Germans, in the meantime, had not sat idly. They continued to wreak havoc and spread fear, not just on the European continent but right on their doorstep. Three times since Wally and his team first arrived in England, Luftwaffe airplanes had dropped bombs on London. The rattle and vibrations of their assaults were felt in the rivets of the Naval Center and throughout East Wapping. It seemed East Wapping had its own air-raid wardens like him, distributing fliers and pulling sirens throughout the city. He was grateful to be in a fortified military facility, surrounded by trained officers, but each time the center's own sirens rang, he and the others had raced to the underground chambers of the center to ride out the assault below the surface of the Earth, like groundhogs. Owing to their good fortune, or perhaps to the Royal Navy's success in keeping the purpose of their facility secret, the German bombs had been directed far enough away from them not to do any damage to the building. It seemed to reinforce their plan to move the facility to Scotland as soon as the new facility was ready. But the onslaught had one specific effect on the team. It had made them all more determined than ever to stop the blight of the Nazi machine, to work hard to achieve their mission goals, and to help the Allies defeat the Axis powers once and for all.

Wally returned to the piano bench and eyed the team as the radio music floated through the air of the studio. Each of them had proven their skills as Finch had asked, and he was never prouder to be part of such a group. He, too, had worked to meet the demands of the mission, writing complete songs from scratch, even though Rat had urged him to use the songs he'd already written in his journal back on the troopship. But Wally refused. He had abandoned those songs, just as he had abandoned the feelings he thought he'd had for Bobbi. Instead, the lyrics he now wrote carried both secret messages for the Allies and his secret longing for Audrey. With each passing day, he found it more difficult to contain his feelings for her, and to keep those feelings to himself. The close quarters of the studio, his daily interactions with Audrey, and his growing admiration for her only added fuel to his romantic fire. Now that he had finally recognized how great she was, it was all he thought of.

"What are you daydreaming about?" said Drummond. Wally hadn't seen the petty officer come in and startled when he approached the piano.

He squinted at Wally through his round glasses. "You look knackered," Drummond said. He then looked around the studio. "The whole lot of you look knackered."

"What's 'knackered'?" said Wally.

Drummond tossed his clipboard onto the piano lid. "You being cheeky? It means you've been holed up here long enough. It's time to check out a proper English pub, mate."

"Pub?" said Frankie, lifting his chin. "You payin'?"

"Indeed," said the petty officer.

"Don't have to ask me twice," said Max, standing from his chair. "I've been dying for some fresh air."

"Can I bring Dorothy?" said Frankie.

"S'pose so," said Drummond.

Though Wally still found Drummond annoying, he realized the guy did know how to motivate a team and had proven both effective and efficient at the task.

"Come on," said the Drummond. "Fetch the girls."

Frankie rose from his table, leaned over, and punched Rat, who was still dozing.

"Ow!" said Rat, waking with a start. "What was that for?"

"Four-eyes is springing for drinks," said Frankie.

Wally walked over to the riser and shook Mayfield awake. "Alvin," he said. "Rise and shine."

"I'll milk the goats in a minute, Mama," Mayfield muttered, still stuck in a dream.

"Okay, but the goats are waiting," said Wally, playing along.

Mayfield lifted his head, "Huh?"

Max rubbed his buddha-like belly. "What kinda food will they have at this 'proper English pub' of yours?" he said.

"Steak and kidney pies," said Drummond. "Best in East Wapping."

"Will the beer be warm?" said Max with a frown. "I heard that's how the Brits like it."

"Ale is best served at room temperature," said Drummond. "Just as it was intended."

"Debatable," said Frankie, and he split to go collect Dorothy.

Max pulled his suspender straps over his shoulders, now appearing wide awake with the talk of food. "I'll get Bobbi and Audrey," he said, and strode out of the studio.

"Get cracking, lads," said Drummond. "Civilian attire. Out front at nineteen-hundred."

Wally followed Mayfield back to their quarters, eager for the chance to get out of the facility and to be close to Audrey, even though he knew he'd have to keep his feelings to himself. As frustrating as it had been, thinking about his forbidden feelings had proven productive as a source of musical inspiration. They had led Wally to write two of the best songs he'd ever written: "My Girl Back Home" and "Bad Time for a Good Man Tonight." It was exciting when Wally first heard the songs played on BBC radio, and a thrill again when he learned they had been transmitted to the middle of the conflict in Italy. The fact that Audrey loved those songs was icing on the cake, even if she didn't know Wally had written them for her.

Over the weeks, Audrey had tried to concoct opportunities for them to be alone, but when Wally consistently created excuses to avoid such moments, Audrey seemed to back off. He had not intended to leave her feeling rebuffed, but if he was going to be the man he wanted to be, the man she deserved, their time together would have to wait.

Wally gathered his civilian attire and reflected, as he dressed, on the pendulum that seemed to govern both his personal life and the progress of this despicable war. Despite the team's impressive productivity, the war was now at a standstill. Italy had officially surrendered to the Allies, but Hitler continued to hold Rome. For every German submarine destroyed by the Allies, an Allied ship was sunk by the Germans. The map in the conference room had red Nazi pins all over Europe, and the pins kept growing. It was a never-ending arm-wrestling match, and hope among the team was starting to run thin. Even more disturbingly, the papers reported camps had been found where Jews had been taken by the Germans to starve, die, or worse, with more Jews getting captured and transported away from their homes like cattle. Everyone in Europe had it bad, but for Jews, it seemed, the clock was ticking loudest.

This made Wally think about his own family. His mother had written that they were safe, happy, and proud of both Max and Wally. Knowing she had to keep their correspondence free from compromising details in case it was intercepted by the enemy, his mother had said the families were safe just where Wally and Max had left them, her way of saying they were still at Fort Hamilton. According to Brubaker, Wally's folks had volunteered for work as a seamstress and a garment presser for the armed services with Copulsky, the garbage-man-turned-army-security-officer checking in on them daily. Audrey's mother and brother, Carl, were helping in the mess hall, with Carl saying every day that he wanted to be an airman, sailor, or soldier depending on who he saw in the chow line. Frankie's father was apparently restless but was now assisting with weapons training, and Rat's mother had taken to helping with the grim task of writing condolence telegrams to the families of fallen soldiers. It seemed the families of the team were aiding the war effort in their own ways, but Wally wouldn't be satisfied until he laid eyes on them himself, still feeling the guilt of dragging them into something they didn't ask for in the first place.

He went to the bathroom, shaved neatly, and splashed his face with a brisk, lemony aftershave before returning to his room. As he tied his tie in a Windsor knot the way his father had taught him, Wally allowed his mind to drift to Audrey and their night ahead. He opened the box with the loafers she had given him, slid them on, and sighed at the thought that they fit perfectly, the same way Audrey fit him. Still, it felt odd to wear shoes meant for Johnny, and the symbolism wasn't lost on him. He wasn't as brave as Johnny, and certainly not as strong. But he had every intention of protecting Audrey, filling his shoes in that way, and for that, he knew Johnny would approve.

"I'm gonna wear my boots," said Mayfield, pulling his army-issued standards from his bureau.

"Why would you do that?" said Wally.

"First new pair of shoes I've ever owned," said Mayfield. He held the boots to the light. "My whole life, it's been hand-me-downs and church donations," he said. "Uncle Sam has been like Santa Claus. New clothes, new friends, and new boots."

Wally hadn't considered all the army could offer a guy like Mayfield. He'd been focused more on what it took from guys like him, how it had redirected his life so wholly.

"I think boots are fine," said Wally. Mayfield was a simple guy with simple pleasures, and Wally found their friendship to be one of the few good things that had come from this godforsaken war.

Mayfield began polishing his prized footwear. "I'll shine 'em up quick, and then we can go."

Soon, the team had gathered outside, at the naval facility's front entrance. Wally was grateful to wear his civilian clothes, to feel more like his old self. April had proved much warmer than prior months, and it felt good to be outside, to breathe fresh air, to see the setting sun's sparkle on the Thames.

Frankie arrived with Dorothy on his arm. She wore a conservative dress the color of chestnut, her dark hair down to her shoulders, looking more attractive than Wally remembered.

Bobbi was characteristically overdressed in a shiny green number that matched her eyes and caressed her curves like ivy clutching the statue of Venus. Her curls bounced and her skin was flawless like a Hollywood starlet's.

However, despite the beauty of Dorothy and Bobbi, it was Audrey who captured Wally's attention. Like Bobbi, Audrey was also dolled up, having borrowed a smooth sapphire gown from Bobbi's wardrobe. And yet Audrey seemed natural and authentic, unaware of her own beauty and the power that came with it. She sported healthy brown curls, her hair now longer than when she'd first left New York. Her makeup was light and precise, serving to make her blue eyes especially electric.

A flash of that electricity shot through Wally when their eyes met. "You look...very nice," he said.

"We're going out," Audrey explained, her dimpled cheeks growing flushed at his attention. "Don't get much chance these days."

Wally bit his tongue. He really wanted to tell her how perfect she was, how remarkable, but knew to do so would only open the floodgates, draw him closer to her. It was a move he was unready to make.

"Let's go," said Frankie. "I'm starving."

"I could eat a horse," said Max.

Wally turned to Rat, afraid he might comment on Max's appetite or his likeness to a horse. But to Wally's surprise, Rat said nothing, appearing as though such a joke hadn't even occurred to him.

The group made its way deeper into East Wapping along the waterfront and past a row of shops and vendors, with dusk drawing entrepreneurs, selling candles and trinkets, calling for shillings to fund their riverside enterprise. As the team walked down the street, Drummond strolled up next to the ladies.

"You girls look lovely," he said, pinching his glasses.

"Well, thank you," said Bobbi.

"Aren't you sweet?" said Audrey.

Wally's annoyance began to bubble, but he gritted his teeth and tried to ignore it.

Mayfield hustled forward in his buttoned-down shirt that ran short in the sleeves. He wore a tie, a pair of slacks, and the shiniest army boots Wally had ever seen. His hair was combed and parted for the first time since Wally had met him.

"Can I talk to you?" Mayfield whispered, tugging on Wally's elbow. There was a nervous shake in his voice.

"Sure," said Wally, allowing the rest of the team to pass. Mayfield pulled him aside.

"I'm gonna ask Audrey out tonight," said Mayfield. "You know her better than anyone. What can I say to win her over?"

The blood rushed from Wally's face, and he thought he might pass out right there on the waterfront boulevard.

"You...like Audrey?" Wally stuttered.

"Well, yeah," said Mayfield. He squinted at Wally. "Wait. You're not thinking of asking her out, too, are you?"

"No." Wally barked the word too quickly, knowing his denial was true, though it wasn't the whole truth. It would have been more accurate to say "not yet."

"Okay. Good." Mayfield breathed his relief. "What should I say to her? How should I act?"

"I don't know, Alvin," said Wally, realizing he sounded upset. Not wanting to draw attention to his disposition regarding Audrey, he quickly added, "Just be yourself, I guess."

"Be myself?" said Mayfield. "Who am I?"

"Shuffle on, mates," Drummond called from ahead. "We've only got two hours' leave."

Wally and Mayfield caught up with the others farther along the harbor where fishing vessels nodded in the Thames. Wally focused on the low nautical bell that rang in the distance, calling like the nagging vision of Mayfield trying to make time with the girl he secretly cared for.

"I'll warn you," Drummond said to the gals, "we may cause a stir. Most of these pub folks are fisherman and charwomen. They don't dress for pies and pints. Not like you lot."

"Oh, nonsense," said Bobbi. "We'll eat our food and have our drinks like everyone else."

Drummond chuckled and shook his head. "As you like." He seemed to have learned not to argue with Bobbi.

As they moved farther down the riverside, the air smelled increasingly of fish, just as it had on the day they'd arrived in East Wapping. It was an odor Wally and the others had been spared over the months of their indoor isolation. Wally held his breath, trapped between the stink of the street and the stink of his thoughts.

Just as Wally was ready to bury his head in his coat, the team arrived at the pub. A carved sign hung over the entrance that read "The Lout and the Lady," leaving Wally to wonder if the universe was sending him a message about his relationship with Audrey, whatever that relationship was.

When Audrey reached for the door, Mayfield dashed forward to hold it for her. "I've got that," he said. His smile was as awkward and as crooked as his tie.

"Thank you, Alvin!" Audrey batted her eyelashes as she strode through the open door.

Bobbi followed and winked. "What a gentleman."

Wally clenched his teeth but pretended it was a smile.

"Thanks, pal," said Frankie, still hooked arm in arm with Dorothy Davies.

Mayfield's own face was a wide grin, his cheeks flushed pink, either from the cold or from the girls' attention.

"Was that okay?" Mayfield asked as Wally passed. "You hold a door open for a woman, right?"

"Yes, Alvin," Wally said flatly. "You do."

The Lout and the Lady was just as Drummond had described, a tavern filled with old leathery fishermen, grungy dockworkers, and women in coal-smudged aprons. Flocked floral paper ran along the walls, peeling in places to reveal the ash wood beneath it. Photos of old seafarers and fishing vessels were hung everywhere, and a large taxidermized fish of some sort sat above the hearth in the back of the room. The ceiling was also planked with wood, creating a warm sense of protection.

Laughter rose and fell, and the place felt welcoming. There were a few young ladies in lace-fringed frocks who were adept at balancing trays of stouts and ales on their long porcelain arms. A full-figured red-haired bar matron doled out the booze alongside a grizzly old bartender. In the far corner were two men locked in a game of darts with friends haggling over who might win. The smell of beef and barley floated through the air and nearly made Wally forget all his troubles.

The bar matron caught Drummond's eye. "Grab a seat if you can find one, dearie."

"There," Rat said, pointing toward two tables by an old piano.

"Perfect," said Drummond.

The barman came over to wipe the table as the crew took their seats.

"What d'ya say, Wally?" Drummond called, pointing to the rickety upright. "Play us a tune?"

The barman looked up at Wally and motioned with a fistful of used mugs, streaked with froth, toward the piano. "Help yerself, lad," he said with an Irish brogue. "We could use a bit o' playin'."

"All right," said Wally, glad for a distraction from Mayfield. "What should I play?"

"Play Audrey's song," said Bobbi, "so she can sing it."

"Oh, no," said Audrey. "Not in front of everyone."

"You're good," blurted Mayfield. "You should sing."

Audrey offered him a half smile that Wally wished had been aimed at him. "I don't know, Alvin."

The barman dragged forward a standing microphone, although the small pub didn't require any amplification.

Audrey continued to look uncertain.

"You can do this," said Mayfield.

A few of the patrons caught on and hooted their encouragement. "Give it a go, lass! Let's hear what ye got."

One man added, "Rather *see* what ye got!" And received a round of laughs from his mates.

Both Wally and Mayfield shot the man an angry look, and Wally worried they might start a brawl. Instead, Audrey relented.

"Okay, okay." She stepped over to the piano and took her place at the microphone to enthusiastic applause.

Wally took a seat on a wobbly stool in front of the old upright. He played some fast staccato combinations to start and to get his mind off Mayfield's intentions. The piano was slightly out of tune and nothing like the Chappell at the studio, yet it was surprisingly loose like his Wurlitzer back home, and Wally figured he could make it work.

He played the intro to "I Run a Little Blue," the tune Audrey had written with lyrical help from Wally, the one that had been playing on the radio the whole last week.

After the soft intro, Audrey took a breath, and sang:

> *"I run a little blue;*
> *That's all because of you.*
> *I find your heart so hard to read.*
>
> *We opened up a door,*

And now I long for more.
To grow a tree, you first plant a seed."

Heads turned from the bar as all eyes fell on Audrey. Wally had played the song a hundred times with her when they'd written and recorded it for broadcast. And yet, here on the dilapidated piano in the local pub, it sounded perfect.

"And when it's all in place,
You're home in my embrace,
That's the time you'll know it's true.

I'll give you all I can,
And woo you with my plan.
'Til then, I'll run a little blue."

Wally played the interlude, his hands moving with a memory of their own. When he glanced up from the keys to find Audrey, their eyes locked in a way that held him as if time had stopped, his gaze so steady he felt transported.

It was in that instant, the inscription in his uncle's watch seemed to fit. *The right place at the right time.* The music filled his heart which pulsed for Audrey. He'd never felt so connected to another person, and the feeling left him mesmerized. The moment must've been profound to others watching, too, because he heard the audience woo and whistle at their lingering stare.

The noise that rose from the crowd broke Wally's trance, brought him back to the moment. That's when he noticed Mayfield scowling. Still, Wally couldn't help himself, or maybe he just didn't want to, and he turned back to Audrey.

She cracked a smile, one clearly meant for him, and she resumed singing.

"I look into your eyes,
And see with some surprise
The things you want me to see,

The things we dare not speak,

The love that we both seek,
The things that just cannot be.

I see it on your face,
Feel it all in your embrace,
The things we both know are true.

Until you're back with me,
This feeling cannot be,
And for now, I run a little blue."

Wally played the reprise, and on the last note, Audrey took a bow. The pub's patrons burst into applause. Glasses shook and people stood.

"Lass sounded just like the one on the radio," called a woman at a nearby table.

Wally wanted so badly to explain how lucky the patrons were to have the real singer of that song in their midst.

The bar matron bustled over, her face alight with glee. "Play more songs like that one, and Harry says he'll pay for your meals," she said.

Frankie stood. "You've got a deal!" he said, and his enthusiasm made Dorothy laugh.

Drummond surveyed the group. "All right," he said. "Steak and kidneys all around."

"And an apricot brandy," said Bobbi.

"Sounds good," said Audrey, taking her seat. "Me too."

"Me three," said Dorothy.

The fellas all ordered ales, and Frankie added, "As cold as you've got."

Wally also agreed to an ale, though he would have preferred the brandy given how effective he found it was for settling one's nerves.

Mayfield asked for a whiskey and then rushed over to pull Wally aside. "What's the big idea," he hissed, "making eyes at Audrey?"

"I didn't make eyes. I was just playing her song."

"Well, keep it that way," Mayfield seethed. "I've got plans." He returned to take his seat and crossed his arms.

Wally tried to take his own seat, but before he could, Bobbi grabbed him by the arm.

"Not so fast, Curly," Bobbi said. "It's my turn."

"Okay," said Wally. "What did you have in mind?"

Bobbi shot him a knowing smirk. "This crowd looks ready for 'Kaboom, Kaboom, Kaboom,' wouldn't you say?"

"That song's a little risqué," said Wally. "And don't you need Audrey for that number?"

Bobbi raised an eyebrow. "You're not complaining, are you?"

Wally turned toward Audrey, who was out of earshot, his gaze lingering.

"Attaboy." Bobbi elbowed him and then walked over to get Audrey.

True to her word, Bobbi had kept Wally's feelings for Audrey a secret ever since the night he'd confided in her. Now, Bobbi was acting playful, creating opportunities for Wally and Audrey to interact, and tonight he didn't mind. Time Audrey spent with him was time she wasn't alone with Mayfield.

Wally placed his hands on the keys again just as Bobbi pulled Audrey back in front of the patrons, drawing the eyes and the whistles of the drunken crowd along with her. Wally pounded out an extended version of the song's introduction to allow Bobbi and Audrey the time to take position at the microphone.

Out of the corner of his eye, Wally saw Mayfield glowering.

Bobbi raised her hand to her mouth and called, "This one's for all our fightin' boys!" and the crowd cheered. She and Audrey began to sway and sing in harmony to the piano music.

> *"With the flowers in bloom,*
> *And the way you make me swoon,*
> *It's kaboom, and kaboom, and kaboom, and*
> *kaboom!"*

With each "kaboom," both Bobbi and Audrey put their hands on their hips and thrust them left and then right. It was sultry and suggestive, lighting a fuse in the already explosive crowd. Some of the women even sang along, no doubt recalling the tune from its recent radio play.

> *"With the stars and the moon,*
> *And the lights off in the room,*
> *It's kaboom, and kaboom, and kaboom, and*
> *kaboom!"*

The girls then sang the intervening verse softly.

> *"The bombs,*
> *They may be droppin',*
> *But the love,*
> *It won't be stoppin'."*

Wally pounded the keys dramatically like an old saloon piano player from the Western films he loved to watch with his father.

> *"When the room is on fire,*
> *And my heart's full of desire,*
> *It's kaboom, and kaboom, and kaboom, and*
> *kaboom!*

> *When I pucker up for kissin',*
> *Not a target you'll be missin',*
> *It's kaboom, and kaboom, and kaboom, and*
> *kaboom!"*

With each thrust of the girls' hips, the patrons stomped their feet on the wooden floor and thumped the tables. Wally feared the walls of the pub might crumble from the quake. Still, seeing Audrey dance so suggestively sent heat through his fingers and toes.

> *"The bombs,*
> *They may be droppin',*
> *But the love,*
> *It won't be stoppin'."*

The girls traded off between the final lines, their bawdy movements making Wally's limbs warm.

"It's the love that we'll be makin',
And the risks we'll both be takin',
It's the room that will be shakin',
And your boots that will be quakin',
It's my heart that will be achin',
And my dear, there's no mistakin',
It's kaboom, and kaboom, and kaboom, and
kaboom!"

When the song ended, the crowd erupted in crazed applause, glasses crashing to the floor and men climbing atop the tables. Their drunken revelry seemed to take a more menacing turn.

Instead of shining with pride, Wally felt a sudden rush of fear, noticing some of the inebriated men were stumbling toward Bobbi and Audrey as if trying to get their hands on them.

The few women in the place who'd accompanied the men looked uncertain of what to do.

Bobbi grabbed Audrey and scurried behind the piano for cover.

Dorothy let out a scream in fear.

Wally ignored his own panic, put a snarl on his face, and raised his fists against the most boisterous of the men.

Mayfield put down his now-empty shot of whiskey and jumped up to join Wally. Drummond, Frankie, and Max clambered forward to help Wally and Mayfield create a circle around Bobbi and Audrey to protect them.

With his heart thudding fiercely, Wally feared he might pass out. Again. In the most public place yet.

Just then, Harry the barkeep reached beneath the bar and pulled out a shotgun. He cocked the weapon, held it above his head, and fired into the rafters. The loud bang made everyone halt in place.

"Enough!" blared Harry. Splinters fell from the ceiling. "Siddown, all o' ye!"

The worst of the men quickly climbed off the tables and returned to their seats. Others followed like nothing had happened.

The panic soon subsided as though this were just another Tuesday night at the Lout and the Lady.

Wally looked to be sure Audrey was safe and saw Bobbi leading her back to the table, unsettled looks on their faces. The bar matron delivered their pies and remaining drinks, setting down their food as conversation resumed among the other patrons.

Mayfield grabbed another whiskey and finished it in one throw.

"Should've warned ye about this crew," the matron said. "Ain't seen your type here before, least not singing songs like that one."

"I'm so sorry," said Bobbi.

"Sorry?" she said with a laugh. "That was brilliant! How 'bout another one?"

"I think it's time for us to go," said Drummond. The flirtatiousness in his voice was now replaced with the flat seriousness of an officer, and he motioned to the others to head for the door.

"Not letting this go to waste," said Max. He grabbed a fork from the table and devoured one of the steak and kidney pies in a few bites, wiping his mouth with a napkin once he'd finished.

Rat gaped at him, wide-eyed. "Very impressive."

Frankie took a long swig of his ale. "I'll be damned," he said, turning to Dorothy. "Room temperature. Ain't bad."

"All right," said Drummond. "Let's go."

Mayfield made his way over to Wally. "I thought we were friends," he said, and then charged toward the door before Wally could respond.

Wally hadn't intended to upset his roommate, but he knew if things were going to remain civil with Mayfield, he'd have to tell him about his own feelings for Audrey.

Bobbi turned back to the patrons and waved. "Good night, East Wapping!" she called, and then blew the crowd a kiss to a wave of applause before joining the rest of the team outside.

The sun had set, and the darkened sky was filled with patches of clouds, glowing with distant moonlight. The team headed back toward the Naval Center, the cool evening air softening their agitation. After a few blocks and some awkward jokes, the team was able to laugh off the fear that had ended their exhilarating performance.

"Won't forget that anytime soon," said Rat, and the team chuckled.

"I'd like to forget it," said Audrey.

Only Mayfield remained quiet and brooding.

It wasn't the night out Wally had expected, but it served to renew the team's energy just as Drummond hoped it would.

"That pie was terrific," said Max.

"Never got a chance to try it," said Rat.

"Suppose we can rummage up something in the mess hall," said Drummond.

But before anyone could reply, air-raid sirens rang out.

"A drill?" Rat shouted over the alarms. He raised his hands to his ears.

As if in answer, boats in the harbor switched on their searchlights and aimed them toward the London sky.

Between the wail of sirens, a loud hum, like the start of a growl, sounded overhead, which Wally quickly realized was not the thunder of a spring storm. He stopped dead in his tracks, the blood rushing from his cheeks. He and the team narrowed their gaze to see dark-gray objects burst through a pair of nimbus clouds like wolves leaping from a snowbank.

"Germans!" Drummond shouted.

Luftwaffe planes howled overhead, and the sudden squeal of bombs pierced the quiet night.

"Take cover!" Drummond shouted, and the team bolted toward a row of shops. Other people on the boulevard scattered too, some of them screaming in fear.

An incendiary bomb hit the side of a shop building with a loud explosion, shaking the earth in a deafening blast that sent dust and masonry everywhere. The rattle of gunfire rang out in the distance like hornets raging from the sky. Wally put his arm over his head as if he were dodging a heavy Brooklyn rain and then realized how useless that was.

A car sped past them, swerving to narrowly miss a crowd of people just in front of them.

"There!" cried Max. He pointed away from the damaged shops to the other side of the street, toward a harborside fishery that stood in darkness. The team raced to a warehouse, where Max threw open the door to the cold rush of fish-scented air. "In here!" he called.

They ran inside, past pallets, barrels, and crates full of fish in the dim blue moonlight that shone in through the warehouse's two small windows until Drummond spotted a stairwell heading beneath the floor.

"Over there!" Drummond called. "A shelter!"

"Get moving!" called Frankie. He hovered over Dorothy, shielding her with his body.

Without a thought, Wally grabbed Audrey's hand, and they quickly descended the steps to the shelter door as a sudden squeal sounded out followed by another nearby explosion that shattered the warehouse windows behind them. Glass flew, but the team was safe in the stairwell.

Drummond twisted the knob and opened the door at the bottom of the stairs. Once in, he flipped on the light switch.

A thin corner lamp illuminated a small room, barely big enough to hold all nine of them. A chair and a bench flanked the lamp, and shelves of canned food and books lined the far wall. In the far corner was a trunk with stacks of gas masks piled on top of it as if this space were designed for riding out a chemical attack.

Another explosion erupted, shaking the tiny space, sending dust down upon them.

Dorothy covered her ears and rushed over to the chair where Frankie stood by her side. Max and Bobbi took the bench. Mayfield and Rat sat on the cold concrete floor, their backs against a brick wall, and Audrey huddled close to Wally, standing by the shelves.

"Hurry!" said Max. "Close the door!"

Drummond pulled the door closed behind them and leaned against it just as another explosion hit.

The loud clatter of falling rubble sounded overhead in the warehouse.

Everyone grew silent.

Audrey buried her head on Wally's chest, trembling. He put his arm around her, closed his eyes, and tried not to faint.

One Mississippi, two Mississippi, three Mississippi...

He forced his thoughts to drift, to transport him and Audrey away from this basement, away from London. His mind took them to the rooftop of their Brooklyn apartment building, when air-raid sirens were only drills, when Audrey was just Johnny's little sister.

Yet, even as these visions began to calm him, the shaking walls and rumbling sounds around them kept dragging Wally back to East Wapping. The reverberations of each explosion rattled his bones and frayed his nerves. After more than a thousand Mississippis and countless explosions, the attack finally ceased and the sirens fell silent.

For a long while, no one spoke, and Wally found the silence just as troubling as the sound of the bombs.

Drummond was the first to rise, open the door, and take the stairs back into the warehouse. The others followed, but no one said a word.

When they emerged from the stairwell, Wally saw a strip of timber missing in the warehouse roof, acrid-smelling ash from the smoky sky cascading through like snowflakes.

The German fighters were gone.

Wally was careful not to breathe in the ash, holding his arm across his mouth. Audrey gripped his free hand, and the pair followed the others to the street. When they got there, however, the team stood in dismay at what they saw.

Craters had replaced large sections of the boulevard where they had just walked. Charred bricks and chunks of masonry were strewn up and down the street. Streetlights were dark. Several cars were now in flames, and people were staggering into the street, many frightened and confused, some injured.

But when he raised his gaze to the distance, Wally spotted the naval facility a few blocks away and lost his breath.

"Oh, God!" said Bobbi, pointing to the building.

A large section at the top of the facility was missing. Dark plumes of smoke rose in tendrils into the ochre-colored sky, spilling white ash and red embers everywhere.

Audrey covered her mouth with her hand.

"Jesus, Mary, and Joseph," said Frankie, crossing himself.

"Dear Lord," said Dorothy. "Our people."

"My mother!" cried Bobbi.

Drummond raised his palm. "Wait here, everyone."

"Like hell," said Wally, finally gaining his composure. "They may need us."

"Where you go, we go," said Max.

Drummond looked over the team, and then nodded. "Fine. Follow me."

They all ran toward the naval facility, the smoke and falling ash growing thicker as they got closer.

"If they followed protocol," Dorothy panted, "they'd have taken refuge below when the siren rang."

"If they had time," said Drummond. "Those bombs came on fast."

Wally's pulse pounded with each stride. He recalled the bombings in January and March, when he thought the rattle of the building was the worst of their concerns. Now his fears for Finch, Brubaker, and the others in the facility made those prior fears seem meaningless.

The team ran past piles of stone, steaming pipes, and bent steel blown free from the building. People wandered the scene, some holding cloths and towels to bloodied wounds or covering their mouths to avoid ingesting the smoke.

Once at the north side of the facility, they found the security door blocked by a mound of mortar and bricks.

"Help me move these," said Drummond, his breathing erratic.

Each of the guys joined to form a work line, lifting and handing one another the busted masonry, moving it away from the door. Others from the street rushed over to help, though a small crowd of onlookers stood by to watch.

"Help them or stand back," Audrey called to the gathering crowd.

"You heard her," said Bobbi. "Get busy or get out of the way!"

Soon, Wally heard pounding from behind the door.

"We're clearing debris!" Drummond called to those trapped inside. "Hold on!"

Soon, the way was clear enough to pull open the door, releasing a plume of dust and smoke. Several servicemen and servicewomen rushed out of the building, coughing. Some were covered with dust and shards of glass, a few with abrasions, others with faces blackened, most without apparent injury.

Wally couldn't see Finch or Brubaker.

"Where's the superintendent?" Bobbi cried.

"Dunno!" said one of the emerging soldiers.

"What about Colonel Brubaker?" asked Wally. "The American?"

"Sorry, mate. Haven't seen him."

Concern turned to panic, and Wally searched the area for a sign of their commanders.

Once the line of escapees had dwindled, Bobbi rushed forward. "I'm not going to wait another minute," she said, and pushed her way into the building.

"Hold on!" called Wally. "It isn't safe!"

Without a thought, Wally swallowed his anxiety and charged after her.

"Walter!" Audrey cried, but he gave her no time to debate.

Wally moved through the dark corridor filled with smoke and debris, his eyes immediately burning with dust and ash, searching for Bobbi. The damaged lights flickered on and off around him and the siren was deafening.

"Bobbi!" he hollered, but she didn't respond or, perhaps, she couldn't hear him over the alarms. He yelled louder though his throat was now raw with dust. "Bobbi, where are you?"

"Here!"

He found her at the door to the lower levels, which was pinned shut by a jumble of heavy piping that had fallen from the ceiling.

"It's blocked!" she called. She pushed hard on the pipes, unable to move them. "I have to find her!"

Wally saw the strained and distraught look on Bobbi's face. There was no convincing her to leave.

Without a word, he tried to push away the pipes, to no avail. A rush of anxiety filled his limbs, and he worked to keep calm. He tried to breathe, to quiet his nerves, and instead, drew in a throat full of smoke. He coughed, imploring himself to stay conscious.

The smoke swirled, and through the soot and falling ash came Mayfield with Max, Frankie, and Rat behind him.

"Need a hand?" said Mayfield. He seemed ready, at least for the moment, to set aside his anger.

"Yeah," Wally wheezed. "Help me move these."

One at a time, Wally and the others were able to shift the pipes until Bobbi could open the door. When she did, a new stream of soldiers, sailors, and staff raced out, coughing and gasping for air.

At the end of the flow of people, Brubaker and Finch finally came forward, coughing, carrying flashlights to light the way.

Bobbi grabbed her mother around the waist and squeezed her.

"Mother!" she cried.

"Oh, my dear!" cried Finch. "Thank God you're safe." The superintendent was uncharacteristically emotional, her eyes welling with tears.

Another conduit fell from the ceiling nearby, prompting Brubaker to reach for Finch's arm.

"Delphina," he said softly. "We have to go."

Finch nodded, clutched Bobbi's hand, and led them all toward the exit.

Once through the door, Wally drew a breath of cool air and held it, willing his heart to cooperate. Somehow, he'd managed to stay conscious.

After striding a safe distance from the facility, Brubaker leaned toward Wally. "Nice work, Slim." He shook Wally's hand, but then worked his shoulder, which continued to bother him, despite his recovery from his injuries.

"He didn't do it alone, ya know," chimed Rat.

Brubaker laughed. "Duly noted, Mr. Rubinstein. Thank you. Thanks to all of you."

Audrey rushed toward Wally and grabbed him so hard she nearly knocked him over.

"Oh, Walter!"

As they embraced, Wally saw Mayfield staring as if sizing Wally up for a coffin, his anger clearly returning, but Wally refused to move an inch.

When Audrey realized everyone was looking at them, she released Wally, eyed the team, and said, "Thank goodness you're all safe. Follow me."

Wally wished he could follow her all the way back to Brooklyn, but he knew his time with her had not yet come.

She led them all to the street, where Drummond and Dorothy had gathered others from the facility around a barrel bonfire. Dorothy recovered a clipboard and had begun to take note of the survivors.

When Finch approached, Drummond saluted, clear relief on his face. "Good to see you safe, ma'am."

"Damn Germans caught us with our knickers down." She looked to Miss Davies. "What's the status?"

"Fifty-two accounted for, ma'am. Forty still missing."

"Forty?" Finch shook her head. "Sirens got us below levels, but not fast enough. Bloody building shook so hard, I thought it had fallen."

"We went to a pub," said Bobbi. "I'm sorry we weren't here."

"Don't be," said Finch. She touched Bobbi's cheek. "I'm grateful you weren't."

"I'll head to the south end of the building, see if I can find others," said Brubaker. He raised his flashlight toward the superintendent. "Will you be all right?"

"I will," said Finch. "I'll radio command with our status."

Brubaker nodded and smiled at her in a way Wally thought was uncharacteristically tender.

"Miss Davies," Brubaker said. "Hand me that list."

Dorothy gave over the roster to the colonel.

"I'll come with you," said Wally.

"Me too," added Mayfield.

Brubaker eyed them. "All right, fellas. You're with me."

"How can we help?" said Max, flanked by Rat and Frankie.

"You three keep people fifty yards from the building, away from falling debris."

"Yessir!" The trio saluted.

Finch handed Wally her flashlight, and then he and Mayfield followed Brubaker to the south side of the building.

With Brubaker several paces ahead, Mayfield turned to Wally and whispered, "Why didn't you just tell me how you felt about her?"

Before Wally could reply, Brubaker stopped.

"There." He pointed to a group huddled in the street and then handed the roster to Wally. "Get their names, Lipkin. Find out who needs medical attention. Have them stay put and I'll send help to you."

"Yessir," said Wally, and he saluted.

Brubaker turned to Mayfield. "Let's move, Tuscaloosa."

Mayfield shot a look at Wally that seemed to say, *We're not done talking*, and then followed Brubaker around the rear of the building.

Wally shined the flashlight toward the crowd. After a few minutes, he had gathered twenty-two names from the roster, identified several with minor injuries, but found most were just shaken and unnerved. That left eighteen unaccounted for.

After an hour, Brubaker returned with Mayfield, a grim look on his face.

"Twelve alive," Brubaker said and then looked away. "Six dead."

Wally coughed like he'd been punched. He had come to know a fair number of the people at the facility and fought the urge to ask who hadn't made it. Instead, he read his roster.

"Twenty-two alive and accounted for here," said Wally. "With the ones you counted, sir, I think that's everyone."

"Okay," said Brubaker. "Let's report back."

Brubaker led them to Finch and the others. The ash was still falling like an untimely snowfall, and it was now close to midnight. The fire brigade was busy putting out fires, and both the police and members of British military helped to restore order, at least as much order as one could expect on such an appalling night. Ambulances took others to the nearest hospitals with navy medics performing first aid on those who needed it.

The team watched the last of the flames smolder under the fire brigade's water hoses. Several buildings on the boulevard also bore damage, and a handful of boats had been sunk in the harbor. Brubaker said the deaths were few, relatively speaking, and that they were lucky this time around. But, to Wally's thinking, nothing about this felt lucky.

Max walked over next to him. "You said there'd be no running," he said with a half smile.

"I wish there wasn't," said Wally.

"What do we do now?" said Rat. "How do we continue the mission without a facility?"

"Yeah," said Frankie. "It's like New York all over again. Where will we work?"

Finch raised an eyebrow at Brubaker. "Colonel, I think it may be time for phase two."

"Not sure we have a choice," said Brubaker.

"Phase two?" said Max. "I didn't even know there was a phase one."

"What does 'phase two' mean?" said Wally.

Brubaker's features grew serious. "It means we're taking our show on the road."

15

Causing Trouble

The loud howl that had been ringing in Wally's ears like insanity for seven hours began to dissolve, and the pressure that filled his head loosened its iron-fisted grip on his brain. The engines of the C-47 transport aircraft wound down now that the plane sat on terra firma, its propellers slowing to a merciful stop.

Wally opened his eyes, not realizing he had closed them, his shoulders tight like a cable ready to snap.

The rear cargo door yawned open with the grind and buzz of the lowering mechanisms, and a cool rush of spring air enveloped him and the team.

Wally was the first to release his seatbelt from the metal bench seat, squeezed quickly past the cargo pallets loaded with crates, hurried down the ramp to a clearing beside the muddy runway, grateful to be back on land—and threw up.

The pilot of the Dakota aircraft had taken Wally and the team high above the clouds, away from the threat of Axis radar detection, farther from solid ground than Wally had ever wanted to be, especially on his first trip in an airplane. But the steep and hasty descent of their landing had caused Wally's stomach to roll. He had counted Mississippis until the engines had stopped, yet it wasn't enough to keep his breakfast from returning once they arrived.

He spat into the mud, wiped his mouth, and drew in gulps of frosty morning air. Layered under the scents of airplane fuel and bile, everything smelled earthy and wet. And, as miserable as it was to throw up, he was grateful he hadn't passed out. It was a small victory, all things considered, but a victory, nonetheless.

"Welcome to Italy!" said Rat. He lumbered off the plane like a man on vacation and walked haltingly over to the clearing next to Wally, struggling to carry a duffel pregnant with extra blankets, shoes, and empty journals he'd managed to acquire before leaving

London. Rat dropped his heavy bag at his feet and looked to the tree-covered hills in the distance. "Looks like Upstate New York."

"You sure packed like it was," said Max, striding up beside them.

Rat shrugged. "Mom always told me to pack for anything."

"Anything or everything?" laughed Max.

Standing between Rat and Max, Wally got his bearings, reached into his jacket, and pulled out his uncle's pocket watch to change the hour. For some reason, he popped open the compass side of the watch to read the inscription: *The right place at the right time.* It was a tragic irony that, not so long ago, Wally was thumping away on his Wurlitzer, writing jingles about war bonds as a way of avoiding a trip to the European continent and certain death. And yet, here he was anyway, in the very place he'd hoped to avoid. He changed the hour as if hoping to change history itself, and closed the watch, uncertain what influence he could have over his fate.

Wally surveyed the terrain and tried to quiet the troubling chatter in his head. He was standing in a wide clearing, in a place Brubaker said was called Lucera. The area had been secured by the Allies a few months earlier and now served as an Allied airfield in the southeast of Italy in the ankle of the boot. The airfield had dual runways, suitable for sending and receiving bombers and transports like theirs. A few hangar buildings had been constructed along the airfield's perimeter, flanked by makeshift structures that served as the airfield's control center.

Beyond the clearing were craggy hills and dense forest clutches, thick with evergreens that Wally imagined were crowded with German soldiers poised and ready to kill them. The fields and forests were a stark contrast to the New York and London cityscapes to which Wally had grown accustomed, but the Nazis had run him and his friends out of every city where they'd set up shop so far. Now, the team had to keep the mission moving to keep it alive. They had to take the fight to the enemy.

After the attack that had damaged the Naval Communications Center, the team had spent two weeks at a safe house outside of London preparing for the trip. They'd packed their bags, keeping their belongings to a bare minimum, save Rat, who apparently missed the point that they'd be on the move. Frankie had to say a painful goodbye to Dorothy Davies and had been mopey every moment since. Each member of the team had sent pleasant letters home, revealing nothing of their work, their mission, or their fears. They'd shared details only of the suitable food, the kindhearted people, and the pride they felt to be of service in the war effort. Each of them had assured their families that they were in their thoughts, that they were safe and well cared for, and that they were eager to see them soon. It was yet another string of lies that seemed to weave through each episode of Wally's life. He'd lied to his friends, lied to his family, and even lied to himself when he thought he could set his feelings for Audrey aside and solve the mystery of his anxiety neurosis. It seemed that, even when he was ready to stop lying, the world still forged him to be a liar.

He looked to the sky and wished he had his beloved Wurlitzer on which to work through his apprehension. Of course, with the taste of bile on his lips now, he would have settled for a toothbrush.

"Don't get too comfortable," said Brubaker, walking past Wally, Rat, and Max. "We'll be hitting the road in fifteen minutes."

Comfortable? Wally thought. *Is he kidding?*

The colonel joined a dozen gangly British soldiers along the airstrip next to a line of transport vehicles awaiting the team's arrival. Brubaker then shook hands with a British officer who approached with a half dozen British servicemen at his side.

The rest of Wally's team carried their belongings down the ramp toward Wally, Rat, and Max. When a couple of British soldiers spotted Bobbi and Audrey, they rushed up to greet them.

"Let us help you with that, miss," said the short, ruddy-faced soldier approaching Bobbi. He reached for her bag.

"Thank you." Bobbi turned to Audrey. "How 'bout that?"

A taller soldier with a few days' beard and childish features came forward for Audrey's duffel. "And yours, miss?"

"Oh, yes, please," said Audrey, making Wally wish he had been the one to offer her help.

Brubaker soon returned and directed the attending British servicemen to the second armored cargo truck. "Bags travel with my team, gentlemen," he said. "And don't forget the crates." He gestured to the covered pallets still strapped in the cargo hold of the Dakota.

"Yessir!" The two soldiers saluted.

Wally and the team moved toward the armored cars and cargo vehicles.

"Wonder what Dotty's up to," said Frankie with a gloomy tone to his voice. "Dotty" was the nickname he'd given to Dorothy, which she loved, calling Frankie "such an American."

"Bet she's writing to me right now," said Frankie. "We agreed to exchange letters."

Wally nodded and offered a smile but wasn't sure when letters could be sent or received out here in the middle of nowhere. He figured he'd refrain from asking poor Frankie, lest he pile more grief upon his lovelorn friend.

Mayfield approached with his rucksack and cases for both his bugle and trumpet, but he didn't look at Wally. In fact, he hadn't said a word to Wally the entire trip. Instead, Mayfield moved past him to stand by Rat.

"What's up with Mayfield?" Max whispered.

"Long story," said Wally.

With everything going on since the air-raid on London, Wally hadn't yet discussed the topic of Audrey with his roommate, and the tension between them had grown as a result.

Brubaker marched forward, and the guys saluted.

"Helluva flight." Brubaker laughed. "You know what they say. Any flight you walk away from..."

Wally just shook his head, unable to find humor in the moment.

"Colonel Brubaker?" said Max. "If I can ask... What's the plan?"

"Yeah," said Frankie. "What are we doing in Italy?"

Their briefing after the German attack on London had been, true to the word, brief. They had all focused more on packing and travel preparations than on the work ahead. Neither Brubaker nor Finch had provided any real details, except that Finch and Drummond would stay behind in the UK as mission coordinators, supporting the team's efforts and the JASCO mission from the new secret facility in Scotland, one they hoped might be safer from the potential of future Axis air raids now that it appeared London was back on the Nazi's priority list. Wally and the others were simply told their part of the mission would continue in Italy, as if those were the only facts that mattered.

"Once we're all aboard the ground transport, I'll fill you in on the particulars," said Brubaker. "Use the latrine if you need. Get some water, and fall in. We depart at oh-nine-forty, sharp." He turned on his heel and rejoined a group of officers at the front of the transport, no doubt to discuss their journey ahead.

Wally relieved himself in the latrine, filled his canteen with water from a spigot, and started his walk through the mud and muck to join the others who were gathering by the trucks. Audrey approached him, wearing her army-issued uniform, which was similar to his, though hers was adorned with striped jacket cuffs, brass buttons, and accompanied by a long skirt. She looked like a magazine model for women's military service attire, and Wally didn't know if she looked more brave or beautiful. Either way, he knew he couldn't say so.

"It would be so lovely if this wasn't war," she said.

Wally laughed. Audrey's joke was the very thing to lift his spirits. "Yes," he said. He waved his hand in front of his face as if swatting flies. "And it would be so much nicer if not for all these pesky Nazis buzzing around. Did you bring a swatter?"

Audrey joined the macabre laughter and then moved closer, her breath against his ear. "I know you must be as scared as I am," she whispered, "but Bobbi doesn't think we'll see any real combat. She heard the Allies took this area months ago. We should be fine."

He understood from her discretion that she was being careful to help him manage his anxiety, and her consolation somehow made it seem that the very thing he feared was more likely to occur. It was a clear reminder that Audrey deserved someone brave, capable, and heartier than him, and he wondered if he'd ever be worthy of her affection. It seemed unlikely that the tools to defeat his demon could be found in the very place his demon seemed most ready to pounce.

"I'm sure you're right," he said.

"I am right. We'll all be fine."

"Oh-nine-forty, people!" yelled Brubaker. "Fall in!"

Wally followed Audrey through the aromatic mud across the runway to join the team. Awaiting them were two covered troop transports, two jeeps, and what Wally figured was an artillery truck. Each vehicle lined the muddy dirt road that wound out of Lucera toward who-knew-where.

A British soldier opened the door flap of a canvas-sided transport and helped the team up and into the rear of the truck. As Wally approached, he tried to shake the mud from his boots.

Both sides of the truck's interior had a bench, and in between the benches, someone had stacked their bags one atop the other. It smelled like gasoline fumes, and the space was confining.

Each member of the team sat hip to hip facing one another on opposite benches in the truck. Audrey sat on one side of Wally, but when Mayfield entered, he took the open seat next to Bobbi rather than the one by Wally.

Audrey leaned over to whisper, "What's eating Alvin?"

"I think it's me," said Wally. "Roommate squabble."

"Better work things out," said Audrey. "Can't be that important."

Rat took the open seat next to Wally and set his feet on the bag in front of him, folding his hands in his lap like a child trying to control his excitement at the start of some sort of weekend excursion. "Ain't this something, Lipkin?"

"Oh, yeah," said Wally. "It's something."

The transport vehicle fired up its engine with a rattling cough and a grind of its gears. The door flap closed, leaving the team with just the dim light that peeked through the gaps in the canvas each time the vehicle rattled and rocked.

"We're like goats to market," joked Rat, talking over the sounds of the engine.

"They kill the goats at the market," said Mayfield.

"Oh, right," said Rat. "Never mind."

The truck lurched forward and began its trek down the dirt road, through an open field, and into the hills. After an awkward silence, Frankie finally asked, "How long's the ride?"

"Two or three hours, give or take," said Brubaker.

"I'm hungry," said Max. "When do we eat?"

"Here," said Frankie. He handed Max a D ration Hershey bar from his bag. "Thinking about dead goats made me lose my appetite."

Max took the candy and looked around. He then broke off a piece, which he presented first to Bobbi and Audrey, and then to the others. There were no takers.

"Okay," said Max. He crammed the piece into his mouth. "I offered."

Each of them stayed silent as the small procession continued across the Italian hillside for nearly an hour. Occasionally, the transport engines would rev up and the vehicles would climb; at other times, they'd slow or stop for no apparent reason. Being unable to see the road ahead seemed a fitting metaphor for Wally's whole life.

"Why did we stop?" said Bobbi when the delay seemed particularly long.

"Making sure we're clear, I suspect," said the colonel.

"Clear of what?" said Frankie.

"Snipers," said Brubaker. "Land mines, trip wires... Allies cleared this area, but you can never be too careful."

The team's faces all turned pale in the faint light. Wally's stomach tensed like a fist, and he changed the subject. "Colonel Brubaker," he said, "can you tell us about the new mission now?"

Brubaker nodded and leaned forward through the shadows.

"This team is officially on the camp show circuit now," he said. "Starting with a key Allied encampment, where we'll put on a variety show."

"Variety show?" said Max. "What about the songs and secret messages?"

"You'll continue to write those," said the colonel. "Our show will be broadcast to the encampments nearby with new songs and new messages baked into your routines."

Frankie guffawed aloud. He was obviously thinking what Wally was thinking. New songs and new messages were hard enough. Now they had to put on a show?

"Now that we're in the field," Brubaker explained, "we can better keep up with events as they happen rather than wait for transmissions and reports. We can also send songs exactly when we need them rather than wait for civilian radio rotation. Being in the field will mean we can go where we're needed, when we're needed most. We'll knock the Krauts on their heels before they know what hit 'em." He looked around at the others, whose faces reflected Wally's own skepticism. "The need has become more urgent," Brubaker explained. "And our team has gotten the attention of General Eisenhower."

At the sound of Eisenhower's name, a sudden fear shot through Wally. He knew their work was important, but didn't know it had risen to the general's attention.

"Eisenhower?" said Rat. His eyes widened.

"Finch and I received direct orders," continued Brubaker, "and we've assured the general that we're up to the task. Does anyone disagree?"

Wally shared furtive glances with the others until Max spoke up, his mouth full of chocolate.

"Colonel?" said Max. He swallowed. "You want us out here performing shows in the middle of Italy with snipers and mines and all that, writing songs faster than ever before?"

Brubaker cocked his head. "Your parents were vaudevillians, right, Moxie?"

"Yeah," said Max.

"Surely you've learned a thing or two about how to put on a show."

Max fidgeted. "I suppose."

The colonel thumbed over to Wally. "Your brother here performed an impromptu show on a troopship with Mayfield and the girls. Drummond said you even put on a show at a pub back in London. Seems to me you folks know how to put on a show, and a damn good one at that."

The team grew silent.

"You all can do this," said Brubaker. "And if you need help, Bobbi can show you the ropes too. No one's a better performer than she is."

Bobbi nodded with confidence, and Wally wondered whether she already knew the details of the operation.

"Songs and codes were already a tall order," said Max. "Fitting it all into a variety show in the middle of a battlefield? I don't know…"

Wally silently agreed with Max. Brubaker's plan wouldn't be easy, especially out in some wilderness base camp.

The colonel stared intently at Max, looking more menacing than usual owing to the quivering shadows of the transport. "Private," Brubaker said slowly, "I know none of you intended to find yourself in the middle of a war in a foreign country. But do you think you're alone in that particular feeling?"

Max shifted in his seat. "Well, no sir—"

"Every one of these soldiers out here would trade places with us in a heartbeat. We've had a roof and three squares for most of this war while they wait for a day where they aren't dodging bullets. Don't you think every other poor sap who is stuck in a foxhole wants to know that Uncle Sam is doing everything he can to get him home to his family?"

"Of course—"

"Because, every minute that passes, Germans are gaining the advantage." Brubaker pointed over Max's head. "Men out here are sitting in their own shit and pissing their pants every time they have to face some fascist in the mud with better weapons than they have." I wish I could get them better guns. I wish we had better planes and more men, but we don't. What we have is here in this truck. That's what we have to offer. I'm hoping I'm not alone in my willingness to show up for them."

The group grew quiet, and the rumble and growl of their convoy filled the awkward silence.

"I'm not angry with you, Private Lipkin. On the contrary. I'm quite proud of you…of all of you." Brubaker scanned them all in the fleeting light. "If the soldiers out here have half a chance, it'll be because of you and what you will do."

Wally felt an odd rush of patriotic duty and pride, tempered with nagging doubt. Audrey stiffened at Wally's side and stared at her feet. Brubaker's words had triggered something in her too.

"I'm sorry, sir," said Max. "I didn't mean to make it sound like I wasn't willing. We can do it. All of it."

"Yes, sir," said Rat, his eyes now wide.

Brubaker gave a single nod. "I know you can."

Wally and the rest of the team nodded too, though Wally saw the concerned looks on everyone's faces, reflecting his own qualms.

For the next half hour, neither Wally nor the team said another word, their bodies swaying and rocking with each gearshift of the transport vehicle, the light and shadows dancing across their faces, reminding them of their fears and their duties.

From the crunching under the tires and the jerking of the truck, Wally figured they were climbing over rocks and traversing uneven terrain. Perhaps the convoy leader's concerns for trip wires and traps had led them to abandon the road for a less trodden path.

Mayfield, however, fell asleep, and soon, his metronome snoring allowed Wally to silently run through new songs he had written for Audrey, using his fingers to play an invisible piano on his swaying knees to calm himself. The team's new duty seemed insurmountable, and with General Eisenhower himself calling the shots, Wally feared what would happen if this team failed to make the difference Brubaker expected them to make.

Rat leaned over and whispered in Wally's ear, "Isn't this exciting?"

"Chance of a lifetime," said Wally.

It was noon when the procession of Allied vehicles pulled into the army camp where Brubaker said they'd be setting up base. Wally was the first to hop out of the truck, eager after their dark seclusion to draw in some fresh, cool Italian air; set his eyes on their new surroundings; and get his bearings. But the air wasn't fresh at all, smelling instead of tree rot and lingering cigarette smoke. What Wally saw, however, was something that truly took his breath away.

There, in a sodden meadow field, were rows upon rows of olive-colored canvas tents, hundreds in number, lined up in a grid across a massive camp. The camp was flanked to the west by a long road lined with a procession of dying larch trees and husks of damaged American army vehicles at the roadside. Weeds and dry shrubs had been hacked and tossed to the perimeters of the camp, and pools of wet mud carried the tale of morning rain. It looked like a scene from the newsreels Wally had watched back home, a surreal and desolate monochrome landscape that looked nothing like his Brooklyn neighborhood, or any place he'd ever been.

Gathering clouds huddled in the sky, and wisps of a cold remnant mist floated in a miasma over the hilly pastureland like a threadbare blanket of cotton wool. Uniformed men in crumpled hats trudged through the mud between tents like sleepless phantoms wandering a cemetery. The smell of their sweaty, filthy uniforms drifted among the rot and tobacco, and the aroma stimulated in Wally a new sort of fear.

Over by one tent, which slumped with remnant rainwater, a skinny soldier used a dead branch to beat wet clothes dry on a line. Nearby, four other dispirited men, covered in dried mud, drank from tin cups while sitting around a dwindling campfire, each looking more miserable than the last. Another man sat on a decaying log and shaved using a pocket mirror, dunking a straight razor into murky water from his overturned helmet. Some of the men coughed as though sick. Others required the use of crutches. Some had bandaged heads with crusting blood, and more than a couple sported eye patches from injuries, presumably earned in battle. Few of the soldiers gave Wally's convoy much attention, as if its sudden boisterous arrival was of no real importance to them. Most of the men looked worn, their eyes hollow, their movements slow and labored. There wasn't much laughter or conversation among them. They just appeared tired and spent, as if languishing in a purgatory awaiting their final damnation.

Whatever patriotic enthusiasm Wally had brought with him seemed to dissolve. Brubaker had delivered them directly to the worst place in the world.

Rat hopped out next to Wally and stared at the men just as Wally did. His shoulders slumped and he immediately lost his usual perk. "God," said Rat after a moment of gawking, "are we losing this war?"

Wally surveyed the rest of the area. A row of jeeps was parked on the opposite side of the road, some in disrepair, others splattered with wet dirt and rocky chunks of mud. A single American tank sat on the edge of the camp, its turret facing the rocky hills to the north, its flank riddled with damage from artillery strafing.

"This is horrible," said Audrey, approaching Wally and Rat. She crossed her arms over her chest, the color draining from her face, and she shivered.

His uncle Sherman's voice entered Wally's thoughts, narrating the scene.

Every brave thought you have, every courageous impulse, will be taken from you until all you have left is fear and despair.

The rest of the team hopped down from the transport truck and stood dumbfounded in the mud like Wally, Rat, and Audrey, their eyes taking in the camp scene.

Brubaker stomped forward with a young soldier at his side, seeming ignorant to their growing misery, and the team saluted.

"This is Security Officer Simpson," said Brubaker. He gestured toward a pale-looking narrowly built soldier who looked as though he'd sucked too long on a lemon. "He's aware of our mission. He'll show you to your tents." The colonel acted like everything around them was fine. "I'll let Colonel Otis know we've arrived."

After Brubaker left, the man named Simpson eyed them all with something that looked like a blend of suspicion and disdain, and then led them down a puddled path, crisscrossed with the tracks of vehicles, around the back of the camp.

"This is no place for girls," grumbled Simpson.

"It's no place for boys either," said Audrey.

Simpson huffed and steered the team around the perimeter to a pair of tents at the far corner of the camp. He assigned Wally and the guys one large tent for sharing and the gals a separate tent of their own. Each had been supplied with cots, a set of blankets with no pillows, and a trunk to share for their few belongings. They were meager accommodations, but Wally hadn't expected much. At least the space seemed private and dry.

A separate outhouse had been constructed for the ladies, and a hand-painted sign had been crafted that read "No men allowed."

"You're guests." Simpson scowled. "But don't think that makes you better than any of the men here."

"We don't think that," said Max.

Simpson ignored him and said, "Grub is on in the mess at the far end of camp when you hear the bugle." He then turned on his heel and left.

"Friendly fellow," said Max.

Wally and the others used the moment to test out their cots and empty their bags. Frankie immediately sat down, placed his journal on his knee, and started writing a letter to Dotty.

Mayfield tossed his rucksack onto his cot and strode back out of the guys' tent, a stiffness to his movements, saying nothing to anyone.

"What's eating him?" said Rat.

"This place must have already gotten under his skin," said Max. But Wally knew the truth. Mayfield remained angry with him over Audrey.

After placing his own duffel into his trunk, Wally wandered out of the tent, hoping to find Mayfield and settle their issues once and for all. Instead, he found Audrey standing a few yards away, peering at the craggy mountains in the distance, her hands in her pockets.

"Not what I expected," she said, her voice small and filled with dread.

"Not one bit," said Wally. "Papers and newsreels say nothing about how miserable our troops are."

Bobbi approached, rubbing her hands together and looking suspiciously at the clouds. "It's a roof over our heads, right? Besides, we're surrounded by soldiers. What could be safer?"

Wally could think of a thousand safer places but decided to keep his mouth shut. Bobbi and Audrey deserved a little optimism, and who was he to take that away? These soldiers already seemed defeated, and the feeling was contagious. Wally figured their only hope was to complete the mission and leave Italy as soon as possible. Figuring out how to make that happen was now priority one.

Brubaker stomped forward through the muck, cutting short Wally's dark reflection. "All right, team. Get the others," he said. "It's time to meet our host."

The crew all gathered and then followed Brubaker to the entrance of the command tent, which was larger than the sleeping tents they had each been assigned. There were two guards, each appearing younger than Wally, standing at either side of the door flap.

The guards nodded and Brubaker led the team inside.

Behind a desk made of crates and boards, sitting in a scratched wooden chair, was a severe, thick-necked man with dark features, bushy eyebrows, and piercing eyes, deep like black inkwells. His military jacket hung on a rack next to the desk, its medals catching the flickering firelight from a small woodstove that popped and hissed beside the desk. His shirtsleeves were rolled to his elbows, and he leaned over a map that lay flat on the desktop, its corners held in place with a canteen and an open sardine can being used as an ashtray. The man rose when Brubaker and the team entered.

Following protocol, they all stood in a line and saluted him, including Colonel Brubaker.

"Ladies and gentlemen," said Brubaker, "this is Lieutenant Colonel Warren Otis."

The man returned their salute, and yet something in those dark inky eyes conveyed distrust. Like the men under his command, he also looked tired. "At ease," said Colonel Otis. He stepped out from behind his desk in a swirl of cigarette smoke that rose from the sardine can. He walked the line, appearing to evaluate each of them as he passed. "I've been fully briefed on your mission," he said in a voice filled with gravel. He stopped when he got to Bobbi and Audrey. "And I've told your colonel how I feel about women in the field."

Brubaker turned to his team. "I've assured Colonel Otis that we're quite happy to restrict ourselves to quarters and necessary workspaces."

"Whether it makes you happy or not," said Otis, "is of no concern." His mouth tightened. "We may be of equal rank, Colonel Brubaker, but this camp remains mine. Everyone follows my rules."

"Of course," said Brubaker in a tone Wally thought seemed exceedingly deferential given the man's rude tone.

Otis continued to scrutinize the team, and Wally froze as though he were being sniffed by an angry dog.

"As requested, we've constructed a radio broadcast tower at the east end of the encampment and a stage that I've made available for your use," Otis said. "I've assigned you three men with comm duties as well as Security Officer Simpson, whom you've met. They're the only ones to whom I've granted clearance. Everyone else thinks you're just the entertainment. Camp show performers here to raise spirits."

"That should do fine," said Brubaker, but for some reason Wally felt a little insulted.

Otis frowned. "There will be no fraternizing with my troops, and I expect that you have no other special requirements."

"None," said Brubaker. "We appreciate your hospitality. Thank you."

As uncongenial as Otis sounded, Wally had one thing in common with the man. They both wanted the team to get things over with and be on their way.

Otis shot a cheerless look toward Brubaker. "My men have seen continuous combat for months, Colonel. They don't have much energy left, and I don't have much patience. We have an offensive underway in the north, and that's our focus. Not you. Not your team. Your safety is not our primary concern."

"I understand," said Brubaker.

Wally's heart sank. *Whose primary concern was their safety, if not the soldiers of the camp?*

Otis seemed irritated at Colonel Brubaker's pleasant disposition and drew closer to him when Brubaker failed to flinch at his terseness. "You should know I refused this request until General Truscott made it clear that hosting you and your team was an order."

Brubaker nodded. "Seems you have your orders, and we have ours, Colonel."

The two men stared at one another, and the heat in the tent rose.

"Very well," said Otis, frowning. "Then we understand each other."

"Is there a space where we can set up shop?" said Brubaker. "The men and women of my team work together. I'm sure you'd agree, it would be improper for them to do so in quarters."

"There's a coordination tent next to comms," said Otis. "Down the path a ways from mess. You can work there."

"Much appreciated," said Brubaker. "Oh, and I almost forgot, to express our gratitude, I brought a gift for you and the men of your camp."

"A gift?" Otis looked skeptical, and even Wally wondered what Brubaker had in mind.

"In the transport." Brubaker gestured to the door. "If you'd care to follow me?"

Wally and the others trailed behind Brubaker as he led Otis to one of their transport vehicles.

Brubaker withdrew a whistle from his pocket and blew, cutting the eerie silence of the camp and sending a dozen ravens from the larch trees, complaining, into the sky. The drivers who had brought the team to the camp stood ready and peeled back the canvas tarps that covered two pallets, stacked tall with crates. They used crowbars to pry open one of the crates, revealing its contents: cases and cases of bottles, each holding Coca-Cola.

A few soldiers noticed the commotion and came to investigate, their faces transforming when they saw the bottles of soda. Soon, more soldiers heard the commotion. Word got out, and soon, a crowd began to form.

Otis turned to the growing clusters of soldiers, put his hand to his mouth, and shouted, "Fall out! And help yourselves!"

The men cheered and rushed forward with an energy Wally did not expect from such sullen men. The drivers pried open the second crate, allowing the scores of men to grab the colas. Some men cracked them open with their pocketknives or rocks; some even used their teeth to get at the soda. They laughed, cheered, and knocked back bottles, and began to behave like the living, each of them now bubbling like the soda.

Wally was thirsty too, but stayed put to watch how such a small thing could make such a big difference to men who had nothing.

Otis turned to the colonel. "Very clever, Brubaker." His features softened and he shook Brubaker's hand. "And much appreciated."

"I've served in the field, Colonel. Figured you and your men could use a little something familiar. We don't want to cause any trouble."

Otis raised a thick eyebrow, and for the first time since they arrived, he smiled.

"This is a war, Colonel. We're here to cause trouble."

Wally pushed his way through the door flap of the guys' tent and breathed in the musty air. Despite the early enthusiasm among the soldiers over the colas, a persistent gloom still hung over the camp and an infectious anxiety lingered, working its way into Wally's bones.

He grabbed his harmonica, stuffed it into his pocket, and then returned to the clearing outside the guys' tent. Soon, the others joined him, similarly disposed, carrying with them the supplies they had packed to assist in their work. The gals had songbooks, Frankie lugged a satchel filled with pads and pencils, Rat cradled two new journals, and Mayfield carried his bugle. Brubaker had left to help the transport team settle into their own temporary quarters for the night before they returned to Lucera, and had put Max in charge, giving him instructions and showing him the most discreet path to reach their work tent.

"Follow me," Max said with authority.

They trudged through the dreary bog in line. Bobbi kept pace with Max, and Rat looked around with solemn curiosity. Frankie kept one eye on the path and the other on his journal, where he continued composing his lengthy letter to Dotty. Mayfield scuffled up next to Max as well, obviously keeping his distance from Wally, who brought up the rear.

Audrey lingered to match Wally's pace, eyeing Mayfield. "Whatever you two have going," she whispered to Wally, "it needs to stop. Alvin seems really upset with you."

"I know," said Wally, but with everyone present, the private conversation he needed to have would have to wait.

He longed to spend time alone with Audrey but knew he couldn't. Not yet. Instead, he turned his thoughts to the mission. The sooner they could finish their work, the sooner he and the others could leave this dismal camp and the hellhole of Italy.

The work ahead wouldn't be easy. Without a piano to use, Wally would only have his harmonica to craft and perform their tunes. That would be a new challenge, both for him and for the others who relied on his playing. The piano had more octaves, greater movement, greater precision, and was far more inspiring to Wally's creativity than a harmonica ever could be. Of course, he also had the added challenge of performing on a camp stage. Could he keep from passing out as he had after his recent Diamond Club fiasco?

A slow, familiar doubt began to percolate. His strategy to keep his feelings for Audrey in check, and to steer clear of stressful situations whenever possible, had allowed him to avoid fainting for weeks. However, here, he had to acknowledge his luck may be running out. His demon could not be so easily discharged, and the magnetic draw of his grave fate could not be escaped indefinitely. But that doubt now felt like an indulgence. He remembered Brubaker's point that every soldier here would kill to trade places with him. It was cold comfort, but true—he had it better than most, even with his anxiety neurosis. As if to illustrate that thought, Wally noticed, off the sodden path, a group of five men playing cards around a smoldering fire. Among them, one player had white bandages wrapped around his head and a dark, bloody spot where his ear would be. Another man wore damaged glasses. He had one eye closed, swollen shut behind his broken lens. Farther along the puddled trail, four Black men sat clustered and alone. One of them played a woeful ballad on a guitar, and the others sat quietly listening. They were too distracted to care about Wally's team or to question why women were there at all. It was a sober scene, and yet Wally appreciated the sound of their music. It was a welcome distraction in this miserable place.

The crew soon arrived at the end of the camp and at the entrance to a broad tent, just as Brubaker had directed.

"This must be it," said Max. He pushed aside the door flap and held it for the others to enter. The space was much like Otis's command tent, twice the size of the guys' quarters with a few darkened lanterns hanging from hooks off the inside tentpoles. However, this space contained three small tables; some Italian orange crates set up as chairs; and a colorful, ragged recruitment poster of Uncle Sam in his white top hat, pointing an accusing finger over the caption: "I Want You for U.S. Army."

"This ain't the studio," said Frankie, finally lifting his gaze from his journal.

"It's not about the space," said Max. "It's what we do with it that counts."

Maybe it was his newfound leadership role, but Max was starting to sound like Brubaker, and Wally longed to believe him. The task was greater, the work more difficult, and yet they had far fewer resources and far less safety than that which had supported their prior efforts.

Max arranged the crates and Frankie lit the lanterns, bringing both a warmth and a brightness to the space. The girls laid their songbooks on one table, and Rat sat with his journals at another. Mayfield, still festering, quietly set his bugle on a chair.

"I'm just eager to broadcast more songs," said Frankie, "get back to it, to the feeling we had in London."

"Wait," said Mayfield, finally engaging the team. He lowered his voice. "Who will we be broadcasting to?"

"Troops like these," said Max, gesturing to the camp, "but who are closer to the action."

"First we have to craft ciphers and send the code sheets," added Rat. He looked around as if to assure no one outside the tent could hear him.

"Ciphers?" Mayfield furrowed his brow.

"Cryptographic algorithms," Rat whispered. "Just like the ones we made in London, remember?"

Mayfield's expression remained blank, and Rat shook his head. "Didn't you pay any attention to what I did in London?"

"Sorry," said Mayfield. "You were gone a lot. I just focused on learning the songs."

Rat huffed, clearly irritated that anyone on the team had missed the important role he played. "Okay, ever seen those ads for decoder rings?"

"Course I have," said Mayfield. "I read."

Rat leaned in closer. "A cipher is a way to make decoders like one of those rings. It gives you the means to understand the messages when they arrive. We make code sheets and those go first on a secure Allied comm channel. Messages follow on a public channel."

"And the messages are in our songs," said Mayfield, locking into the mission particulars.

"Right," said Max. "Code sheets go through on the army's signal line and the songs get broadcast on the local radio. We keep 'em separate to keep 'em safe."

"But everyone listens to the radio," said Mayfield.

"True," said Rat. "But remember, not everyone has our code sheets. Our songs sound like other songs on the radio, and that's how we trick the Germans. Unless someone is looking for a message in the songs on the radio, and happens to have a cipher, it all sounds normal. Sounds like it'll work the same for our camp show."

"Is that what we've been doing all along?" said Mayfield.

Rat turned and squinted at Wally. "Is he serious?"

"He hasn't been at this as long as we have," said Wally.

"I'm not dumb," said Mayfield, seeming to direct his outburst directly at Wally. "I never thought about all the details, that's all. I was just happy to be on a team."

Wally felt a pang of regret for not being more inclusive with Alvin. He'd been so focused on his own feelings, he had failed to deal with Mayfield, failed to be honest with him.

"It all worked great in New York and London," said Rat. "But out here, plans can change if the signal lines go down. In those cases, they told me, they send a runner."

"A runner?" Audrey put her hand on her chest. "You mean, a soldier delivers the ciphers by hand?"

Rat nodded. "That's what makes the songs easier than the ciphers. Songs go out on regular radio during a predesignated time frame. Don't need a signal line for them. The troops on the receiving end usually record what they hear on the radio anyway, just in case. But out here, if the Allied signal lines fail, there's no other way to send a cipher. Gotta have a runner. The guys in London told me all about it. Scary stuff when it happens."

The team grew quiet at what that scenario represented.

"I get it," said Mayfield, much to everyone's surprise. "Transmitters and lines go down sometimes. It's standard operating procedure. Gotta have contingency protocols."

"Contingency protocols?" said Frankie. "What do you know about contingency protocols?"

"Comm configurations and signal lines were my specialty at Fort McClellan," said Mayfield with a smirk. "I'm signal corps. Don't look so surprised. I have skills like y'all. I told you. I'm not dumb."

Frankie raised an eyebrow. "Duly noted."

Hearing talk of all the risks gave Wally pause; despite their skills, such details made their mission seem more preposterous and far less likely to succeed than it did from the presumed safety of the New York studio or from their London facility. Then again, it had turned out those places weren't safe either.

"So, what do we do now?" said Mayfield.

"Same thing we've always done," said Max. "Only now, we have to build a show around it all." He pulled out a notebook and opened it. "And I have a few ideas I'd like to borrow from our folks' old stage routine—"

"Belay that order," said Brubaker, suddenly at the tent's entrance. He held two crowbars in his hand.

The team stood and saluted the colonel as he entered, but one step in, he held the door flap open. "Hate to interrupt, but you may wanna come see this."

Wally was confused until they followed Brubaker outside and saw a handful of soldiers pointing at the sky. An Allied bomber was flying away in the distance, and in its wake, a large crate floated down by parachute.

"What is that?" said Wally.

Brubaker kept his eyes on the sky. "That, Private Lipkin, is our secret weapon."

Perplexed, Wally and the others followed Brubaker through the mud and tall weeds into a clearing east of the camp, where the crate landed in the muck. They detached the crumpled chute, and Brubaker handed over the crowbars, which Max and Frankie used to open the crate. When the front panel fell, Wally gasped at what he saw.

It was a piano.

"They call her the Victory Vertical," said Brubaker. "Built by Steinway for military use. Army drops a few here and there when the situation calls. Finch and Drummond made sure we had air clearance."

"So exciting!" Bobbi was all smiles, but Wally began to wonder if this whole scene was some anxiety-induced dream.

"Never seen a piano like that," said Rat.

The wooden upright piano was painted with a drab army-olive lacquer, and was absent any slender legs that could have been damaged in transport. The keys weren't the usual ivory but some yellowish-white coated material. It wasn't pretty by any measure, and yet it was the most beautiful thing Wally had ever seen.

"President Roosevelt halted manufacturing of American pianos to secure wood and metal for the war effort," said Brubaker. "That is, until Colonel Dawson and the folks at Steinway convinced the army that music was necessary for troop morale."

Bobbi perked at the mention of Dawson. "My father was right about that," she said. "Music has power. Just the sight of this piano makes me feel better."

Wally stood, speechless.

A handful of soldiers from the camp pulled forward in an armored jeep hauling a flatbed trailer. Brubaker instructed them to load and secure the Victory Vertical and bring it back to the rehearsal tent, but Wally kept his eyes on it the whole time.

Once at the tent, the soldiers lifted the piano off the cart and set it down inside where Brubaker directed them.

As soon as the soldiers left, Wally rushed over to assure the Victory Vertical wasn't damaged, circling it and scrutinizing its every curve and panel.

"Not many of these pianos to go 'round," said Brubaker. "We're lucky to get this one."

Wally hardly heard him. The world around him had disappeared. He put his arms around the piano as if holding an angel that had fallen from heaven. He held it in his ardent grasp, smelling its varnish, feeling the weight of it before his teammates' laughter made him realize what he was doing.

He withdrew his embrace from the piano and stuffed his hands into his pockets. "Good construction," he said with a cough. "Solid."

Brubaker nodded. "Figured you'd like it."

"Looks more like he loves it," laughed Rat.

Wally couldn't argue. Aside from his friends, the piano was the first thing he'd seen since landing in Italy that felt familiar, that gave him any measure of comfort. And who wouldn't love that?

Brubaker's eyes gleamed at Wally. "Take her for a spin, Curly. Let's make some magic."

Wally tried to calm his racing heart, pulled a sitting crate up to the Victory Vertical, placed his fingers on the soft keys, and immediately felt something visceral and urgent. He played "Everybody Loves My Baby," one of the early radio songs he'd ever learned to play on the piano, knowing it called for both major and minor chords, to feel out the edges of what this fallen angel could do. He was surprised to find the piano was well tuned despite whatever it had likely endured in transit. He closed his eyes and let its bouncy music fill him, felt the vibration of its strings and the way it responded to his every movement. The canvas fabric of the tent absorbed its sounds, offering little echo and no reverberation, making the music feel close, intimate, and perfect, enveloping Wally and the others like the cradle of a mother's arms. The piano's sound soothed him, brought warmth like truth spoken in the ears of someone who had heard and told too many lies, transported him out of the tent, out of Italy, all the way back to Brooklyn.

When the song ended, he sat quietly, his eyes still closed.

No one spoke a word until Brubaker broke the silence with a single order, given in a whisper: "Gather 'round."

Wally reluctantly withdrew his fingers from the keys and opened his eyes, the harsh reality of their circumstance returning like a persistent winter storm, the accusing finger of Uncle Sam still pointing right at him. *I Want You...*

Brubaker pulled up another orange crate next to the piano, and the team came forward.

"As you may have gathered," said Brubaker, "operations in Italy haven't gone as well as the Allies had hoped. Our men have been fighting nonstop since leaving Sicily, pushing toward the Liri Valley to get to Rome, but the Nazis have us locked down. They've been using the high northern terrain to fire on Allied troops no matter what angle we've come from."

Wally's jaw tightened, the calming effects of the Victory Vertical quickly slipping through his fingers.

"US bombers nearly destroyed an abbey at Monte Cassino," Brubaker said, "a place we thought the Germans were using as a base. We had hoped that would make a difference." He shook his head. "It didn't. Allies have tried three times and still haven't broken through. Each time, the Nazis keep bringing out bigger guns."

"Bigger guns?" said Frankie.

"PAK forty antitank guns," said Brubaker. "K5 railway guns."

"What are those?" said Audrey, her eyes wide.

"PAK forties can strike from over a mile away," the colonel replied. "Knock down Sherman tanks like they're toys."

"Jesus," Frankie muttered.

"It's actually the K fives that are the real monsters. They fire a quarter-ton shell up to fifty miles and still hit their target. They call 'em rail guns because the Germans move 'em back and forth on rails they lay into and out of tunnels so our bombers can't target 'em from the sky." He huffed his exasperation. "Killed hundreds of our troops at Anzio alone."

Bobbi gasped and covered her mouth with her hand.

"Sounds grim," said Wally, "like there's no way to win."

He had hoped Brubaker would follow his gift of the Victory Vertical with some sort of rallying speech, one that would take the edge off the misery the team had seen at the camp, give them some renewed sense of optimism to fuel their creative efforts. Instead, Brubaker seemed determined to scare them with details of failed battles and superior weaponry.

Brubaker leaned back in his chair. "Here's the fact," he said. "The Germans are well equipped and well trained. We can't win with artillery alone. I suspect the whole reason we're fighting here is to keep the Nazis—" Brubaker cut his own words short.

Rat leaned forward. "Keep the Nazis busy in Italy instead of where the real fight's brewing?"

"That's not what I said." A vein throbbed in Brubaker's temple. "Look around this camp, Mr. Rubinstein. This *is* the real fight."

Rat looked away as though unconvinced.

"The whole reason we're fighting here is to keep the Nazis on the defensive," said

Brubaker. "Get them nervous. Show them what we're made of."

The colonel walked to the front of the tent, drawing the team's scrutiny with him. He drew open the flap haltingly, his shoulder still apparently giving him trouble, and stared out at the camp.

"For every German soldier we've killed or wounded," he said, "the Nazis have killed or wounded three of ours. Now, troops from New Zealand, India, France, and Poland have joined Britain and the US to plan a fourth push through the mountain passes into Rome." He drew in a deep breath. "Success could help finish the Germans for good," he said. "Failure, on the other hand, could mean our final defeat." He turned back to the team. "Not just in Italy but everywhere."

Wally's gut clenched.

Brubaker eyed the team. "Like I said, this is the real fight."

"But, sir," said Frankie, "you said artillery, alone, wouldn't win the war." His ruddy cheeks grew more flush.

"Yeah," Mayfield chimed in. "What can we even do about those antitank and rail guns you talked about?"

Brubaker didn't blink. Instead, a slow smile formed at the edge of his lips. "Everything we need is right here in this tent," he said. "It's clearer to me now than it's ever been. This mission can help make a difference."

Wally looked to the faces of his teammates. What he saw was different than what Brubaker must have seen. Max was overconfident, Frankie was a serial cynic, and Rat was too arrogant to see past his pointy nose. Audrey was determined and Bobbi was bold, but neither of them was prepared for the horrors of war. Mayfield was strong, smarter than he let on, but he was clearly distracted by Audrey and consumed by his anger with Wally. And Wally himself was a mess of emotions and anxiety, cursed with a propensity for fainting. It was clear Brubaker had placed his bet on the wrong team.

"We won't fail you, sir," said Max.

"This time, the troops have us," added Rat.

"My father believed in us," said Bobbi, "and so do I."

"I know," said Brubaker. "And that's more than enough." His reassuring nod and sparkling look left no doubt of his support of the team.

Wally had to admit, the colonel had earned their trust despite everything that had happened between them. But being trustworthy didn't mean his confidence was well founded.

Wally turned away to hide his skepticism. If hundreds of trained soldiers hadn't succeeded in pushing through the Liri Valley after three tries, even with other troops coming, how could a handful of New Yorkers and a grumpy trumpeter from Alabama make a fourth attempt work?

"It's time to coordinate those ciphers," said the colonel. He gestured toward Rat. "Mr. Rubinstein, you're with me."

"Yessir!"

The team saluted, and Rat marched out of the tent with his journals, following Brubaker. The others set up their supplies, each appearing more certain of their duty in the wake of Brubaker's encouraging speech.

Wally just eyed the piano that had floated, like a miracle, from the sky. It was a magical gift for sure, but pianos didn't win battles, and he knew it.

"Let's get to work on our act," Max announced. "We have a lot to do."

"Yes, please," said Audrey. "I'm nervous about performing, especially after what happened at that pub in London."

"Oh, come on," said Bobbi. "That was a great performance."

Audrey cocked her head with a laugh as if to say Bobbi was nuts, but Wally figured they were all nuts if they were ready to ignore the upsetting details they'd just heard. He stood from the piano stool.

"Are you kidding?" The words sprang from Wally's mouth, and he realized he was trembling. "Didn't you hear anything Brubaker said?"

"He said we needed each other," said Audrey.

"He said we were more than enough," added Bobbi.

Wally's face grew hot. "That's all bullshit."

"Walter!"

Wally met the puzzled looks of the team.

"Brubaker listed one reason after another that the Germans have us beat—better weapons, better training, better positioning. And what about Clyde? He said this whole mission could come down to ciphers and code sheets, and those may not even make it to the troops. From where I sit, things are more desperate than ever, and the army wants to put all that on us. It's ridiculous."

"Take it easy," said Max. He walked toward Wally with an outstretched hand, which Wally refused to take.

"Come on, Max!" said Wally. "Haven't you seen the men out there?" Wally pointed a shaky finger toward the camp outside. "They've been here for months. Parts of them are still on the battlefield. Most can hardly lift their eyelids, let alone a rifle. Brubaker thinks we're the best hope because no one is left to pin our hopes on."

The team fell silent, their faces drained of the certainty Brubaker had inspired in them moments earlier.

"Who do we think we are, anyway?" railed Wally. "We don't know anything about war."

Audrey looked away, Mayfield stared at his shoes, and Bobbi bit her lip.

Max stepped forward, adjusted the belt around his wide belly. "That's why those other troops are coming." Max's voice was calm and carried a strange confidence. "The British, New Zealanders, Poles, Indians? You heard Colonel Brubaker. Help is on the way."

"So what?" said Wally. "What if those other troops are in no better shape than the men here? Tired. Beaten. Broken."

"Then they'll need our help too," said Max. His eyes narrowed. "Tanks and guns are not what we have to worry about. It's the messages. The music. That's our part. That's our *only* part." He put his hands on his wide hips. "Brubaker brought us out here to put on a show. Our parents put on shows, and so will we. That's what Lipkins do."

The gals exchanged affirming looks, and the others nodded their agreement.

"Don't you see, Walter? We were born for this," said Max. "And when there's a job to do, a job we're good at, we gotta do it. All of us. Simple as that. Those other troubles are concerns for other teams. The show is all we need to worry about. Keep your thoughts here"—Max pointed to the earth beneath his feet—"where we can make a difference."

Wally tried to calm himself and consider Max's point of view. In the plainest of terms, Max had given Wally and the team permission to ignore the most frightening parts of their mission and focus only on the parts they could manage.

"My father has been after me all along to be a cop," said Frankie. "He wanted me to help people, to do the right thing, to take the risks others wouldn't, like every other O'Brien before me. I couldn't understand my part in that. Always thought of policing as his gig, his thing, not mine. But the damnedest thing happened because of this crazy mission. Helping people became my gig too." Frankie stepped forward, a clear resolve filling his limbs. "I like helping people, Walter, and I think you do too."

"I have some ideas for our show," said Max. He walked over next to Frankie, his gaze still fixed on Wally. "Will you help? Just like we used to do back home? The Jingle Boys?"

Wally looked to the rest of the team. Mayfield just stared, lost in thought. Bobbi, on the other hand, offered an encouraging smile. Audrey glanced at him with something that looked like pity, and all he could do was turn away.

He looked over to the piano, to the Victory Vertical, and drew a long, deep breath. There was only one choice, only one way to set things right with Audrey and to face his anxiety once and for all, despite the risks.

"All right," said Wally. "I'll do it. But you have to promise me one thing."

"Okay," said Max. "Name it."

"Promise me we'll make this the best goddamn show these men have ever seen."

Max grinned and pointed his finger gun. "See? Now you sound like a Lipkin."

16

The Show Must Go On

Wally climbed the ten feet of stairs to reach the backstage riser, ran his sweaty palms along his army-issued trousers, and fixed his gaze toward the darkening Italian sky. From the space between the clouds, the sparkling stars gleamed back like the expectant eyes of his Jewish ancestors looking down upon him, reminding him that both his fate and the fate of the Jewish people hung in the balance. This time, there was no magic ring of Solomon, no burning bush giving divine instructions, no desert to escape to, no miracle awaiting them. The ancestors and the Allies were counting on him, his jeep-colored piano, and his scrappy friends, and this time the miracle had a stage.

The last week had flown by faster than any week of Wally's eighteen years. He had set aside his fear, focused on his tasks, and helped his team do the work they were dragged halfway around the world to do, just as Max had instructed. He had listened to the lies, tried his damnedest to believe them, and did what he knew how to do, and only that. Now, it was time to put all that work to the test.

Miracles weren't too much to hope for, he thought. It was some sort of miracle that Frankie had received a letter at the camp from Dorothy, which he'd been pouring over in his every free moment since it had arrived via supply truck. Whatever the letter had said only fueled Frankie more. He had become driven in a way Wally had never seen him, working until the last light of the camp had gone out and rehearsing to the point of exhaustion every day.

Rat had spent most of his time with Brubaker and the camp's comm specialists, crafting and coordinating the mission ciphers to align the Allied battle plan instructions with the tunes the team had written. Early that very morning, he had said, those ciphers were sent via army comm lines to the Allied troops in the north, and, assuming Rat's work had been successful, those forces would now have what they needed to decode tonight's show. The broadcast performance would be sent via open radio channels, heard by anyone who tuned in. The secret messages buried in the team's show would instruct US planes to drop their bombs over and near Monte Cassino one last time. This would be the first phase of the Allies' fourth attack on the abbey, and, if it worked, the next phase would occur over the following days when troops would move through the mountains and along the Liri Valley in a final coordinated effort to retake Rome and turn the tide of the war.

It all sounded great in theory if they won; failure, on the other hand, would mean certain victory for the Germans, and the consequences of that were unthinkable—not just for Europe but for all of humanity. Recent chatter from Otis's reconnaissance soldiers told of Jews they'd found in the woods, emaciated and hollow-eyed souls, clothed in striped uniforms that hung from their bones. Those few they found alive and who could speak English had told tales of horror Wally could hardly believe, tales that, if true, made the Germans more insidious and horrible than any newsreel could convey.

The ghettos that Jews had first been confined to, they said, had been cleared of people who were then sent to work camps. The work camps, however, turned out not to be work camps at all but death camps equipped with tools of torture and murder. The Nazis didn't just want to take over the world. They wanted that world to be rid of Jews.

The escapees who had been found alive, Wally learned, had been brought south to greater safety, far from the camps from where they'd escaped. The word of their discovery was supposed to remain quiet so as not to upset the men of the camp, but word had gotten out nevertheless, and "upset" was hardly the word for how Wally and the others felt.

It was the reason his mother prayed every night for the safety of their people.

Wally swallowed hard and realized his hands had been clenched into fists. He shook his head to rid his mind of these rumors and drew a bagpipe breath to take his thoughts away from the dangerous points of this war, the unimaginable stakes, preferring to follow Max's advice to leave the worry of guns and tanks and battles to others. Instead, for now, he would only allow himself to concentrate on the show. It was through such concentration that Wally intended to stay conscious and prove to Audrey he was not some panicky, fainting dope but a brave guy from Brooklyn, worthy of her love. Or maybe he was just trying to prove that to himself once and for all.

Following Max's plan, he and the team had integrated their songs into a new version of his parents' original Borscht Belt stage routine. Many on the team had objected to the abundance of his parents' now outdated jokes about President Hoover, Prohibition, or the Suffragette Movement. So, to assure a more contemporary performance, Max and

Frankie had replaced those jokes with new ones that they hoped would appeal more to the men of the camp and within earshot of the radio broadcast. Bobbi and Audrey had overseen the show's blocking and choreography, which Wally was spared since his place would be at the Victory Vertical—a welcome thing since he wasn't sure he could trust his uncertain legs.

Mayfield had layered in his horn accompaniment throughout the show's musical score, offering clever punctuation at just the right points in the songs they'd written. All the while, Mayfield had managed to avoid personal conversations with Wally and any hope of reconciliation every step of the way. It would be after the show, Wally hoped, that he and Mayfield could finally have their heart-to-heart, clear the air, and rekindle the friendship that had meant so much to him.

It seemed everyone on the team had adopted Max's strategy to focus only on the show and not on the war, and the approach had paid off. Even Brubaker had complimented them on their excellent work. Now, after long days and nights of writing and rehearsals, everyone knew their parts by heart; everyone was ready—at least as ready as they could be.

Just then, Mayfield climbed the steps to the riser and approached Wally's spot behind the backstage wall. He carried his trumpet under his arm but seemed a bit unsteady on his feet. After a withering look at Wally, he peered around the wall, across the front platform, stage right, where Audrey and the others waited in the wings for the show to begin.

Wally resigned himself to the silence between them, but, to his surprise, Mayfield turned back, looked him in the eye, and spoke.

"Hey, Lipkin. I've decided to ask Audrey out after the show. I'm not asking your permission. I'm just informing you."

Wally's mouth gaped. "What are you talking about?"

"You've had plenty of time to make your move with her," he said. "I've been watching you, and you've done nothing since we left London."

"Alvin, I—"

Mayfield moved closer to Wally, close enough for Wally to smell the sour scent of whiskey on Mayfield's breath.

"It took me weeks to work up the courage last time," said Mayfield, "and you ruined it. Then I gave you space to take your own shot. You had your chance and never took it. Now, it's my turn. Fair is fair."

"There's a reason I haven't pursued Audrey," said Wally. "I'm working out some things before I tell her how I feel."

Mayfield cocked his head. "What things?"

Wally craned his head around the backdrop to peek at the audience. Soldiers were now beginning to sit on the soft mud and weeds of the open field in front of the newly constructed stage, readying for the performance they'd been promised. The only proper chairs present were lined in a short row at the foot of the stage, marked "Reserved" for the camp's top brass. But neither Otis nor Brubaker were anywhere to be seen, and they were the ones designated to start the show.

It was not the timing Wally had hoped for, but Mayfield had finally handed him a chance to settle things. He turned back to Mayfield and raised his chin. He marshalled his courage, looked his friend in the eye, and spoke his words in the form of a blurt: "Alvin, the fact is, I have a fainting problem, and I want to solve that problem so I can be with Audrey."

Mayfield squinted. "A what?"

"Almost every time I get nervous. Been happening since I was a kid. Something surprises me, gets me anxious, I get rattled, and I pass out."

Mayfield squinted, and he took a moment, appearing to play Wally's words over in his head. Finally, he said, "I don't believe you. You didn't faint when the Germans shot up London. Weren't you nervous then?"

"Course, I was," said Wally. "But Audrey kept me calm. Stopped it from happening."

"So, you don't faint when Audrey is around?"

Wally shook his head. "I wish that were true. I can't make any sense of it. I tried to kiss her once and I passed out. That's why I haven't told her how I feel and why I need to solve this before I can be with her." Wally hung his head. "Can't be much of a boyfriend if every kiss puts me out for the count. That's why I haven't made my move."

Mayfield kept his bloodshot eyes fixed on Wally, a shadow darkening his features. "You're lying."

"No, I'm not."

"You think I'm stupid like everyone else. You wanna keep me away from her because you're too chicken to ask her out yourself and you don't want anyone to have a shot." Mayfield's unsteady voice rose, and Wally began to worry the audience would hear him.

"That's not true," Wally whispered. "You're drunk. Keep it down."

"I don't need to keep it down."

Suddenly, cheers and whistles rose from the full crowd of soldiers that had grown during their conversation. Wally turned his attention back to the stage. A bright spotlight switched on, and Colonel Otis walked into its glow. But it wasn't Otis who had riled the men of the camp. Striding onto the stage behind him was Bobbi, blowing kisses to the audience as she joined the camp's commander center stage in the limelight. She wore a sequined dress that twinkled green, her beauty drawing the men's attention like a lighthouse calling ships home.

"Thank you!" Otis said into the microphone. "Thank you, all." He shaded his eyes from the glare of the spotlight, and the ruckus quieted to a dull rumble. He cleared his throat. "You men have been to hell and back, and I am grateful," he said. "General Eisenhower is grateful. Your families at home are grateful too!"

Again, the men burst into applause, whistling and cheering. It was more energy than Wally had seen from them the whole week he'd been there.

Wally spun back to Mayfield. "Alvin, let's talk about this later. Right now, you need—"

Mayfield grabbed Wally's collar and twisted it, shoved him with unexpected aggression against the stage backdrop, which shook under his force. "Don't tell me what I need," Mayfield seethed, his face red.

"Alvin." Wally gasped for air. "Stop! You're rocking the stage."

The colonel's voice stammered at the movement of the backdrop wall. "Looks like they're getting things ready back there," he said. "And that's good news because tonight we have a special treat for each of you. Miss Bobbi LaFleur and her friends from New York City have a show for you that you'll never forget."

Cheers rang out again.

"Alvin!" Wally coughed. "Let go."

Things started to blur, but Mayfield's grip remained firm.

"Show me!" said Mayfield. "Show me how you faint."

"Please, Alvin. The show."

Mayfield eyed Wally and then released him. "See?" Mayfield said, his voice slurring from the effects of the whiskey. "You're lying."

"Alvin, you have to—"

"Don't talk to me!" Mayfield stepped back and swung at Wally but lost his footing. Wally ducked his friend's slow-motion assault, and the momentum of Mayfield's swing spun him around backward, causing him to fall off the backstage riser.

"Alvin!"

Wally heard a loud, sickening "clunk" as Mayfield disappeared into the shadows behind a stack of pallets. "Alvin!" Wally called again into the darkness, but there was no answer and he could see nothing.

"Despite what some may think," Otis blared into the microphone, "I'm no dummy, at least not dumb enough to stand in the way of a good show."

Wally's stomach knotted. He froze for a second but willed his legs to respond. He dashed down the ten feet of steps and around the pallets, expecting to find his roommate in an unconscious heap among the stage's metal framework, but there was nothing to be found. Mayfield was gone.

Otis's voice boomed from the speakers: "Without further ado, please give a warm army welcome to Miss Bobbi LaFleur and the Victory Players!"

The crowd's howling resumed with cheers that were almost deafening.

Bobbi disappeared to the other side of the stage, which was Wally's cue. His head buzzed like an air-raid siren, his attention split between the show and his missing friend, but he knew the show must go on. He took a breath, strode back up the steps, and raced onto the platform, into the light, to take his place at the Victory Vertical upstage.

He gave a wave and began to play a welcoming ditty, connecting with the Victory Vertical, which had, over the past week, become an extension of him. Its warm yellowish keys both ugly and familiar, activated the piano's hammers, which pounded the strings and, released a resonant sound, a language as primordial or ancient as a cry or a laugh.

As the polite applause intended for him began to fade, it once again grew, coinciding with Audrey's arrival onstage. She approached the microphone stand in a shimmering dress, hers made of blue spangles that matched the sparkle in her eyes. She had added some curl to her nut-brown hair, and when she flashed her smile between those dimples, Wally's fears momentarily dissolved, and he was smitten all over again. He understood why Mayfield wanted his chance.

He searched the stage, hoping Mayfield might enter from the opposite side. But Mayfield's spot remained empty.

Wally placed his fingers on the olive-painted upright and played the instrumental introduction that was Mayfield's cue to join in with his trumpet, but Mayfield didn't arrive and there was no trumpet sound.

From center stage, Audrey turned when the trumpet failed to play and spied Mayfield's empty spot with a look of concern.

Apprehension and guilt crept into Wally's chest like stalking wolves. While plinking the tune in the piano's lower octaves, he managed to play Mayfield's solo in the higher ones, hoping to make up for his friend's absence.

With a nod to Wally, Audrey turned back to the audience, put her hand beside her mouth, and shouted the first line of their routine: "Yoo-hoo, Maxie!" she called. "Where are you?"

On cue, Max entered from stage right and joined Audrey in the spotlight with Wally, alone, accompanying the scene with the twinkle of light background music.

"Here I am, baby!" Max wore a furry Russian ushanka hat and sported a very thick, very fake mustache. The audience laughed at the sight gag, and Max ate up the attention with an appetite he usually reserved for his mother's cooking.

Max stuck his hands in his pockets and rocked on his heels like Charlie Chaplin. "Audrey," he said. "I have something to ask you and I'm not sure how you'll react."

"Don't be silly, Maxie," she said coyly. "I don't bite."

A few soldiers in the audience whistled.

"All right." Max dropped to one knee and took Audrey's hand. "Will you marry me? We can have our wedding in Moscow."

"Moscow?" Audrey clutched her chest. "What about Stalin?"

"There's no stallin', baby. I wanna get married now!"

The soldiers in the audience burst out laughing and Wally's crew breathed a collective sigh of relief. The joke had hit its mark, and the mission's first code had been delivered.

Yet Wally felt no relief. Mayfield was still missing.

"Oh, silly. I meant Joseph Stalin."

"That's fine," said Max. "It's your wedding too. Invite whomever you want."

The audience laughed again, but Wally was still distracted, almost missing his key change. He played harder, pulled his attention back to the piano, lest he put the whole mission at risk.

"We only met two weeks ago," said Audrey. "This is all so fast. Why Moscow?"

"'Cause I'm Russian."

Audrey mugged to the audience, "No kidding."

Wally was proud of Audrey and her seemingly endless skills, which now notably included comic acting. The audience was eating it up.

He ventured a look to the front row, where Otis and Brubaker sat together. Otis was uncharacteristically laughing, caught up in the show, but Brubaker was frowning. He caught Wally's eye and mouthed, "Mayfield?"

Wally shrugged and shook his head. He kept playing, trying to keep his mind focused, keep his music flowing.

Brubaker's jaw set. He rose from his chair and rushed off into the darkness.

"Just say 'yes,' baby," Max crooned. "You know I love you."

That was Wally's cue to begin playing their real first number, a little tune he'd written called "Russian to the Chapel."

Audrey nailed her part of the duet, even though Max's baritone sounded a little shaky on the first refrain.

> *"You know you can trust me.*
> *I'm not Germany.*
> *We're Russian to the chapel of love."*

The song was not only meant to be funny and musical, it also carried the next set of messages to the Allies, buried in the lyrics of the third stanza and in Wally's C-to-D key changes, which he was careful to nail with precision.

Wally's final note of the song marked the end of the first vignette and was Rat's cue to replace Audrey and Max at center stage for the next routine. As the pair exited stage left and the audience applauded, the hot spotlight moved across Wally's face to settle on Rat entering stage right.

Rat took his mark downstage, dressed in an ill-fitting private's uniform he had gathered from the men of the camp. He stared melodramatically into the night sky, just as he'd done in rehearsals, which caused a few giggles among the soldiers in the audience.

Frankie then entered, stage right, and joined Rat, accompanied by Wally's staccato instrumental tune. Frankie wore a commander's hat and uniform. "Hello, soldier," said Frankie with deep gravel that sounded hilariously like Colonel Otis's voice.

"Oh, hey, Commander," Rat replied without the customary salute, a brooding look on his face.

"Son, what's wrong with you?" said Commander Frankie. "You're supposed to acknowledge your commanding officer with a salute like this." Frankie demonstrated with a hand to his temple. His stoicism and his knotted brow were reminiscent of Colonel Otis and prompted laughter in the audience.

"That's just it, sir," said Rat. "Something's wrong with my arm. Every time I try to salute, this happens instead." Rat pointed his right arm to the air, his flat hand forming a German "Sieg Heil" salute.

The men of the camp roared, and the air crackled with their amusement. Even Colonel Otis couldn't contain his laughter.

"Private! That's a German salute," snarled Frankie.

"I know, sir." Rat opened his beady eyes wide.

"Well, that won't do." Commander Frankie rubbed his chin. "Not one bit. You look like some sorta Nazi. What does the medic say?"

"He says to lay off the bratwurst and sauerkraut, sir."

At the sounds of the troops' further merriment, Wally scanned for Mayfield and then glanced to the audience again. Brubaker's chair remained empty, and Wally worried that neither Mayfield nor Brubaker was coming back.

The boisterousness of the crowd grew. If the acting wasn't great, the jokes were making up for it. Max and Frankie's writing had hit the mark. And while it was the messages to the front lines that mattered most, putting on a convincing show helped keep those messages secret.

"When did this saluting problem start?" said Commander Frankie.

"On my furlough day, sir. I went into the village and met this Eye-Talian girl. She was something else…" Rat wiggled his eyebrows at the crowd like Groucho Marx, and the men in the audience hooted and whistled at the innuendo.

"Say no more, soldier," replied Commander Frankie. "You need to be more careful. Local girls can spell trouble."

That was Bobbi's cue to enter, and when she did, the crowd went nuts, rose to their feet, and whistled.

"I know I'm trouble," said Bobbi. She placed her hand on the curve of her hip and worked a suggestive Mae West sensuality into her voice. "I just can't resist a man in uniform."

The crowd howled like a pack of hungry coyotes, but Bobbi seemed to enjoy the attention and rewarded them with a wink.

Rat acted dumbstruck at her arrival and looked wide-eyed at Frankie. "See what I mean, Commander? Trouble."

Frankie pointed at Rat. "Son, you're a soldier in Uncle Sam's army. What about that girl of yours back home?"

"Forget that girl," said Bobbi. "What about me?"

That was Wally's cue to play a song called, "I May Be Trouble." It was a tune he'd written with Bobbi to highlight her melodic voice and her propensity for dramatic performance, using musical hints of honey borrowed from her Diamond Club shows. And, just like the Manhattan audience, whose responses could be counted on, the soldiers ate up the sweet, savory songs of Bobbi LaFleur.

At the conclusion of Bobbi's number, Audrey returned to a burst of whistles and applause and delivered a humorous song Max had written called, "Don't Kiss a Fritz in a Blitz." She kept her dimpled smile while managing to nail the high- and low-register elements of the song. Through Wally's corresponding key changes, the pair delivered additional instructions to the Allies while succeeding in keeping their audience's spirits high.

Wally worked to stay focused on his Victory Vertical and fix his roving mind on his part of the mission to ensure he wouldn't miss an important note or key change. But his anxiety quietly defied him, rising in intensity with each number despite the reassuring reliability of the Victory Vertical.

His menacing demon seemed to be whispering in his ear: *Mayfield is still missing and it's all your fault.*

The muscles in Wally's shoulders tightened and his breath felt labored. He slowed during his instrumental interlude as Audrey left the stage and tried to keep calm, working to infuse his breath with a rhythm as reliable and steady as a metronome. There was only one number left, and he had to get through it.

The final song was provocative and was called "My Man's Gun," filled with double entendres and innuendo, written for Bobbi. It was slow and sultry, crafted to conclude with a horn solo, which, in Mayfield's absence, couldn't happen.

It was then Wally realized tragedy had struck. The mission's final messages were built into that horn solo and couldn't be delivered by a piano.

Their mission was about to fail.

Wally struggled to maintain the hard-won calm he had mustered, simultaneously trying to keep the show going as he played the song's playful introduction, prompted by Bobbi's slow and sensual entrance. But the tune's playfulness only served to feed Wally's disparate feelings.

With each stanza, with each refrain, the song approached Mayfield's solo. Bobbi delivered the suggestive lyrics, and Wally's heart pounded harder. He tried to lock his knocking knees, remind himself to focus only on the music. He relied on the intuition of his fingers, on the connection they maintained with the vertical piano that had fallen from the sky. But his control was starting to slip, the whispers of his demon growing louder.

All your fault.

Between stanzas, Bobbi shot a look to Wally. Her face was all smiles, though panic shone from her green eyes. She, too, understood what Mayfield's absence meant.

Wally's throat began to close, and he heard himself wheeze.

Suddenly, Brubaker marched onto stage, a trumpet in his hand. To the hoorahs of the audience, the colonel lifted the instrument to his lips, aimed for the stars, and played the solo intended for Mayfield without a moment to spare.

Stunned by the colonel's arrival, as much as by his skills with a horn, Wally snapped out of his spiraling fear. He swallowed to open his throat and gain his breath, then pounded out the song's final rhythms using the Victory Vertical to anchor himself. With the last lingering note of the trumpet and piano, he drew a deep bagpipe breath, lifted his fingers, and wiped his dripping brow with his sleeve.

He had managed not to faint. More importantly, the final messages had been broadcast. For their part, the mission had succeeded.

The audience leapt to their feet. Bobbi's song, and the night's show, was over. Bobbi took center stage and gestured to acknowledge each member of the cast, who joined her in the spotlight, relief washing over Bobbi's face and the faces of the others.

The team all joined hands and bowed. When the ovation was over, they raced backstage.

"Where the hell was Mayfield?" said Max, yanking off his hat and fake mustache. "That was nearly a disaster."

"Some of the men found him staggering through the camp," said Brubaker, "bleeding from his head and muttering to himself. Said it looked like someone had clocked him pretty good. I found him in the infirmary and managed to grab his trumpet."

"Oh, no!" said Audrey.

"Jesus," said Frankie. "Who would hurt Mayfield?"

"Did he say anything, Colonel?" said Max.

Brubaker looked straight at Wally. "The only word he said was 'Walter.'"

"What?" Wally's stomach dropped. His heart was still racing from the energy of their performance, but his emotions were a swirling mess. "I didn't touch him. Why would he say that?"

"You two haven't exactly been speaking," said Frankie.

"Yeah," said Rat. "What's been going on with you two?"

It's all your fault.

"We have some things to work out," said Wally. "Private things." He wasn't about to explain that they were at odds over Audrey, especially with her standing across from him, but his lack of forthrightness seemed to further the discomfort of the team.

"Walter," said Audrey, "I've been telling you to work things out for days. Did you hurt Alvin?" Audrey seemed stunned, not only by the prospect but by hearing her own words.

"Of course not!" said Wally. He peered into Audrey's eyes, searching for the compassion and understanding she'd always provided, yet the look on her face said it all. She didn't believe him.

"Look, Walter," said Max, "I'm sure whatever happened was an accident. A misunderstanding."

Wally saw the faces of his teammates, and they all held the same doubt as Audrey.

"I told you," Wally snapped. "I didn't touch him."

He turned back to Audrey, hoping to find at least one ally among them. Instead, she turned away.

"Okay," said Brubaker. "Let's all take it down a notch. Private Mayfield wasn't himself. I'm sure there's an explanation for all of this." He placed a hand on Wally's shoulder. "Private Lipkin, let's take a walk."

Wally stood beside Brubaker at the foot of Mayfield's cot in the dimly lit infirmary tent, upset to see his roommate so incapacitated. Mayfield was propped up on pillows, his head bound in bandages. His eyes were open, but he squinted toward the infirmary tent flap as if he were trying to find something far in the distance. Unlike the earthy tobacco-and-sweat smell of the camp, the infirmary smelled of surgical spirits and ether, reminding Wally of his visit with his uncle at Brooklyn State Hospital; only, this time, it was Wally who felt crazy.

A half dozen other cots were occupied by unconscious men in worse shape than Mayfield, each of them bandaged or bloody, still recovering from battles in the prior weeks.

"Did you hear me, Mayfield?" said the colonel. Brubaker moved around the cot, closer to Mayfield's ear. "Can you tell us what happened to you?"

"Walter," said Mayfield. It was the only word he had said since they'd arrived and the one he kept repeating. "Walter." His gaze remained fixed elsewhere.

Brubaker glanced at Wally as if seeking some explanation.

Wally looked to the ground with shame. He hadn't touched the guy, but he may as well have. Mayfield was there in the infirmary because Wally had been a lousy friend and a coward. All Mayfield had wanted was a shot with Audrey, the same thing Wally still wanted. It had driven him to drink, and drinking caused him to fall. The thread was clear, and it all tied right back to Wally.

The camp doctor, a man in his late thirties with thinning hair and a pencil mustache, pushed aside the canvas tent door and entered the infirmary. He waved away the moths that flitted around the infirmary lantern and approached Brubaker.

"I put your man on painkillers," the doctor said. "Twelve stitches in the back of his head. He also smelled of whiskey. You're not gonna get much out of him tonight."

"Walter," Mayfield mumbled. His eyes rolled.

The doctor pushed forward to adjust Mayfield's dressings. "I told you. He needs his rest. I'm afraid I need you both to leave."

Brubaker and Wally exited the infirmary and began to walk the path toward Wally's tent.

"He'll be fine," said Brubaker, misunderstanding the look on Wally's face. "The mission will be fine." He stopped walking. "Though I am concerned about you, Private."

"I didn't touch Mayfield, sir. You've gotta believe me."

"Tuscaloosa smelled like a distillery," Brubaker said. "You don't have a scratch on you. And you don't strike me as the sort of fella who would hit a guy with his back turned to you. It's obvious you didn't fight him. He fell."

The tension in Wally's head start to ease. At least the colonel believed him.

"We argued before the show," said Wally. "He fell backward off the stage. When I went to help him, he'd already run off. And with the show starting, it was too late..."

Brubaker nodded. "You and Tuscaloosa have been at each other for weeks. Even I've noticed that. What's the story there?" When Wally didn't reply, Brubaker replied for him. "A girl?"

"Audrey," said Wally.

"Thought you had eyes for Barbara Ann."

"I did," said Wally. "Now it's Audrey."

Brubaker chuckled. "With only two gals on the team, you're not giving the guy much to work with," he said. "I can understand why he might be upset."

Wally kept silent, and they continued down the path until they arrived near the entrance to the guys' tent. To Wally's surprise, Colonel Otis was there waiting for them under the moonlight with the rest of Wally's team at his side.

Each saluted when Brubaker and Wally approached, and they both saluted back.

"Colonel Brubaker," said Otis with none of the mirth he had exhibited during the show. "Afraid I have some bad news. Would you and the others please follow me?" Otis turned and marched toward the command tent, and the others followed.

Wally made a beeline for Audrey, still eager to set matters straight with her as he had with Brubaker. However, before he could say a word, she raced over next to Bobbi, her face carrying a look of anguish.

Wally hung his head. After their mission victory, he should have been elated. Instead, he seemed to have lost Audrey's confidence in him.

They arrived at the command tent, where Security Officer Simpson was waiting. His demeanor was as brooding and sour as usual. Nevertheless, he saluted, as did the two guards who stood on either side of the entrance. Otis nodded at them, and they lifted the flap for the team and Simpson to enter. Otis lit his lanterns with a cigarette lighter and gestured for Brubaker to take the chair in front of his desk. He then motioned toward the row of wooden chairs lining the tent wall. "At ease, people. Take a seat."

The team all sat on the creaking wooden chairs, some speckled with mud and moisture from the camp. Simpson stood with his hands behind his back as Otis piled kindling and a log into his stove. He lit the kindling with the same lighter, fanned a fire to life, and turned to face the team.

"Your show tonight was a hit with my men," said Otis. He returned to his desk, drew two squat glasses from the top drawer, and filled them with whiskey from a decanter. He handed one glass to Brubaker and kept the other for himself. He then corked the decanter without offering a drink to anyone else. "It was a show they'll remember for the rest of their days and exactly what they needed to lift their spirits. It was truly appreciated."

"Thank you, Colonel," said Brubaker, lifting his whiskey glass but not drinking. "You said you had bad news?"

"Right to the point, eh?" said Otis. "Okay, then." He met Brubaker's unmoving eyes. "We learned that this morning's code sheets never made it to the French." He took a swig of his whiskey.

The sudden and blunt proclamation washed over the team, and Wally felt the blood leave his face. "Never made it?" Wally blurted.

"Kiwis, Poles, Brits, South Africans, and Americans all confirmed they got the transmission." said Otis. "We got no such confirmation from the French. Without them, it's doubtful we can take the north."

"What does that mean," said Bobbi.

"The show was a success, but I'm afraid the mission will be a failure."

"Hang on," said Frankie. "Do we know if the French got the radio broadcast of the show tonight?"

"Anyone with a regular radio got the show," said Otis. "It's a safe bet. But the army signal relay appears to be down between here and there. Without the signal line, there were no code sheets, and without a way to decipher the codes—"

"So, we send a runner," said Wally. "Isn't that what we do if the relay goes down? Send a runner?"

Otis lowered his voice. "French are too far north," he said. "A runner wouldn't reach them in time."

"Then what about repairing the relay?" said Wally. "Couldn't we resend the transmission through the signal lines if the relay is fixed?"

Brubaker grabbed his glass, gulped his whiskey, and said, "If the relay was compromised, Private, it likely means the Germans were the cause. Even if we send a team to fix the relay, the enemy will surely be there waiting. Standard ambush."

The room fell silent, and Wally tried to puzzle out some way the mission could be saved.

"The French were supposed to take the Aurunci Mountains," said Rat, his voice soft with defeat. "That leaves one whole flank of the mission uncovered."

"This was a calculated risk," said Brubaker, clearly working to conceal his own disappointment.

"Shouldn't we try to reach them?" Wally hoped to sound more resolute than desperate.

Otis stood and cleared his desk to reveal his map. Wally and the others took that as permission to approach.

"We're here," said Otis. He pointed to a red circle in the lower left side of the map. "The western relay is twenty clicks northwest...here." He traced the path with his finger along a rudimentary line drawing of foothills between the camp and a red X farther up the map. "That appears to be where the signal died. Even if a team could make it to the relay in time, and even if the Germans aren't there to greet them—and that's a big 'if'—we'd still need a signal specialist to make repairs and patch into the line to resend the transmission. It would have to be someone who knows those code sheets by heart. Can't carry secrets on paper into enemy territory."

"Don't you have a signal specialist?" said Brubaker. His voice betrayed a glimmer of hope.

"One of the best in the army," said Simpson, chiming in for the first time. His face looked pained. "But he succumbed to his injuries three days ago. He was the last of a half dozen."

Otis finished his whiskey and set his empty glass on the map. "'Fraid we're outta luck."

The tent grew quiet.

"We have a signal specialist," said Wally. "He's lying in the infirmary."

"Walter!" said Audrey. "How could you—?"

"Mayfield will come to," said Wally. "When he does, he'll want to do this. Besides, he'll have me to help him."

Audrey grew quiet. Brubaker and the others looked unconvinced.

"Alvin and I have had our issues," said Wally, "but I didn't hurt him. You've gotta let us try."

"What about the codes?" said Frankie. "Neither of you knows those by heart."

"I do," said Rat. He stood a little taller. "I'll go too."

"Enough!" snapped Brubaker.

He downed what remained of his own whiskey in a single gulp and slammed his glass on the desk so hard Wally thought it would shatter.

"I'm not sending either of you into the field," Brubaker barked, "and there's no way Mr. Mayfield is up to a dangerous mission. You saw him. We're gonna have to count on the other Allied troops to make this operation work without the French, at least as best as they can."

The rest of the team seemed relieved at the colonel's decision.

Rat shrugged. "Well," he said, "how reliable are the French, anyway?"

Max chortled, though Wally didn't think it was funny.

"The rest of the troops will make do," explained Brubaker. "We'll learn more in the morning."

"That's it?" said Wally. "That's the plan? We just hope for the best?"

"Sometimes hope is all we have," said Bobbi.

Wally looked to Audrey, but she wouldn't look at him. Whatever infraction she thought he had committed, she was not ready to forgive him.

Brubaker raised his chin. "Twelve of the thirteen cipher transmissions made it through,

Lipkin. Tonight's radio broadcast of the show was a success. Even without the French, the Allies are in a better position to break through Monte Cassino than we've been in all year. That's not hoping for the best, that's the best we've ever had." But when Wally didn't respond, Brubaker added, "Sometimes we win by changing the plan."

Wally didn't try to hide his frustration. Changing the plan seemed to have been the plan all along, starting when the Nazis shot up WKOB and continuing when they destroyed their London facility. Now, the enemy had taken down the signal line, putting an end to the team's work and Wally's hopes once again. Nazis were always one step ahead of them, and Brubaker seemed to be saying that was just the way things worked.

"So, I guess that's settled," said Otis. He turned to the team. "You should all be proud of a job well done, despite this setback. You have Uncle Sam's gratitude and my own. Tomorrow, we'll regroup. For now, let's call it a night."

Brubaker looked at the team. "Dismissed."

The crew marched in a line out of the command tent. Wally hoped to talk to Audrey, to try and appeal to her sense of forgiveness, but she left in a hurry, dragging Bobbi with her.

Once outside, Wally kicked the dirt. Judging from the look on her face, Audrey seemed more concerned for Mayfield than she did for him. Maybe Mayfield was the right guy for her after all, and it was time Wally got out of the way and just accepted defeat in all things.

He followed Max, Frankie, and Rat to their tent, a new angst rising in him. He stared at Mayfield's rucksack and his empty cot. While the others seemed ready to accept the failure of their mission, Wally decided he would not. He could not.

He turned and took Rat by the arm. "Clyde?"

"Yeah, Lipkin?"

"Get your pack. We're heading out."

Max stepped forward. "What are you doing, Walter?"

"You can't be serious," said Frankie. "Heading out?"

Max scowled. "You're gonna run the codes, aren't you?"

"Someone has to do something," spat Wally. "Might as well be me."

Max shook his head. "You can't drag Clyde into this. He's no soldier."

"I'm as much a soldier as any of you," said Rat.

"Exactly my point," said Max. "None of us is a soldier, including you. It's suicide."

"He's got skills," said Wally.

"Yeah," said Rat, "I have skills. And I make my own decisions."

"Neither of you has signal skills, and Mayfield sounds like he's down for the count. What are you trying to prove?" said Max.

"I'm trying to finish what we started," said Wally, "to see this mission through to the end."

"Getting killed is not the mission," Max snapped. "Even Brubaker thinks—"

"Max." Wally held up his hand. "I know you think you're in charge, and most of the time, you are. But fellas like me and Clyde? Every now and then, we have ideas of our own."

"Yep." Rat nodded. "Ideas. Both of us."

Wally shrugged. "You said it yourself. When there's a job to do, a job we're good at, we gotta do it."

Rat walked over and stood beside Wally in solidarity, facing Frankie and Max, unwilling to be left out of the debate. "Double what he said. No one's tying me up this time."

"Otis has real soldiers," said Max, ignoring Rat. "He can send them."

"Brubaker and Otis are convinced this is as good as it'll get," said Wally. "They won't agree to send anyone. And you heard Simpson. Their last signal specialist is dead. Who will they send?"

Max struggled with a retort, and Wally used the time to further his position.

"Mayfield will want to do this. Rat and I want to do this."

"Then we'll come with you," said Max. "We'll all go."

"That's right," said Frankie. "We'll all go."

"You'll only slow us down, draw attention," said Wally. He fixed his eyes on Max. "Besides, if we don't come back, someone's gotta keep the mission going, and you two and the girls are the best ones for that job."

Max's eyes darted as if searching for some way out of the trap, but Wally had the momentum and pointed his own finger gun at his brother. "Max, you're the one who told me to focus on the work, not the danger, remember?"

"There's gotta be some other way."

The light from the lantern sputtered as a moth hit the fire and burst into smoldering flame. Wally didn't think that was a good omen, but he ignored it and stared back at his brother.

"Keep Audrey safe," said Wally.

There was no time to say goodbye and no time for further debate. Wally threw his pack over his shoulder, grabbed Mayfield's rucksack, and motioned for Rat to get his things.

"Twenty clicks away," said Wally. "If everything goes well, we'll be back by morning."

"You'll be court-martialed by morning," said Frankie.

"I dodged a couple of those already. What's one more?"

"What if you aren't back tomorrow?" said Max. His voice had grown small, his eyes glossy.

"Then you'll have the satisfaction of knowing you were right."

Max threw his arms around Wally and hugged him. "I don't wanna be right, Walter," said Max, his voice unsteady. "Not this time."

After a moment, Wally withdrew from Max's embrace and chewed his lip to keep his feelings in check.

"Gotta go," said Wally quietly, "but there's still one thing I need from you."

Wally moved with quiet determination through the slumbering camp, Rat scuttling close at his heels as they passed row upon row of tents. A thin layer of overhead clouds filtered the moonlight, bathing the camp in an eerie blanket of blue. Through the quiet, Wally heard the labored breathing of sleeping soldiers and the occasional whispered conversation among those unable to sleep.

"Ow," said Rat.

"Quiet," said Wally. He turned to see Rat standing on one foot, shaking his upside-down boot over the path.

"Rock in my shoe," said Rat.

"What about 'quiet' don't you understand?"

Rat shoved his foot back into his boot and then lifted two rucksacks—his and Mayfield's—over each shoulder. "You try carrying all this with a stone in your boot. Mayfield's bag is heavy."

Wally shook his head, and the two continued toward the infirmary tent.

Once behind the tent's rear guy line, Wally glanced around the corner to see Max and Frankie at the infirmary entrance, talking to the doctor.

"So, you saw the performance, huh?" said Max. His voice was unnecessarily loud for a conversation with the doctor two feet in front of him, but his volume was clearly intended for Wally's benefit.

Wally leaned over to Rat and whispered, "Max and Frankie have the doc distracted," he whispered. "Keep a lookout."

Rat stood sentry at the infirmary tent's rear flank as Wally sliced his jagged army-issued knife into the canvas and cut the thick fabric to allow a new door flap to form. He then slipped into the tent, careful not to wake the four injured men sharing the space with Mayfield.

"I did some light opera back in Kalamazoo," Wally heard the doctor brag. "Some said I could've been a professional."

"No kidding?" said Frankie. "Professional? Let's hear what you've got."

Only one lantern in the infirmary tent had been lit and was lowered to a flicker. All was quiet until Wally heard the doctor sing "O Sole Mio." He feared the sleeping men of the infirmary would awaken, but after a look confirmed the men were still out cold, Wally rushed over to Mayfield's cot and shook him.

"Alvin," he whispered. "Alvin, wake up."

"I hate those goats, Mama," said Mayfield sleepily.

"Oh, come on, Alvin," whispered Wally. "Wake up."

Mayfield's lids fluttered and then lifted. His confusion slowly transformed to anger when he saw Wally under the dancing lantern light.

"Lipkin," Mayfield said flatly. "What do you want?"

"Your country needs you," said Wally. "I need you."

"Blow it out your ass." Mayfield turned his bandaged head away from Wally. "Yow!" he blurted. He sat up with pain and reached for his head. "Holy Christ. What the—"

"You're hurt," said Wally. "And you blamed me for it."

Mayfield gently touched his bandages, confusion replacing his anger. "I did?"

"You lost your footing backstage and fell," said Wally, "but you told the colonel that I hurt you."

"I don't remember saying that." Mayfield looked away.

"You were mad at me, and I know I deserve it," said Wally. "But right now, the mission is at stake."

Mayfield's eyes flashed. "Oh, God," he said. His face grew white with realization. "I missed the show. My horn solo."

"Brubaker saved the show," said Wally, "but we still need your help to save the mission. I'll explain everything on the way, but we gotta get outta here now."

Mayfield seemed to gather his senses, slid his legs out from under the blankets and placed his feet on the ground. When he stood, however, he nearly fell, and sat back on the cot. "Whoa."

"They gave you painkillers," said Wally. "Not sure how long they'll last. You drank a bit too."

"Whiskey. I remember," said Mayfield. He rubbed his temples.

Seeing Mayfield so confused and uncoordinated gave Wally pause. Maybe Brubaker was right. Maybe Mayfield wasn't up to such a dangerous mission.

"You really have talent!" Max's voice boomed from outside the infirmary tent.

"Yeah, Doc," said Frankie. "How about another song?"

"What's going on out there?" said Mayfield, pointing to the infirmary entrance.

"Max and Frankie are distracting the doctor," said Wally. "So, we have to leave that way." He pointed to the flap he'd cut.

"Need my boots," said Mayfield. He was fully uniformed but looked down at his socked feet.

Wally found his friend's jacket and boots beside his cot and helped him with his laces. Wally then put his shoulder under Mayfield's arm and led him to the makeshift exit. He drew back the flap and helped Mayfield through, out into the blue darkness of the camp.

Once they were both outside, Wally looked over and lost his breath. Rat was not alone.

Standing beside him was Simpson, the cranky security officer who always seemed to have the stink eye for Wally and the team.

"Simpson," said Wally. "What do you want?"

"I know what you're doing," Simpson said flatly, "and I highly doubt either of our commanders would approve."

Wally and his pals exchanged looks in the awkward silence.

"Lucky for you," said Simpson, "I do approve."

"You do?" said Rat.

"Look around," said Simpson. "The men here are spent. If your mission fails, we all fail. We'll have to fight again, long before we're ready. It'll be the death of us, at least some of us."

Wally shifted uncomfortably. Was he or his pals any more ready than the men of this camp?

Simpson stared at Wally. "When you arrived, I resented you, all clean and green and talking about music; you even brought women with you." Simpson sighed. "You were nothing like the soldiers I knew. It was insulting to every fella here. You even had a piano air-dropped into the camp. It was ridiculous."

Wally shifted uncomfortably.

"Now," said Simpson, "I see what you're ready to do to save the mission. To help these men. To serve our country." He drew a breath. "I was wrong about you." He moved his gaze to Rat and Mayfield. "All of you."

"Simpson, if anyone asks—"

"I never saw you." Simpson unsnapped his sidearm from his holster and handed it to Wally. "You may need this," the security officer said.

Wally clutched the Colt pistol and eyed it, uncertain if he was comforted or alarmed. "Thanks, Simpson."

"Don't make me regret it."

Wally checked to be sure the safety of the gun was on, as they had taught him to do back at Fort Hamilton, and then stuffed the weapon into the back of his trousers.

"Let's go," said Rat. "Our last, best chance to take Monte Cassino starts in twelve hours. After that, our message to the French won't matter."

17

The Right Place at the Right Time

U nder a sky full of stars, Wally, Mayfield, and Rat hiked the foothill trail north of the camp, trying to stay clear of the main road. The earlier cloud cover had now passed, and the moon held a diffused halo, giving it the appearance of a giant eye, watching them. Its sallow light created a glow on Mayfield's bandaged-wrapped head. If this had been any other night, the moon's radiance would have been welcome. Tonight, however, it only amplified the trio's risk of detection and threatened the failure of their mission.

Wally's heart pounded a warning, pulsing to a rhythm out of sync with the chirp of crickets who seemed cheerfully ignorant of the stakes of the human world around them.

"You remember Otis's map?" said Rat.

"I do," said Wally. He pulled his uncle's pocket watch from his jacket and flipped it open to the compass. "We stay north until the road cuts west." He lifted his gaze and pointed over the tall flaxen weeds. "That direction."

Wally looked back to the compass and read the inscription: *The right place at the right time*. For months, he had worked to avoid this very situation, this very place, the scenario of his worst nightmares. He'd made choices to keep himself safe and free from the threat of combat, and yet everything he'd done, every choice he'd made, had led him here, to an Italian battlefield where his anxiety neurosis might, finally, prove to be the death of him. If he were truly in the right place at the right time, he wished things would have felt more...right.

He snapped the watch closed, returned it to his pocket, and saw that Mayfield was slogging behind, grunting with the effort of movement.

"You okay, Alvin?" called Wally.

"I'll be fine."

After Simpson helped them sneak out of the camp undetected, Wally had spent the first hour of their journey explaining their plan to his injured roommate. With Mayfield's help as a signal specialist, they could repair the western relay that had failed to deliver the mission ciphers to the French. They would then patch into the repaired line with Mayfield's radio equipment, and Rat would send the coded ciphers from memory. This would trigger the part of the Allied mission for which the French were responsible, the taking of the Aurunci Mountain pass. It was the only way to assure the mission had any hope of succeeding, no matter what Brubaker had to say.

Mayfield was eager to help despite his injuries, but now he was staggering, holding his head, and enduring a pain that only appeared to be getting worse as his inebriation and painkillers wore off.

On one count, it seemed, Brubaker was right. Mayfield wasn't up to the mission.

"Let's take a break," said Wally.

"But, Walter—" Rat's beady eyes looked urgent.

"Mayfield needs a break, so we take a break."

Wally knew Rat's concerns about stopping were well founded. None of them knew what dangers lay ahead nor how long it would take to find and fix the signal relay. Stopping might be wasting what precious little time they had. However, for their mission to work, Mayfield had to do what his signal corps training had taught him to do. If the guy needed to catch his breath, they had to stop.

Wally motioned toward a clearing in the brush. "There."

He set his rucksack down in a patch of dirt, pulled out a canteen, and handed it to Mayfield. "Here, Alvin. Drink some water."

Mayfield took a swig and nodded his thanks.

Wally turned to Rat. "What did you bring?"

Rat opened his own rucksack and looked inside. "Tool kit, chocolate bar, picture of my mother, canteen, toothbrush…"

"You're not going to sleepover camp," said Wally. "This is a mission."

Rat shrugged. "I said 'tool kit.'"

Mayfield snorted and spat out his water, his laughter momentarily taking Wally's mind off the danger they faced.

"We have Mayfield's bag too," said Rat. He opened the second rucksack to review its contents. "He's got a roll of wire, clippers, a radio, a heavy metal box with a dial…"

"My field repair pack," said Mayfield. "It's got everything I need. We'll be fine."

In the darkness of the unfamiliar countryside, under threat of German detection, "fine" was hardly the right word for what Wally felt. The night air smelled of juniper and the dry dust of Italian weeds. It was nothing at all like the car fumes or city scents of Brooklyn, and there was no sparkle of city lights. Only the moon and the stars lit their way.

Opposite the road, cradled in the breast of two hills some distance away, Wally saw the remains of a Gothic-style church that seemed to glow under the moonlight. He retrieved his field lenses and aimed them at the fallen structure, which looked like the victim of a recent bombing, its façade like an open mouth, spilling colorful broken frescoes from its front doors. It had fragmented spires and fallen columns telling the tale of the terrible fate that had befallen this place of worship. What was once clearly a thing of beauty and safety was now just a pile of rubble. He turned away and aimed his lenses farther down the road in front of them and then to the road behind. Their path looked clear, but who could be sure out here?

He returned the binoculars to his pack and then reached to the small of his back, to the gun that Simpson had given him. He eyed it in the starlight and ran through what he could remember of his weapons training at Fort Hamilton. He never liked guns but having one handy made him feel a little better.

"Good thinking," said Mayfield, seeing Wally secure the gun. He stood and handed back the canteen. "Let's get moving."

Wally nodded, assured the gun's safety was on, and returned the weapon to the back of his trousers. Rat hoisted the two heavy rucksacks, and the trio resumed hiking, with Mayfield now keeping up more closely. Soon, just as Wally predicted, they reached the crossroad cutting west into enemy territory.

"How far to the relay?" said Mayfield.

"Otis said it was twenty clicks from camp," said Wally.

"Twenty clicks is about twelve and a half miles," said Rat. He looked to the air above him as if reading an equation. "A man can hike two or three miles an hour on flat land, one if he's climbing. I read that in our field guide. We've been at this for about two hours now, so…"

"You're giving me a headache," groaned Mayfield.

"Just doing the math."

"How much time until the relay, Clyde?" Wally huffed.

"Four more hours, give or take," said Rat. "Allowing for any breaks or changes in the terrain."

"Not a lot of time," said Wally. "Once we find it, we still have to make the repairs and send the ciphers. Let's pick up the pace."

Rat continued in the lead, and the trio hiked more quickly for another hour along a green hillside, with thin weed stalks as tall as men growing thicker and wilder as they progressed, forcing them closer to the road. Their pace was good, but they needed to do better.

Wally turned to Mayfield, noticing him once again lagging farther behind with each stride.

"Alvin?"

Mayfield stopped. He held his hand over the back of his head, but this time he didn't reply.

"Clyde," Wally called to Rat, "hold up!"

Rat doubled back as Wally helped Mayfield take a seat on the soft soil. Once again, Wally opened his rucksack and handed his canteen to Mayfield. But when Mayfield lifted his hand from his head to reach for the water, Wally saw his roommate's fingers were glistening red under the moonlight.

"Alvin, you're bleeding!"

Mayfield gazed at his palm. "Must've popped a stitch."

Wally raced behind Mayfield, lifted the moist bandages from his friend's head, and saw his wound under the vigilant moon. Six of Mayfield's stitches had come loose, and the gash on the back of his head had opened like a mouth, a dark crimson stream trickling onto his neck.

Wally gasped. Instinctively, he pinched closed the skin of Mayfield's wound, blood covering his own fingers. "Holy shit!"

"That bad?" said Mayfield. He sounded woozy.

"No," Wally said, feeling a little woozy himself. "Let's just sit for a minute." He turned to Rat and tried to work a calm into his voice. "Clyde, can you bring over my pack, please?"

Rat complied and walked over. One look at Mayfield's wound, and Rat's face lost its color. "Oh, God."

"So, it *is* that bad," said Mayfield.

"Grab my sewing kit," said Wally.

"Sewing kit?" said Rat. "You're not a doctor."

"No, I'm not," said Wally. He continued to pinch Mayfield's wound with his fingers. "Maybe you'd like to handle this?"

Rat fell silent and handed Wally his sewing kit.

"Alvin," said Wally, "do you have any more whiskey?"

"An extra flask should still be in my bag," said Mayfield. "Help yourself."

"Not for me. For you. This may hurt."

"I'm gonna throw up," said Rat.

"No, you won't," said Wally. He looked intently at Rat, one hand still on Mayfield and one grasping his sewing kit. "Give Alvin the whiskey and then get my flashlight. I need you to shine it here, on his head."

"Oh, God," Rat repeated.

"Keep it together, Clyde. I need you." But Wally wasn't sure he could keep it together himself. If he didn't close Mayfield's wound, the guy could bleed out.

"I'll try," said Rat.

Rat handed Mayfield his whiskey and then shined the light on his wound.

"Can you see?" said Rat.

"Yes," said Wally. "Aim it close, away from the road."

"Got it."

Wally continued to pinch Mayfield's wound closed and used his other hand to remove a pre-threaded needle from his army-issued sewing kit. He brought the needle into Rat's light and paused short of Mayfield's head.

Wally leaned forward next to Mayfield's ear. "Now would be a good time for that whiskey."

Mayfield took a long, slow slug and then said, "Do it."

Wally held his breath. He pinched hard on the wound and pushed his needle into Mayfield's flesh.

Mayfield sucked a sudden breath of his own through gritted teeth, confirming that his painkillers had worn off.

"Easy," said Wally. "Try counting Mississippis."

"I'm from Alabama," groaned Mayfield.

"Then count Alabamas," said Wally. "I don't care. Just keep still."

Rat held his shaky flashlight with both hands, pointed at Mayfield's head, though Rat's own eyes were aimed somewhere else.

Mayfield counted aloud, groaning, "One Alabama, two Alabama..."

Wally imagined himself at A-Rite Cleaners, helping his mother darn Mr. Fleming's pants. Of course, pants didn't squirm when Wally stitched them, but his mother's dip-and-tuck method helped him make things go quickly. He kept his needlework clean and tight, using the intricacy of his mother's technique to keep his mind off the fact that he was sewing flesh, not fabric. It wasn't Mr. Fleming's approval at stake tonight; it was the success of the Allied effort and the life of his friend.

Wally filled his lungs with juniper air, focused on Mayfield's Alabamas, and forced himself to remain conscious.

"Doing great, Alvin," said Wally, but Mayfield just kept counting.

After eighty Alabamas, Wally removed his hand, confirmed the bleeding had stopped, and tied off his thread. He then rewrapped Mayfield's bandages tight to swaddle his head, feeling an odd impulse to say a Jewish prayer over his handiwork.

"Done?" said Mayfield.

"Done," said Wally. "You were a trooper."

Mayfield handed over his whiskey and patted his bandages. "Thanks, Walter."

"Didn't do it alone," said Wally.

He turned to Rat, who abruptly buckled over and vomited into the tall weeds. When he rose, Rat spat to the ground, ran his sleeve along his lips, and donned an unconvincing smile. "You know me," said Rat. "Always here to help."

Wally stood and ensured his pistol remained secured at the small of his back. They'd avoided one disaster, but still had a three-hour hike ahead of them. Whatever fate had in store, Wally doubted things would be so easily sewn up as Mr. Fleming's pants or Mayfield's head.

Before Wally could gather his rucksack, the strange rattling trill of a night bird silenced the crickets. Wally then realized the sound wasn't a bird at all. He spun to face the road behind them and saw an approaching light.

"Oh, shit."

A dark-gray open-top German tub car barreled down the road toward them in the distance, its mounted searchlight scanning the foothill path they traveled.

The trio had ventured too close to the road.

A shock of adrenaline rushed to Wally's limbs.

"Hide!" he snapped, and the three ran from the road into the tall weeds and dropped onto their bellies beneath the weed line, hugging the earth beneath them.

The car approached quickly down the dirt road, its burning spotlight slicing the darkness like a hot knife through butter, sending needles of light between the flaxen reeds.

Wally froze, the gun in his waistband digging into his spine. He wished himself invisible as the light beamed over their backs again and again like the roaming gaze of a predator. The spotlight's intensity grew as the vehicle closed in on their position. Then, with the crackle of gravel from the main road and the squeak of dirty brakes, the utility roadster rolled to a stop just yards away.

The beam of light locked in place, aimed into the distance just beyond them as he heard someone set the car's brake. He turned his head away from the road, dragging his cheek along the mud, and saw Rat's wide eyes staring sideways back at him through the brush. Rat mouthed the words, "Don't move."

The raspy voices of at least two Germans broke the silence. Though Wally didn't understand a word of German, he was relieved that the soldier's exchange sounded conversational and friendly, not urgent. His trio hadn't been spotted.

The tub car's door squealed open. Wally tried to count Mississippis, or even Alabamas. He prayed for invisibility, wondering if Solomon's ring would have affected such a result. He would have settled for the ability to talk to plants and imagined how he might instruct the tall weeds to reach out like the tendrils of an octopus and strangle the German soldiers. But he found it hard to focus. His mind was a cacophony of heartbeats and air-raid sirens.

He closed his eyes, relying on his ears.

A soldier exited the vehicle, his boots hitting the road grit, which crunched like bones beneath the German's weight. The sound of his steps moved closer to Wally, off the gravel road and into the tall whispering weeds, so near that Wally feared the soldier may step on him or one of his friends. Wally's heart pounded so hard he was sure the approaching German could hear it. He tried to concentrate, to get a sense of how close the guy was and how many others might be there with him.

Suddenly, he heard splashing a few yards away, followed by the putrid smell of urine.

Wally turned his head back to where Mayfield had dropped and opened his eyes again. But just as he gained focus through the haze of light on his friend's bandaged head, he saw Mayfield rise above the weed line, into the spotlight, and charge toward the road.

Bile rose in Wally's throat, but before he could try and stop Mayfield, a shot rang out.

Something within him forced Wally to his feet. He tried to get his bearings, find Mayfield among the tall weeds, bright light, and wild silhouettes.

Wally spotted his friend by the tub car, struggling to pull a rifle from the grasp of an equally tall German.

"Walter!" cried Rat. "Look out!"

Wally spun to see the German who had been urinating now lunging toward him.

Wally wanted to flee, but his body would not respond. His legs went numb. He stumbled backward, remembered his gun, reached to the small of his back.

The German groped toward him, his arms outstretched, aimed at Wally's throat.

Wally grabbed the gun's handle, but it slipped loose from his sweaty hand and fell somewhere into the weeds.

He dropped to the ground, fumbled to find the gun in the light from the tub car, but the soldier was upon him.

The man grabbed Wally, flipped him over, pinned him to the ground, and raised his fist.

The German, a dark-featured, bloated man, barked something into Wally's face, his sour spittle falling onto Wally's cheeks. His swastika armband, emblazoned in crimson, black, and white, shone in the light as his fist came down on Wally's jaw. He tried to push the German off, but his arms were paralyzed, now as useless as his legs.

The soldier struck Wally again with his fist, knocking his head to the left, a sudden copper taste in Wally's mouth.

The world began to fade, consciousness leaving him. This was it. This was how he'd die.

The German drew his fist again, and Wally braced for a third strike.

That's when he heard a sickening "crunch," and the German fell off him, into the brush.

Wally's eyes suddenly drew focus on Rat standing above him, silhouetted in the glow of the spotlight, his chest heaving, his eyes wide with terror. He held Mayfield's metal signal transmitter box over his head.

"Oh. God," said Rat when he saw the fallen soldier at Wally's side. "Is he dead?" He dropped the metal box.

A prickling pain crossed Wally's skin, and he thought unconsciousness would finally take him. He closed his eyes and imagined piano song, heard Audrey's soft voice singing.

To his surprise, the darkness didn't come.

He opened his eyes again, the kaleidoscope of stars slowing overhead, sensation returning to his limbs.

A second shot rang out.

Wally forced himself to sit up in the weed patch and, again, urged his searching eyes to find Mayfield through glow of the spotlight, past the swirl of dust and night bugs.

Mayfield staggered forward, placed his hands on his knees. He breathed like a prize-fighter after the ninth round, puffing, coughing, and occasionally laughing.

"That was...a helluva thing," Mayfield said.

Wally wiped the blood and mud from his mouth, rubbed his aching cheek where the German had struck him.

"Just two of them?" said Wally.

Mayfield offered Wally a hand and pulled him to his feet. "I got the one," he said. "Clyde got the other. You okay?"

Wally worked his jaw. It was sore, but nothing felt broken. His mind was a jumble, but he had managed not to faint.

"I think so," said Wally. "You?"

"Took 'em by surprise," said Mayfield, betraying an odd pride in what should have been a horrible moment.

Wally looked down to see the German that Rat had dispatched. The guy's skull was crushed on the side where Rat had struck him with the box, his lifeless eyes staring into the sky.

Rat stepped over, his own face blank, his voice quiet. "I killed a Nazi."

Mayfield looked over to the body of the other fallen soldier, the one he'd managed to shoot, strewn on the road by the tub car. "Me too."

Rat froze, and then turned away to vomit. Again.

"Now I know why you packed a toothbrush," said Mayfield.

Rat spat into the weeds. "Jesus Christ."

"You guys saved my life," said Wally, but his gratitude was tainted with a deep shame. In the middle of his most important mission, when his friends needed him most, he had proven useless.

Rat spat again into the weeds, wiped his mouth, and looked up at Mayfield. He shook his head. "Alvin, why didn't you just wait 'em out? They didn't see us 'til you jumped the guy in the car."

Mayfield shrugged. "Figured we could use the wheels." He thumbed over to the utility vehicle still idling in the road beside the dead man. "Uniforms too," he added.

While trembling in the weeds, Wally had thought only of his own survival. Mayfield, on the other hand, had turned their misfortune into opportunity. "Smart thinking, Alvin." Wally said, gaining back his breath.

Mayfield gave a crooked smile. "Thanks."

Wally circled his friend to examine his sutures. "And your stitches held."

"Don't congratulate yourself yet," said Rat. "There are only two soldiers and three of us. That's not enough uniforms."

Wally moved his gaze between the two dead Germans, noticing both were tall like him and Mayfield.

Rat ogled the dead men as well.

"Okay," said Rat. "Guess I'm the short guy with the short straw."

"You sure?" said Wally.

"No," said Rat. "But if Alvin gets to be smart, I get to be selfless."

Wally nodded. "That's fair."

Mayfield used a handkerchief to clean the blood off his signal box and return it to his pack as Rat managed to find Wally's missing gun in the weeds. In the meantime, Wally took on the grim task of pulling the uniforms off the dead Germans, working hard to keep as much blood off the garments and off himself as possible. Once he'd removed the men's clothes, Rat and Mayfield helped him drag their bodies into a ditch beneath an oak tree where the dead Germans were unlikely to be spotted from the road. For good measure, they covered their remains with fallen branches and clutches of tall weeds with nettles.

"That oughta do," said Mayfield.

Wally fixed his eyes on the dead men. "Guess so." He smelled blood on the breeze and felt the weight of it all, the strange mingling of victory and sadness. He knew he shouldn't feel sorry for a pair of Nazis, especially ones who had tried to kill him and his friends, but part of him couldn't help it. Somewhere out there, he figured they had families waiting for them to come home too.

Rat stashed their rucksacks in the rear keep of the rumbling tub car as Wally and Mayfield donned the dead Germans' uniforms. Wally found the woolen garments to be heavy and thought they smelled like sweat and cigarettes. Ironically, Wally's jacket and trousers fit him as if they had been tailored for him by his own mother. He remembered wearing the Edelman bar mitzvah suits at the Diamond Club, feeling like an imposter. Now, that seemed like a rehearsal for this moment when being an imposter might save his life.

Again, he saw the red swastika armband and reached to rip it off but stopped when he realized his disguise depended on it. His Jewish victory would have to wait.

Mayfield's jacket fit fine, though his pants fell about an inch too short on his legs.

Wally pointed at Mayfield's ankles. "That'll have to do," he said, though the tailor in him was entirely disapproving.

"What're you talking about?" said Mayfield, examining his clothes under the watchful moon. "Fits perfectly."

Wally shook his head. "If you say so."

Rat was the first to climb into the tub car, where he switched off the spotlight. "No need to draw any more attention," he said.

Mayfield took the wheel. Wally grabbed the passenger seat, and Rat pushed himself low into the space beside the spotlight where he'd stashed their belongings.

"What if we come across more enemy soldiers?" said Rat.

"Do either of you speak German?" said Wally.

"No," Rat and Mayfield chimed together.

"Then I suggest we avoid anyone else along the way."

"Here," said Rat. He handed Wally his pistol, to Wally's great relief. "Try not to drop it again."

Mayfield reached beneath the driver's seat and pulled out the German rifle. "If all else fails..."

"Right," said Wally. He returned the gun to the back of his trousers and hoped neither of them would have to fire a weapon again.

Rat retrieved a thick blanket he'd found in the vehicle and crouched down. "Holler when we get there," he said, and pulled it over his head.

Mayfield released the parking brake, yanked the tall gearshift, and maneuvered the tub car onto the road. "Here we go," he said. "Next stop: the western relay."

With Mayfield driving, Wally eyed the terrain, searching past the reach of the car's headlights for any sign of the relay somewhere off the road. He was tempted to have Rat turn on the spotlight but feared they were already at risk by driving with their headlights on. After only thirty minutes, however, he spotted something.

"There!" said Wally.

Fifty yards or so off the road, deep into the tree line by a gathering of oaks, a tall, thin pole caught a quick flicker of moonlight. If Wally had searched any farther left or right, he would have missed it altogether.

"Wow. Good eyes," said Mayfield. He let up on the gas, downshifted, and pulled off the road to a cluster of bushes. "Let's hide the car here, behind these shrubs," he said.

Mayfield switched off the engine. Rat threw back the blanket and emerged with Mayfield's rucksack.

"Time to get busy," said Wally. "Don't wanna linger."

The three hopped out of the tub car, gathered fallen branches, and covered the vehicle as they had the bodies of the dispatched German soldiers until it was well hidden. Wally tucked his pistol into his new German holster, grateful to no longer have his own weapon aimed at his ass. Mayfield grabbed the shotgun, and the trio raced to the tree line and the tall relay post.

Mayfield examined the post, stem to stern, eyeing the cord that wrapped it like a snake and the four spiked antennae reaching for the stars. "Damn. Just what I was afraid of."

"What's wrong?" said Wally.

"Antennae looks fine," said Mayfield. "Problem must be with the relay box."

"Where's that?" said Wally.

"Close," said Mayfield. He turned on his flashlight and used the light to follow the insulated wire from the base of the pole into the bushes. His light then traced the wire farther to a thick oak tree, around its trunk, and high into the depths of its overhead branches. He shone his light into the dark mass of leaves. "Problem's up there."

"You can't climb that tree," said Wally. "Your stitches will come out again."

"You're right. I can't," agreed Mayfield. He turned to Rat. "But he can."

Rat stared at Mayfield. "You've gotta be kidding."

"I'll go," said Wally.

"No," said Mayfield. "Clyde is the one who has the codes memorized. Once the box up there is fixed, he's gotta transmit them, remember?"

Rat looked at the tree. "He's right. Time is running out."

Wally put his hand on Rat's bony shoulder. "This is it, Clyde. Can you do it?"

Rat sighed, reached into his pocket, and handed Wally a folded sheet of paper.

"What's this?" said Wally.

"It's my eulogy. Wrote it back at camp."

"You wrote your own eulogy?"

"I'm an excellent writer," said Rat. "Besides, no one else would get it right."

Wally stuffed the sheet into his pocket. "Not gonna need it," said Wally. "I promise.

This will work."

"You took it," said Rat. "So, you know there's a chance you're wrong."

Wally shook his head but couldn't deny it. They weren't out of hot water yet, and he began to think he should have written his own eulogy.

Mayfield brought Rat his field pack and helped him strap it over his shoulder. "Tools are in there," Mayfield said. "Everything you'll need. I'll talk you through it." He handed Rat a headband with a small battery-operated light in the center. "Switch on the light to see what you're doing. Just don't aim it at the road or else you might be spotted."

"How do I even get up there?" said Rat.

Mayfield withdrew from his pack a long, wide belt. "Wrap this around you and the trunk of the tree and climb like those fellas on the telephone poles. Ever seen them?"

"I live in a city, hayseed. I've seen plenty of telephone poles."

"He means, have you ever seen a guy climb them?" said Wally.

"Oh. Well, yeah," said Rat. "I've seen that too."

"And they say I'm the thick one." Mayfield shook his head. "Once you get to the high branches, look for the box."

Rat hoisted Mayfield's field pack onto his back, pulled the belt around the tree, and clutched the tree with Wally helping lift him.

To Wally's surprise, Rat proved adept at climbing and quickly managed to get all the way to the branch clusters without sliding down.

"Wow," Wally called in an urgent whisper. "You made fast work of that."

"I'm motivated," Rat replied. "Let me find the box." After a few moments, he whispered down again, "Found it. Now what?"

"Turn on the headlamp. What do you see?" said Mayfield.

Rat seemed to fumble with his equipment, and then Wally saw a dim light switch on from between the oak's leaves. Rat whispered down, "A covered metal box stuffed into the crook of two branches, banded with some sort of cord."

"Anything damaged or out of place?"

"Hang on," Rat said. "Yeah, looks like a part of the box got blasted."

"Nazis probably shot it out from down here," said Mayfield. "Pop open the lid of the box and describe the damage."

Wally heard the scrape of metal as Rat maneuvered the box. "Well, a bunch of wires are fried, and half the screws they were tied to seem to be missing."

"Damn," grumbled Mayfield.

"Sorry?" said Rat. "What was that?"

Mayfield's eyes darted like he was reading his own service manual in the darkness.

"This will work," Mayfield replied, but it sounded more like Mayfield was trying to convince himself.

"You don't sound very confident," said Rat.

"I can usually see the box I'm working on. Give me a second to think."

"Wanna trade places?"

"You can do this, Clyde," called Wally. "Mayfield, you can too."

Rat mumbled something Wally couldn't hear.

"Okay. Get the clippers," said Mayfield. "Front pocket."

After a minute, Rat said, "Okay, got 'em."

"Clip the end of those fried wires, and the other ones, strip an inch off the colored rubber sleeves so you can twist the exposed wire onto new screws."

"There are five of them!" called Rat.

"Shhhh!" hissed Wally. "Be quiet and keep things moving."

As Mayfield whispered out directions to Rat, Wally kept his eyes on the road. So far, it was clear, though he worried someone would soon come looking for the two guys they'd encountered earlier.

"Okay," said Rat. "Now what?"

"You're going to need to replace the corner board and reconnect the wires. There should be a replacement board in the pack. Do you see it? It's the one with a cylinder welded to it."

Rat grew silent and Wally worried he had given up.

"Okay, here. Got it."

"Use the screwdriver, remove the first board, and replace it the same way you removed it."

Wally closed his eyes and listened to the breeze in the air, the twitter of crickets, and the whisper of the leaves, assuring there was no sound of approaching danger. He reached to his hip, to the gun he kept in his new holster. He hoped never to use it, but he was happy it was there. He just prayed that if the need arose, he wouldn't fumble it again.

"Okay," said Rat. "Now what?"

"Last steps," said Mayfield. "Take the tiny screws from the pack and screw them into each of the holes in the new board. Then, we'll tie those colored wires to them. When you're ready, let me know and I'll give you the color order."

It was then that Wally opened his eyes. The rumble of an approaching car had silenced the crickets.

"Hurry!" huffed Wally. "We have company."

"Oh, for Chrissakes," called Rat. "You can't do this in a hurry!"

"Find a way," said Wally.

"And turn off that headlamp," said Mayfield.

"You've gotta be kidding," said Rat. The glow of his headlamp snapped off. "How do you see color in the dark?"

Slowly, the sound of the vehicle grew louder until Wally saw the headlights on the road. His heart began to knock out of sync. He counted Mississippis, but all he could think of was Rat up in the tree, trying to make this all work in the darkness.

"Give me the colors," called Rat. "I'll have to do this with the moonlight. What's the order? Quick!"

"Red, black, yellow, blue, green," rattled off Mayfield.

"Red, what?"

"Black, yellow, blue, green," Mayfield repeated more slowly.

"Everything looks blue," said Rat.

"Quiet!" called Wally. "They're close."

Mayfield and Wally backed farther into the woods, past the tree line, to obscure themselves from eyes on the road. They kept their gaze on the path that led them there with Rat perched overhead, buried in the tree. If they were lucky, the Nazis would miss seeing the signal pole altogether, just as Wally had almost done.

The vehicle came around the bend, but instead of breezing by, it slowed. It was another tub car like the one they'd hidden in the shrubs below, this one without the mounted spotlight, and it carried four German soldiers.

Then, to Wally's horror, the car stopped.

His heart leapt to his throat when he heard the brake crank into place.

It was just as Brubaker had warned. The Germans had used the damaged relay to draw them here. They knew exactly where the relay was. It was an ambush.

The four soldiers got out, seemed to notice the tire tracks in the road, and drew their guns. Without pause, all four started marching slowly into the woods, guns drawn, toward the signal pole. Toward them.

Once again, it seemed Wally's only contribution had been to put his friends in danger, dragging them into the wilderness to be captured by the enemy. Rat had skills with codes and ciphers. Mayfield had the signal repair know-how. But what had Wally offered? His skill seemed to be to complicate everything, to bring danger to others when all he really wanted was to give meaning to his life.

It was then that he knew what he had to do.

He sprung forward from the shrubs, into the moonlight, the glow shining off the pair of medals on his new German uniform.

"Heil Hitler!" Wally announced loudly and thrust his hand into the air.

The soldiers froze at his sudden appearance as if Wally were some wild Nazi apparition. Surprised, the soldiers lowered their guns and raised their hands back. "Heil Hitler!" Wally nodded back, which only seemed to make the surprised soldiers nervous.

"Was ist es?" said the closest soldier, clearly surprised to find Wally there.

Wally thought about reaching for his gun, but quickly realized to do so would reveal he was an enemy and invite their own gunfire. He may get out one shot or two, but with four soldiers to dispatch, he wouldn't last more than a moment.

Instead, Wally held his finger to his lips, ignoring the tumultuous trembling in his limbs. "Shh," he said, and the four looked completely flummoxed.

He then strode past them, toward their vehicle, drawing their attention with him. He turned back and gestured for them to follow.

"Was machst du?" a second German called, but Wally just kept waving them toward him without speaking.

He knew if the baffled Germans' eyes were on him, they weren't on Rat or Mayfield, and that might buy his friends the time they needed to complete their work. The caper may get him killed, but he realized the success of their mission didn't require his survival. His friends just had to get the signal repaired and transmit the ciphers. And to do that, they only needed time.

Wally's stroll became a lumber, and his lumbering became a sprint. He ran toward their car, and the four soldiers bolted toward him, yelling, finally realizing his deception.

He threw open the door of their vehicle, grateful they'd left the tub car running, and jumped into the driver's seat. He'd never driven a car before; however, after watching Mayfield for the last couple hours, he was ready to try.

In fast progression, he released the brake, engaged the clutch, yanked the gearshift, and stepped on the gas pedal, peeling out in a cloud of dust and exhaust just as the soldiers reached him, their guns aimed at the car.

Two of the Germans gave chase, a shot or two ringing out, but in his rearview mirror,

Wally saw the other two Nazis turn back toward the woods, back toward his friends.

His heart pounded in his ears, but he knew his work was not done. He managed to wrench the steering wheel, spinning the car back around, aiming it, like a torpedo, at his pursuers. This time, however, they did not look at all confused. They raised their weapons, locked their eyes on him, and opened fire.

Wally stomped the gas and ducked down. He saw a Nazi helmet on the passenger seat and stuffed it between the dashboard and the gas, locking the pedal in place. He then reached for the driver's door and opened it.

Like *Nick Carter, Master Detective* had done in the show's seventh episode, Wally leapt from the speeding car and onto the road.

He hit the ground hard, which knocked the wind out of him. He rolled end over end. Trees, gravel, and stars spun around him, the car now a missile aimed at his assailants.

With the horrifying crack of bone like the sound of an anvil landing on a dry two-by-four, Wally landed in a roadside ditch, a shooting pain blazing up his leg, his vision blurring.

Still, he was able to see the result of his work. The car had pinned one lifeless German to a tree, the other crushed beneath its front wheel, which still spun, grinding the second dead man into the dirt.

It was then he heard the gunshots. He ignored the fire in his leg, willed his aching head to turn and face the tree line where he'd left Rat and Mayfield.

He scanned for the other two Germans he thought were firing at him and reached for his holster. This time, he was able to grab his gun, but when he lifted it to aim, it wasn't a German he saw. It was Mayfield, emptying his rifle into the last-standing German soldier, the other already lying flat on his back.

Wally dropped the gun, blinked against the pain in his body, tried to ignore his pounding heart. He moved to stand, but his leg wouldn't hold him. He fell on his side writhing in pain, his body feeling like it was smashed into a million broken pieces.

When he looked down, he saw his leg was bent in the wrong direction.

He slumped back down and everything around him started to spin. Blood rose in his throat and nose and his breathing became labored.

"Lipkin!" called Mayfield.

Unable to keep steady, Wally felt his head fall to the side, his ear filling with gravel from the road on which he lay.

Mayfield ran sideways toward him.

"Lipkin!" he repeated.

"Not sure I did that right," said Wally. His breath was thin, his voice weak. He recalled Nick Carter was up and at 'em, right after ditching his own car. Why did everything seem so much easier in programs?

"What did you do?" said Mayfield.

A warm, wet stream crossed Wally's forehead and ran into his eyes. Things turned red, and the world began to fade. His mouth tasted like an old penny.

Consciousness began to fade, but this time it didn't feel as though he was fainting. It felt more like a thin filament connecting him to the Earth was quietly unraveling. He was becoming untethered to his disloyal body.

Mayfield knelt beside him. "If you ain't the bravest, craziest piano player I ever met."

The scene started to close in on Wally like a love letter being folded and folded again. And while he was grateful for Mayfield's compliment, the face he wished to see most was Audrey's.

"Tell her she's pretty," said Wally. "Tell her I'm sorry I never told her that."

"Tell her yourself," said Mayfield. "You're the one she wants to hear it from."

Piano song filled his ears, and he somehow smelled the sweet scent of peppermint. His heart sputtered and his breath grew shallower. The warm glow of the moon and the sparkling eyes of his ancestors seemed to call him home.

"C'mon, Walter! Stay with me!"

Wally closed his eyes and found a sudden, unexpected comfort in the irony that when the darkness took him one last time, it would take his demon too. And that, he thought, at long last, felt like a victory.

18

A Broken Heart

In the quiet of the infirmary tent, among aromas of surgical spirits and wet wool, the team surrounded Max, who stood beside the entrance facing his friends. He held a sheet of paper in his thick hands, cleared his throat, and raised his chin.

"We all cared for him," Max read, "and as we look back upon his short life, it's clear that bravery was his defining trait. His greatness was undeniable, though many missed it because of his enviable intelligence and humility." Max swallowed uncomfortably. "Some were blessed to know his brilliance. Most just knew him as generous, selfless, and wise. Our gift was having known him at all in his all-too-brief time on Earth, and our loss, like his sacrifice, is profound."

Max lowered the sheet and scanned the faces of the team.

Mayfield scratched at his new clean bandage, Frankie pushed a hand through his red hair, Bobbi nodded, and Audrey just stared at her shoes.

"Who is going to believe any of this crap?" said Max, waving the paper. "It's completely over the top, and, to be frank, most of this is a lie."

"You're reading it all wrong," said Rat. He strode over and snatched the paper from Max's grasp. "You aren't very convincing."

"It's your eulogy. You wrote it yourself. I shouldn't have to be *convincing*."

"Shh," said Audrey. *"You'll wake up Walter."*

The group all turned to Wally, who sat propped up in the camp infirmary bed once occupied by Mayfield. Wally's leg was wrapped in a brace and elevated by a sling on a metal pole. His eyes were wide open.

"I'm awake," said Wally. "Who can sleep with all that racket?" His voice sounded scratchy and his head throbbed with pain. How long had he been out?

Audrey was the first to rush over.

"Oh, Walter. Thank goodness! When I think about how badly I'd treated you—"

"I love you," Wally blurted. His mind was foggy, but he was ready for truth, ready to be rid of the lies and the distractions that kept him from Audrey, from being who he truly was all along, even if that was a broken, damaged piano player with a fainting problem.

Audrey's eyes grew wide. "What?"

He reached for her hand and tried to ignore the pain in his ribs, in his leg, in his skull.

"I don't know if I'm dead or if this is a dream," said Wally, "but if you're real, I need to say something before I lose my chance. You're beautiful and brilliant and I love you, Audrey Milhouser. I should have said so a long time ago, but I'm a putz."

Audrey's cheeks grew flush.

"I'm sorry," Wally continued. "I know you deserve better than me."

"Walter, I—I love you too."

He cleared his throat. "Back in London, when I tried to kiss you—"

"Walter..." Audrey looked both flattered and embarrassed as she eyed the rest of the team. "They gave you narcotics. Can we talk about this later?"

"Sounds like my cue to interrupt," said Brubaker. The colonel pushed aside the infirmary's door flap and shouldered through the gathered team with the camp doctor at his side.

"Too many people in here," said the doctor. He waved his hand as if swatting away the usual flurry of moths.

Audrey and the others stepped back from Wally's bed, giving Brubaker and the doctor a clear path.

"Colonel Brubaker," said Wally, but he couldn't figure out how to sit up or salute with his leg lifted high and his arm in a sling.

"At ease, Private Lipkin. Doc says you gotta stay put 'til that leg heals, and your heart gets the once-over."

"My heart? What are you talking about?"

The doctor raised his stethoscope and pressed it to Wally's chest.

"Private Lipkin," he said. "Have you had any trouble with fainting?"

Wally gulped and he saw Audrey was equally surprised.

"You might say that," he said, his eyes scanning his friends.

"Ever occur to you to tell anyone about it?" The doctor moved the stethoscope to another part of Wally's chest.

"Once or twice," said Wally. He tried not to look at Max.

"Best I can tell," said the doctor, "you've got a malformation in your heart, either a mitral valve anomaly or a heart murmur." He withdrew his stethoscope. "Causes problems getting oxygen to the brain. Maybe that's why you forgot to mention it. No air up there." The doctor tapped his own forehead and shot Wally a sardonic smirk.

Memories of his fainting episodes flashed through Wally's mind like scenes from a newsreel, one shameful incident after the other. He'd always attributed those episodes to his failing brain, his cowardly disposition, his demon. "Malformed heart?" repeated Wally.

"Could be congenital, genetic—or just how your heart developed," said the doctor. "Gotta be careful with such things. Some grow out of it, some don't." The doctor turned and aimed an angry frown at Colonel Brubaker across Wally's bed. "That's why we give men full physicals before we let them serve. Secret missions are no exception." He turned back to Wally. "Men with a condition like yours typically are relieved from conscription."

"Things moved kinda fast, Doc," said Brubaker. He looked at Wally. "Sorry we didn't take better care of you, Lipkin."

"That's okay," said Wally. "I was the one who kept it a secret. I thought it was just a fainting condition."

Since that basement kiss with Eleanor Getzman, Wally had seen himself as a troubled guy prone to panic attacks, a guy who had what his uncle had. Of course, that may still be true, even if his neurosis was complicated further by a heart condition. Whatever his problems were, he was still Walter Lipkin, a dope who fainted. And maybe that's just who he was always going to be whether he blamed his head, his heart, or the demon Asmodeus.

"Whatever you have," said Brubaker, "didn't stop you from defying orders again, did it?"

"No, sir," said Wally. He lowered his gaze. "I'm sorry." Then he remembered the events that had landed him in the infirmary in the first place. "Wait," said Wally. He looked back at Brubaker. "Did it work? Did the French get the transmission?"

"Yes!" said Rat. His grin was full of pride. "But that was two days ago."

"Can you believe it?" said Mayfield.

"I was out for two days?" The barrage of news rattled Wally's bruised brain, or maybe that was the effect of the narcotics Audrey had mentioned.

"Driving a car into a pack of Nazis was a damn brave thing to do," said Mayfield. "Even if it was crazy."

"You were all brave," said Bobbi. She touched Mayfield's arm, and a dopey grin crossed his face.

"More to the point, all three of you went AWOL," said Brubaker. His stern voice sent a hush through the infirmary tent. "You know the penalty for that?"

Wally eyed his senior officer. "Court-martial?" said Wally.

"Damn right," said Brubaker. "Lucky for you, the army would sooner throw me in the brig than see you reprimanded. Your little stunt has made a lot of people happy."

"So, what happened after the code sheet made it over?" said Wally.

"French got through to the north," said Brubaker. "Not much time to spare either."

"Worked like a song," said Bobbi. "Allied troops broke through and are making their way toward Rome right now."

Max approached Wally's bed, his face sporting a strange, solemn smile. "Walter, the troops also stopped a German train heading north. It was full of Jewish prisoners."

"Jewish prisoners?"

"On the way to the camps."

Wally swallowed, recalling the horrible rumors about the extermination of Jews.

"But they're safe now," said Max. "Allies got them out of there." Max's eyes started to well. "More than five hundred of them, Walter. Five hundred."

A knot found its way into Wally's throat. If they had saved five hundred Jews, how many others were still out there, praying for their own miracles?

The doctor stuck a thermometer in Wally's mouth. "That was some fine suture work you did on Private Mayfield too. Ever think about a career in medicine?"

"Not really," said Wally, the protruding glass wand wagging from his lips. "Never liked the sight of blood."

"Could've fooled me," said Rat.

The doctor withdrew the thermometer, looked at it, and nodded. "A man with skills like yours might think about how to use them." The doctor gestured to Wally's leg. "Compound fracture will heal, but it'll be several weeks. You're gonna need to keep your weight off it in the meantime and keep the excitement to a minimum." He pointed at Wally's chest. "Ribs'll be sore for a while and your heart needs a break too. You and your colonel can decide if you should recuperate here or at home."

"Home?" said Wally. He turned toward Brubaker, his whole body protesting with the effort. "You mean, New York?"

Brubaker smiled. "I think it's safe to say, you finished your mission here, Private Lipkin. And like I've said, we can't break up the team. I can arrange transport for everyone when you're ready."

Wally's thoughts flashed to the aroma of his mother's pot roast, the rumble of the dryer at A-Rite Cleaners, the sight of the Manhattan skyline, and the maritime activity of the East River. But he only entertained those thoughts for a moment.

"But, sir, the war isn't over."

"No, son, it isn't."

Wally thought about those Jews on the train, the scores of others still out there. He met the searching eyes of his friends. "Can the team go home if they want to, Colonel? I mean, if I stay?"

"You nearly died, Private Lipkin." Brubaker shook his head. "I'm not sure you're up to staying."

"I can still write songs," Wally held up his good arm, "and I can still play music, that is, if someone can carry me to a piano."

Audrey stepped forward. "I'm not going home if Walter isn't."

"Me neither," said Max.

"If there are still people to help," said Frankie, "I'm staying too."

"I go where they go," said Mayfield.

Rat narrowed his beady eyes. "What's the next mission, Colonel?"

Brubaker looked defeated and turned to Bobbi. "This all work for you, Barbara Ann?"

"I trust my friends," said Bobbi. "We're a team."

Wally leaned forward in his bed trying not to let the pain show on his face. He raised an eyebrow, the only thing that didn't hurt. "Team's ready when you are, Colonel. Where to next?"

Epilogue

It was a warm night in Brooklyn and all the stars seemed to be out. Wally and Audrey sat side by side in deck chairs on the roof of their Kensington apartment building, their eyes focused on the card table and the chessboard that was set up in front of them.

"Your move," said Wally.

From the other side of the chessboard, Uncle Sherman sat in his own deck chair, facing them. Sherman's hair was neatly combed, his chin cleanly shaven, and his clothes were freshly pressed, a perk of his new job at A-Rite Cleaners.

Sherman's face was gnarled in frustration, his eyes fixed on his black king. "You penned me in," said Sherman. "You know I hate that. Checkmate no matter where I move."

"It was your idea to play chess," said Wally, "not mine."

"That's only because you refused to play poker. Can't you give your old uncle a chance to win some of that money you're earning over at WKOB?"

"Max is the studio manager," said Wally. "He makes the real dough. I just write jingles and play piano."

"I liked your stewed tomatoes song," said Audrey. She hummed Wally's ditty from a few weeks earlier.

"Whatever you make over there in Manhattan is still more than I make at the cleaners," grumbled Sherman. "Your dad's a real cheapskate, you know."

"He and my mom are still saving for a vacation," said Wally. "After hiding away at Fort Hamilton for months, they decided they wanna get away to the Catskills."

Sherman shook his head. "Always the Catskills with those two."

Wally reached into his pocket and pulled out his uncle's watch. "Better make your move, Uncle Sherman. *Nick Carter, Master Detective* is on in an hour, and Audrey and I have a date."

"The show is very exciting," explained Audrey.

"Thought you were done with excitement," said Sherman. He eyed the chessboard.

"Isn't that what the doctor told you?"

"Over and over," said Wally. "Also said the heart thing could be hereditary. I told you, you oughta get yourself checked."

"Already know I have a broken heart," said Sherman. "Her name was Trudy, and I haven't seen her since before the Great War. Besides, I've seen enough doctors for one lifetime. And thanks to you, I don't have to go back to that horrible sanitorium."

The sound of metal scraping against metal interrupted their conversation, announcing Max's arrival as he stepped off the fire escape. His face was red, and he appeared winded from the climb.

"Chrissakes," Max panted. He put his hands on his knees. "Can't you play your games...and have your conversations...in the family room...like normal people?"

"Better view from up here," said Wally.

"You can see the birds," agreed Sherman.

"Who wants to be a normal person anyway?" Audrey laughed, a cloud of peppermint filling the air around her.

Max made his way over, leaned forward, and put his hands on the back of Wally's chair as he finally caught his breath. "Mom says dinner's ready, and Dad'll flip his lid if he paid for a roast that no one eats."

"Roast?" said Sherman. "Don't need to tell me twice." He stood from his chair and boxed up the game. "I was losing anyway."

Sherman went down the escape with the chess set in his carrying case, defeated. Max followed but turned to Wally before descending.

"Make it fast," said Max. "Clyde is already telling Mom the tale of his wartime heroics, and his story keeps evolving. He's shameless."

"Which story?" said Wally. "Monte Cassino? Cherbourg? Paris?"

"Who can tell the difference anymore? He thinks he's the hero of every one of those, like none of us had anything to do with any of it. I may throttle him if you don't get down there soon."

"What about Frankie?" said Wally.

"Frankie is walking the beat tonight, but said he'll come by with Dotty and the baby later. If he lets me borrow his gun, I may use it to shoot Clyde."

"All right." Wally laughed. "Be right there."

Once Wally and Audrey were finally alone under the stars, he put his arm around her. They looked out over Brooklyn and suddenly heard music coming from a radio in an apartment across the alley. To Wally's surprise, it was the song he and Audrey had written and recorded back in London, "I Run a Little Blue," with Audrey singing and Wally on the piano.

Audrey looked at him and laughed. "There's no escaping it," she said. "The war followed us home."

Wally drew a bagpipe breath, his ribs no longer sore after months of healing. He closed his eyes. "No," he said. "The war is over. The music is what followed us home." He put his hand to the sky. "'Wherever you go—music,' remember?"

Audrey leaned toward Wally, closed her eyes, and kissed him, her lips tasting of peppermint.

Wally's pulse quickened and she drew back from the kiss.

"Too long?" she asked.

"Just right," said Wally. "But if I gotta die, that's just how I wanna go."

Audrey socked him in shoulder. "Save the sweet talk for your jingles, Mr. Lipkin."

Wally turned back to the neighborhood, and while Kensington seemed exactly the same as it was before the war, he knew things had changed. Everything had changed.

"I remember you telling me I didn't like myself," said Wally. "Right here, on this spot."

Audrey winced. "I'm so sorry," she said. "That wasn't very nice."

"Don't be sorry. You were right." Wally lifted her chin to look in her eyes. "I didn't like myself because I didn't know myself, not like you did."

"And now?"

Wally smiled. "Now I'm painfully aware of all my flaws."

"And, of course, you know I love you despite your many flaws."

"*Many* flaws?" said Wally. "How many flaws?"

"Who can count?" Audrey laughed. "Too many." She jumped from the chair and raced to the fire escape. "Come to dinner!"

"Give me a minute," said Wally.

"All right," she said. "But don't be long."

Once alone, Wally again drew in the Brooklyn air. He was grateful the war was over, grateful to be home, grateful he and his friends had made it back safely. He had told Audrey it was the music that had followed them back to New York, not the war. But some part of him still carried the war's weight, a new companion on his life's journey. Like his broken heart, he bore it in his chest, lived with its impact, accepted it as part of him, but chose not to let it define him, control him, just as he'd mistakenly done with his demon.

He had learned to focus on the things he and his friends had accomplished, the lives they had saved, not the ways they had failed, not the lives they had lost or the horror they had seen. But, of course, those thoughts were present just the same.

He turned his gaze to the sky, where a million stars winked like diamonds strewn across black velvet. If those were his Jewish ancestors up there, maybe those winks were their way of assuring him that he'd done right by his family, done right by his people, and done right by himself despite his troubles and flaws. Lies were no longer needed and could be left behind, tucked away in a drawer like his grandfather's ring. And perhaps the ancestors were also reminding him that not all miracles were grand spectacles like parting seas, magic rings, or burning bushes, speaking with the voice of God. If the war had taught Wally anything, it was that some miracles were simple, like radio jingles. Some were surprising, like pianos falling from the sky, or the unexpected gift of trust when he least deserved it. Some miracles healed broken hearts, or broken bones, and some miracles smelled like peppermint. And to experience a miracle, to feel its true wonder, you didn't need to be anyone other than who you were, even if you were broken. You just had to be in the right place at the right time.

Acknowledgements

Many an intrepid fool like me seeks a team of adventurers to aid in his journey, though the fellow adventurers I found must reflect some great good fortune on my part for they exceed me in every way. They are deserving in more ways than I can articulate, but here I shall try.

To my mentor Louella Nelson, I thank you for both your wisdom and your encouragement. Your soul is generous; your kindness is without limit.

To my fellow writers' group members, past and present, I thank you for helping me hold my oars steady in the water and my compass aimed north. I envy your talents and cherish your friendship. I offer my deepest thanks to Begoña Echeverria, Beverly Plass, Brad Oatman, Deborah Gaal Silverberg, Debra Garfinkle, Kristin James, and Laurie Casey for their patience, creativity, and encouragement and for sharing their own stories of wonder and inspiration. You restored my love of Mondays and furthered my belief that writers are a special kind of crazy.

To Ben Gocker, former librarian with the Brooklyn Collection at the Central Library of New York, I thank you for making our one-hour appointment last a whole day. That day stands as one of my favorites amongst the many spent researching this book. Libraries remain the world's portal to everything and so librarians are, themselves, magic. An equal measure of gratitude to my friend, Jon Power for joining me in Brooklyn for that adventure and the one that followed at Coney Island. Nothing beats a rollercoaster ride with strangers to top off a time-travel excursion.

To my exceedingly excellent family and friends, I offer my thanks and apologies. How you endure the ebbs and flows of a writer's behavior can only be described as kindness, or maybe tolerance. And in the end, you gift me with your love, encouragement and, if I'm lucky, forgiveness. You are good people.

My particular and deepest gratitude to "the Steves"—Messieurs Cohen and Siegel—for their love, support, and well-appointed condominium in the California desert. That space provided this writer with the creative, quiet location necessary for this particular endeavor. Also, I appreciate your great internet bandwidth and impressive local dining options for those times I remembered to eat while immersed in this world of my own imagination.

To my mother, Sandy, and to Emily, Ben, Olive, Archer, Ethan and Miki, I love you forever and always, and more deeply than any words in any language can express. Thank you for making my life full, and fun, and happy. I write from a place of joy and that joy would not be possible without you.

And to Maggie, my love, my partner in everything, I thank you for bearing the hours I spend gazing at a screen or traveling to far-off places, especially when those places are only in my head. Know that I always feel you with me, even when you aren't, hand on my shoulder, whispering in my ear—"You can do this."

About the Author

Herb Williams-Dalgart is an award-winning author and screenwriter, recognized by national and regional writing competitions for developing rich, memorable stories, layered characters, and fresh dialogue across many genres.

The grandson of a World War II veteran after whom he was named, Herb maintains a great respect for and fascination with "the greatest generation" and with the period. Many of his works, including his debut novel, *The French Girl's War*, draw from the tapestry of this war-torn era to find stories that seek to capture the heart, humor, drama, and sacrifice of the time.

Herb is a graduate of UC Santa Barbara with a degree in English, and an emphasis in creative writing. He holds a certificate in screenwriting from UCLA's Writer's Program, spent a year at England's Birmingham University, and studied at the Shakespeare Institute in Stratford-upon-Avon.

When not writing fiction or screenplays, Herb spends time with his wife, their children and grandchildren, and the family dog in Southern California.

Visit him at http://www.herbthewriter.com

Made in the USA
Coppell, TX
15 December 2023

26203416R00193